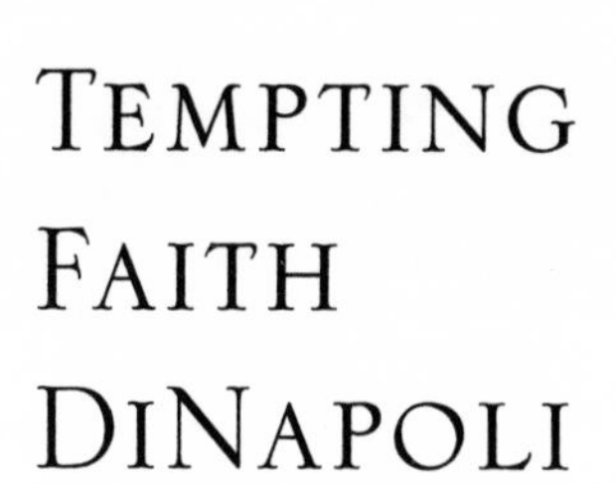

Tempting Faith DiNapoli

Tempting Faith DiNapoli

Lisa Gabriele

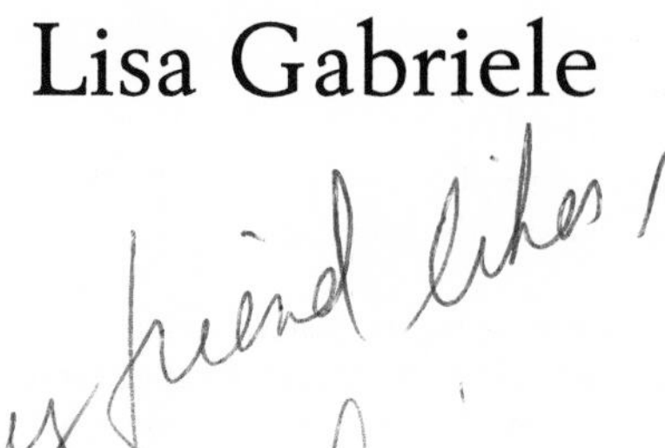

Doubleday Canada

National Library of Canada Cataloguing in Publication Data

Gabriele, Lisa
Tempting Faith DiNapoli

ISBN 0-385-65821-4

I. Title.

PS8563.A253155T44 2002 C813'.6 C2002-900307-5
PR9199.4.G32T44 2002

Jacket image: Ralph Del Pozzo
Jacket design: David High
Book design by Ellen R. Sasahara
Printed and bound in the USA

This book is a work of fiction. Names, characters, places, and incidents either are products of the author's imagination or are used fictitiously. Any resemblance to actual events or locales or persons, living or dead, is entirely coincidental.

Published in Canada by
Doubleday Canada, a division of
Random House of Canada Limited

Visit Random House of Canada Limited's website:
www.randomhouse.ca

BVG 10 9 8 7 6 5 4 3 2 1

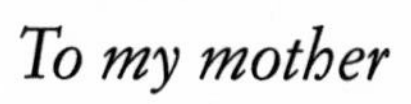

To my mother

Tempting Faith DiNapoli

I am so close to good. I have no need to see God.

—Kenneth Patchen

CHAPTER ONE

THESE ARE THE THINGS I remember about the city. The crumbly, brown-bricked houses in our neighborhood were stacked so closely together, I used to pretend when I was four, they were the chipped, rotting teeth lining the mouth of an urban ogre, and the people who lived inside were busy little cavities. It was as though we all lived in the same house. If we were bad and sent to bed early, we could easily peek across the street into the Trevis' living room and finish watching the TV show with them, guessing at the dialogue.

Privacy was something only rich people enjoyed.

Our house, in Little Italy, shared a wall with the Rossis' next door, and our clothesline connected with the Pilettis' behind us. My mother used to say that if one of the neighbors' houses was swallowed up by hell, we would all be pulled down with them. When I was little, I didn't understand her jokes, so I would include Mr. Piletti in my prayers, whispering, "Also, God, please make Mr. Piletti stop beating his wife in the face, because Mom says he's gonna go to hell, which means that so will we."

In the city, the four of us kids were always together, not just because our house was small and we had no choice, but because when we were small, we weren't given any. My mother only had one goddamn set of eyes, two hands, for chrissakes, and four bloody kids. So stick together, she'd say, don't you ever, ever let go of my hand. And don't let go of each other's, either, she'd say, or I'll kill you. There was all that traffic and those perverts and the crowds to contend with. And always a lot left for her to do before the day was out.

In the city, the four of us kids were all the same people. We had the same bodies, the same moods, and the same ideas. For ten years, we had the same parents, who did and said the same things to each other and us. It was the only time in our lives when we could pretend to be like everyone else, which I came to believe was the gift of the city. In the city, it's difficult to stand out, unless you were like my mother. But her uniqueness was an accident of birth, and completely unintentional, which was true with us, too, but we just didn't realize it at the time.

I remember being small enough that the first things I saw when my mom entered the room were her dirty pink slippers. I got bigger and it was her knees, scabbed and puckered. Then bigger, and there's me grabbing her macramé belt and my little brother's hand as we'd scramble across a busy street because my mother was the type who never crossed at the lights.

Then, church became my measuring stick. At first I couldn't kneel, as I wouldn't be able to see Father Pete or the pretty hats. Then my chin fit perfectly over the back of the pew in front of me. Soon after, all the prayers and songs were in my head, permanently, despite the fact that I don't remember anyone putting them there on purpose. I don't know how old I was when I realized I could not legally marry Jesus, but one day it, too, became something I knew for a fact.

In the city, buildings got built around us or torn down. Nothing ever seemed finished. And unlike God on the seventh day, no one stood back from the city and said, "There, I'm done." But after our seventh year in the city, our neighborhood began to treat my mother like it was done with her. When that happens, I've learned, there's nothing left to do but leave.

My mother told me that ever since she was little she knew she was going to have four kids. All boys. Other people are born with moles or left-handedness, but my mother said she was born with the knowledge that she would have four boys. For proof, she showed us her high school yearbook. Under her graduation picture, next to "Future Plans," it says, "Mother to the Four Tops (only white)." Someone had written next to it: "Sure, Nan, we'll see about that. [Signed] Johnny Mathis."

My mother's name was Nancy Maria Franco.

Back then, Johnny Mathis and being Catholic were her hobbies. In fact, she came up with the names for her four boys in Sunday school: Matthew, Mark, Luke, then John—to be called Johnny, because of her favorite singer. It was there, in Sunday school, that she first fell in love with a boy. Also, in Sunday school, she got into deep religious debates with her younger sister, my auntie Linda, about who was a sexier Jesus, Max von Sydow or Jeffrey Hunter. This debate continued well into my own childhood, my mother sometimes opting for the Jesus on my Bible, who looked to be a calmer type of hippie, and not like the long-haired American kids we'd see dancing naked on the TV. My mother would watch them for a second, roll her eyes, and switch the channel. Though she was around the same age as they were, she always said, "Know who has time to be a hippie? Bored, rich people, that's who. And me, I'm neither."

ONE OF THE FIRST STORIES I memorized about my mother was how she met my dad. It was at her church, Most Precious Blood. Grandpa had forced my mother and her sister to attend Italian mass, after the both of them slept through the earlier English one. They had been out late the night before, celebrating Auntie Linda's eighteenth birthday. My mom noticed the back of my dad's head, liked his black curly hair, and the way he swayed during hymns. My auntie Linda noticed that my dad kept turning around to stare at my mother.

After the service, the church was holding the annual Giovanni

Caboto Day picnic. Normally they never went, but to spite my grandpa, my mother and my aunt stayed and mingled with the other Italians. Someone whispered to my mom that my dad and his family had come from a particularly war-torn part of Italy. The DiNapolis, they said, arrived with almost nothing except the clothes on their back and nobody spoke very much English, even though they'd been in this country for more than a year. My mom was Italian, too, but in name only. She never learned to speak a word of the language, because what for? This is not the Old Country, my grandpa Franco would say. His own family had left Italy a thousand million years earlier, so my mother's only Italian legacy was a vowel at the end of her name. And as her father continually pointed out, nobody gave them a thing when they moved here. Nothing. Sure, my mother's mother, when she was alive, cooked spaghetti, but she served it with Ragú. She used vegetable oil, never olive oil, as it was too expensive. Same with prosciutto. Baloney was good enough. And she passed these fine family traditions down to her two Italian-in-name-only daughters.

My aunt said when my mother finally spoke to my dad, she knew those two would marry. But she knew it in a bad way. A way that made her nauseous and hot-faced. My mother felt the same and told my aunt that she had to sit down a lot while they were dating. Everyone was nice to my dad when he started to come around, but Auntie Linda was disappointed in my mother. Not that she didn't want her sister to fall in love and have children, but not right now, with this all-wrong man. He was a construction worker, not a businessman. He lived with his parents, and he hadn't learned to drive.

The bank where my aunt and my mother had just started to work was on the bottom floor of the second tallest building in downtown Detroit. But the big plans the two sisters had had about moving into the very tallest one simply began to vanish.

MY DAD LOVED my mother right away, too, only in a good, not bad, way. He thought she was beautiful and funny and smart, and even though he didn't much like skinny women, he thought she had the potential for abundance, at least around the hips and bum.

They met during the Detroit riots, so my mother would arrive back in Windsor with exciting stories of black people yelling at white cops. My dad would worry in the depot, holding his plaster-flecked face in his red, callused hands, waiting for his new girlfriend to come bounding off the tunnel bus wearing one of her professional bank outfits. Every day he would pray for her to arrive unbeaten, unshot, and unraped.

Soon, my mother began to latch onto my dad, steering him around the city, happily the one behind the wheel, happily the one paying for hamburgers and records. If you were a sharp girl, with a basic education, and better-looking friends, he was not such a bad catch. He was handsome and handy. He was a dreamy dancer. Plus foreign men were interesting back then. My mom loved the *Gigi* movie, because of Louis Jourdan. (That's where I got the name for my seventh-birthday present, a Siamese kitten.) And her big favorite was Marcello Mastroianni. I'm sure when she married my dad she pictured herself as a small-time Lucille Ball with a construction worker kind of Ricky Ricardo, who would come home, slap her bum playfully, defusing all marital tension. I'm sure my dad figured their young love would sort out big misunderstandings, due to language barriers, cushioning them when they landed on their blissful wedding bed each night. But, in fact, my mother married my dad because she was three months pregnant, and not yet twenty.

AND IT CAME TO BE that Matthew, my older brother, did come to be. There is a picture of my mother in the maternity ward, cradling Matt in her right arm, a lit cigarette in her left hand. My dad's next to her with a beer. This was back when smoking was a bad habit, pregnant women only had a few drinks, and hospitals were more like hotels where people like my mother went for rests when their nerves were bad.

After Matthew came me.

She said that when the doctor told her it was a girl, the news stung. She thought her body had performed a kind of trick on her. Plus she delivered me so painlessly and quickly she was sure she had had a bowel movement instead of me, a little baby girl. (Later when I got older on her and she would get madder at me, she sometimes called me a "little shit." I'd say, "But Mom, I can't help it, I was born that way, wasn't I?")

My mother loved me the exact same as Matt, it's just that she didn't have a backup name. I was supposed to be a Mark, not a girl. Her naming scheme and the rest of her biblical intentions kind of tanked. But determined to fulfill at least one yearbook promise, and Mark not being an easily feminized name, she changed religious tracks and called me Faith, and figured Charity would follow Hope. And after Hope was born, all that was left for us to do was pray for a little Charity. But my mother became overly confident carrying the fourth, even teaching me, at two, how to pronounce Charity, and Matt, at three, how to spell it out, her hand cupped around his, both wrapped around a crayon.

At one, the best that Hope could come out with was "Char-yee," so when number four was born an unfortunate boy, "Charlie" became his name.

"Hope can already pronounce it, so we'll give her this one," was my mother's defeated reasoning.

Matthew, Faith, Hope, and Charlie—the unholy thud of our baby brother's name made us sound more like Mousketeers than disciples.

Our names were her choices, but the fact that most of our H's were completely unpronounceable to my heavily accented dad was nothing but a funny coincidence. My mother was never that mean.

After Charlie was brought home from the hospital there was a period of about six months where my mother said we were all in diapers at the same time. At three, Matt was ready to toilet-train, but was having a hard time with her giving constant birth to diapered rivals. Out of frustration, she made the mistake of trying to train Matt and me at the same time. She figured teaching things to us in twos might be the trick with four kids, each only a year apart. This worked for things like coloring and singing, but not for peeing.

One sorry Saturday, my mom was hit hard with a bad flu, the worst she had ever had, and my dad couldn't, or as she said, wouldn't stay home to help her with us. Matty was not fully trained, and I treated the toilet like a toy. Hope was little. (When he'd argue with my mother about working weekends, my dad's accent sometimes got thicker. "Whose-a gonna pooda food on da tabe. Eh? Jesus Haytch Chryse hisself?" he'd ask.)

My mother didn't know how long she'd be upstairs in the only bathroom, with us out of eye line and earshot.

"Hey, who has to pee? Matt, have to pee? Faith? Pee? Hopey? Come on! Let's all pee. Mommy has to pee real bad."

We were all at an age where we couldn't be left alone because we put a lot of things into our mouths. So we trundled up behind her, me and Matty tugging Hope up each step by her arms. My mom held on to Charlie while she wrestled her pants down around her ankles. She practically fell back on the toilet with instant relief, which set Charlie off bawling hard. This apparently set off me, then Matty, then Hope. We were like a bonfire of babies at her feet. My mother couldn't move from the seat, which set off her own helpless wailing. She alternated between shushing us and patting us on the head, and grabbing herself around her middle.

When my dad came home, he heard the wretched squalling and headed straight upstairs expecting a satanic cult to be butchering his wife and all of his babies. Instead, he found her crying with the four of us collapsed at her feet, drenched in tears.

"I'm sick, Joe, I have no dignity anymore. Look at me! None!" she whimpered from the toilet.

"Nan. Oh, jeez. Why's everybaddy crying?" he moaned.

"Hand me some paper. People get emotional when they can't care for themselves with dignity, Joe, they do," she wept, as he fished out a roll from the top shelf.

He left her there, scooped us up one by one and dropped us, still crying, back down in front of the TV. My mom couldn't move from the toilet for another half hour. My dad was lost downstairs in the sea of afternoon diapers, damp flesh, and snotty noses. None of us had shirts on, we all stank, and we all had the same mess of dark, matted curls. My dad had no idea who was who. Fate? Ope? Matte-ew? Baby? Stop alla dis crying. For Daddy, okay?

He yelled upstairs to her that he would find a teenager, somebody, to help her on weekends. He hollered up a promise to finish the little bathroom on the main floor. He vowed that he would maybe try to work every other Saturday, if he could. Anything to stop her crying, to get her the hell-a downstairs, to help him.

"I give you sam more manny, okay?"

My mom said that we were all so scarred by this, for the next few months Matt refused to learn to pee standing, I would not sit down, and Hope wouldn't keep a diaper on. Little Charlie associated noise with toilets. Until he was approximately five years old, he'd sing songs to himself, out loud, from the bathroom, even when we were in a Chinese restaurant.

Dad never finished the downstairs bathroom.

In general, he was very little help, only because he was hardly ever home. He worked for a man my mom called "The Biggest Asshole in the World" on account of the hours my dad put in fixing that man's messes. Dad's coworkers became simply "those bunch of knuckleheads." She'd leave phone messages for him that read, "Joe: T.B.A. in the W. called. Job in Chatham canceled—rain. Maybe take kids to my dad's? Need break."

My dad would leave replies like, "Nancy, I do not be able to make the trip becuss I must do a job for time and a haff. We need the munny and you know it. I am sorry and kiss for me the kids." When I started getting A's in spelling, I'd sometimes correct his, which he always thanked me for, saying, Fate, you are so smart. Your dad, not so much, eh?

My dad was in construction. Drywall, mostly. He was responsible for building homes in subdivisions that began to spread out and away from the city and closer and closer to the small towns around it.

"These houses look like something even Charlie could draw! No offense, Charl," my mother once said, looking over some plans my dad brought home. Dad was across from us. Charlie was in her lap.

He was only three and already showing signs of being a sucky. He never left her side, he had three "bankies" (stained, crusty baby blankets), and he kept his fingers in his mouth all the time. The third last time my mother ever slapped me hard across the face was when, at ten, I asked her, "Is Charlie a gay like everyone says?"

Whack.

"He is not a gay, he is a boy with more feelings than normal people and there's nothing wrong with that. You hear me?"

She never slapped Charlie. Charlie was her favorite.

MY DAD WAS the opposite of her favorite. My parents made a terrible match right from the beginning. The language barrier wasn't the problem. My mother understood the things he said, she just could not understand the things he did. They fought each other constantly and with the kind of calamity that made the neighbors shy toward us some mornings. They fought late, too, always starting at the breaking-off point between awakeness and sleep before us kids could escape into dreaming. Then we'd hear crash, scream. I would wake up with a vague remembrance of the point of it all. Mom thinks Dad drinks too much. Dad thinks she smokes too much. Mom's sick of still being poor. Dad says the place is a mess. Mom says pick up after your own self, I'm not your slave. Dad feels there's not much to come home to anyways. Mom wonders if maybe having four babies could be a good enough reason to come home. Dad wonders how we'd eat without the money he brought in. Still, Mom says she won't pick him up at the tavern anymore.

Last time we did that, when she had to wake us and bring us with her, we were told not to fall back asleep in the station wagon. Instead, when we pulled up to the tavern, she hoisted sleepy Charlie around her waist, made me grab Hope's hand, and pushed Matty to lead the way to Dad's bar stool.

"Look," she said, "there's Daddy. Go say hi, honey."

Matty ran up to my dad and pulled on his jacket. We were still in pajamas. The bar was dark and glittery. The song that was playing on the jukebox was "Me and Bobby McGee," one of my mother's favorites. Hope had to pee, so my mom asked my dad to please point out the bathroom.

When my dad turned around and saw my mother, then Matty, he jumped off his stool and mumbled, "Oh, jeez, Nan, let's joost go 'ome, okay?"

She replied, "No, Joe, Hopey has to pee. Faith, you take her. We'll wait right here."

My mother never took her eyes off my dad, and the people in the tavern never took their eyes off my mother. She was still in her housecoat and pink slippers. But she didn't seem to mind. She was even nice to my dad's boss, who was hunched over on the stool next to my dad. She asked him about his own wife. How's Maria? Has she had the second baby yet?

I remember the blonde ladies in the bathroom were very kind to us. One lifted Hope up in order to reach the faucet. And the lady with the long orange fingernails knelt to dry my little sister's tiny, wet hands. I tried not to stare at the red band sticking out the back of her short white skirt, but I had never seen underwear that color before.

At first I would listen in on their fights, same with Hope, both of us craning for facts that were needed for nothing. We looked like seals, in silhouette, perched on our forearms, alert. But after a while, I started to force myself to concentrate on other things, like TV shows I liked, or song lyrics I knew, and then exactly what I should wear the next day. And then the day after that. And then the day after that.

But this was the way of us, and full sleep, with that natural-born calm, became the gifts of the people around us, kids whose clothes fit, who were picked up at school on time, who were never as anxious as I was to be called on first in class, arm up, begging, "Sir, sir, miss, miss, I know, I know! I know the answer!"

AS CATHOLICS I would rank us average. We went to church. We made a big to-do about the Sacraments. We were all baptized, which meant we were going to heaven, unless we really screwed up. Which we did. Some of us, anyway.

But I loved church. I used to imagine living there, because we were told, though it was God's house, it was our house, too. But with no kitchen, bathroom, or bedroom, my idea of living in a church consisted of imagining myself running mad inside and having my friends over, each of us getting our own pew, maybe. We'd put on plays at the altar, or sing Olivia Newton John songs, out loud, from the high balcony. I loved church mostly because it was clean and rich-looking. There were important holy paintings to look at, and fourteen stained-glass depictions of Jesus at various stages of being killed.

And everyone dressed beautifully.

In church, we shook hands with our friends and sang with strangers. Sunday was the only day of the week we seemed normal. We got up early. We got ourselves scrubbed and ready. Even Dad paid extra attention to combing the plaster chunks out of his damp hair. Also, we didn't fight too much, and sometimes, after church, we'd go for hot chocolate and doughnuts, right along with other normal people.

But the biggest deal about being Catholic was First Communion, especially for me, as I was the oldest girl. And my First Communion was the most memorable, not just because I got the most money of everyone, fifty-seven dollars, in cash, but because it marked the time my mother, a proud and talented Catholic, decided that she would never go to church again.

THE SPRING OF my First Communion was one of the coldest on record. I remember using a toboggan in April, a week before I was to wear a white dress and walk down the aisle, a miniature bride, minus the groom, champagne, or sex. And I was finally going to find out what the host tasted like. We were told, in Religion, it was the actual body of Christ, only more meringue-y.

We used to practice the Sacrament of the Eucharist on our front porch. We would lay out Wonder Bread slices and use my mother's rolling pin to flatten them out. We'd cut small circles out of the dough and stack them up. The neighborhood kids came over; congregated, if you will. Katrina Trevi from across the street started this great thing by pulling a turtleneck sweater up and over her face. She'd leave the neck part tight around her skull like a headband, letting the rest of the turtleneck fall down her back. It was the best pretend long hair and it substituted as a good way to be a nun, especially if the turtleneck was brown or black.

We took turns being the priest, making a collar out of the cardboard insert from the neck of my dad's one dress shirt.

"This is the body of Christ," I would say to Hope, raising the Wonder Bread host in front of her face, using my holiest voice, surprisingly deep for age eight.

"Amen," she'd say with an equally deep voice, lifting her cupped hands to receive the bread from me. (Hope used to have a yellow turtleneck that pulled her face so tight she looked like a bald bird.) She carefully lifted the bit of "Jesus" out of her palm and placed it tenderly on her tongue. We would do this over and over again, sometimes receiving the host ten, maybe twelve times.

"Lemme do it again. I didn't do it good that time."

"Don't chew, it's Jesus. Let Him melt in your mouth or it's a sin," were my priestly instructions.

"Um na cooing. Is melling in my mow, see?" Hope pleaded, her mouth stuffed with a wad of white bread.

"I saw you chew! Look, Hope's biting the body of Jesus! You're going to go to hell!"

This curse would send her screaming into the house. My mom would poke her head out of the door to a half-dozen half-naked four- to eight-year-olds, cross-legged, hands cupped, T-shirts like veils, surrounded by crusts of bread. She never really liked us playing church—not because it was a little creepy, but because it was a waste of perfectly good food.

"Faith, stop telling your sister she is going to hell or I will make sure you go with her!" my mother hissed.

Slam. Game over.

* * *

HELPING ME PICK OUT my Communion dress gave my mother a lot of pleasure, because when Matt had made his Communion, the year before, he only added a big white bow to the arm of his dark suit jacket. He removed it after pictures because he thought the bow made him look like a girl. Communion, I believed, was harder for girls, because our outfits were far more complicated and important. Also the girls making First Communion were better to look at than the boys, which is why it seemed like good practice for getting married. All of my female cousins who'd already made their Communion had giant dresses, trains, and veils, and some of them wore gloves to their elbows, exactly like brides I'd seen. My oldest cousin, Anna, had had the most famous dress, not because it was beautiful, but because it was, at the time, the most expensive thing I had ever heard of. It cost $450, enough to feed the world as I knew it, at that age. According to my mother, it was a "gaudy mess" that made Anna look like "one of those tacky white Christmas trees." No, we were going to find me something tasteful, classy, holy, and most important, cheap.

We headed straight to Chico Moda's, a used-clothing store, off the main strip. She had to pull me past Adores, a lushly decorated import children's clothing store, where my rich cousin Anna had bought her dress. Styrofoam doves, gold crucifixes, and dozens of white, frothy Communion dresses were suspended by wires, hanging out of my reach in every possible way. We also passed Carmela's, a religious corner shop where Matt got his bow, and where I could see a wide array of snappy Bibles on top of mountains of candy-covered almonds, arranged just perfectly. Big and little pink and yellow Easter bunnies were piled in the corners, mashing up against the windows like orphans, begging for me to take them home and love them. I waved because how could I not?

"God," I was thinking, "being Catholic is so beautiful."

Then we reached our stupid store. Chico Moda's had a filthy "Big Sale" sign Scotch-taped in its windows. When we entered, I was hit with the stench of mothballs and cigarette smoke. Everything smelled used and poor.

"Mom, how come we have to go here all the time?"

"I told you, these are good enough. Besides you won't wear your Communion dress ever again and I am not spending five hundred dollars just like an idiot."

"I will *so* wear it again."

"Stop it."

She always shopped in a hurry, as though someone had deliberately hidden the one thing she came to buy, and if she could just push everything else out of the way, she'd finally, finally find it.

"Here. Nope. No," my mother said to me, cradling the throwaways. I was suffocating under a pile of stinky satin. "Oh now, Faith, this one's nice. Try this one on."

The dress she had chosen wasn't bad. It had a prairie look to it, ruffled collar and a big band around the waist that tied in back. It was a little long, but I wasn't finished convincing her we should be at Adores or Carmela's before anyone saw us here, where poor people shopped.

So I stalled.

I knew if I tried it on, we were buying it. I can't remember a time when we didn't buy the first thing that fit, while shopping with my mom. Once, when she was resting at the hospital, Dad took us back-to-school shopping. We went to Sentry's, a discount department store, with good parking, which was right next to a licensed Chinese restaurant. My dad said he'd meet us there after we were done. He gave Matty one hundred dollars, cash, and said, You be in charge. Twenty-five for each, okay? Bring-a me change.

Inside Sentry's, I pouted with incredible intensity and refused every corduroy jumper Matty'd lift with the tips of his fingers out of the piles of on-sale girls' clothes.

"How 'bout this, Faith? Ewww," he'd tease, throwing leotards or pink underwear at my face, as if it was diseased.

In the end, Matty bought himself a genuine leather soccer ball. Charlie picked out a Lite-Brite set and a bat. We all agreed on new

Lego and the giant-sized box of crayons, to share. We were able to secure, by way of useful outfits, one single sweater for Hope.

I took the twenty dollars left over from my share of clothes money and hid it.

Dad didn't inspect the bags until we came home. Our purchases distressed him so much, he opened another beer and called Grandpa Franco. He asked if Grandpa would do him a favor and take us back-to-school shopping while Mom was away. My dad explained how he had to work. And the next day, when my dad handed Grandpa yet another hundred dollars, I felt as though I had hit a jackpot reward with my hidden twenty. I spent the rest carefully, and lovingly, over the next few months, sometimes on myself, a chocolate bar or ice cream, sometimes treating Hope, Matty, and Charlie, if only just to shut them up.

We wouldn't have gotten away with that if my mom had been there.

At Chico Moda's she pushed me into a dressing room stall, then she shoved the balled-up prairie Communion dress under the door. I put it on slowly and came out to see myself in the mirror. I tried to avoid her face because I knew she'd be showing way too much enthusiasm for it.

"This dress is okaaaayee, but I think it's too loooong for me," I whined into my own reflection.

"I can fix the hem, easy."

So we bought the extra-long prairie Communion dress. Her concession was a small tiara and satin slippers from Carmela's, after I convinced her they could be a part of an excellent princess costume for Halloween.

"I wonder what Jesus would think of that bargain?" she asked the ceiling, while paying for the items.

I cried three times the morning of my Communion. First, when I saw the seven inches of snow that had fallen the night before, which meant I had to wear my ugly blue parka, Matty's hand-me-down, over my dress. Then I cried while I pulled on my winter boots.

"Stop it, Faith. Jesus is not going to see your boots under your dress. You can change into your new slippers at church."

"Still."

"Don't be like this. I don't feel so good this morning."

She looked awful, too, like she had the flu, but I wasn't feeling tender toward her. Having to wear an ugly boy's parka over my new(ish) dress, not being able to show off my lovely slippers, on a day as important as this, was my first real clothing dilemma. And it became a lifelong trigger. There was little that could bother me more than when something went wrong with an outfit. Planning what I would wear could keep me up all night, with me thinking, "That top matches those leotards, which would pick up the yellow in my mitts nicely." If one of those pieces was missing or dirty, I would fling myself across the nearest couch, bed, or lap and deeply question the state of the entire world and all of its unfairness. How could this be? I can't wear Matty's parka! What had I ever done to God to deserve this? And why did You make it snow? Today? Jesus Christ! It's April! (I wouldn't have considered uttering "Jesus Christ" as blasphemous. Back then, I would often directly address the Man whose body I'd soon be eating, as though He was an upstairs neighbor, wanting to be helpful.)

My mom looked at me in disgust and said, "Stop pouting, Faith. This is supposed to be your holy day, so just try and act a little holy, okay?"

She stomped upstairs to wake up my dad. As usual, he had come home late the night before. I had heard him drive up and was fully expecting a big fight. I was awake, thinking about my Communion outfit. But instead of a fight, he and my mother had talked for a long time, in the kitchen. Their voices were low. At one point it had sounded like my mom was crying. It was odd for them to have been holding what seemed to be a real kind of conversation, especially since my dad had come home so late.

Especially since my mother had waited up for him.

I knew it was exactly two-thirty in the morning when they had finally gone to bed, because my mother let me have the alarm clock in my room. I wanted to wake up before everyone else so I could set my hair in rollers, something I had just learned how to do on my own. I needed extra time in case the complicated hairdo I planned to wind around my tiara didn't turn out right.

After she woke up Dad, my mom came downstairs looking worse than when she left. Her face was pink and flushed and she was wiping at the corners of her mouth. She looked at me, turned, and ran back upstairs again. My dad stumbled around her on his way down and went quietly into the kitchen.

"You look very beautiful, Fate," he said, without looking at me. I was sitting at the kitchen table. My hair was in an "updo," the kind Auntie Linda wore. I used thirty bobby pins, bending my tiara around the sides to keep the coils of my hair in place.

"Is Mom feeling sick today?" I asked, while he was pouring a glass of water.

"Naa, she gonna be fine. Everybaddy's ready?" he asked, still in his own pajama bottoms.

"No, nothing's ready. This is just great! How come she has to be sick on my Communion day?"

"Come on, Fate. You help alla keeds get ready, okay?"

Matt, Hope, and Charlie were watching cartoons, even though cartoons were not that good on Sundays. My dad disappeared upstairs with the water. I started to fake cry, sitting in my tiara, coat, and boots.

"You guys, get ready," I screamed into the living room. "We have to go! Now!"

My mom heard me from the upstairs bathroom.

"Jesus Christ, Faith, you don't have to yell!" she yelled.

A few minutes later, my mom came down dressed in her olive-green pantsuit with the fake alligator belt. She was wearing her only piece of good jewelry, a butterfly pin, which had two authentic diamond chips in it. She kept it in the bottom drawer of our silverware box and I loved it almost as much as she did, checking in on it at least once a week. She was taller and skinnier-looking that morning but she smelled like Moonwind, as always, the only perfume from Avon that she liked. When my mother dressed up, which she hardly ever did, it made my heart skip a beat as if I was a boy who had a crush on her.

My heart did that, not just because I thought she was beautiful, but because other people would think she was beautiful, and it felt like we were taking a baby step toward normal. When I was eight, if things seemed normal, they were.

"You look really beautiful today, Faith," she said, the makeup on her face looking as if it was hovering just in front of her skin and not resting on it the way it should be.

My dad, in his only pair of dress pants and wearing his only dressy sweater, went out to warm up the car. He didn't have a good coat, so he didn't wear one to church. Even in winter.

"Hey, let me put a little bit of lipstick on you," my mom said to me, after she finished putting some on herself.

"You feel better now, right, Mom?" I sniffled. My mom never let us wear makeup, not even play makeup.

"Yeah," she said, and I pushed out my lips. She smeared Avon Coral Craze on my mouth.

"Me too, me too," demanded Hope, and she got some, too.

"How come Hope gets lipstick when it's my Communion?" I whined.

"Faith . . . shut . . . it."

"Me too, me too," said Charlie, jumping up and down, and we watched in awe as my mom put a teeny bit on him.

"He's a boy!" said Matt, disgustedly.

"He's a little boy," my mom replied, and we went out the door, the five of us, almost at the same time.

As soon as we settled into the station wagon, and before my dad could back out of the driveway, I noticed Charlie touching my skirt with his dirty snow boots.

"Mom, Charlie's ruining my Communion dress completely."

"Oh Christ, come up here then!"

I smugly exited the back seat and slammed the door, came around to the passenger side of the station wagon, and my mother scooted over to the middle. I shut the door and shot my brothers and sister my best "nyeh nyeh" face.

"Faith—enough," my mom scolded.

Hope kicked the back of my seat.

I yelled, "Stop it or I'll kill you, Hope. It's my special day, goddammit!"

That came out by accident.

"Fate!" my dad yelled. He must have been in a bad mood because he never yelled at us. This was something I reminded my mother of every time she did.

"That's because he's never around to see how bad yous guys are!" she'd say.

On the way to church, no one said anything, which made me feel depressed. I sighed and put my forehead on the window a little dramatically. But I was thinking that, so far, this day didn't feel different or special for me. In Religion, we were told by Sister Lianne that today was holy. After today, I was told, I would be one of them. I would go up to mass behind Dad and Mom and Matty and be a real member of God's family, and not just a stupid old member of my stupid old family. Yet no one in the station wagon seemed to care. Even Hope and Charlie didn't realize that today, when I went up for the host like everyone else, they'd have to sit all alone. No more "Faith, you're in charge! Kids, listen to Faith!" while Matty went up with my mom and dad. I thought, What's going to happen to Charlie after Hope makes her Communion? Would he have to sit all by himself in the pew? Because of perverts, we were never allowed to leave Charlie alone, even for a minute, even to run into the store for a second. What if there was a pervert nearby him in church and we left him alone in the pew? This was too much to think about on my big day, so I started to concentrate on my outfit. I hoped to be prettier than my classmates. I especially wanted to look prettier than Natalia and Nadine Montebello, who, just because they were twins, got all the attention. They did promise to save a seat for me. And as soon as I got inside the church, I thought, I would give my mother my coat, and then I would change out of my ugly boots and into my new slippers and . . . my slippers. Oh, Christ! I forgot my slippers!

"Mom, we have to go back home!" I screamed.

"Why?"

"I forgot my slippers!"

"Jesus Christ, Faith! We don't have time! We're almost there!"

"Yes, we do, we have to have time! I can't wear these stupidlyugly boots! I can't or I have to go barefoot!"

"Jesus. Turn around, Joe. Turn."

"Jesus," said my dad, pulling a sharp and unexpected U-turn in the middle of the street, a block before the church parking lot. My mom grabbed my arm hard, I thought, to steady herself during the turn, but it stayed there. Her eyes were still bulged out even after we had swayed and corrected ourselves straight again. She slapped her hand over her mouth.

"Joe, please stop," she said, but it sounded like "joepeesta," one fast word, uttered through her clenched fingers. My dad slammed down on the brakes. My mother's whole body went for the door handle next to me. She still had a tight grip on my arm, so when I went tumbling out, I took her entire front half with me. Still holding my arm, she threw up in the snow, her torso nearly folded under the car to direct her sickness away from me and my dress. She was crying and talking through her retching, "Honey, oh, are you—*bleeeck*—okay? Faith? Oh, God—*bleeeek*—Faith! Joe—*bleeeck*—oh, God! I'm—*bleeeck*—sorry."

My dad had stopped the car and had run around to her side. He grabbed me under my armpits and dragged me away from my mom, dropping me back on my butt, in fresher snow, a few feet away. He kissed the top of my head fast and hard.

"Okayokayokay, Fate, you okay?" he asked, looking over at my mother. I made a noise as a reply.

"Uhgh."

He kneeled in front of my mom, picked up her head, and moved her hair off her face. A little of her vomit was on the bottom of my dress. I rubbed the stain absently in the snow, never taking my eyes off my mother, bent under the car door. I had tears in my eyes, but they stayed there, helpfully blurring out this unfair sight.

My dad was frantic, yelling Christ! Keeds, gimme some-a-ting to wipe Mumma's mouth.

Nobody moved.

"Looook, for chry-ssakes!" he screamed, for the second time in his life.

Matty handed him a crumpled-up McDonald's bag. My dad smacked it out of his hand and stood up. He pulled his only good sweater over his head, balled it up, and put it under Mom's chin. She grabbed it and, still holding the sweater to her face, and without even looking at him, she started to make her way out of the car over to where I was sitting, stunned, in a snowbank. Her eyes were little red beads swimming in watery, black mascara. I struggled and started toward her. Meeting halfway in the middle, she wrapped her free arm around my back and cried into the sweater, "I'm sorry. I'm sorry, Faith."

My dress had soaked through to my bum.

"It's okay," I said in a small voice, unsure if I really meant it. My dad put his arms around both of us. My mom put her hand on his bare back. He was naked from the waist up.

"Joe, where's your dress shirt for under this?" my mom asked, holding his balled-up sweater in front of her mouth.

"I couldn't find it."

"Jesus, Joe, I ironed it and put it on the back of the kitchen chair. God, would you look at us," she said, half-laughing, yanking herself out of our hug.

Matty's teacher, Mr. Grillo, pulled over and asked if we were okay.

My dad nodded and waved. "Nan, she's gotta the flu bad. We gonna go home."

"If you want, I can take the kids to church with us," Mr. Grillo offered.

My mother looked at me. My tiara was at a tilt. I had no real hairdo left. I would not go to church without my slippers. Plus there was vomit on my dress. No, no, no, I was saying in my head. Matt was saying the same thing in his own head, I could tell.

"No," said my mom, "but thanks, Mr. Grillo."

She climbed back into the front seat. I got into the back, where Charlie was crying. Hope had him on her lap, holding him tight, as much for her own relief as for his.

"You fell out of the car," said Hope, sniffling. "I saw it all."

"Yeah, me too," whispered Charlie.

"I know."

"Look what happened to your dress," Hope said. "You prolly gotta get a new one, right?"

"Yeah," added Charlie.

"I know," I murmured. That was one thought to comfort me.

A few seconds later, Matt asked, "Is everyone okay? Jeez!" His voice was shaky and afraid and it sounded like mine would have if I could have let it out of jail. There were feelings in my body and emotions crawling across my face that I was completely unfamiliar with, so I locked them all up.

My mom nodded yes, still holding the sweater to her face. I didn't know where to look, down at my dress, at the back of her head, at my dad's naked shoulders, at the church that was slowly disappearing behind us.

My mom said, "Faith, we'll figure this out when we get home, okay?" She started to cry very softly into my dad's only sweater. He tried to put an arm around her but she moved over to her side of the car and leaned her head up against the window.

THAT NIGHT, after a long nap, my mom told us she would need to go into the hospital just for a couple of days, because of the special kind of flu she had. She got sick again, a few days later, the morning my auntie Linda came in from Detroit, to pick her up. We watched our aunt park her silver-blue LeMans, something we knew she had just bought with her own money. She walked into the kitchen, breezed by my dad, and dropped a dozen fancy doughnuts onto the dining room table and sat down.

Those doughnuts would be our breakfast for the three days Mom was gone.

"Kids, come here and give me an octopus hug," said Auntie Linda, growling, and gathering us up into her strong, tanned arms, us crowding her skinny middle. My aunt was one year younger than my mother was, but she looked like the older one to me. She wore a lot of interesting makeup; white lipstick, which was unsettling, and thick black eyeliner, slanted out to her temples. My mother once said that Auntie Linda's sense of style took a dangerous turn not long after a man on the tunnel bus told her she looked like Elizabeth Taylor.

"I tried to tell her he meant *National Velvet,* not *Cleopatra,* but she won't listen to me."

As sisters, they were devoted to each other, though they had very little in common, except for sharing a strict father and suffering a motherless childhood. I was told that Grandma Franco died from the disease of not being able to enjoy the sweeter things in life. Later, when Auntie Linda explained diabetes to me, I thought, I'd die, too, without "Lik-m-aids" or Pop Rocks or Snickers.

While my mom was away, my dad took a few days off from work to take care of us the best he could. Life was a blur of TV and McDonald's.

Grandpa Franco stopped by the morning my dad was to take me to pick out another Communion dress. I was coming downstairs when he offered my dad his credit card in order for me to be able to afford any dress that I wanted, "In the world," Grandpa said. My dad tried to tell him he could afford to buy me the dress himself, but Grandpa just whispered to my dad that he was under the impression there was very little we could afford these days. My dad said that's not true, that "it" (whatever "it" was) had nothing to do with money. My dad said that "it" was all Mom's decision and not his at all. I thought that my mother must have felt really sick, this time, to go into a hospital, since it sounded like an extraordinarily expensive thing to do. She was so stingy with money, rather than pay a dentist, she'd pull out our baby teeth herself, our knees bent over the kitchen counter. The teeth would be as loose as kernels on a cob, so she didn't hurt us so much as scare us half to death with the giant pliers.

Later, in the car, I asked my dad about why he didn't think Mom should go to the hospital to get "it" done? He asked me how did I know about "it." I said, I heard yous talking. Without yelling, he got angry, and said I shouldn't be listening to other people's conversations because it was a sin for a girl to be nosy. He said, Fate, when you getta married, you gonna understand about a lot more tings.

That was the first time I noticed that when my dad dropped my "H," my name had a different meaning. I knew from Religion class that "faith" comes from God, because it originates in your heart and prayers. But "fate" was used by lazy pagans to excuse their ignorant deeds. "What can you do?" those sinners would say. "It was my 'fate' to steal that car, meet my mistress, kill that shop clerk." We were taught, with enough faith, you could triumph over your sins, because hell is no good Catholic's fate.

My dad asked me if I had heard what he said, about a girl like me being nosy. I whined that I couldn't help hearing them. I was just there, after all.

He shut off the engine and looked at me with sad, tired eyes.

"Whadam I gonna do with you, Fate?" he asked.

I felt like saying, what am I going to do with you and Mom? I wanted to tell him that I was losing faith in the fact that they'd tell me what I needed to know. And that if they continued to whisper, in secret, like prayers, in rooms, and in staircases around me, then it was my necessary fate to be listening. And their fault if that was a damn sin.

THE DAY I made my Communion, my mother was still away, so my grandpa brought Hope and me to church, after dropping the boys off at the hockey arena. My dad took the opportunity to work, to make some money, double overtime. The dress I picked out with my dad wasn't expensive. It wasn't even as nice as the first one, really. It was more peasant than prairie-style, but it fit perfectly, and since the snow had melted I would be able to wear my new slippers.

At church, because the story got out about my mother being so sick, with the bad flu, I was treated like I was famous for something. People looked at me, or maybe it was because I was the only one making First Communion that day.

I remember this: when Father Pete placed the host in my hand, I couldn't believe how light it was for being a part of the body of Christ. When I put it in my mouth, it immediately stuck to the roof, like Matty said it would, and I spent the rest of mass using my tongue to mash it into something more swallowable.

I hoped to improve my technique with time.

After Communion I changed into leotards and a jumper and we all went to Ponderosa Steakhouse to celebrate. Then we went to the Spring Fair at the Kmart parking lot and rode on all of the scarier rides. It was nice, and nobody threw up this time.

When my mom came back from the hospital, she seemed completely back to normal. Better than the other times she went for rests. She returned happy, thrilled even, to see us. She cleaned the house, cooked a honey-baked ham, and didn't seem at all surprised when Father Pete rolled up in his black Volkswagen Rabbit, Dad following shyly behind in the station wagon. She invited Father Pete to stay for dinner but he declined the offer. He was really only wondering when would be a good time for her to come see him at the church. He thought perhaps they had some things to discuss, things better left unsaid in front of the children. My mother looked at the four of us gathered around the table, stopped her eyes on me, and said, There's nothing that gets by these kids. Go ahead, she said. Father Pete smiled and made a quiet offer of good counsel for the dilemma she might have found herself in. She said that she wasn't aware of any dilemma. Charlie said, Yeah, Mom was sick, and now she's all better, from going in the hospital. Well then, Father Pete said, We'll see you soon, I hope. My mom said, No, you probably won't, and turned up the radio when she heard "Me and Bobby McGee."

My dad opened a beer and walked Father Pete out to his car.

After supper, my mother adjusted the antenna on the TV, found a movie she loved, *Rebecca,* and let us stay up an hour longer than usual to watch it with her. The four of us leaned up against her body like kindling on a bonfire.

"You're all cured from the flu, Mom?" Hope asked, climbing gingerly into her lap, being careful not to hurt Mom's "booboo tummy."

"Yup, all cured. No more flu ever!" she said.

My dad lifted himself off the couch and went to kick around chunks of dirt in our garden for the rest of the evening.

MY MOM DID NOT go to church with us that week, or the next. After a month of Sundays passed, my mom shooing us out the door with Dad, I finally asked her why she stopped going.

"Because I have too much to do around the house," she said. "Plus it's my only time off from yous guys."

Then I asked her if she missed it, and she said, "No, I don't, because now I do all my praying at home, when I'm on my hands and knees, scrubbing the floors."

PEOPLE AT CHURCH noticed my mother's absence. At first they asked after her a lot, then a little, then sometimes, then never. I started to miss the olden times, when my dad would wait around after mass to talk to our neighbors, in Italian, poking at his teeth with a toothpick, nodding and laughing at their foreign stories. I missed how my mother would yell from the car, "Let's go, Joe, I want to get the kids home!"

Now we avoided eye contact with people.

Used to be I loved how Father Pete told the stories about Jesus in a funny, modern way, saying, "Well now what in the heck was Jesus going to say to that, I ask you? Jesus probably scratched His head and thought, darn it all, who in the heck are these people asking me to perform miracles like I'm some kinda carnival sideshow? I'm the Son of God, for Pete's sake!"

Ha ha ha. I'd giggle. My mother would roll her eyes at me, and look at her watch.

I missed her doing that.

Now I paid no attention to the parables and the sermons. Now I thought constantly about what my mother was up to at home. Sometimes I pictured her talking on the phone to Auntie Linda, filing her nails, or going back to sleep. Other times I pictured her crying by herself. I used to pray for toys, or for certain boys or people to like me. Now I prayed for my mother or on behalf of my mother. I used to linger after church to watch what other people wore, imagining their outfits for myself. Now we rushed out to the car after the final "Go in peace." I used to love the feeling of being normal, for that one hour a week, the six of us lined up in varying degrees of height, Dad down to little Charlie. Now we pinched each other and pointed at the people standing in front of us, holding our fingers one inch away from their bums, on a dare. My dad would gasp and shush, but now that we never went for hot chocolate or doughnuts after church, what was our incentive to behave? Without Mom watching over us, and God and Dad not showing themselves to be equally scary substitutes, church was a useless chore.

My own mission remained, however. If my mother was a sinner, not going to church so, therefore, hell, I would need to hold the fort here. I would plead her case and save her soul. Making my brothers and my sister laugh was just a harmless way to bust up the monotony of my earnest vigil.

Chapter Two

When people from church, or our neighborhood, would call my dad by his real name, Giuseppe, it always startled me. It startled me even more when I heard my dad speak Italian back to them. It was as though he was speaking in tongues, or worse, faking it, making up gibberish just to throw us off. Dad's Italian frustrated my mother more because she couldn't speak a word, despite her own full-blooded heritage. She also showed no interest in learning Italian, and practically forbade it to be spoken in our house. My dad once "got caught" teaching me how to say, "Gigi is my cat," in Italian. My mother yelled at him to stop, that she wanted us to be "normal," not like other immigrants whose accents and outfits people made fun of.

"I don't want people to think my kids are Pakis," she explained. Pakis had recently replaced Arabs on her list of people you'd want nothing to do with. Arabs were causing economic problems for the world, due to the oil crisis, she said, and whatever jobs were left went to the Pakis. Her "Paki/Arab fear" used to leave my dad silent for a few seconds. He understood English, but not some of the more stupid things that came out of her mouth. He'd reply, How can people think our kids are Pakis when everyone around here knows they are "filt-ee WOPs"?

"True. Full-blooded," she'd say.

We were WOPs, but when we lived in the city, around other WOPs, we never felt like WOPs. And though we were darker-skinned compared to the other kids, I was never even called a Paki—nigger, yes, but not a Paki. And the "nigger thing" started because of my mother. Billy Bondi, the first kid to call me that, was referring to my hair rather than my dark skin.

"Faith, you got an Afro just like a Jackson's Five!" he told me. "You're probably a nigger and you don't even know it."

Like Matty, Hope, and Charlie, I was born with a head of black, springy curls. But as I got older, my hair went thinner, then limp, so by the time I turned ten, it had about as much body as smoke. My mom seemed to hate my stringy hair more than I did and subjected me to back-to-back Toni home perms for years. Sometimes my hairdo worked out okay. Sometimes I yelled at her, head ducked under the kitchen tap, that if I suffered a disease of the head, it would be because of these perms. But mostly I was left with a nappy tuft of hair, burnt and uneven, that could barely be held down with spit and barrettes.

A particularly bad run of hairdos coincided with the fall release of the popular miniseries *Roots.* We watched it raptly, and it changed the way I stared at black people when my grandpa took us shopping in Detroit. It used to be I was fascinated by how different they looked, but after *Roots,* I stared at them harder, trying to see their deep sadness from having been slaves.

Like in the case of *Grease* and *Star Wars,* it was inevitable that the characters from *Roots* would work their way into our recess games. Angelo Delassi started it all by talking like Kunte Kinte, the star slave. Frankie Fredi and Palmerino Scalia acted like Chicken George. Natalia and Nadine, the twins, automatically fell into the roles of Southern belles who had the best job of just bossing us around.

But I was always, always Kizzy.

"Faith DiNapoli's probably a nigger, so she's Kizzy," was the tail-end sentence of the schoolyard *Roots* roundup. Faith DiNapoli was also the most cowardly, and since Faith DiNapoli was never chosen to be Princess Leia or one of the girls from *Grease,* Faith DiNapoli was grateful for the part of Kizzy, the female lead.

The *Roots* game involved my "owner," Tina Degenero, tying me to a basketball pole. I would sit on the concrete begging to be "free of my chains" (skipping rope), while a bunch of guys wrestled Angelo to the ground. Angelo and me had to reach out for each other while the "slave catchers" led him away, bucking and screaming. The "Southern belles" would keep yelling, "Shut up, just shut up, Kizzy, you're a nigger, and you're a dummy," they'd tease. I was instructed to hiss angrily at them because they separated me and Kunte, a father-and-daughter team, took us from our home in Africa and brought us to downtown Detroit, where we would have to find jobs at a Ford's or Chrysler's plant. After a particularly vicious auction, I was sold to a boy who promised to release me on the condition that I let him punch me hard in the arm. I agreed because my wrists hurt and I could no longer feel my fingers. He smashed me in the same shoulder more than once and walked away. When I asked the twins to untie me, they said they didn't do nice things for stupid niggers. So I stayed slumped under the basketball hoop until Matty and his friends came out for their recess and needed the court to play. Matty bent over me shyly and said I should stop playing with kids who didn't like me. It was the first time it occurred to me that they might not.

When I got home from school, the welts on my wrists were still pink, and a giant yellow bruise had formed on my shoulder. My mother asked me what the hell happened and I proudly described our slavery game, including the part where I was picked as the star slave. Matt told her he found me tied to the basketball pole and Hope added, Yeah, because everyone thinks that Faith's a nigger. My mother snapped a finger in front of her face and said, I don't want to hear that word again, you hear? She sank down into her chair with a sigh, and pulled me toward her.

"Faith, honey, you have to learn to stand up for yourself. You can say no to people when you don't want to play their games. Nothing's wrong with that."

I assured her that I didn't mind being a slave because the alternative was to be a nobody at recess.

"But these are my friends," I said, "and they really like me to play with them."

My mother asked me who are these friends of yours and she carefully wrote out the names that I recited. Hope remembered the ones I forgot, or the ones who I wanted to protect.

"And don't forget Frankie Fredi," Hope added, "because I heard him call you a dirty sinner, Mom."

She rolled her eyes.

THE NEXT MORNING she walked the four of us to school, holding a cigarette and her keys, and not our hands all that much anymore. In the principal's office, she made me pull back my blouse to show Sister Mina the now-purple bruise. My mother informed her of what these "ignorant immigrants" were up to at recess. She suggested that maybe they should be involved in activities that were a little bit more holy, goddammit, or at least something that did not involve the sale of her daughter to bullies. Sister Mina thanked my mother stiffly for the information, promised she'd look into it, but added that she found it odd getting advice about her students' religious upbringing when my mother had nothing to do with our own.

"How dare you speak to me like that in front of my daughter?" my mother hissed.

I nearly fainted from the fear of God. I had never heard a person scold a nun. I had never imagined it was something nuns could have done to them. That's why they were nuns. Their job was to scold us, on behalf of God.

Sister Mina cleared her throat in a classy way, holding her fist away from her mouth like a microphone.

"Mrs. DiNapoli," she whispered, "it's my duty to speak my mind, since I haven't had much of an opportunity to do so with you on Parent/Teacher nights."

True that my dad always went. But my mother said it was because she helped us with our homework every single, goddamn night, and it would be good for him to see what the hell the inside of a schoolroom looked like.

"My husband comes to those and that should be good enough for you people."

Her voice was cracking, as though a younger version of herself, one also taught by nuns, was emerging from her throat.

"Sometimes absence is the greatest sin, Mrs. DiNapoli," Sister Mina added, placing her arm around my shoulders.

I was afraid of everyone in the room, especially God, who I couldn't see, but could feel, shocked and fuming above us. Something bad was going to happen because my mother was yelling at a nun. This knowledge shot hot through my body for the first time in my life. That's around the time I began to form a connection between the bad things God let happen to us and the sins my mother committed.

"Listen, Sister," continued my mother, me feeling her soul spiral southward, pulling mine down with her, I was standing that close. "I did not come here to get lectured by you. I am here because I love my children very much, so I don't want anything bad happening to them. So if you don't do something about these little assholes, tying my Faith up, beating her, and calling her a nigger, you better believe I will!"

While she spat these words out, my mother's shaky hands were unwrapping a new pack of cigarettes.

"That won't be necessary, Mrs. DiNapoli. I'll take care of things from here. Oh, and there's no smoking on the school grounds, dear." Sister Mina waited one second before adding, in a fake-nice way, "Come, Faith, I'll escort you back to class."

"Bye, Mom," I muttered.

The bell rang.

Sister Mina bowed toward my mother and ushered me out the door with her. As she led me down the long hallway, I looked over my shoulder and watched my mother dig out a hankie from her purse and one-handedly blow her nose. The other hand, holding the unlit cigarette, waved frantically after me. When we got to my classroom door, I stopped and blew my sinful mother a kiss. She made a motion to catch it, as though she really, really needed it, and snapped her cigarette in half. I gasped as she dropped it on the carpet and stomped out of the office.

That was an accident, Jesus, I prayed to the crucifix hanging over the chalkboard. My mother means well. She always means well. In fact, I'm sure she'll confess to You about it later, when she's crouched in the garden, tackling the weeds.

It wasn't that my mother had ever had a bunch of girlfriends, like the other mothers on the block, but it suddenly seemed that her only friend was my auntie Linda. They only lived an hour away from each other, but they led very different lives. Auntie Linda worked in Detroit and lived there alone. Sunday mornings were the only time we left my mother alone. Auntie Linda dated lots of different men. My mother had only dated the one man she married. Auntie Linda once went to Las Vegas with a married math teacher. I was listening in on the extension when my mother said, "Oh yeah, big deal, Joe took me to A&W for my birthday. The kids came, too, because I couldn't find a babysitter, so I asked them to try and pretend they weren't there. They actually tried really, really hard. Hope hid behind her fingers, and Faith laid down in back and said, See? I'm invisible."

My aunt giggled and said, Christ, you win, Nancy.

Auntie Linda came to visit us one Saturday a month. That was my dad's excuse to stay out late. He didn't like being around all that much when my aunt would crack my mother up with stories of being single and wicked. But this one visit, my mother was cracking her sister up harder with stories of being married and having all these kids. The biggest laugh of the night came from the time I had made an Egyptian diorama of a pyramid, using sugar cubes and sequins for treasures. I thought it was a beautiful depiction of ancient life, and my mother drove me to school and helped me carry my fragile project to class. But we had ants in the house and they came with us. Sister Mina had screamed and batted her skirt when she saw them gathering at her feet.

"Oh, don't you see?" my mother had explained. "Those ants represent slaves buried along with the Pharaoh. Faith, as you know, has a deep affinity for the struggle of slaves, so thought she'd include them."

My mother imitated Sister Mina jumping around, making a face at us, throwing away my diorama, spraying Raid around my card table, and handing me an apologetic B+. It looked as though my auntie Linda had actually stopped breathing. I laughed, too, but at the time I remember being embarrassed about the bugs, and my mother joking with a nun about them.

"I said to Faith, That's not such a bad mark, considering you contaminated the whole school."

My mother was refreshing the wineglasses. Auntie Linda stopped laughing and put her hand on my head.

"Aw, Faith kiddo, at least it wasn't lice, eh?"

She left her hand there for a few seconds, and looked at me even longer. I was in awe of my auntie Linda and the single life she led. And I couldn't understand why a man hadn't grabbed her and married her and given her a bunch of kids, too. When I asked her once why she didn't have a husband, she shrugged and said she wondered that herself. But she said she had other talents, not the least being that she was one of the few people who could change my sad mother into a happy one, even if it was for a day and it required a lot of drinks.

While they continued to talk, about movies, money, and makeup, I stole three sips of their wine and was flooded with that great feeling of being "one of the girls," giggling quietly around our kitchen table at dusk. To belong to important things, our church, this family, their conversation, allowed me to sleep better and stand taller, and I memorized the feeling of that night. It was better than being a slave. Then I wondered if those little sips were going to make me as hung over as I knew my mom and her sister were going to be the next morning.

SHORTLY AFTER Auntie Linda left that Sunday, my dad came home and announced that we were moving, from the city, out to the county, an hour away, to a place called Emeryville, where he had just bought a little lot. At first I pretended that I had greatly misunderstood my father. His accent was very thick. He didn't say moving, he said what? Mooling, mooding, moofing? But I knew there was nothing wrong with his V's. He said we are moving, though he might as well have told us we were going back to Italy. Emeryville sounded as far away and foreign, and the fact that my dad needed to change his name when he moved to Canada no longer seemed inconceivable to me. I needed to be anyone else but Faith DiNapoli, the girl frozen in fear, holding a piece of yellow Lego, because she would be leaving behind the only place she knew. My dad noticed that the four of us had been gathered at the table, working on a complicated Lego house for our cat, Gigi. This is just a coincidence, I wanted to scream, us building this thing, which I now had the urge to violently shove off the table. But my dad said, Looka how nice, keep it up, kids, we're gonna need the practice.

My mother put her hands over her mouth and muffled, "Oh, God! Joe! We got it? We got that lot? How much?"

"Well, Nancy, T.B.A. in da W.," he said, mocking my mother's insult, "he give us a good deal."

"We can afford this, right?" she asked, nodding, answering her own question.

My dad said, "I tink so. I 'ope so."

"Oh, Joe, this is great," squealed my mother. She jumped up, spilling the Legos she was sorting on her lap, and threw her arms around his neck. "This is the right thing for us [kiss]. It's just going to be so much better out there [kiss]. We have to leave, you know it."

"I know, Nancy," said my dad, dodging her mouth. "I know."

Charlie bit down on a cheese slice, and asked, "But do I gotta leave here?"

My mother fell back in her chair, and said, "You, Charlie, are probably the only one who doesn't, but I think we're gonna bring you anyways."

So this is the punishment, I thought, for my mother screaming at a nun and never going to church.

My dad had predicted this.

A few months back, many Sundays after Hope had made her First Communion, in my old dress, my dad had crept downstairs wearing his white spattered coveralls. He found us lined up on the couch in our best outfits, waiting to go to church. Cartoons were on low because Auntie Linda was sleeping on the cot in the downstairs hallway.

He looked at us, shook his head, then turned and ran back upstairs, taking the steps in twos.

"Nancy!" we heard him yell. "You gettuppa now! I wanna you see deez kids. Dis is no good!" he screamed. "I wanna you take-a dem to church, goddammit all!"

Some weekends, my dad signed up for time-and-a-half piecework, on the new subdivision in Forest Glade. Normally he didn't do roofing jobs, but the money was good, better on Sundays, and my mother must have forgotten to tell us that church was off that morning, since my dad wouldn't be able to bring us. Besides, she and Auntie Linda had stayed up late the night before, laughing about high school and Grandpa Franco's strictness. We had been allowed to play Monopoly until way past bedtime. So that morning was supposed to have been an opportunity to sleep in, along with my mother, something we had been doing more often than I cared to. Those sinful Sundays, I could almost feel God and all His better people carrying on without us.

My mother came staggering downstairs, crunching the sleep out of her eyes. She frowned sympathetically at the spectacle of our little feat, which I had been mostly responsible for. I had woken everyone up, poured the cereal, and kept the noise down. I had even spit-combed Charlie's black wavy hair over to the side and behind his ear, like my mother always did. Hope was uncomfortably tugging at my least-adorable hand-me-down dress. As a beginner tomboy, she was starting to wreck my prettier things, so I was reluctant to part with the favorites even though they didn't fit me anymore.

"Oh, jeez," my mom sighed. "You guys look so cute. Look at yous."

My dad yelled at her, saying, Ees dat all you can say? Cute? Da're perfect and you're ruining dis family! You and your damn stabberness! You bring dem to church, Nancy, I no care how.

My mother ignored my dad, crossed her arms, and looked at the four of us, particularly at me. My pride in myself started to melt into embarrassment, so I stared hard at Matty, who was staring hard at his shoes.

"Joe, just go make some money, okay?" my mother said, almost kindly. "Or we're all going to have to start working Sundays."

My dad's boss pulled up and honked. He rushed toward us and kissed "I love yous keeds" into the tops of each of our four heads, me getting the "love" part, and feeling every bit of it. On his way out, he hissed out a reminder, saying, I mean it, Nancy, a sin. Bigger dan the odder one. He slammed the door and left.

Auntie Linda appeared out of the dark hallway wearing the shiny blue pantsuit she had worn the night before. She grabbed her full-length, fox fur coat and threw it around her shoulders, using her hand to tamp down the part of her hairdo that was sticking up.

"Well, kids, guess what? Your auntie's gonna bring you to church this morning," she announced, her voice gravelly like a man's. "How'd you like that?"

She made a face at my mother—a "what the hell" face.

"Oh, sweetie, thanks," said my mother, wetting her thumbs with her tongue and smearing Auntie Linda's stray black eyeliner up under her bottom lashes. "Maybe everyone'll think you're me." She laughed, pulling Auntie Linda's coat tight around her shoulders, and cupping her chin.

We all piled into the station wagon and Matty had to remind her how to get to the church. I knew she hardly went herself, so I reminded her how to act inside, me whispering, Now comes the part where we sit, then we kneel, Auntie Linda, and now let us pray.

She nodded appreciatively and folded her hands.

"Yes, let's do that. Let's pray real hard, Faith."

"Pray for Mom, too," I whispered.

"Yes, for your mom, and a little bit for me, too, dear," she said, closing her eyes and rubbing her temples.

* * *

ALL WE WERE TOLD about the move was that we needed the move. Needed to start all over again. Too many people knew too much about us in the neighborhood. I had heard my mother tell my auntie Linda that my dad was beginning to get sick of the way people looked at and talked about her. But I knew we were moving only because my mother wouldn't budge. She wouldn't go to church, wouldn't ask for forgiveness for the "odder" sin, though for the life of me I couldn't imagine what could be worse than sleeping in on Sundays. Maybe yelling at Sister Mina? Hollering at the neighbors' kids and us? Other mothers did, too, so what was different about mine? Sure, she didn't make her own tomato sauce or watch soap operas all day. She also had a clothes dryer and used it, even in the summer. Sometimes she didn't wear underwear under her tighter pants. And she drank like my dad, though beer seemed to affect her a lot less than it did him. She often wore curlers without a kerchief. And though other mothers took cigarette breaks on the fire escape, my mother smoked on the benches lining our dance class, watching me and Hope practice our steps, cheering us on like we were doing sports. Also, she read the paper and had a lot of things to say about what she had heard on the news that night. She'd tell anyone who'd listen. Though more and more, it was just us kids as her audience. And what did we know about arrogant politicians, OPEC's unfairness, or the unnecessary slaughter of cute baby seals? No, she wasn't like other moms, but it seemed to bother the rest of us a lot more than it ever bothered her.

MY DAD'S REAL NAME was Giuseppe but he officially changed it into Joe after he became a full Canadian citizen. Joe is, in fact, English for Giuseppe, but according to my mother, he chose Joe probably because it was easier for him to spell. He wasn't sure if it was an insult, but my dad always told me leaving behind his old name made things easier in the new country.

So, like my dad, I changed mine. I got the first part, "Rebecca," from my mother's favorite movie, and the stories of Sunnybrook

Farm. I added "Gauloises" as a last name. "Rebecca Gauloises" would fit in and be normal, living near all those farms and French-Canadians we were told populated them. When I announced my new identity, my mother said fine with the first name but I couldn't change my last name. It might make transferring school records too difficult, she explained. Mostly, naming myself after Auntie Linda's cigarettes didn't seem like a very good idea to her.

"Plus," she said, inhaling one of her own, "if I let you change your last name, the other kids are going to want to. I'm having a hard enough time keeping track of all your new first names."

It's true, my personality plus creative ideas had a lot of influence on my siblings. After I became "Rebecca," Hope changed hers to "Chastity," after Sonny and Cher's kid. Matty and Charlie fought over the name of "Steve Austin," from the *Six Million Dollar Man.* My mother suggested they split it up and rotate every once in a while. Matty'd be "Steve" for the week that Charlie was "Austin." They were only playing, but I worried "Faith DiNapoli" was too Italian-sounding and I didn't want to risk being called a nigger ever again. I knew we were already going to stand out because Katrina Trevi told me there were almost no ethnic people living way out there, unless you counted French-Canadians, which we didn't. They were Catholics like us, but my mother said they had Italians beat on many counts.

"They breed like rabbits out there, on purpose, not accidentally, like me," she joked. She also said we wouldn't have to worry about remembering other people's last names as there were only about three or four to choose from: St. Pierre, Chaumier, Lachapelle, and Laroque. She was not completely drunk when she joked like that, but she was not completely wrong either.

I DID AGREE THAT the city house was too small. A dresser wouldn't fit in me and Hope's room; we still shared a bed. The hallway acted as the spare room. We even had to keep our toys stored under the dining room table, which was never used anyways, except for Christmas and Thanksgiving, when we'd all sit facing each other, mute like tombstones with nothing written on them. We needed more space, but it felt as though we'd have too much space living out in the county. We'd have no neighbors to witness my parents' fighting, and no more counting Mrs. Piletti's bruises in order to feel a bit better about it. No more sandbox down the street to retreat to. No ice cream man to chase. No more running through the water from a gushing fire hydrant that one of the older "punks" would vandalize and unscrew. No shopping for crusty buns and mortadella in Little Italy, where we would run into my dad at a bar with his coworkers. He'd be speaking Italian until he would see my mother and then he'd say, in English, "Yeah, yeah, I be rye home, Nancy." No more me and Hope taking the Number 4 bus downtown to dance class. No more Mom saying, Don't let Hope out of your sight or I'll kill you and sit behind the driver and here's five dollars for French fries and gravy at Kresge's. Don't go anywhere else but there. Don't talk to perverts. Come straight home. Bring me change.

None of that anymore.

THE NEW HOUSE, in the county, came to us first in the form of a picture, a pastel watercolor from one of my dad's subdivision catalogues. They had even painted in a family standing out front; a blond man and a blond lady with two kids, both white-haired and waving. The lady was holding a baby, and they had a kind-looking yellow dog. The new house was called "The Valhalla Model," a "split-level, 4 bdr/family rm, fplc, carport." We were adding a small fountain to the lawn, something my dad insisted on. But I took to calling Emeryville Emerald City, because didn't Dorothy want to leave it, too? Because no matter how perfect it seemed, and how much it had to offer, by way of space and beauty, didn't she want to go home just the same?

For a while, we had two houses, after my dad started building the county house from scratch, using his own hands. I didn't know where we got the money for it, but once when I was playing with Katrina Trevi, I overheard her mother, Frances, tell another lady that the DiNapolis "sold whatever was left of their souls to a mortgager."

I told my mother what I had heard. I didn't know what a mortgage was, but I knew about souls and money, and I asked her how much did she think I could get for mine. She told me I could get a lot more than Frances Trevi, because, fact is, at least I had one.

ON SATURDAYS, we'd drive out to see the new house, and to store some smaller things like flowerpots and toys in the new shed. And every time we drove out there I tried hard to memorize landmarks and turns, hoping they'd keep changing, that we'd just get lost and drop the whole idea.

We spent afternoons playing on the dirt hills and walking around barefoot because the foundation often flooded, turning the basement into a giant wading pond.

This kind of structural damage would make my mother anxious.

"Are you sure you know what you're doing, Joe?" she'd ask. "I don't think I asked for an indoor pool."

Before the walls and doors of the new house went up, we would find piles of cigarette butts and empty beer bottles stacked in the corners of the foundation. Once, I came across evidence of a tiny bonfire that someone had built right in the middle of what would eventually be my room. I figured it was hoboes. We had "hoboes," I thought, like other people had ants or termites. I imagined them huddled around the fire on the cement floor of my new bedroom, swapping traveling stories and eating beans out of a can, me catching them at it.

"This is my damn bedroom, you hoboes, so get out!" I would have yelled at their dirty faces, watching them scurry over the cement wall, holding sticks with bulging handkerchiefs tied to the ends.

But my mom said it was probably a bunch of "asshole punks" from the neighborhood and just great, I thought we were leaving all that behind.

Then, I became protective of the home we were building with our hands and because of that I came to like the idea of living there. I was to finally have my own room, in the basement, just off the family room. It was small, but it would be all mine, and I already knew exactly how

I would decorate it—Holly Hobbie everything (including light fixture). And I would keep my First Communion Bible and pink rosary, along with my best marbles and a picture of Shaun Cassidy, in the drawer of that white wicker nightstand I saw in the Sears catalogue.

Though my dad paid us some money to sand the drywall, each of us getting a little patch to work on, we mostly spent time out at the new house to get a head start making friends. But at first, we were all too shy to leave the property. Besides, everyone lived so far away, not like in the city, where we could see Mr. Rossi next door peeing in his downstairs toilet from our upstairs bathroom window.

We'd need bikes for sure.

Soon, I'd be done with one task and tugging my dad's shirt for another. I felt I alone could heroically complete the vital parts that would make the new house into a real home. The city house didn't sell right away, which became a kind of blessing because the county house wasn't ready to be lived in yet.

But then came talk about "The Recession." It was The Recession this and The Recession that and I had started to think of the recession as a white smoky hand, like from the movie *The Ten Commandments,* which crept down from heaven and killed firstborns. My mom said that showed a lot of "insight," because though a recession didn't actually kill kids, it certainly took their fathers down a few notches.

One afternoon, a lot of people came to the city house and sat around our dining room table. They placed a lot of papers in front of my dad to sign while my mother fetched a lot of beers. It seemed the house in the city was sold, but instead of being happy when the people left, my mother started to cry and sent us to bed.

Chsh. My dad opened a beer for himself.

Chsh. My mother opened one too.

I was listening at the top of the stairs when she told my dad, "We're going to lose the new house, Joe, I just know it. How can we afford it on this shit offer? Jesus, Joe, and The Recession? What if you lose your job? I have a bad feeling we're going to lose the new house. I just do. And the closing date? It's too soon!"

He murmured, Whadum I supposed-a to do? Wait-a summore?

For wad? Two mortgage payments is what's killing us, Nan. This offer ees as good as it gets, I promise. No one's gotta money deez days. Nobaddy. Then he said, You need-a start working at a jab. We should-a talk about maybe you getting a jab, he said. A job? She laughed. Who's going to take care of your kids? My dad said, Wadd-about your seester? Why can't Leenda help out? My mother started laughing louder, and said, Linda is not stupid like me. Linda has what is called a career and a life. Do you think she'd want to move in and be a nanny to these four? Once a month's enough for her, Joe, be real! My mother started ticking off where she might begin her new career in the county. The arena? she teased, or that doughnut shop? I'll make two bucks an hour at a coffee stand and pay a sitter three. Jesus, Joe, think about it. We got four! Four kids!

My dad said nothing, and went to bed soon after. My mom got on the phone with Auntie Linda and they talked until late in the night. She cried some and I heard the *chsh, chsh* sound a few times more.

That night, I lay awake and imagined how you'd go about losing a house. Did it mean we'd head out to the county and just never really find it again? Would it rip itself out of its foundation and go somewhere else? Or did it mean the new house would stay in the same place, but it would be us that would become lost? Could a house lose its very own family? This was all too much, so I went back to wondering what I would wear tomorrow. What about on the last day of school here, now two weeks away? What about on the first day at the new school? Does God know we're leaving? Does the church transfer our records to the new one? Are there records? What about my mom's records? Maybe I could alter hers on the way, or delete them altogether. Or we could tell people we were partial orphans to make her certain absence at the new church far less noticeable than it was in the city. Or we could tell people our mom's a cripple and can't move good enough to make it out of bed on Sundays.

I wondered, Am I getting enough sleep for a growing girl of my age? Will being nosy stunt my growth?

Prolly not, as Hope would say.

My dad tried hard to finish the house on time, even sleeping out there on a mattress we borrowed from Grandpa Franco. But he also had to work at his regular job, too, to make money to finish the roof. We never saw him. And then there was the problem about the closing date. It came faster than the roof, so we had little option but to rent a trailer-tent and head out there anyway. My mother said it would be like camping, except we'd be the only ones camping, and we'd have a toilet and a shower, at least when it wasn't raining.

The day we pulled out of the neighborhood, no one came to say goodbye. My mom didn't care, and didn't yell at us when we told people we were going to be living in that tent for a while. To us it was an adventure and something to brag about. To my dad, it was a little embarrassing, so he stayed out at the new house. To my mom, the tent was a fact, and oh well. All she cared about was that she was leaving the city and the damn neighborhood forever.

On moving day, she was the happiest I had ever seen her. She was all "good riddance electric heat," and, "sayonara rotting floorboards," and, "see you later, stinky wall-to-wall shag."

She tried to make it fun to be leaving the city house forever.

"Well, kids, say goodbye to the house," she said, starting up the engine. "And if no one wants to say goodbye to us," she added, "we'll just have to say goodbye to them."

She drove the station wagon slowly down the crowded, narrow street, the roof piled high with carpets and boxes, every living space inside filled with clothes and kids, pulling the tent on wheels that would be our home for a few weeks.

"Kids, I want you all to say goodbye to nosy Frances Trevi!" she yelled out her window.

"Bye, nosy Frances Trevi!" we yelled out the window, right at nosy Frances Trevi's face, sitting right there on the porch!

And we covered our mouths and giggled.

"Goodbye, snotty Fontanas and all your millions. You crooks!"

"Goodbye, crooked snotty Fontanas and millions," we followed.

"Say goodbye to the assholes on the corner who never gave out Halloween candy!"

"Goodbye . . . assholes . . . on the corner, you never even gave Halloween candy to us!" we yelled, variously stumbling over the "asshole" part, kind of expecting to be slapped.

But she was oblivious. And beautiful, driving away like that with Gigi, our Siamese, hanging around her neck.

"Say goodbye, store, that wouldn't give us groceries on credit for that one goddamn week, three years ago!"

"Goodbye, store," the rest of the sentence fading out, us not really understanding it.

"Goodbye, school, for never seeing how great my kids are!"

Our enthusiasm was pitched high just then, so when we yelled, "Goodbye, school, for never seeing we are great!" I wasn't looking at the school, I was looking at her profile, completely in awe. She thinks we are great?

"Kids, finally"— she cleared her throat, passing the church—"I want you to say goodbye to Father Pete, the biggest hypocrite in the entire world!"

"Bye, Father Pete . . . the biggest . . . *hippo* . . . in the world!" the boys yelled out loud.

This cracked her up so hard, she couldn't light her cigarette, couldn't suck it in for laughing. She did hear me and Hope say "hypocrite" clearly, she even looked at us through the rearview mirror, through her giggles, probably knowing she was the only one in the car who really understood what that word meant at the time.

I DIDN'T MIND living in the trailer-tent. Nobody did, really, except my dad.

"Probably reminds him too much of the Old Country," my mom explained, washing dishes with the garden hose, our new kitchen sink on back order. So Dad stayed in the house on the mattress, and woke up at dawn to hammer away at the roof.

Dad thought Matty was old enough, almost twelve, to get right up there with him, to help shingle. My mother screamed that if Matty broke his neck, so help you God, I'll kill you in half, Joe! Dad yelled down, how nice, a great-a start, Nancy, I doan tink our new neighbors can hear you!

The rest of us helped any way we could. I made sandwiches and handed up two-by-fours. Smaller ones. Sometimes I opened beers when my dad's co-workers would come by, though when they did, it meant little else would get done that day. Their visits made my mom leave a lot, to go to the grocery store, or to drive to the place where we'd have to pick up mail. The little mail building fascinated me. It was always open, even after five. Mail didn't come to the house anymore. We went to mail.

County life was interesting, but we were having a hard time making friends. Since school was starting soon, I figured I'd take the stress off myself now and make friends later. And so far no one was coming to us, though we could see kids, some by the creek, some playing in the high cornfields, or the two living right behind us, over the fence, in the little blue house. They looked to be around me and Hope's age, too. But they'd disappear whenever they saw us. My mom said maybe they were resentful toward us, as ours was the only new house in a small neighborhood of old ones. We'd have to try harder to make them like us, she said, in case they think we're snotty.

"Go talk to them," she said, while hanging out the wash on the makeshift clothesline.

"No, I don't want to talk to them," I said, staring hard over at the girls our age, peeking around the corner of their house.

"Go. What are you scared of? Go, or I will."

Clearly she herself was afraid of nothing out there. The first day we arrived, she went right over to the neighbors next door, a young French-Canadian couple who'd just had a little baby. She walked right down their gravel driveway to ask if she could use their phone in case of emergencies. Until we got our own, that is. I'm sure they didn't realize "emergencies" could mean calling Auntie Linda, collect, of course, and having long, giggly conversations with her while the neighbors ate their supper in the next room. On her way out, she never failed to remind them that me and Hope, us hiding behind her legs, would soon be old enough to babysit. And wouldn't that be just great for them?

Finally, three weeks into our tent life, I made an excuse to walk to the store. It was blocks away, if you call dirt roads that separate four big properties blocks. I took the shortcut over our back fence and through the back lawn of that blue house. The girls, our age, were playing sock ball on their front porch.

I panicked when they saw me.

"Hey," one of them yelled. "You! Hey! Hiiii! Helloooo!" There were all different voices coming at me from behind.

I refused to turn around and walked even faster to the store, where I bought nothing, really. Maybe Jujubes for Mom and sunflower seeds for Hope.

I passed Matty and Charlie hovering in front of the pinball place, where my mother said us girls were not allowed.

I yelled, "Hi, Matty," knowing it would bug him since he was going by plain old "Matt" out here.

"Get lost," he said, tossing a pebble at my head. "You ain't allowed here."

"You aren't allowed to say 'ain't.' I'm telling," I sneered, sticking my tongue out.

Charlie was ignoring us, biting his nails and swaying back and forth on his feet. He seemed to be waiting for someone he knew, by the way he studied each boy coming in and out of the door. My brothers were lucky, I thought. They were making friends easily because they were allowed a different kind of freedom than me and Hope were. As soon as we moved out here they disappeared. Sometimes for the whole day, and my mother never got mad or worried. They had made two friends, neither boy the exact right age as Matty or Charlie. They were stuck somewhere in the middle, and very retarded-looking.

My mom gave them funny nicknames.

"Where are yous guys going with Mutt and Jeff today?" she'd ask.

"Nowhere," Matty would yell, running down the gravel driveway, Charlie chasing after him, those two boys, waiting, straddling their bikes, skinny arms dangling over the handlebars like houseplants.

"We'll be around," Charlie would add.

And it's true, they were never far enough away that they couldn't hear my mother scream for them at the edge of the driveway. None of us went far enough to miss that, especially me and Hope. But our drift was just beginning. In the city, it was hard to be apart, but in the county, there weren't that many houses, streets, perverts, or parks to bracket us close together anymore.

NOT WANTING to appear chicken, I decided to go back by the blue house and see if the two girls our age would say hello again. I kept telling myself, "You are strong enough to say 'hi.' Say it really fast. You are not a stupid idiot. It would not kill you. They won't kill you."

But when I reached their place, they were gone, the front porch empty, and I felt stupid for ignoring them. Then I noticed as I approached our property from behind, the girls were standing in front of our tent, each taking turns peeking inside.

"Hey," I yelled. "What are you doing there?"

My mom stuck her head out of the tent and smiled when she saw me.

"That's Faith, the oldest girl. She's almost your age, Janey," she said to the one who looked about my age. I was mad she didn't use my new name of "Rebecca," then remembered I hadn't used it in a month, either.

I nodded to this Janey person. Meeting these new people was hurting my stomach. I didn't remember actually making friends before. In Windsor, my friends had always just been my friends; they were around, like the elm trees or the ice cream man.

Hope jumped out of the tent from behind Mom and said, "Lula's my age, Faith. Almost exactly. Her and my birthdays are, like, a week and a day apart, exactly."

Good for you, I jeered in my head. I almost expected them to grab hands and skip down to the creek together, giggling.

Lula smiled. She looked like a boy. Even up close, I would've thought she was a boy, had no one said anything about her being a girl.

"Hi," I said to no one in particular, ducking by them and going directly into the tent.

I zipped down the flap and sat opposite my mom.

"When did they get here?" I whispered.

"A few minutes ago, when I asked them to," she said, through clenched teeth, without looking up from her folding.

"You don't have to make my friends for me, you know!"

"Oh? Could've fooled me. I saw you walk by them just like a snot. Don't be snotty here, Faith, it's not a good thing."

"I'm not being snotty."

"Well, you're being snotty right now sitting here. Go out there and talk to them."

I didn't move.

"I . . . mean . . . it . . . right . . . now . . . Faith . . . go . . . out . . . there . . . with . . . Hopey . . . now," she hissed.

"Fine, in a minute."

"Now!" she yelled.

I waited a beat, in defiance, then slowly unzipped the flap. I was grateful they had moved over to the picnic table, in the carport, and grateful that my dad had started up a backhoe or some other piece of machinery that was strewn about our troubled lot.

I prayed that they hadn't heard my mother yell.

"Act yourself," was all I can remember thinking upon my approach.

Hope seemed different. She was happily showing off Gigi to Lula, the girl-boy. Ever since the doors and windows were finished, we kept Gigi inside the house because she was in heat. All I knew about "the heat" was every once in a while Gigi'd roll around acting mad and meowing loud and she had to stay away from other cats until she stopped screaming like that.

"This is a Siamese cat, from near China," explained Hope. Lula and Janey crowded around Gigi. Lula asked if she could hold her.

"Sure," I said, which was my entrance. "She's my cat from when I was seven," I explained.

"But we share her," said Hope.

"Yeah, but she's mostly my cat, from my seventh birthday."

"Uh, we know that by now," snipped Janey, the one almost my age, the one I wanted to spit on and vowed to hate from now on.

I crossed my arms hard around my chest and sat down hard on the picnic table.

"What's to do out here for fun?" asked Hope. I started to get impressed and angry with her at the same time. It was like she had read a book about moving to a new town that listed good things to say and ask and show to new people. A book that also taught her how to act like she was the oldest daughter in charge.

"We had soccer league but it's over now," said Lula. "We could go to the creek with our canoe. Sometimes we play in the cemetery. Or under the bridge. Also there's the shed behind the church. We could take you there. We know how to get inside it. Also, I know how to climb the roof of the school," Lula said.

"We're not supposed to do that no more, idiot," Janey said.

"I know. I'm just saying I know how," Lula replied.

"I don't know," Hope said, kind of coyly. She was looking over at me to rescue her from underneath all this new information.

"We could do something," I said, stopping the conversation completely. "I don't know," I added, "something."

Everyone started to shrug and pet Gigi more aggressively, which made her spring out of Lula's useless arms. Gigi had never been free outside here, so watching her scramble from the dirt pile to the window ledge to the picnic table then to the station wagon, made me feel sorry for her, made me feel just like her, terrified of all this unfamiliar space and these strange, new people.

It took us ten minutes to trap Gigi under the trailer-tent. Four giggling girls chasing down a bothered and unfriendly purebred, wailing away in heat, made my dad laugh out loud, from the top of the house. I think he was thinking to himself, "This is what it's all about."

When my mother looked up at him, using her hand as a visor, I think she was thinking that these messy kids chasing an angry animal around dirt piles and filthy vehicles, all this is definitely reminding him of the Old Country. They looked at each other for a few seconds, both smiling, Dad down at her, Mom up at him, like they were happy in love. I froze this picture in my mind and folded it into the place where I kept a few other pretty good memories.

Hope screamed, "There goes Gigi, Mom!"

My mom made a rough grab for one of her hind legs, caught her, and tossed her into the house by the scruff of her neck like a hero. She turned to the four of us girls, and exclaimed, "I know what we can do! Let's go into Belle River and get some ice cream!"

We loved going into Belle River, but that wasn't why me and Hope screamed "Yippee" so earnestly along with Lula and Janey. It was because my mother had never suggested ice cream so joyously before. I looked over at Hope and Hope looked over at me, both of us thinking the same thing. Maybe things would be normal here after all.

Chapter Three

The new roof was nearly finished, but it seemed as though we didn't need it. A joke, really, but it sure felt like The Recession had made a comfortable home right on the top of our tired heads. The Recession sat on our chests while we slept. It was all my parents talked and fought about. Every time we turned on the car radio in the station wagon, we'd hear about The Recession, then Interest Rates, and all The Inflation that came with it. I had no honest idea what all this meant, but because of The Recession, more official-looking people came over to our house with more papers. This time, instead of gathering around our dining room table, which was still in storage, with the beds and winter clothes, they sat around the picnic table, in our now-finished carport. We still didn't have a phone, so my mother said, Wasn't it nice that these people were kind enough to come and see us in person?

It had just stopped raining the first afternoon they visited. My mother didn't offer them anything to drink, even though she and my dad enjoyed several beers, one after the other.

The first set of people with papers was a man from our old bank, in Windsor, and a woman from the new one, in Belle River. The bank people sat side by side with their heads bent near each other. They thought, then they scribbled out the new mortgage payment on the edge of a newspaper and pushed it under my parents' noses.

My dad laughed. "I'll say inflation!"

My mom laughed, too, so I laughed, and my mom told me to go away, go play somewhere else, didn't I have something to do?

I left the bank people with my folks, reluctantly, head hung low, exaggerating my banishment. The fact is, I started to need information like other kids needed vitamins. My nosiness had become a sixth sense. In fact, I believe I used it more than smell or feel. Things changed around here too quickly, and if I relied on my parents for information we'd be well on our way out before they'd ever tell us where and why we were going.

I moved to the other side of the half-built wall and played with Gigi. We had her tied up with some yarn so she wouldn't run away. She was pacing the dirt piles, meowing like she was in a zoo, and angry about it.

The bank people were putting the papers back into their folder when my dad's boss, T.B.A. in the W., pulled up. His real name was John Dormer. "JD Construction" was written out big on his stumpy cube van. Everyone said hello to him except my mother, who addressed him by saying, "The only worse thing that can happen to us today, John, is if you've driven out here to fire Joe."

"Jeez, Nan," John said, pulling off his baseball cap. "I didn't come out here to fire anybody, but I do need to talk to you both about something important."

Nobody said anything for a second. Then my mom said, "Fuck, shit. That is why you're here isn't it, John?"

My dad probably winced at her cursing in front of his boss and the bank people because they were a group of folks who were either holding important papers, or our sorry future in their very hands. Their hushed voices and obvious authority added a churchy feel to the cavernous carport. But I realized my mother hadn't had much practice bowing before anything powerful in a long time. Least of all my dad.

"Wait a second," she said, ignoring the way her cruddy words made everyone feel. "Before we go any further, I need another drink. Anyone else?"

John said sure. Dad said no, he was fine. The bank people got up and said they'd call them in the morning with the new payment schedule.

"How? We don't have a phone," said my mother. "Why don't you send it by carrier pigeon? How 'bout you do that?"

She was throwing these words over her shoulder as she headed over to the tent where the cooler was. She saw me, scrunched down behind the wall. I avoided her eyes, thinking, Why don't you just move the goddamn cooler into the carport? Save a trip.

On the way back, with the jangling beers, my mother stopped in front of me. I was moving pebbles into a pile with a stick.

"Faith, come sit with us, visit with John, okay? I want you by me."

When the bank left, I stood up and walked back into the carport. I felt shy with his boss there so I fell into my dad's lap and hugged him a little too much. That summer marked the time in my life when I started to become aware that I could appear adorable upon my command. I was cultivating a deep vanity, a sin, for sure, because we were told, in Religion, a girl's powerful knowledge about herself could distract her into insanity. That's how decent women became whores, and why actresses would never be happy, we were told.

And I was sick with it.

The week before, a big wall-to-wall mirror was installed in the upstairs bathroom, and I had made excuses to pee six times, in one hour. Each time I went up there, I stared at myself in the mirror for longer than I ever looked at anything in my life, not counting TV. I stared at myself sideways, sticking my bum high and out. I stared at myself up close from the front and way back from behind. One time, a song came on my dad's radio, while he was working in the basement. It was "Evergreen," by Barbra Streisand, and I sang it low to my own reflection, even holding the last note for as long as Barbra did. I climbed onto the counter and looked into my bottom eyelids! And for what? I think I was just taking serious stock of what was already there, and what was coming. For instance, I had started to get those dimples in my thighs like my mom had when she wore bathing suits. And I was afraid. I also memorized what expressions looked best on my face when experiencing certain emotions, even emotions I had never fully committed, like "yearning" or "heartbroken." But the knowledge that people, especially boys and men, might one day stop what they were doing to just look at me, like they looked at my mother, was as close to feeling powerful as I could get back then.

The worst part about one girl's vanity is that it is contagious, because when Hope came around from the back of the house, she screamed, "Me too, Daddy, *me!*" And Dad opened his arm and we both stayed cuddled for a few seconds, until he tickled us away from him, which he had started to do more and more.

"So how you doing?" said John to my dad. "Place is coming along. Looks good. What are you using for the soffits?"

"Aluminum. Plain. Nan wants to paint them."

My dad wasn't looking at his boss, he was fending off me and Hope.

"Sounds nice. Thanks," John said to my mother, when she handed him a beer.

"Sure. Girls, get off your dad," she barked, motioning for me to sit next to her on the bench. I didn't really want to stay in the carport anymore. The air became foggy with someone's anger, hers, and it told me all I needed to know about what was going to happen to us.

"Hey, Nancy," John said, "why don't you have the kids go and play so that I can talk to—"

"They can stay, John," my mom interrupted, without any kind of emotion. I stood with my arms crossed in front of me. Hope sat down next to my mom. My mom never took her eyes off T.B.A. in the W., and John didn't sit down either. He just took a big gulp of beer and explained how his little company lost the big subdivision contract because the big subdivision wasn't going to be built because no one wanted to buy the houses because no one had any money and it was what he most feared, but don't worry he still had jobs, a good one, even, for my dad, in Calgary, a city I had never heard of, even in geography class.

Silence.

"We lost the house," my mom said, dropping her bottle onto the picnic table.

Me and Hope looked at the open screen door and into the house. I could tell Hope was thinking the same thing I was. How could the house be lost when it's right here? We're right here. I can see it.

"Calgary. Jeez," said my dad. "When?"

"Right away. It wouldn't be for long, either, six months, maybe a year. You could bring the kids. If you want. Some of the guys are. There's housing for families. Not too expensive. Well, the housing's being built, but meantime, we could put you up in a motel, near a school, of course. It's very busy out there. Lots of work."

Silence, again.

"I . . . feel bad," John continued, "but there's nothing here. No work. I feel bad about all this."

"I know," said my dad, "I knew. I juss—" He slapped his hand over his mouth, shutting himself up. He looked over at my mother but she was acting like she wasn't listening. She was concentrating on pulling the label off her beer bottle, cleanly and slowly. It came off in one wet piece.

"Would you look at that," she said, examining the label. "That's supposed to be good luck. Here," she said, handing it to me, "go press that in your Bible as a remembrance of this day. I think it's very fitting."

My dad moved his hand hard through his thick, curly hair, which was lopsided from wearing baseball caps all day.

"I doan know what to say," said my dad. "Me and Nan—we got a lot to talk 'bout, John. Where you will be working tomorrow?"

"Out on County Road Nine, the duplex," said John.

"I come out for noon," said Dad, standing up. They shook hands.

My mom stayed sitting, looking at her fingernails. But as John was backing out of the driveway, my mom got up from the bench and ran after him. John stopped the van and rolled down his window. She went over to his side, as if to say something, but she just stood there with her hands on her waist. She took a couple of deep breaths and before anything could come out of her mouth, her head fell forward. My dad ran down to her. John went to open his door again but my dad put his hand up as if to say no, no. My dad pulled her away from the van but she struggled from his arms and walked back toward where me and Hope sat root still, our hands grasping the underside of the bench. John put the van in reverse and backed out. My mom turned and picked up a big chunk of dirt and threw it, badly, at the back of the departing van.

"Stop, Nan, eet's not his fault," said my dad.

"Then whose is it?" she screamed, turning to face him.

They stood a few feet apart from each other at the edge of the gravel driveway.

She turned away from my dad and walked calmly over to the tent, reached in, grabbed her purse, and threw it into the open window of the station wagon. She climbed in and drove away without even saying anything to us.

I looked over at Hope, who was biting her bottom lip. She got up and went into the house, and I watched how the new screen door slowly wheezed shut behind her. I kept my eyes on the door of the house that was still here. The house was still here. Still. But we were the ones lost.

I watched my dad, standing in the middle of the driveway. His eyes went from the roof, to the churned-up lawn, then over to the tent, then at me, then back up to the roof, then to Gigi, now chewing on the yarn leash.

"Where'd the boys go?" he yelled over to me, finally, his hand like a visor, the way my mother's was the day she laughed up at him on the roof. The day he laughed down at her. The last day of normal around here.

"Don't know," I yelled. "Are we moving to Calvary?"

"Calvary? No, Fate, eets Cal-Gary."

That was the first time my dad had ever corrected me, and I started to think it was funny, us so far apart, yelling answers back and forth from a stupid distance. Then he told me go find-a boys, bring them back for supper, and I said okay, thinking that it would be an opportunity to go to the pinball place. Hope should come with me. I'd be too shy to go to the pinball place by myself.

I opened the screen door and yelled, "Hope, come! We gotta go find the boys! At the pinball place!"

No answer.

I went inside and carefully climbed the wooden stairs. There was still no banister. It, too, along with the kitchen sink, bathtubs, and fireplace bricks were all on back order, where they'd probably remain.

Hope was on the floor of one of the bedrooms. She had grabbed Dad's comforter and was pretending to be sleeping soundly.

"Hope, get up, we have to go find the boys."

"Are we moving again?" she asked in a fake sleepy voice.

"I don't know."

"Where's Mom?"

"I don't know, let's go."

"I don't want to move. I got friends here."

And it's true we had made friends. And every day since Hope had met Janey and Lula, she'd go over to their house for breakfast. I didn't, using my mother as an excuse. "Who's going to keep Mom company?"

Besides, I didn't much like them. Or I felt that they didn't much like me. But they loved Hope, because she would do anything they'd ask her to. Sometimes I'd join them down by the creek to look for tadpoles or "clues." "Clues" could mean anything from an old shoe or a cigarette pack. County kids used their imagination, my mother said, because there's not much to do out here. Janey and Lula would pick these "clues" up as though they had great importance. Hope would play right along with them.

"Maybe it's from the bad guys," Hope would say with deep suspicion and passion, poking at a dirty plastic bag or a balled-up sock. They'd all squeal, drop the "clue," and run away toward the cemetery, me following halfheartedly behind them.

That's how we spent our time in the county, down a dirt road off the highway in the small town of Emeryville. It was French, and most people who lived here did have the same last name, Chaumier. Including Janey and Lula.

"That explains why Matty's new friends look the way they do," said my mother. "Inbreeding."

Hope finally "woke up" and came downstairs with me. We found Lula and Janey waiting for us on the picnic table in the carport.

"Hi, we're going to the cemetery. Come on," said Janey. I liked playing in the cemetery. It was a newer one; all the headstones were flat on the ground, so it was not at all creepy.

"We can't, we have to go find the boys," I said.

"We're moving again," Hope added.

"You are not. That's stupid," Janey said.

"We lost the house," Hope said. I hit her arm. Mom wouldn't like them to know about something that we didn't even know about for sure.

"But it's right here," Lula said, holding her arm up like a magician's helper. "See? Anyways, maybe the boys are out there, in the creek or something."

"They're prolly playing pinball," Hope said.

"Then we'll go by the pinball place on the way back, come on."

Me and Hope looked at each other. I was thinking that maybe if we delayed getting the boys, we could delay everything bad about moving, for a little bit longer.

"Okay," we said.

My dad was getting something out of the tent. I yelled we were going to get the boys and we'd be back for supper.

"Okay, and here," my dad said, walking over to me. He handed me a five-dollar bill. "Get some-a-ting for everybaddy."

I was stunned and glowing. I would use it at the pinball place, on my first game ever.

We ran down to the creek, teetered along the shallow bank, up to the little bridge that led to the cemetery. This was the back way. Old Man Chaumier, Janey and Lula's great-uncle, lived along the front entrance, at the cemetery's lane, by the gate. He cleaned and maintained the cemetery, mowed the lawn, polished the headstones, and picked up all our chip bags, gum wrappers, and pop cans. The Old Man, as we called him, hated us playing in the cemetery. Anytime he saw the four of us walking down the street, even if we weren't anywhere near the cemetery, he'd shake his fist and yell, "Stay the hell out of the cemetery or I'll run yous over with my car!" You wouldn't have known Lula and Janey were related in any loving way to him from how he'd holler, "I'll kill yous all if I catch yous in there again, I swear."

We would ignore him, or run, depending on our mood, and whether or not we were wearing shoes. But he always made us laugh with his hate.

The best part of the cemetery was the statues. There were fourteen life-sized versions of the stations of the cross. There was the Jesus with the crown of thorns statue, the one of Jesus in a courtroom, Jesus and Mary talking about His death, and the one of Veronica, who wiped His face when He walked the main street. Jesus fell three times carrying the cross on His back. He was on His way to being killed in Calvary, kind of like we were, I thought. I knew we wouldn't be killed in Calgary, but I felt I'd probably die there anyway. I didn't want to move again.

The statues were exactly the right height to climb on, to hug and talk to, like when we played "prisoner" or pretended we were dancing with them. The best dance partner was the statue of Jesus at His "Resurrection." His arms were held out at our waists, perfect height to lean up against in a slow-moving embrace.

When we got to the cemetery, Lula automatically climbed up and started to kiss Jesus. I felt nauseous. From the look of the white Jesus statue, you could tell He was molested like this a lot and was very sad about it. His mouth was stained pinkish and the paint was peeling off so you could see the cement underneath. Maybe other girls, like me, also went through periods when they were in love with Jesus and wanted to marry Him. Over the years, I had grown to respect Jesus as a person, and I liked Him only as a friend. But mostly, I was afraid of His revenge. I was already worried that Jesus brought The Recession down upon us, since it was something that seemed to only be affecting our family. I thought He might be pissed off about us having only gone to the new church twice. But it was not our fault. We had a lot of work to do to finish the house, and every day counted, even Sundays.

"Look! I'm French-kissing," said Lula, licking Jesus' mouth.

I closed my eyes. I had wanted to pray for us to stay in Emeryville, but watching this sick spectacle, I was now preparing myself for our certain banishment. I opened my eyes and saw the county church, which was next to the cemetery. It was newly built and reminded me of a small barn that God had sat on. Inside, there was no Jesus hanging off the crucifix, only metal rays of light shooting out of the top, at odd angles. The pews were made of light-colored wood. The choir consisted of a long-haired lady, who sang by herself and played her own guitar. She wasn't even a real nun. And though it was walking distance from our house, I resisted going to the new church because there was nothing beautiful to look at inside.

Lula planted a few more light kisses on Jesus before rolling off Him.

"Your turn to do it with Jesus, Faith," she said.

"No. Forget it. It's a sin. Plus it's gross," I said.

"You're gross," Janey said, shoving me a little, in defense of her sister.

"Shut up, you are, Janey," Hope said, defending me.

"It's not a sin," Lula said, "you can learn how to kiss on it."

Then Hope climbed up and took Lula's place with Jesus. I watched as my little sister necked with the body of Christ, moaning stupidly and moving her head back and forth. I couldn't help but slap her ankles.

"Get off Him!" I screamed. "You look like a damn idiot, Hope." I was embarrassed for her, plus a little worried about her soul. Didn't she realize the danger we were in? The last thing we needed was further wrath and bother from God, or His Son, who we were rudely molesting.

Hope screamed down at me, "I do not look like an idiot, you do! You're being such a baby!"

We were not aware of this, but that summer was the last time we'd be as close to each other. After that summer, I would never really know exactly where she went, or exactly who she was kissing, statues or not.

FROM THE CEMETERY, we could see Old Man Chaumier's driveway. It was vacant. The thing he hated the most was when we'd jump off the little cemetery bridge into the creek, because we splashed water all over his rhubarb patch, growing right next to the banks. One time he got so mad he drove his Cadillac onto the bridge, with us treading water underneath. His rumbling car on top of the metal beams made us feel like we were swimming inside an airplane. When he had stuck his head over to scream at us, we splashed the Old Man with creek water. He spent a few more seconds gunning his engine, and then took off. We swam the creek home, but the Old Man was waiting for us where the creek meets the highway. He pinged rocks at our heads. I thought he was crazy for sure. That day, while we were drying off, my mom told us we were doing nothing but swimming alongside human poo, and that that was more dangerous than a pissed-off old man.

After getting a better look over at his driveway, Janey said, "Old Man's gone. We should go swimming really fast."

The creek was nice and deep at the bridge. Sometimes when we'd jump off, we'd yell out the name of a boy we liked. I always yelled "Shaun Cassidy," because I didn't know any boys here yet.

"We're not wearing suits," Hope said.

"So? We're going naked. We always do," Janey replied, as she and Lula quickly stripped. "Don't be chicken."

Hope had her clothes off first. We were all mostly little girls. But even Janey, who was almost twelve, was less developed than Hope. In fact, at nine, Hope was closer to getting her boobs than me. She even told me her nipples itched sometimes. My own nudity was benign still, so I wasn't sure what I hesitated over. I had no breasts, no weird hair anywhere, and I didn't crave any, either. But it felt strangely sinful to be wearing nothing, right in the middle of broad daylight, near all those dead people and suffering Jesus.

"What if the boys come by?" I asked.

"Who cares? Come on," yelled a naked Janey over at a scaredy-cat me. I was taking my time undoing my shoelaces. I decided I'd keep my underwear on. The rest came off only because it was hot.

My first, almost-naked leap was so wonderful that the only pain I felt was hitting the water hard, and it was welcome. We were jumping off the little bridge that separated the church parking lot from the cemetery, yelling boys' names out loud, and I was loving this place, Emeryville. I wanted to stay here forever. Stay smooth and little like this. Stay friends with these two girls. Stay taller than Hope. I wanted to stay ten, to jump naked off a bridge with my little sister, for the rest of my life. I was having such a good, good time, even with Janey, who patiently showed me how to do a back somersault in the water without getting any up my nose. We were all having such a good, good time, that none of us noticed Old Man Chaumier's Cadillac parked at the foot of the cemetery lane.

We climbed out of the creek, not too quickly but in a way that spoke of our self-anointed right to swim there. We casually helped each other onto the banks and laughed a little too loud while recalling each other's antics, all the while totally ignoring him. None of us knew how long he had been waiting there, like a humming wasp, his head barely visible over the steering wheel.

"Shit, your uncle's mean," I said to Lula, who was struggling to get her shorts on. She didn't even bother with her underwear. She balled them up and shoved them in her back pocket.

"He won't do nothing," she said nervously, pulling her T-shirt over her wet head and sticking her tongue out at him. I fell over laughing while trying to get my socks on over my wet feet. Hope was still fussing with her underwear.

The Old Man gunned his engine to a loud growl, then stuck his head out of the window and yelled, "I am telling yous get the hell off that bridge or I'll run yous sons-a-bitches over with my car!"

"What a fucker," whispered Janey, now fully dressed. "I'm going to tell my mother he swears at us and wants to kill us all the time."

"You shut up, old man, you don't own this bridge. We can be here if we want!" Lula yelled.

Out of nowhere, Hope added, "Yeah, and you're not my grandpa, neither!"

I looked at Hope. My mouth was giant open and she seemed as shocked at herself as I was at her.

"Hope! Watch your mouth, and get your damn shirt on, we gotta get out of here," I whispered, pulling my shorts on over my wet underwear. I regretted keeping my underwear on. It looked like I peed my shorts.

The Old Man started honking like a crazy person when he saw us jump the short brick fence that separated his own back yard from the cemetery lane. He roared up to the bridge in his car. We made a run, straight through his garden, Janey stopping and yanking up some rhubarb, our feet smashing down the rest. Janey started tossing stalks over her shoulder, making the sound of bombs as they landed behind her.

We were laughing at that point.

It took Old Man Chaumier a few seconds to execute the five-point turn required to rotate his huge Cadillac to the proper direction, which was our only head start. He roared back down cemetery lane. When we made a run for the house across from his, he accelerated after us. The Old Man wanted to kill us for real, and, I thought, if he caught us, he would. But feeling so alive before my certain death flooded my body with a fresh mission. No way was he going to murder such vital creatures as we were, at that age, on that day. No way was this how I was going to die.

We cut through a few back yards, jumped over another small fence, then crossed another street, until we finally reached the field.

"We made it!" Hope screamed.

I was laughing—inappropriately, but with real joy.

The open soy field was only budding so we could see the chain-link fence and the back of the mail building on the other side. After that was the highway, a few streets more, our "home free."

Hope screamed, "Look, he's coming!"

"Oh my God, that fucker's gonna drive the field," Janey squealed, almost laughing out of disbelief.

The Old Man was driving through that last back yard like it was a carved road. He drove right under the clothesline, his antenna catching, releasing, then wagging in the wind. White dress shirts, towels, and sheets tickled across the dusty hood, roof, and trunk of the slow-moving Cadillac.

"He's gonna kill us," Janey shrieked, and that's when I started to panic.

Old Man Chaumier's Cadillac stopped at the edge of the field. He began to inch the heavy car onto its edge, like the tires were toes, testing water. He must have felt confident the soy would hold up his car because it seemed nothing but a tiny second before he was on us, right behind us, moving faster than we ever could. As much as I knew the great importance of keeping my eye on my destination, I couldn't help but look back. Seeing a big, shiny car, bumping fast through a pocked and holey field, was like watching a car kill itself, and murder whoever was inside.

We were almost at the mail building, puffing way too hard for four young girls who hadn't yet smoked their first of thousands of cigarettes.

"We're there!" I screamed, my nails digging into Hope's wrist. I wouldn't let go of her, even though Janey and Lula separated, making them much faster and definitely less of a target.

When we reached the high chain-link fence, we leaped out of the field and clung to it, looking like four flies struggling on a giant swatter. We scrambled up and over, carefully negotiating the perilous points of the twisted metal crowning the top.

Lula was scratched and landed crying. Hope was gored in the thigh and fell hard on her butt, blood already running down her outer leg. Hope had left her shoes behind, had made that whole run, down dirt roads and through the bumpy soy, completely barefooted, without saying a word. I was horrified, and then impressed, and then white-hot angry at the Old Man, now idling fifteen feet away on the other side of the blessed fence.

He couldn't get at us now. No way he'd drive through metal.

"He's fucking crazy," Janey said, her hands on her banged-up knees. Out loud to him she screamed, "You're fucking crazy, Old Man. I'm telling my mother this time and you're going to jail. For good! Asshole!"

The Old Man pushed down hard on the pedal, revving the engine. But instead of the Cadillac crashing through the chain-link fence, we watched as the entire back end of his car sank inches down into the soggy earth. The spinning tires kicked dirt high up into the air, some raining down all over us.

My first thought was that we were going to live, maybe not in this town, but at least we'd be alive somewhere. My second thought was we were not wanted here either. We lost the house, so we will have to leave this town, because it was as small as their problems were. We would stand out like stooped and shameful giants by comparison. Especially my dad. If my mother had made a mess of our lives in the city, my dad had done little to clean it up in the county.

I offered Hope a piggyback home because we weren't going back to fetch her shoes. They weren't worth dying over. I think we expected the Old Man to jump out of the car and at least throw his hat down on the hood in defeat. Instead, he stayed inside, never moving, his fuming, growling car the ultimate expression of his outright hatred for us.

We walked away slower, but not slowly. And every time one of us would turn around to ensure he stayed stuck, we'd whip out our middle finger and shake it at him, until we couldn't see him anymore.

We four split into twos behind Janey and Lula's house.

"See you," I said, sounding little.

Janey ran over and hugged me.

"You guys are the greatest," she said. "I'm glad you moved here."

"Us too," I said. "But tell your mom right away, because he is going to jail. I don't care if he's a relative. Okay?"

"I know," and they waved to us until we reached the fence and climbed over.

I let go of Hope's hand when I saw the barbecue smoke. I ran. My mother was home. She had probably just taken off to go to the store. And to calm down a little.

When I reached the carport, she was coming from inside the house with a bag of frozen hot-dog buns.

"Where the hell have yous two been? Did you pee your pants, Faith?" my mom asked, only kidding a little, my underwear soaked through my shorts. "And Hopey, where's your shoes?" She took a closer look and gasped, "Hope! Your feet!"

"Mom—" Hope started, then stammered and bawled.

"What the hell happened to yous two, Faith?"

I told my mother we went swimming. I told her about us jumping in the creek, doing nothing, not making any noise, or mess, nothing. And then I told her how Old Man Chaumier blocked the cemetery lane with his car and when we ran, scared, he tried to kill us, all the way across town, all the way through the field, all the way up to the mail building, but his car, see, it got stuck, so he couldn't kill us, but he wanted to, and maybe he still does. And he came this close. And he should go to jail. And I was crying, too, by then.

My dad had heard part of the story from the roof, and jumped off where it stooped low over the carport. He was gripping a hammer when he demanded to know, When-a hell dees happen?

"Just now," cried Hope. "I think he should go to jail. He's so mean, prolly he's got my shoes." She was wiping her dirty face with her dirty hand. Her damp curly hair was stuck to her head. She looked two, standing there, shifting her weight from her right foot to her left foot. My mom put her hand on Hope's head and looked down at her chewed-up feet.

"Jesus, Joe, look at her feet!"

There were scribbles of bloody cuts all over her feet, diminishing in density toward her knees. She had a big gash, too, now scabbing high up on her thigh.

"Faith, go fill up that little tub with water. Hope, soak your feet."

"It's going to be a good scab to pick," Hope whispered, bent over the cut. My dad smacked her hand away from her sore and grabbed the first-aid kit from the lockbox.

My mom knelt down to our eye level and put her straight, tense index finger up in front of both our faces, first mine, then Hope's, and hissed, "Yous two better be telling me the truth. You hear? I am going to go over there and talk to Lula and Janey's mom. Stay." She looked at my dad with ferocity, and said, "And you go get Hopey's shoes from that asshole! And tell him to get a fucking lawyer!"

My dad nodded and bent over Hope's thigh with a Band-Aid. He looked shaken and angry. The Band-Aid was way too small for her cut, so she asked if she could have five Band-Aids, and he gave her five. I was filling the small tub with hose water, envying Hope's gash. I had nothing to show for our ordeal except what looked like pee in my pants.

My mom walked behind our house and I watched her jump a fence for the first time ever. She didn't do too badly. The landing was a bit clumsy, but she wiped her grassy hands on her bum and walked up to the back door. Janey and Lula's mom was already holding it open to her.

My dad made us tell him where the Old Man lived. Hope said, next to the cemetery lane, it's all brown, but he's prolly still in the field. My dad grabbed the car keys and yelled at the boys, who were shooting pucks in the basement, to getta the hell-a outside and keep an eye on the girls.

The way he squealed out of the driveway, awkwardly fishtailing the station wagon, made me fall in love with him. I rooted for my dad to smash the Old Man, and any other force that brought us down. For some reason I thought this would please my mother enough for her to love him again, too. Fight for us, Dad, I cheered in my head. Let nothing bad happen to this family or Mom will stop loving you. If she hasn't already.

Matty and Charlie came out of the house sucking on Popsicles. Me and Hope grabbed Popsicles too, and told the story to Matty and Charlie of how their two sisters almost died that day. For doing nothing wrong. Matty said that the Old Man probably had a weapon, a rifle, or a big sword, in the front seat. Hope said she didn't see a weapon. Matty teased, That's because you were crying too hard to notice. Charlie figured his plan was to run us over, take our bodies to his house, and cut us up. Then, after, he'd bury us in the cemetery and no one would ever find us again. When Charlie finished, his eyes were wide with delight.

"Shut up, I'm scared now," I said, shivering. "I wonder if Dad's gonna punch him out?"

"Or if Mom is," Hope replied, which cracked us up with its better likelihood.

"We have to move again, you know," said Charlie.

I began to think it might be good idea to move, so Old Man Chaumier couldn't kill us anymore. Matty stood and said he was going to catch up to Dad.

"No, don't, then the Old Man'll come kill you. He hates kids!" said Charlie, starting to cry. "Or he'll come kill us!"

I remembered the money Dad had given me and felt around for the five-dollar bill. It was gone too, probably sailing out of my pocket during the run for my life.

How weird to have almost died, I thought, looking at Hope wincing with her cut-up feet in cold water. What would my mother have done without her two girls? I couldn't even picture what would happen to her face if she had to stick it out the front door and force herself to listen to police officers telling her that they found the dead bodies of Faith and Hope out behind the mail building. "Big tire prints over their middles, ma'am. Crazy Old Man laughing on top of them!" Couldn't even picture how it would look, her face, while taking in such sorry news. Right then, I made a special promise to God, to take damn better care of my immortal soul. And much better care of my little sister's.

When we heard the sirens, Hope and I locked eyes the way adults do. Her face even looked older. The sirens wailed closer and closer until we saw two police cars pull up beside Janey and Lula's house. Tall uniformed men got out of the cars, knocked, and disappeared inside.

Charlie whispered, "The Old Man is going to jail. That's how come the police are here."

We went over to the back fence and stood staring with amazement at that back door. It was swallowing up all the important people that day.

My mother stepped out of the house and called us over.

"Girls, I need you to come here," she yelled. She was wrapped tightly again, her arms around her waist. As we approached her, I tried to read the look on her face, but I couldn't.

"Hope, Faith . . . the Old Man? He chased you out to the soy field? Right?" She was talking to us like she talked to Charlie, or Gigi.

"Yeah and then he—"

"Yeah, I know what he did next." She barely looked at us. Was she mad? We didn't really do anything wrong, dammit. What had that Old Man told the police?

"Lula and Janey just told me the same story you did. But listen to me. Something bad's happened."

My mom sat down on the stairs, and we walked closer to her. Charlie was holding my hand hard.

My mom said, "Charlie, honey, go back to the house for a second, we'll be right there."

"But no one's there, Mom. Matty went after Dad."

"Shit."

One of the police came out onto the porch.

"Nancy, which one's Hope and which one's Faith?" he asked. I felt dizzy by his largeness. So did Hope. She grabbed a fistful of my T-shirt, her mouth gaping wide, her eyes taking in the fact of his gun. He had removed his uniform jacket. His wrists were thick, and hard enough to stop bullets without the bracelets that Wonder Woman needed.

"Did they find him, Mom? Is he going to jail?" Hope asked.

"Honey, they found him," she answered. Then she turned to the police and hissed, "What's the difference who's who? Jesus, you heard what happened to them. That asshole tried to kill them. I'm glad he's dead because I would've killed him too, if I got my goddamn hands on him."

A flurry of letters shot through my brain. They scrambled into words, then organized themselves into one bold sentence, my mind's eye reading, "Thou shalt not kill," written in fancy, holy script. I remember thinking to myself, I am just a little girl, and when my knees gave way, I yelped like one, because I thought the devil had gotten ahold of my legs. The first person I grabbed for was my mother, thinking she'd save me from hell, or I'd bring her down with me.

"Faith!" she screamed. I hadn't quite fainted, but blackness was so close I would've given in to it, if my mother hadn't had such a strong hold on my arm.

"Jesus, look what you did," she yelled at the police. "She's a kid!"

"Ma'am, I didn't mean—" the policeman stammered, reaching for my other arm.

"Don't you touch her!" she spat, smacking at his monster wrists. Oh God, I thought, first she yells at a nun, and now she's hitting the police! More blackness, the devil on both of us!

"Stand up, Faith, this is not your fault, stand up!"

She yanked my arm, like she had used my body to play tug-of-war with the devil, and won.

"Listen to me," she said, "It's neither of your faults. He was an Old Man, who put great stress on himself, so he had a stroke or some heart attack is all. Would've happened today, even if you weren't there."

I was unconvinced about the last part, and I could tell my mother was, too.

"Still," said the policeman, "I need to ask them some questions, Nancy. Get their statements so I can fill out my report. Mind if I take them aside?"

"Yes, I mind. We have had a very long day. I am taking my children home. What you can put in your report is this: Old Asshole tries to kill my kids. Story has happy ending."

"Okay, well, look," said the cop, "I'll give you a call tomorrow."

"We don't have a phone," we all said, at the same time. My mom smiled at the police, proud almost.

"Well, then, is that your house with the tent over there?" he asked.

"For now," my mother answered.

"I'll be by tomorrow with some papers," said the cop.

"Line up with the rest of them," said my mother. "Everyone's coming by tomorrow with some papers."

Lula and Janey knocked on their upstairs bedroom window. Janey gave us a thumbs-up. Hope started to give a thumbs-up back, but my mother smacked her hand and held on to it as she waved goodbye to the police.

When Lula and Janey's mom came out, she shooed her daughters away from the window.

"Hi, girls," she said to us, "you doing okay?" She was nice to us, overly so, but she always asked a lot of questions, like, How long do you think that tent's gonna be up in the front yard? Is that a skipping rope your mom's using as a clothesline that I see? Have you enrolled in school? Oh, and why not? And who exactly sleeps out in the tent with no heat on at night? We explained, me, my mom, and Hope got one bed, the boys on the other side, and my dad sleeps in the house on a mattress and the only reason we live like this is it's the summertime . . .

"We're okay," we replied.

"Look, Nancy, what a day! I think it's a good idea if the girls don't come by here for just a while. I think Janey and Lula need a bit of a rest from playing around."

"You serious?" my mom asked. "But they have fun together. They weren't doing anything wrong, playing out at the creek like that. I was worried about them swimming in all that shit, not some crazy old man wanting to run them over."

"Well, someone died today, Nancy. And he's a relative too, don't forget."

"Well, Dana," said my mother, "I sure hope he doesn't forget about you and the girls in his will!"

"Nancy, there is just no need—"

"Yes, there's need, Dana, there's great, great need."

We were all facing my mother. She swelled up like she had inhaled a hundred pounds of fire.

"Okay, fine, the girls will stay away from each other," my mom replied, as though her mouth was typing out the words. "Starting right now. This minute. Let's go!"

And we all made our way to the fence. My mother took her time getting over. At one point, we had to unhook her pant leg, and Hope had to keep her hand on Mom's bum until she found earth.

My dad was waiting for us in the carport holding Hope's shoes. He found them on the bridge where a neighbor had informed him of what had had happened. He didn't look mad. He looked amused.

Matty said, "We went to kill him but he was already dead!"

My dad said he musta jooce snapped, then he started to laugh, for a very long time. My mother fell into the lawn chair across from him.

"I know the feeling," she said, smirking at the four of us. "God, we turn our backs for one little second and our kids go and kill a guy."

She saw the result of her joke spread across my horrified face. She covered her own face with her hands, making a dramatic motion to wipe what was funny off it.

"Faith, come here. Come here," she ordered.

I walked over to her lawn chair. She took my hands in hers.

"Faith, you have to get it out of your head, now, that you guys killed someone today. I know you. You take things so heavily. But I'm telling you—" She couldn't finish. She was seized with the same giggles that had begun to die down in my dad.

"Maybe it's a sign. Maybe it's time to move!" She laughed.

"And go to Calgary?" I asked, sickened, yanking my hands out of hers. The moving memory had vanished with all the talk of murder, but Calgary came back into our heads like a collective fever.

"No, not Calgary. We're not going to Calgary," she said, sobering up.

She stayed looking steady at my dad. He stood up and walked over to the cooler for two beers, the boys trailing behind him like dogs. They followed him all the way back to the carport. My dad sat back down on the picnic table and sighed. The boys, sitting on either side of him, sighed, too.

It seemed like three against three.

"I tink-a you right," he said, finally.

"I think we'll stay here," she continued, "and get a little place in town. We can rent. I drove to the Laundromat and there's three places in Belle River that sound okay. I can get a part-time job. And my dad said he'd lend us some money. And then we'll wait for you."

She was completely out of breath.

"You can come home for Christmas," she added.

My dad said nothing.

"You can write the kids letters and call Sundays."

He said nothing.

"Then, before you know it, it's Easter and then spring and you'll be home!"

My dad opened his beer. Just before he could take his first sip, he choked and started to cry. My mother bolted from her lawn chair. She went over to him and knelt down at his feet. At first he kept his head bent and covered, so she just placed her hands on his knees, and waited, staring into the top of his head, already starting to bald some. It was like we weren't there. It was just the two of them and they were nineteen again. These twelve years, us four kids, had never happened. He opened up his face to her face, grabbed her arms, and threw them around his neck. He hugged her and held her harder and harder, saying over and over again, I'm-a sorry, so sorry, Nan, so sorry, my keeds.

Chapter Four

The morning of the one and only vacation we had taken as a family, we woke to Dad warming up this big Winnebago in the driveway. My mom said that thing would be our home for two whole weeks. She said it had everything home had, plus wheels. She turned into a tornado, tossing summer clothes into a giant hardback suitcase, throwing a case of beer and a carton of cigarettes onto the floor of the kitchen part, dropping forks and knives into the miniature drawers and whipping toilet paper rolls high up into the cupboards. Why didn't they warn us? Why wake us up and sneak us out in those blue dawn hours? Because last-minute money problems would change small plans for the drive-in, and break Matty's, Hope's, and Charlie's hearts for days. She didn't want to break them over something big like a vacation.

I was seven and had never cared about going places. My mother knew I resisted big change or new people. I liked to keep things just as they were. I held on to clothes that I loved long after I outgrew them. I ate from the same blue plastic plate with the white speckles that Grandpa gave me. Even when we went to Chinese restaurants, I always ordered the hamburger and French fries, ignoring the ugly egg roll that my mother would drop onto my plate.

"In case you change your mind," she'd say, eyebrow up.

So we drove to the animal boarder's and dropped off our new kitten, Gigi, and I cried. We stopped at a twenty-four-hour store for pop, chips, and crayons, and I smacked them away from me. As we headed for the border, I kept looking out the window, asking my mother, Why are we going, where are we going, what's going to happen to us out there?

"Faith," she said, "shut it. Have a sense of adventure."

When we crossed the Ambassador Bridge, it was still dark out.

I vowed to myself that surprises like this could not happen again. And it was around the time I stopped believing what my parents told me to my face, and relied more on information I gathered behind their backs. I guess that's why I refused to remember that vacation. I almost have to take out the photo album for proof we saw Niagara Falls, Manitoulin Island, Storybook Gardens, the Soo. We were there. It happened. See? That's me, in the hat, pouting in front of the Wawa goose, with my arms fiercely crossed. Look, there's Hopey petting a stray dog at Sauble Beach. Matty and Charlie in the bumper cars. Hope with no front teeth. Dad grew a mustache. Mom in those giant sunglasses, smiling. She loved change. I didn't.

I had almost forgotten that we'd ever been anywhere farther than Emeryville, until the morning my dad left for Calgary. That morning, another Winnebago sat running in the driveway, my dad and his boss deciding to drive out and live in it, until they could find permanent housing.

Again, that morning sneaked up on us.

And again, it was still dark out when my mother woke us up to say goodbye to Dad, sending him on his long, long vacation away from us.

"Kids, get up, Dad's leaving," she whispered from outside the tent.

"We know that," said Matty, very sleepily.

"No, now, kids. He's leaving right now, come on. Say goodbye."

There was a definite weight to my heart, so it hurt when I tried to sit upright. Dad was leaving? Now? How come they didn't tell us sooner? Because they wanted to avoid an unimaginable tear bath. Because we would beg and bribe him to stay, every day leading up to that morning. Because Charlie had already threatened to hide away in Dad's duffel bag. Because none of us imagined that he'd actually leave.

Ever since we heard the word Calgary, I had been praying for the singular gift of money, just enough so that my dad would not have to go away to make any. I had asked nicely, so when money never appeared, I felt ignored by God, or punished, possibly for having killed the Old Man. Maybe he had been somebody's dad, so we just had to give up ours for a while, on account of his family's grief. That's how I saw God's job back then. He was in charge of an intricate system of balances, and since, in those days, hell rained only on the DiNapolis, I figured we must have done something really, really bad to deserve all this sadness. But who to blame? Charlie was little, Matt wasn't mean, just sad, and Hope never left my side. We sinned in pairs, so we kind of canceled each other out. So blame fell solely on my mother. She got us on God's bad side, she's making Dad go away today, so I vowed to get her sins forgiven, and to put us back in God's good books again.

Hope didn't stir but I knew she was awake. I climbed over her tense little body with very little care.

I was barefoot and even though it was August, it was still a bit cold. I could smell school coming, all dense in the air like an obvious hint. Or maybe it was my dad's new work shirts, stacked up on the picnic table. We usually did back-to-school shopping around now. The smell of all my fresh outfits would send me straight to September, completely smearing out the last days of all my Augusts.

I met my dad in the carport, where he was shoving his new work shirts, by twos, into his green duffel bag. I started to help him out. Mom went into the house to turn on the radio and make coffee.

"I wish I was going with you," I said, though I didn't mean it. I didn't want to go with him. But I sure didn't want him to leave. I didn't want anything to change. I could've lived in the tent for the rest of my life.

"Me too," my dad said quietly, without looking up from packing. "But, like I say, it would be too hard, too esspensive, and I'm only go to make-a money and come home. We talked about dis, 'nember?"

Matty walked up, stretching in an exaggerated way. He'd been quiet and absent a lot lately. Even on his birthday, two days earlier, we had to wait and wait for him to come home before Mom would let us cut his cake. She didn't yell, but I could tell she was worried as cake was the one thing that brought us together in a hurry. For the whole day that he turned twelve, Matty didn't smile once, and nothing we did could make him.

"Hey, Dad," Matty whispered. "Leaving today?"

"Hey, Matt. Yeah. Picking up John, then we go. Sorry it's-a soon after your birdday."

Silence.

Matty said, "So bye, I guess."

"Bye, Matt-eew."

"I'm going to go back to bed, I guess. It's still dark out."

"Okay. I love you."

"Me too, Dad," Matt said, really fast. They shook hands, then hugged, and when my dad went to kiss him, Matty pulled away.

As he was walking back to the tent, my dad yelled, "Listen-a your momma and be nice to girls. Even your seesters. Okay? I will call."

Matty nodded and ducked back into the tent. I felt he was going there to cry, so I stayed in the carport to give him the privacy.

I was relieved that my dad didn't tell Matty that he was the "man of the house now" like on *The Waltons,* because Matty would have lorded that over my head like a suspended gob. He'd be all "Dad said I was the boss around here and you have to listen to me now, 'cause Dad said."

Hope came out, but not Charlie. Little Charlie was harder to wake than a drunken hound, and slept about as elegantly as one, too.

She jogged over to us, rubbing her eyes, "Daddy, you're going today?"

"Yes, sweetheart, but I be back-a soon," he said, very gently.

"When soon?"

"Maybe for Tanksgiving?"

"How 'bout maybe for Halloween?"

"Maybe," he replied, with no sureness.

"Because I'm being an angel for Halloween," she said.

"Yeah?"

"Yeah and know what Faith's being?" she asked, looking over at me.

"No, tell me," Dad said, also looking at me, me shrugging back at him.

"A stupid dumb ugly bum bum idiot!" she replied, bursting out laughing. I laughed, too, out of shock, but she sounded wicked.

"Hey, you swore," I said, as though I'd never heard her swear before.

"Hey," said Dad, nervously zipping the duffel. "Dat's no nice. Say sorry, 'Ope."

She must've been still dreaming because she said, "But I'm not sorry, Daddy, 'cause it made you laugh! It's jokes."

From the look on my dad's face, I could tell he mostly liked Hope's joke. But when my mom came out of the house, they exchanged a wary glance that said she'd be hearing a lot more of those kinds of words out of these precious mouths with him being not around so much anymore.

It was still dark out when he hugged us both, lifting us off the ground in our pajamas, whipping us back and forth a little.

We all groaned.

"God, yous girls getting so beeg. Next time I come home probably you will be having leetle bras or something! Going around with boys!"

"Dad!" we yelled, smacking him a bunch of times. "You're gross!"

My mom started clapping lightly.

"Okay! Let's go. Finish up your coffee, Joe, I don't want you to take that mug with you, we only got the two."

They clinked mugs and downed their coffees like whiskeys and dropped them on the picnic table at the same time. Bang.

"What about Charlie?" I asked.

My mom looked at my dad. Charlie would probably cry, loud and a lot, so my dad told her to let him sleep, that he'd call from the first stop.

"Nice. That'll be the first and only time we'll use the new number," she said.

A phone had arrived a few days before. It was to be disconnected in two days, and we'd have another number at the rented house in Belle River. We wouldn't even have this number long enough to memorize, so my mother had written it out with masking tape and stuck it to his steering wheel, the second one written out larger underneath.

My dad and his boss decided to drive to western Canada through America, because it would be faster. My mom pointed out all the cities in the states that he'd pass through, and circled the places to stop and call.

"I guess Chicago, then, would be your first stop. You can call Charlie from there," she instructed like a teacher.

"I guess," he said, looking at me and Hope. "I love yous girls, and take care of your momma for me, okay?"

"We will," we said.

"And you, Fate, take care of 'Ope, okay?"

"I will," I said proudly.

"Hey, I don't need her taking damn care of me," Hope said, stomping.

"Hey," said both my parents out loud, at the same time, with the same finger snapping out in the front of Hope's face.

"Stop. Geeve a hug to me," my dad said, scrunching down to Hope's height and holding out his arms. "Bote of yous," he said, pulling me in.

I don't remember this moment, my first big goodbye, with total, outlined clarity. I mostly remembered everyone else in that moment. Hope squeezed Dad hard and ran into the trailer. She probably joined Matty, who was probably in the fetal position, probably wrapped around Charlie. I think my mom pulled me away from Dad's hug gently, and said, "Wait for me in the carport," because that's just what

I did while they walked down to the Winnebago. They walked slowly, my mom keeping one hand on my dad's back, as though she had to kind of push him or he'd change his mind, which I was praying hard hard hard for him to do. Turn around, I said to myself. Dad, just turn around and say this is nuts! I can't leave my wife and four perfect little kids like this, for a dumb, however well-paying job, in Calgary! I'm staying because I love them far too much to go, and money's not everything. But I knew it was, and I knew money was the only reason my dad wouldn't and couldn't turn around. He climbed into the driver's side, but it was facing the street, away from me, so I couldn't see if they kissed goodbye with any married passion. He honked once, lightly, because it was still so early, and still so dark, and then he just drove away.

My mom watched him disappear down the street from the edge of the driveway, arms wrapped tightly around her in that familiar way she had of looking like a human Band-Aid. She didn't wave.

Twenty minutes later, after me and mom straightened up the carport, in silence, and just before the sun came fully up, we both decided it would do us some good to lie down for just a little bit. It was still too dark in the tent to make out the boys' shapes but I could hear them snoozing. By feel, I noticed that Hope had tucked herself in on their side, so me and Mom stretched out alone on ours. She closed her eyes, put her hand on my forearm, and dozed right away.

She was more tired than me.

I couldn't sleep, so I prayed for God to forgive my mother if she had anything to do with this mess. I prayed for Him to forgive me if I did. I prayed to God to give my mother the strength to handle the four of us alone, without having to smack and yell too, too much. I prayed for the family that bought the new house. May they love it and clean it. May the kids not take crayons to the walls, especially the four in my old room. May they never know what it's like to lose this house. But mostly, I prayed for my dad and his glorious return. I stared at the roof of the tent hard, and with the full-born concentration of a true believer, I prayed: "Dear Lord in Heaven, let my dad make lots of money fast so he can came back sooner. Keep him safe. Keep him away from the Calgary whores and the taverns. Let nothing bad happen to him or I'll never, ever speak to You again." I prayed this directly and fiercely to whoever was awake, up there, at this godforsaken hour. Didn't matter. Jesus, Mary, or Joseph. And because I was a true believer, in the perfect way that eleven-year-old Catholic girls are, I was not at all surprised to hear a certain far-off engine get even closer. God heard me! God owes me! Maybe I have prayed enough for this whole family!

I lifted the little flap over the little screen and looked through the little window that faced the street. I watched as the headlights of my dad's Winnebago flipped off because the sun was coming up, because he didn't need them on, because he was coming home, and because we are all the light he'd ever need. Right?

He was coming home.

And I knew it. I knew he'd change his mind. Or God had changed it for him.

Thank You.

But instead of shutting off the engine and running out of the Winnebago and ripping open the tent flap and piling on top of us with relief, he stopped and let the Winnebago idle.

"Mom"—I pushed her arm—"Dad's back!" I whispered, still not fully sure how to believe I did this. How to explain my special powers?

"What?"

She bolted up and flung herself out of the tent, in a half-sleep, into the half-light. I watched her stumble over to Dad's trailer as tentative as a blind woman.

My dad opened the side door, saw her, exhaled, and disappeared back inside. A second later, Charlie came out, carrying Gigi, very awkwardly, and wearing only a pair of saggy blue underwear.

He climbed down, still sleepy.

Dad jumped down behind him.

I watched my mother from behind as she fell onto her knees laughing and crying. Charlie let go of Gigi and ran to Mom. Gigi ran, too, then stopped, and rolled around in the grass.

I could hear Hope and Matty stir awake behind me.

"Hey!" they yelled, opening the flap and seeing Dad. Gigi saw them too, and got all confused at the noise.

Hope and Matty headed toward Dad, but Mom said, "Get the cat, kids, before she gets run over," so they were diverted. They cornered Gigi, first in front, but she smartly rushed Hope's legs, and they were forced to scramble after her in back.

I watched my mom throw her arms around sleepy Charlie and wrestle him playfully to the ground.

"Where'd you try going?" she laughed.

"To Calgary," he said, giggling.

I believe my mom was thinking her kids were funny and stupid and heartbreaking.

I watched my dad hand her a cup of coffee and a box of doughnuts. He ruffled Charlie's hair and then smiled down at my mother, the same way he did from the roof that day. The day she smiled back up at him. The last day my dad was in charge of it all.

Charlie made good on his promise and had smuggled himself as far as the doughnut shop. I watched Charlie throw his head back laughing at his own cuteness from what he had done, and my mother tickling him down into her lap.

"Stop, Mom!" He giggled.

"You little monster," she kidded. "Charlie!"

I watched my dad honk honk honk and drive away, again.

Why I didn't leave the tent still bothers me. Maybe because everything changed so fast that I could only take it in through a tiny window. Or maybe because I could still feel my stupid prayer bouncing around inside the canvas, and if it escaped out of the tent with me, it might ruin something kind of beautiful.

And totally inevitable.

Because he was leaving us, again. And God wouldn't help me with this one. But God could've done something about the fact that I ended up being the only one waving hard goodbye, from inside the tent, and crying desperately harder. I always wished my dad could've seen someone, anyone, fall apart over him, in his rearview mirror, because maybe maybe maybe he just might not have left us that day.

* * *

THE FOLLOWING WEEKEND, we moved to Belle River, and all the things we'd stored came after. Everything except for my parents' bed. My mother sold it for fifty dollars, and bought a foldout couch, since the living room would now be her bedroom. She chose the two-bedroom, white brick bungalow because it was the least expensive of the rentals listed, it was available immediately, and it was presentable.

The new rental house was on the outskirts of the town and built dangerously close to the Belle River. The landlord, Mr. Meloche, who owned the funeral home, warned us about floods, and said until he patched the foundation, we shouldn't store important documents down in the basement. After he left us with these instructions, and a new set of keys, my mother laughed and threw everything that we owned down there, arguing we needed the space and none of our things were all that important anyway.

The good things about the house were that it was walking distance from our new school and also our new church, which was older and taller, and felt far more familiar to me as a place to go to and pray in. I didn't mind that corn, instead of neighbors, bracketed us on either side. And we faced a soy field that was owned and tilled by the Lauzons, who lived across the street in the only house we could see from our porch.

While I unpacked the fondue pot we never used, I asked my mother why we couldn't afford to buy another house. After all, didn't Dad make a living building them with his hands?

"Faith, ever see a convertible Corvette?"

"Yeah."

"Well, the chances that the man who built that car also makes enough money to drive it are very, very slim."

"But Dad doesn't make cars."

"I know, and that's why we're renting," my mom said, referring to the subject of one of the last arguments my parents ever had.

Back in the tent, after the bank people had left for good, my parents stayed up late in the carport, drinking beer and talking low. My mother had wondered if the answer to our financial problems was for my dad to get a factory job. She figured factory workers have steadier incomes and better security, and at least she'd know where the hell Dad was all day. My dad did not disagree with her about the money, but laughed about the security part, since most of the guys he knew with factory jobs were also getting laid off. Besides, he said, he preferred outdoor construction work. It's good for the soul to be under the sun all day. My mother joked that too much sun might have been what was wrong with him. My dad clinked his beer with hers and said, "Amen." I think that they were trying to get along because Calgary had been sadly decided upon that week, so neither wanted to make the other feel worse.

On our first night in the new rental house, we were treated to pizza and all the pop we could drink. Six weeks in a tent had made us anxious to experience bedrooms, with all those doors and walls to count on, so we went to bed early. But at one in the morning, I found myself stuck wide awake. My insomnia could've been caused by the four Tabs, which had made me pee twice already. But it was more likely caused by the quiet. Noise was like a member of my family. Sometimes it was here, sometimes it wasn't, but I had never thought about noise when it was here, only when it wasn't, and that was hardly ever. Until that night. It was so quiet that the absence of noise actually kept me up. I realized that traffic and my parents' yelling had been my lullaby in the city; crickets and my parents' murmuring put me to sleep in the tent. Their voices had become, over the years, like my own personal radio signal, relaying news from the battlefront. And though I hated their fights, I loved knowing why the hell they were having one. Now there was nothing being said, and worse, no way to gather information at a time we needed it the most. Dad was gone and Mom never told us anything.

In the middle of that first silent night, I got up to pee for the third time. It felt good to have carpeting under my feet and only a few steps to walk to a toilet. I noticed the light on at the end of the hallway; my mother was awake too, sitting at the dining room table. She was partially hidden behind boxes, a cigarette burning on her left. A half-empty bottle of wine was on her right. The TV was on low and the phone was sitting at her feet, its cord stretched tight like a leash. She was writing something down in a little red book. I could hear her sniffling as I approached her from behind. Before she could cover up what she was writing down, I noticed "Faith," "Joe," "God," as well as my brothers' and sister's names scattered on the page it was open to.

We both noticed my shadow crawl across the open book at the very same time.

"Heeh!" I gasped.

"Faith! God, you scared me! What are you doing still up?"

"I don't know. I can't sleep," I said, calming my beating heart with my shaky hand. She shut the red book, but kept her finger lodged in the spine. She put the pen behind her ear and turned to fully face me.

"Yeah, I know what you mean. We had a big day, didn't we?"

"Yeah, we did. What are you doing?" I asked, staring at the book in her lap.

"Oh, nothing, just organizing some things," she said, ignoring the book.

She smiled at me, a little drunk. She took a strand of my hair and put it behind my ear.

"Go back to sleep, kiddo. Try thinking of sheep or something."

"Okay. Night."

"Night."

I went pee, then climbed into the bottom bunk, wondering what in God's name she was writing about.

A few days later, unable to stand the silence anymore, and knowing there was information to be gathered, I tore through the house while my mother was in town doing laundry. I started on the boxes in the basement. After that yielded no little red book, I tackled the hall closet where she kept her clothes neatly folded. The silverware case was jutting out of the highest shelf. The only things kept in there were her butterfly brooch and some important papers, the silverware long ago sold for groceries or dance classes, whatever was more important at the time. Just by the way that case sat at a freshly bothered angle, I knew I had found the diary's Arc of the Covenant. Though it didn't contain the Ten Commandments, I knew I'd be breaking a pretty damn big one if I cracked open my mother's personal diary. I'd be stealing her thoughts. But weren't her thoughts ours as well? Because what happens to my mother now happens to us, right? I wasn't stealing, I was borrowing information that I used to freely gather. My intention was not to hurt anyone, only to help everyone, especially myself.

I brushed the brooch off the book as though it was a real butterfly and not a silly tarnished pin that suddenly seemed smaller to me.

I recognized the first entry as a rundown of my parents' last fight.

And so Joe said he'd rather die than work in a factory.

She wrote that she wished he maybe would die, as he had a fairly decent life insurance policy, and all their premiums were paid up. Underneath that she wrote that she was just kidding, underlined three times. *God forgive me!* She added perhaps if he was slightly disabled, not too, too badly, they might qualify for a big settlement. Underneath that, *Only kidding, really,* underlined, hard, five times.

Dammit, she continued, *I am going to make a success of this if it kills me. The kids are going to be happy here. Matty, Faith, Hope, and Charlie will be fine. I will be a good mother to them. I will do everything right, from now on. I am all they need. And frankly, I think that I am all they have because I wonder whether Joe and I will ever be together again. I am not too unhappy doing this on my own. I like the feeling of it already.*

When I heard my mother pull up the long gravel driveway, I closed the book and put it back into its hiding spot. I was filled with calmness. I now knew things, and I would need to know more. That was the first night I slept deeply, my whole body pressed up against the cool, hard wall.

Chapter Five

With my dad gone, my mother was becoming the man of the house that we had never had. She woke up in the morning, made our lunches, then dressed carefully for her job in town, the first one she had had since she was a nineteen-year-old bank teller in Detroit. Almost immediately, she started working at the 2–4 Diner, in Belle River. It was new, open twenty-four hours a day, and you could order a "2–4," a whole case of beer at once, brought out in two big tin buckets. Men who got off shifts in droves would pile around the Formica tables, the *chsh-chsh* sound of them opening their beers would radiate like a tinny beat. My mother took extra care with her hair and makeup, more so than when she used to go to church. We'd eat there on "2–4–1 Tuesdays," which meant two meals for the price of one. Matty, Hope, Charlie, and me would come in twos, or all together, and eat at the counter, while doing our homework. And we'd watch how the men watched my mother. Or we'd watch Matty watch how the men watched my mother.

She was the second-shift day waitress. The money wasn't as good as first-shift breakfast waitress, or third-shift dinner girl, but we were too young to be left alone at night, and she was too inexperienced to handle the busier crowds that came later.

I started walking to the diner after school with my new friend Nicole Laroque. I first met her at the diner when she'd pick up take-out for her folks, who owned the hardware store across the street. Nicole was nice, and probably grateful that I had come along, as she didn't seem to have any other friends before me. At the diner, we'd watch my mother for a few minutes. Nicole thought it was both terribly sad and terribly interesting that my mother worked like she did, in a restaurant, like she did.

"After this," Nicole would sigh, "my ma says your ma probably has to go home and do it all over again, cooking and cleaning and waiting on four kids."

I nodded, yeah, but I didn't tell her that after work my mother actually put on comfortable clothes, poured herself a tall drink, cooked a big pot of Hamburger Helper, or pasta with Ragú, and left it on the stove for us to help ourselves when, and in the case of the boys, if, we came home for supper. My mother would stretch out on the couch with the paper, sometimes falling asleep before the sun went down.

During one of Auntie Linda's weekend visits, my mother was called in to cover a double shift at the diner. We needed the money, so she went, saying out loud, Forgive me, Joe, now I know what it's like. Auntie Linda spent the whole weekend scrubbing out the stove and cooking big trays of freezable dishes for us. She made the boys mow the lawn and straighten up the basement. At one point, Matty turned to Auntie Linda and said, Boy, does my mom ever need you.

"Nah, you know what your mother needs, Matt?" she asked, while folding clothes. "She needs a wife!"

Matt laughed and said, "So do I!"

Nicole's mother would often invite me to dinner at their house. I would help set the table and marvel at their matching silverware and look for my reflection in their unchipped dishes. I would stand like a soldier while her mother handed me heaping plates of three-course meals. I'd breathe it all in, as though their normalcy was something I could carry like a cold, spreading it later to the people living in our screwed-up house.

Once when I had tonsillitis, I stayed home alone and got bored with my sickness halfway through the day. I started to clean the house, way before I had dug into my mother's diaries and read the part where she said, *These kids do nothing to help out. They come home, they don't take off their shoes, and even when I make a nice stew, no one says anything about it. I'm gonna go on strike for godsakes. Or at least I'm going to get on those girls like my dad always got on me and Lin.*

That afternoon, I set the table with my blue plate at the head, surrounded by four mismatched others. I filled the wine carafe with red Kool-Aid. My dad had won a bunch of pastel glass goblets at the fair, by strategically tossing dimes into their mouths, and those went on the right of each setting. I carefully folded paper towels and cradled a fork and a spoon in each triangle. We didn't have enough butter knives so I opted not to use any. Besides, I was making Kraft Dinner with frozen French fries and iceberg lettuce salad with French dressing. No knives were needed.

I lit one of the emergency blackout candles, put on clean pants, and waited.

My mom arrived home first and while she took off her coat, she couldn't take her eyes off the table.

"Well, isn't this fancy, Faith! My, my, my."

"Do you like it?" I asked, already sitting in my spot, legs swinging off the floor.

"It's very fancy," she said, nodding. "How are you feeling?" She put her hand on my forehead. "Are you sure you're not delusional?"

"No. I'm feeling a lot better," I said, and it was true. I was glowing with newfound health.

Minutes later, Matty, Hope, and Charlie came bursting into the house, and, as usual, they rushed the pot heating on the stove.

My mother yelled, clapping, "Hey, hey, hey, hey, hey!"

Matty was already holding a plastic cereal bowl in one hand, the ladle in the other.

"What, Mom?"

My mother slapped the things out of his hands.

"Gimme that. Slow down, Matt. Faith did the dining room up nice, so we're eating in there."

There were groans all around, but my mother held the ladle as hostage over her head and handed it to me.

"Perhaps you would like to serve, Faith?"

"Yes," I said, in cahoots with my mother. "Perhaps everyone can get seated at the supper table," I instructed. "And we can begin our supper. Mom, yours is with the ashtray. But first everybody wash your hands!"

I was doing like Nicole's mother and Grandpa too, when we ate there.

"Yes," my mother said with enthusiasm. "Let's go wash our damn hands!"

I even said grace, really fast, since no one else wanted to.

"BlessusohLordinthesethygiftswhichweareabouttoreceivfromthy bountythroughChristourLord, Amen."

Matty added, "And please, Lord, make Faith get over her fever soon, 'cause we're all a little bit worried about her."

I threw a lettuce at him.

My mother lit a cigarette and looked around the table. "Isn't this nice? This is nice, Faith. You should stay home sick more often. Say thanks, kids."

"Thanks, kids!" yelled Matty, Hope, and Charlie, without looking up from their plates.

I was going to make a success of our new life too, I thought, while dousing my salad with dressing. When I put my mind to it, I could be good enough for this whole family.

The phone rang and threatened to snap us out of this proper behavior. But when I heard my mother say, with her mouth full of noodles, "Matt'll have to call you later. We're right in the middle of our supper, Trev," I almost threw my arms around her neck and sobbed out of deep gratitude.

* * *

IN BELLE RIVER, boys came to me in my peripheral vision, floating in my eye like sunspots. They were just shapes. From the diner window, Nicole and I would watch boys riding their bikes in the distance, cycling around in unpredictable patterns, us staring at them the way you can sometimes be mesmerized by a pack of black flies. Boys in town gathered at dusk in front of the variety store, or they'd huddle like dead moths at the base of one of the four streetlights that lined the main strip.

The first thing my mother ever said to me, the day she noticed me noticing boys was, "Jesus, Faith, close your damn mouth." She snapped open a tea towel, wiped the diner counter, saying, "Hang on for a few more minutes because I'm driving you home."

They went to my school, boys, but it was away from the gray backdrop that was school where boys fascinated me. They didn't wear their Catholic school uniforms to the arena or to the store, so seeing boys in baseball caps, shirtless and unruly, was a kind of shock to the system after the blandness of their creased pants and white button-down shirts. They even smelled different. I don't remember when my looking over toward them in their anonymous groups had become me honing in on one of them in particular. I don't know why I started to notice them in the first place, but I remember it was around the time my dad left, and my mother began to work as hard as he ever did.

At first I saw them as attachments to my brothers; I'd think, he plays hockey with Matty, that one is more Charlie's age than mine, that guy once called our house after ten o'clock looking for Matty and my mother hung up on him, calling him a "stupid idiot" for phoning so late, "and don't do it again, the kids got school and so do you."

This one time me and my mom picked up Matty from the arena. Matty approached the station wagon with two boys, all damp and exhausted.

"Can we take Pete and Trev home, too?" he asked my mom.

"Sure," she said, in a not-nice way.

Pete and Trev threw their big bags in back and climbed into the car with Matty.

"This is my sister Faith," Matty said.

"Hi, Faith," they singsonged. Then they talked back and forth about nothing that would interest me, though you would've thought otherwise from how my chin rested on the back of my seat, facing them. And they were nothing to look at, except for their sweaty necks and ragged jerseys. Their faded jeans and dirty shoes. Their knuckles and their ears.

Again, my mother hit my arm and said, "Faith, close your mouth, for pete's sake," which made Pete snicker, and me feel pain. But it was a benign pain, like a friendly tumor had formed on my young heart. And it told me it was staying there for life. I'd see a boy, say the one with the crooked teeth who worked at the variety store, and my heart would hurt inside me. It wasn't that I loved boys yet, but I loved what they were and what they had that I didn't. Boys had the ability to make my own heart rebel inside my own body. How is it possible a boy could make my heart forget its basic job, to pump blood through my system, for those two or three awful seconds? I knew the pain couldn't kill me, because I didn't die when my dad left. But that's around the time I got used to feeling bruised inside, especially after six months in Calgary turned into a year, then two. I knew I'd never be able to inflict that same kind of pain deep into a boy's own heart, because I felt I was not remarkable. Nothing about me was special enough to keep my own dad around, even though better money is a good reason to leave anything behind, my mother always said.

This was the beginning of my sadness for real. Not the sadness I'd feel from whiny boredom or sadness from watching Kimba the White Lion avenging his mother's death on cartoons. This was sadness of the yearning kind that felt permanent. I liked boys. But I was not perfect. Therefore they would leave. Therefore I would stay sad and this was the truth of my life.

I listed these concerns in my notebook and passed it to Nicole in Religion.

1. Is my nose too big for a girl's. ("No," she wrote.)
2. My bum? ("No, it's all in your head, shithead. Get it? Your bum is in your head! Ha ha.")

3. Maybe I am too religious, which is boring to boys. ("To me too, yawn.")
4. We are poor. ("So was Jesus.")
5. I talk too much about my feelings. ("Maybe you have too many.")
6. I'm too sarcastic for my own good my mother says. ("Agree.")
7. I believe that sex is a sin, until you get married. (I put "agree or disagree, circle one," next to this. Nicole did not agree.)
8. Penises are gross to me. Do you think Jesus had a penis? ("Yup.")

Nicole drew a picture of Jesus on a cross, minus the wrapping around his middle. Instead, there hung a penis, with an arrow, pointing to the words, "Get on your knees, Faith."

I mouthed, "You are gross," to Nicole and I shut my book.

ONCE WHEN WE WERE still living in Emeryville, just before we moved, while Janey and Lula were grounded from us, me and Hope had gone down by the creek. It was a Monday and we had found some excellent "clues" along the banks. There were four cigarettes with a pack of matches sealed in a Baggie, a dead bird, plus a dried-up section of a picture magazine. We lit one of the cigarettes and shared it back and forth. Neither one of us knew how to inhale, so we didn't. Hope, holding the cigarette, carefully pried open the stuck-together pages of the magazine. The pictures were of naked men mostly lying on their sides. They looked like giant, muscular babies, with tanned orange skin and slicked-back hair. They were smiling at us and offering up their large wet penises, poking out between the fingers of their big-knuckled hands. The penises looked like baby animals from a different species than the rest of their man bodies. They looked wet with pee or sweat and we alternated between squealing and throwing it a few feet away, then scrambling to retrieve it for another peek. We were awestruck and repulsed. My first thought was I pitied boys this monster-looking thing they owned. It was the opposite of a girl's smooth-bodied mystery. Then I pitied girls who would have to deal with this newfound limb in any sexy way. Not me, I thought. You wouldn't get me anywhere near these sorry things. After all, these naked men were men, like my dad, like teachers I'd had. The difference between boys and girls was simple to me. Boys had penises; I had seen Matty's and Charlie's since they stood up when they peed and sometimes me and Hope would be taking a bath right next to them. When Charlie was six he peed at us as a joke. We shoved armfuls of water at him, which reached and darkened the carpeting in the hallway, causing a little flood. Also, the boys stank and hit things. Me and Hope were quieter and cleaner in most every way. But though I preferred the company of girls, boys were far more interesting to look at and to know things about.

When me and Hope were done memorizing the penises, we threw the magazine into the water and watched it soak and float away. I was thinking I hoped it was the last time I'd ever see anything as stupid-looking in my life. Maybe I wasn't beautiful but at least I was not in possession of something that homely, even if you could keep it hidden inside of your pants. Still, it was one of the best "clue" days ever.

I used to think number seven of my concerns was the greatest obstacle toward womanhood, but by age twelve, when I started babysitting the boy next door, I worried that number eight would be the bigger hurdle.

Todd Mitchelssen, Jr., was a giant of a baby who lived with his young parents in their rented house, which was walking distance down the dirt road behind us. He was the first baby boy I ever babysat, so his was the first penis I was ever in charge of, as far as changing diapers goes. And maybe because he was such a giant baby his penis seemed so strangely super-small. But with nothing real to compare it to, it just lay there like a little question mark. So this is a real live penis? I thought to myself the first time I slid a diaper under his doughy bum. Big deal. It looked like a midget's finger and about as dangerous. It looked nothing like the pictures from that magazine, so I started to think those might have been fake penises, built with doll plastic and rubber glue.

His mom, Sue Mitchelssen, was married to Todd Senior, my brother Matt's assistant hockey coach. Sue and Todd seemed very cool to me. And I couldn't understand how they got to live together on their own, like they did, when they probably should have still been in high school. Todd Senior didn't even seem old enough to shave. Sue watched cartoons, and one time I caught her coloring with crayons while talking on the phone, carefully staying in the lines.

My mother pointed out to me that Sue was really only about six years older than me, and if I was real stupid with my favors, I could end up just like her, too, one day. Or I could end up just like my own mom. Sue and my mom were both not yet twenty when they had had their first baby. They even talked about that when they met, though my mother had far more regret in her voice. Probably because my mother had had three more after, and Sue was waiting until Todd Senior got a job at Ford's before they'd consider having a second.

I couldn't imagine being a mother, especially since I knew that becoming pregnant involved a penis entering inside a woman. But at twelve, I thought it had more to do with the belly button area than anything below it. My clinical knowledge of sex came from TV shows where women did a lot of kissing and rubbing and lying on top of a man, then they'd switch and he'd be on top of her. Sex was stupidly fascinating, but still like a restricted movie, something I heard about, knew I might be old enough to get myself into someday, but didn't make a particular effort toward it. My mother also used TV to teach us about sex, like if a girl was dressed skimpy and dancing on a variety show, just like a whore, my mother would point out all the slutty factors to her performance.

"Look at her, girls," she'd say to me and Hope. "Her parents probably are having a heart attack watching her acting like that. I know I would die! I'd kill yous two if you ended up like that!"

Me and Hope would squirm around, wiggling our bums like strippers, to bug her.

Sometimes soap operas assisted my mother in outlining to me and

Hope the path of the straight and narrow, which was always opposite of what the best-looking girls did.

"Stupid, stupid Erica Kane," she'd say, with a slow whistle. "Erica thinks that doctor loves her, but he doesn't. Girls, he's just using her for sex. And when she figures that out, she'll divorce him too. That'll be, like, husband number three!"

My mom didn't discuss sex with us in any helpful way. But from her diaries I knew she thought a lot about it herself. She'd write, *Oh God it's been so long since I've been with a guy. I can't even imagine dating. I can picture Matt's face if I introduced him to a guy. Forget it. It would fuck him up for life. I'll have to wait until they're older. Wonder if Joe's sleeping around.*

I wanted to cry at that idea.

Another time she wrote about Adam Lauzon, calling him *the cute neighbor's boy who lives across the street. That kid's looking better and better to me.*

It was one of the few times I wanted to admit to my mother I was snooping in her diary in order to tell her how much she sometimes disgusted me. Adam was eighteen years old and my mother was thirty-three, for crying out loud! An old lady lusting after a young guy who helps us with our lawn and sometimes drives the boys to the arena was the most disgusting thing I had ever heard of. And there's my filthy mother writing, *Oh Christ, one day I should just grab him and do it. He's a bit nerdy, I'm not attracted to him, but man, he's eighteen. That would be fun! For him too! Oh I can't even think about it. I should go to jail for these thoughts.*

"Or to hell," I desperately wanted to write, in red ink, in the margins next to these sins. Underlined five times.

For a while after I read that entry, I had a hard time looking at my mother. Or other times, I'd have a hard time not looking at her, careful to wipe the accusations of eternal hell off my face.

But because of her, I did start looking at Adam Lauzon, the "cute neighbor's boy," a lot differently. Sometimes he'd come over to haul wood or plow the field that they owned next door to our rental, and he'd take off his shirt. He once caught me looking at his stomach, and the little trail of hair that went "down there." Our eyes met and my face shot red with me thinking, "Oh no, I'm turning into my mother!"

Once, when my mother walked me over to the Mitchelssens' for babysitting, I only casually mentioned what a good job I thought Sue did hanging the beautiful kitchen wallpaper, and how I'd love to be able to do that too, someday, to my own kitchen, when I got married and had my own little baby.

My mom said, "How'd you like her life, Faith? You being someone's mom in six or seven years? Think about it. It's not all about pretty wallpaper. Mostly it's hell."

Really, though, Sue's life didn't seem all that bad to me. She lived in her own place, rented too, but still, they had enough money to stay stocked in Fig Newtons, Fritos, and fancy ice cream, and not the pink, white, and brown kind that turned to spiky gel after a week. Good kind. Breyers. Plus the Mitchelssens had a VCR, something we wouldn't have for two more years. And they owned a dozen movies, permanently. I watched their *Jaws* and *Grease* probably ten times each.

Hope and I sometimes babysat Todd Junior together. We called it "two for one," but I never split the money. Hope did it to get out of the house for the night and I didn't mind the company. And if Todd Senior was too drunk, me and Hope would walk the gravel road back home together. The pitch blackness meant we clutched each other, wordlessly, when cars came by. We were becoming less and less close to each other.

Because he was so young, but so big, Todd Junior's nickname became Little Big Todd, after we saw the Dustin Hoffman movie about being an old Indian. I took the joke further when Hope and I were sitting on either side of him on the couch. He was just learning how to sit upright on his own and we were using our bodies as brackets. He kept falling into our sides which, on account of his size, could hurt a lesser person.

I said, "Look, Hope, me and you are making a BLT sandwich. Big Little Todd in the middle, get it? BLT." This cracked us up for such a long time that "BLT" became his nickname, edging out "Little Big Todd" forever. The clincher was that BLT cracked up too, which made everything even funnier, because he was totally unaware that he was our joke.

SUE MITCHELSSEN asked me if I could babysit this one time, and after I said sure, she explained over the phone that BLT had had a little operation, had had the top of his penis taken off in a circumcision. She said it would be needing a bit of special attention. I blushed and said I understand, but I didn't. I asked my mom what did it mean his penis would need special attention that night?

"Means our little Todd has become a man, Faith." she said, adding that, seriously, I would just have to clean the top of his little penis a few times to avoid an infection. She said he'd probably be in a lot of pain, since most people were smart, and circumcised their boys at birth. She said it was a rotten idea to wait until he was one to do it. Poor thing's probably screaming bloody murder, all night long, she said.

I got the chills at this and was reeling with the medical instruction of it all.

"Infecting it how?" I whined.

"The skin's exposed is all. It needs ointment, probably."

"Why's the top of his penis off anyways?"

"Some people do that to boys. It takes the extra skin off. It's cleaner. You know, Jews do it on a religious basis."

We weren't taught about penises in school but we were taught about the Jews. And it was confusing because, though Jesus was a Jew, being Jewish meant you didn't believe in Jesus.

"Are the Mitchelssens Jews?"

"I don't think so. Probably for them it's just cleaner."

"Eww. Cleaner for what?"

"Never mind, Faith, just do how Sue shows you."

Maybe the Mitchelssens were Jews, I thought. They didn't go to church, at least not to ours.

Hope came with me for the night of babysitting with the extra-special penis attention. She wanted to get a look at his hurt penis, too, but mostly she came to eat their cool food.

When we got to the Mitchelssens', Sue and Todd Senior already had their coats on. Sue gave me a small tube of ointment and said BLT (she called him "Toddy") is still sleeping, and when he gets up he'll be needing a change. She told me after I do all the regular diaper stuff, I should put a small bit of this just on the tip of his penis before I wrap him up.

"He's been a bit uncomfortable, Faith, but he's not crying so bad now."

It all seemed so criminal, this taking the top off their baby's penis. Criminal and unnecessary, but so interesting that I felt almost grateful for the trust they seemed to be placing in me. And anxious for him to wake up so that I could be in charge of giving him this medicine on his penis operation problem.

"Don't worry at all, Mrs. Mitchelssen. My mother told me about it too," I said, chest stuck out a bit, feeling all nursey and smart. I couldn't wait to tell Nicole this information I was gathering about the penis.

Hope was standing behind me, mute as ever. She didn't like adults much, even if she knew them.

"Glad Hope's here. She's your little helper, eh, Faith? Wish I had one."

"That's right." I eyed Hope sideways. Little helper, my butt. In her mind I knew she was elbow-deep in their green olives with the red pimentos, her favorite, and a rare delicacy in our house, unless we had good company. Hope was greedy and I had to teach her how to eat things strategically, instructing her to take from the bottom of the cardboard layer of the Peek Frean stacks, retard, so there'd be little evidence of our stealing.

People always said, "Help yourself to whatever we have," but I knew they never really meant it. It would be a year or so before we graduated to taking my mother's cigarettes and siphoning her booze, so we were unaware of how much practice we were getting with all our nicking of cookies and pilfering of pickles.

When BLT stirred even a pinch I ran up to get him from his sweaty nap. His hair was a pile of wet stringy curls and I had an urge to give him a light trim, but I remembered my mother's only advice when I started to babysit for folks.

"These little kids, Faith, are not your little dollies. They'll shit and cry and so will their parents if you let anything stupid happen to them, you hear?"

I toted BLT downstairs where Hope was waiting, blanket spread out on the shag rug, the movie *Jaws* already playing in their VCR. It was at the part where all the people were running out of the water for the first time.

I peeled back his diaper. His penis was still small, because of his body size, but the inflamed head made it look like a bony-red, crooked finger, rather than some future sex instrument of any kind.

"Eww," was our refrain.

We said, "Eww," again, loud, when I peeled back the bit of gauze from the tip of his penis, "Eww," maybe a bit too loud, when I wiped around his sacky thing and up the sides of it. When I squirted out the salve and went to reapply the white gummy ointment, BLT started to scream high, just like a girl. He screamed like the people in the movie screamed when Jaws bit off their leg, or their penis, if they had one.

"Holy shit," I said.

"Shh, Beee!" Hope begged. "Beee, Beee, shh, shh." "Beee" probably short for BLT

"Shhh, Beee," I repeated. But he wouldn't.

The worst part was that he was trying to grab at his own penis with his strong, stubby fingers. He had nails too, which I felt when he dug them into my skin while I was trying to hold down his arms. I was instinctively aware of how awful that would feel to a little baby. But I had no maternal kinds of instincts at all. My instincts were only honed for things like sniffing out my mom's cigarette smoke when she was still awake in the early hours, and knowing she was anxious. But I had no instinct toward this baby's crying. I knew nothing about comforting anything in pain, including myself, in any healthy way.

Hope started to cry too, and scrambled over to shut off *Jaws* at the part where the mother thinks her kid has been eaten by the shark.

"What are we going to do?" she asked. "He won't stop and won't stop and won't stop, Faith. What are we going to do?"

Her way of eliminating disasters, like anyone who lives through them on a regular basis, was to keep repeating herself.

BLT had wrestled out of my softish grip and began twisting away from me and the kindest part of my own desperate will. He was trying to crawl, and ended up dragging his pinkish burnt penis across the shag. I didn't want to hurt this baby but ended up doing just that because I had a tight hold on his ankles, trying to twist him back upright. Struggling like that caused his stinging penis to scrape the rug worse. He was a broken wheelbarrow, his torso facing up, his boo-boo penis smooshing down. His scream changed to guttural, like when anger marries to murder, the way Gigi sounded once when overcome by a stray tom.

"Call Mom, Hope. Now!" I yelled. She disappeared into the kitchen.

BLT got a firm grip back on his penis, little nails digging in, his legs clutching tight around his body like a bothered crab.

I tried pleading, "Hey, Toddy, I'm sorry, baby, stop crying now," but I kept thinking, sweet Jesus, even if they were Jews and had to do this on account of their own kind of religion, they'd never get near my heaven after this, those asshole Mitchelssens. I prayed for them to go to hell; for them to rot someplace scorching, too, the tips of their own genitals bared raw for raggedy old birds to pick at.

I heard our car pull up, the door open, and my mom rush in, being only a one-minute drive away, laying dust fast down the gravel road that linked us.

"What the hell happened here?" she yelled, filling up the rest of the space in that little living room.

"Nothing, he woke up like this," I whimpered, struck young by my own failure.

"Both of yous just stop it, you're making it worse."

I watched my mother's rigid body change into softness, easily curling like a lover, making a C over BLT, who was still whelping angry. When she took off my dad's old lumber jacket and threw it over her shoulder, she had on her short yellow nightie; two pink curlers were jutting out of the top of her head. Everything felt like a shuddering emergency of my own making.

"Hi, sweetie, oooooh, heeeeey now. Hiiiii, baby," my mom cooed, like it was one long word, sung out low in song. She never sounded like this with us. It was as though me and Hope weren't in the room, seeing her act like the little mother we never remembered her being.

"Oh now," she said, and BLT melted toward her like I'd seen him do when his own mom would surprise him in the back yard, where he'd be splashing in the pool. His wet arms would go flying up toward Sue Mitchelssen in a way they never did toward me, the stupid old babysitter girl.

I never thought to envy that baby love until now.

With Mom ministering to him using something that seemed like voodoo to me, BLT's screaming turned to crying, then to heaving, then to sobs, and then his wet-choked stutter came to a complete and silent stop. She was like a radio disk jockey expertly lifting the needle off the spinning record of his awful pain.

"Poor little guy, eh," she said half looking over toward us with a watery smile on her face. She seemed to be glad. This put her in a good, not bad, mood. She easily inched the blanket under his bum, and parted his hands away from his "wittle boo boo." BLT never took his eyes off my mother. She kissed his forehead and murmured a giggle out of him. Her speaking all soft and low instantly ironed out his pinched-up face back to being a baby again.

I was breathing less hard, but I felt pissed in the very center of me, thinking that when I'm screaming mad about something, she'd only ever match my madness with her own, and then some, stomping mine out. And here she was, completely in love with a stranger baby, a nothing person in the eyes of our family, and she's all squishy and sweet like a mom I'd order from a catalogue in a second. Yes, I knew the difference, him being "a little baby," and me not being "a little baby" no more, as I was continually reminded, but I was stilled by this "momness."

"Wow," said Hope. "Faith was trying to make his legs still to help him and he wouldn't stop and he wouldn't stop and he wouldn't stop."

My mom looked at me steady for a second, which made me defensive.

"I tried to make him stop crying, I did," I pleaded, "but he was just bad off from when I got him up. I didn't know how. I tried. And I think I almost had him stopping before you got here."

"Shh, shh, baby," my mother said, through his bitty whining, ignoring mine. She firmly held a thigh open with her forearm, and tenderly, and in a way that was a little embarrassing, she caressed the cream onto the base, then up to the tip of his red, red tiny penis. And I hated his penis more than BLT did. I hated all penises, so full of fire and bother they seemed. Why do they have to be so complicated and frightening, even to their owner?

"See?" she said. "See, Faith? Be real slow, and just talk like this." She lowered her voice to a whisper. "And just keep looking at him because he's just a wittle scay-erred baybee boyeee, eh, baby?" she said, never taking her eyes off him. "Gotta boo boo? Yeaaaah, eh?"

And there was BLT wiggling under her like a dumb puppy. And the way she hovered over him like that, my mother reminded me of the Virgin Mary, minus the short yellow nightie. All she needed was an awestruck sheep and a lowing cow to surround them, BLT now substituting as the Christ Child in my mind's manger scene. I wondered if the Virgin Mary had had similar problems with Jesus' penis. I wondered if Jesus even had a penis under that skimpy loincloth he always seemed to be wearing. Maybe I could see it, if I got a better look at church. Jesus was a Jew, so probably he had the top of his penis off too. Did the Virgin Mary lose her mind like me, or did she know exactly what to do with a penis, like my mom did? My mom had practice, having had a husband and two boys, but the Virgin Mary would have been as new to this as I was that night. This was soothing, to have something in common with Mary, after the incompetence I displayed in the face of my mother's finesse with the damn thing.

She decided to stay with me until the Mitchelssens came home.

Hope convinced us she was tired and could make it home down the road alone. My mother told her to call us when she arrived safely, her acting all relieved that Hope survived the ten-minute walk.

BLT fell asleep in my mom's arms and we watched the rest of *Jaws* together, volume low, because the baby was sleeping. She'd never seen this movie before, and probably, to make up for my poor child care skills, I started to speak out the words ahead of when they happened, as though to announce, "Here's something I know about that you don't."

"See, Mom, okay, here's when the shark scares the guys in the boat, right? and that guy gets eaten. Only later. Even though he's an expert at dealing with sharks."

My mother nodded stiffly at my helpful narration. I knew she thought maybe I was too young for this movie, this job, and all these stupid challenges. But still, she never stopped the movie, despite the horror and murder. And most of the time, I might as well have not been there, because she seemed to be really enjoying herself, especially the part where BLT stayed sleeping in her arms.

When Sue and Todd Senior came home they were nervous at first, but my mom said, "Everything's all right, you got three for the price of one," and she handed BLT over to Sue with instructions.

"He'd been screaming, Sue, and the girls called me. I'm glad," she said, clutching my dad's jacket around her. They didn't seem to notice she was in her nightie. "You should take him in, though," my mom continued. "I don't think there's an infection, but when Matty was done, the doctor didn't do such a good job. Toddy cried a lot, tonight. It looks okay to me, but I'm no doctor."

Sue Mitchelssen nodded like the nineteen-year-old that she was, nodded more mutely than Hope did, standing over their screeching boy, hours earlier. She nodded dumber than I had, with my legs stuck mad-straight and helpless.

So the tip of Matty's penis was off, I thought. Charlie's probably too, even though we weren't Jews. And for the life of me I couldn't understand what the hell was cleaner about what we just went through.

"I never want to see another penis again, as long as I live," I told my mother while we pulled away from the Mitchelssens'.

"Yeah, I used to feel the same way myself," she said, inching down the dirt road that led to our driveway. "Probably just after Charlie was born."

"Mom! Don't be gross."

"Oh, Faith! Grow up," she said, laughing at her own joke.

We both noticed Adam Lauzon's Gremlin backing up out of our driveway, at the same time Matty was tugging his hockey bag clumsily up the front stairs. He drove Matty everywhere, sometimes without my mother even asking. I suddenly wondered about Adam's penis; if the tip of Adam's penis was off.

"He's not bad to have around," my mom said, stopping the station wagon at the mouth of our driveway to let his car out. "Too bad he's too old for you, Faith."

"Eww, too bad he's too young for you!" I teased back, with a little too much accusation in my voice.

"He's not really," she replied.

"Mom!"

"Faith!"

Some Saturdays, when my mom picked up a diner shift, I'd hover at the mouth of our driveway, watching for Adam's mom to leave for work. I'd make sure I was wearing shorts and that my tan was showing. When her car disappeared over the tracks, Adam would stick his head out the door and wave at me to come over. Sometimes we'd play Pong and talk about certain movies or political issues about the earth and baby seals, my favorite topics. He told me he was going to be a writer, focusing specifically on science fiction, "with soul and substance." On the side, he was going to study business as a way to have a day job. This one time, he told me I should probably start thinking about wearing bras; that I should probably tell my mom to buy me a bra.

"You should think about shutting up, Adam" was the only thing I had thought of saying before I ran home, burning. He was trying to be helpful, trying to be a father figure, but my mother said that we had a Grandpa for father-type things, until our own dad came home. Not that I'd ever talk to either one of them about my boobs.

Adam reversed his Gremlin, then backed up a few feet to meet our station wagon. He leaned over and rolled down the passenger window of his car.

My mom rolled down her window and yelled, "Thanks, dear! I don't know how to repay you for driving Matty around. Wait. Let me give you some money for gas."

"It's nothing, it's on my way home," Adam hollered over the engines.

My mother got out of our station wagon. While she leaned inside his car, shoving a ten into his face, I could see him protest, his hand up, resisting the money. My mother balled it up and threw the bill into the back seat, laughing.

"There. Take it. Buy yourself a beer or two on me."

I could see her nightgown riding up her bum. When she turned around, I watched Adam watch my mother's legs fold back into our car. He honked and drove away. My mother put the station wagon into drive.

"Mom. Jeez! Look what you got on!" I tsked-tsked her.

"Oh, who cares, Faith. It's just Adam."

"Still," I huffed.

"Still," she mimicked.

"Still."

"Still!"

I waited a few beats, and whispered into my shirt, "Still, he probably saw your bum."

My mother laughed and said, "He's probably seen a few."

Chapter Six

One Sunday morning, I was cycling circles in the driveway, waiting for Adam's mom to go to work instead of getting ready for church. We were going less and less. Matt couldn't be bothered. Charlie had recently decided he didn't believe in God. So it was mostly me and Hope, eventually mostly me, my mom sometimes dropping me off at Nicole's on her way to work, me going with Nicole's family, pretending they were mine.

That day Grandpa stopped in with some money for my mother. He caught me hovering at the end of the driveway, showing off my tan, and wearing a tube top, in case Adam came around.

"Faith, what are you doing here?" he yelled out of the car window.

"Grandpa, I live here," I kidded.

"Does your mother know you're going barefoot? Where's your little dress?"

My little dress? I wanted to scream. I don't wear little dresses, I'm a teenager now, you old jerk. But I said nothing because he was carrying a check that we needed. I looked down at my dirty feet and bruised ankles; my thighs seemed fleshy and distracting, poking long and brown out of my white terry-cloth shorts.

"Here, give this to your mother and tell her to call me."

He handed me the check.

"And Faith, go change into a clean outfit."

My outfit was clean, but I knew what he meant. After he drove off, I did what he said, because he was a man, the last one left in our lives. I didn't count Adam as a man back then. He was an older boy, with man potential, though his power was still kind of vague to me. My dad was, thankfully, missing out on all the new things sprouting on my body and in my brain, and our once-a-week telephone calls were forming an easy script to follow. How's school, Fate? Fine, Dad. You are makin-a friends? Yeah, tons. And you are getting along with everybaddy? Yes, I'm trying. Good. I love you, Fate. Me too, Dad. Okay, now poot 'Ope on. Okay, Hoooope! Dad wants to talk to you!

But I probably changed outfits like Grandpa said, and sought his approval so desperately, because Grandpa didn't approve of his own daughters. Knowing this, my mom always held her breath when she thanked him for the money he gave to her, and the favors he did for her, including the time she asked him to take me shopping for graduation shoes. I was listening in on the extension when Grandpa exhaled loudly, then agreed, saying he was going shopping anyway to pick up a particular kind of American motor oil, available only in Detroit. My mother thanked him and explained how she needed the extra shift, what with Joe now between jobs. For the second time in six months, added Grandpa. And no we weren't going to visit Auntie Linda while in Detroit because there's no parking at her apartment building, he said, and he's not leaving his car on the street to be vandalized by black people.

I had never gone anywhere alone with Grandpa before. It was usually all four of us: me, Matty, Hope, and Charlie, perfect right angles, buckled into his car, staring straight ahead in silence. He'd yell if we stuck our hands out of the window or dropped crayons on the floor. He'd yell if he caught us eating snacks, smuggled inside our little purses. Even if they were clean snacks, like licorice or gum. But we didn't mind his kind of yelling, because it wasn't personal against us. It was discipline, in a firm, smart way. Grandpa explained it's important a car stays clean, for resale value, even though we knew he had no intention of ever selling his precious vehicle.

I wanted to make this shopping trip as organized and flawless as Grandpa's life. For one day I wanted to be the opposite of our chaos and clutter. I wanted to show him what a thoughtful, yet particular, young woman I was hoping to become. Opposite of my mother and her sister.

FOR TEN YEARS, my grandpa had owned a rust-colored Ford Comet, beige tweed interior, with an eight-track player and speakers in back. It looked as new as a Matchbox miniature version, still sealed in its plastic package. He talked about the Comet like he had thought it up in his own head and then made it with his own hands. He used to inch the car so carefully into his garage that you'd think it was made of glass feathers dipped in plutonium with a motion bomb strapped below that would detonate upon impact. Impact included leaning your bum on it while bending over to tie your shoes.

"Watch the car! Get away from the car! Don't lean on the car!"

He was like that with everything. Especially his tools. There wasn't a spot of rust on the wrenches, or dirt on the rakes, and he divided every screw, washer, and nail by size and length, suspending them in baby food jars that had been cleaned, and dried. The jars hung like specimens, or larvae, that if hatched would blossom into God's hardware store, a type of place where you weren't allowed to touch anything. His whole house, too, was like a laboratory, both riveting and terrifying in its layout and careful division.

But it was clean.

We had to eat ice cream outside, even in winter, and running and playing were only allowed in the unfinished basement, which looked like an empty underground pool with a giant three-bedroom dollhouse strapped on top.

None of this perfectionism had rubbed off on his own daughters. And though my mother hardly spent time with him herself, Grandpa loved spending time with his perfect and beautiful grandkids.

He would introduce us to people using our individual names and attributes.

"This is my oldest grandson, Matthew. He's very responsible. This is my studious granddaughter, Faith. Hope is my other granddaughter; she's very athletic. And of course, this is our dear, sweet Charlie, who is quite sensitive," he'd say to the Detroit border guards, or the older lady who worked at the one McDonald's he always went to.

He was also the only person who freely gave us money. By the pound. When we were little he used to save pennies, nickels, dimes, and quarters in giant jars and, once a year, he handed them over with strict instructions to divide it equally. We used to shortchange Charlie when he was really little. At three, he didn't spend it so much as shove it into small spaces around the house and on his body. Sometimes Grandpa would count the coins and challenge us to match his original total. If he was in a good mood he'd let us have the money after two attempts, four hours of counting, when we would still be off by six frustrating cents.

That's how I learned about math, and shopping.

That's also how I had saved my half for the shoes I wanted to buy for my grade-eight graduation. They were cream-colored wedges with a butterfly painted on the top. I cut them out of an ad in the *Detroit Free Press.* When I showed them to my mother, she said, I'm sure your grandpa will find them very interesting. At $14.99, no tax, if we got them in the States, also a bargain.

The morning of our shopping trip, my mother carefully dressed me in my cleanest outfit, in a way that suggested she was more nervous than I was. For one thing she ironed my Roadrunner T-shirt. Rare. She French-braided my hair with shaky hands, starting over twice, me sitting on the floor between her knees. The smoke from her third cigarette of the morning was smoldering in an ashtray in front of my face. I waved it away in an exaggerated asthmatic drama.

"Your smoking could kill me, you know, Mom."

"Sit still," my mother said, braiding my hair tighter. "I could kill you too, with my hands. I don't need cigarettes to help me."

To hide the smell of smoke on her kids, she would sometimes spritz us with a teensy bit of her Moonwind. Not today. Grandpa hated perfume on women.

"Behave, or he won't take you anywhere ever again," she said, securing the ends of my braids.

"I will."

"I mean it or I'll kill you."

"I know!"

"I don't want to hear anything from him."

"Okayokaaaaay."

Grandpa pulled up in front of the rented house and honked, once. He did not get out of his Comet. He hadn't entered the house since the first month we moved here, when he had words with my mother over the state of our place and her marriage. In the living room that day, I heard him remind her of how she had been brought up, and what a shame that she was setting such a bad example for us, especially the girls. My mother just rolled her eyes and walked away from him, clutching her sweater around her. She never talked back to her father, so we didn't either. One frowning look at me and Hope's backless, flimsy halter tops, and my grandpa could send us silently back into the house to put on T-shirts.

My mom walked me out to Grandpa's car. Our driveway was littered with fat, primary-colored toys, booby-trapped with bikes, skates, and Gigi, now allowed out to roam and mingle. Our once spoiled and pampered Siamese had started to look like the rest of our belongings, dirty and ignored.

"Hi, Dad, thanks for taking her. I really need this shift," my mother said, opening the back door of the Comet.

Grandpa watched her buckle me into the back seat. Grandpa never let us sit in front. He didn't like us playing with the radio or going through the glove compartment. My mother said goodbye to me by silently holding a finger in front of her face through the window, eyebrows up, looking hard into my eyes.

I mimicked her back, and we drove off.

I didn't mind Grandpa's rules. I was proud of Grandpa and how clean he looked, my own dad always seeming to have jumped out of a plaster wedding cake.

Even though it was years after the riots, the crime rate was still high, but Grandpa didn't mind risking certain death to shop in Detroit, because the exchange rate was still rather healthy back then. The trick, he said, was to roll up all your windows and lock all your doors and avoid all eye contact with all black people. I was told they hated us, couldn't tell the difference between white Canadians and white Americans, and that they would shoot us too, even though, we, as a nation, had never really owned that many slaves.

The downtown was an ugly shell, with groups of black people, mostly young men, standing around burnt-out houses and empty lots. But we only saw these facts for the five minutes it took Canadian shoppers to reach the expressway. You drove it fast, too. You never took a detour or wandered around in search of anything, Grandpa said. You never asked for directions. If you didn't know exactly where you were going, you were told to turn around and go home. That kind of stupidity, of being lost, was what got you rolled, robbed, raped, and shot.

At least, that's what he told us.

Grandpa, with his hands tightly at ten and two o'clock, caught the expressway through downtown Detroit, took it a little too fast and exited a little too sharply, five minutes after the bridge. I was sickened by that turn and put my hand over my gut, which felt sensitive to me.

When he pulled into Payless, we parked far away from the rest of the crappy, dirty cars. He grabbed my hand and we ran into the store, probably to avoid potential crossfire or my own kidnapping. Probably.

We were the only white people inside the Payless.

Grandpa let me do all the work. I showed the saleslady the picture from the ad. Grandpa didn't say anything. I told her my size. Grandpa didn't say anything. She came back and told me the shoes I wanted didn't come in my size, quite. Grandpa looked at me. She offered me a half size smaller. I accepted. Grandpa spoke up.

"Excuse me, miss, my granddaughter told you her size. Why do you think she'd be a half size smaller? She is not lying."

"Sir, uhh, sometimes certain makes of shoes come in slightly different sizes."

"That's the stupidest thing I ever heard."

I wanted to tell the saleslady that Grandpa talks to everybody this way, not just black people.

"Well, whether you think it's stupid or not—"

"Grandpa, I just want to try them on, okay?" I whined.

"Why? That's not your size. Look at some other kinds, Faith."

"I'll just try them," I meekly insisted. He was hard sometimes.

He nodded to the woman to put the box down. As I tried them on, he sat next to me, looking straight ahead. They felt a little tight, but they were two of the most beautiful shoes I had ever seen. I was going to wear butterfly barrettes and my butterfly necklace. The butterfly decorating the wedges would complete the outfit. Plus they'd stretch. I wanted them very badly.

"Those look small to me, Faith."

"No, I think they fit, Grandpa. See? I think they're my size," I said, desperate for them.

"I don't think they are."

He went down on one knee and pressed his thumb hard onto my toe. He noticed some dirt on the end and took out his hankie to wipe it off.

"They look too tight," he said.

"I don't think so."

"You're buying shoes you might only get to wear once, and that's ridiculous. It's impractical, Faith. Unless there's something else here that you like, we're going. You are not buying shoes that do not fit you. I can't let you do that."

I tearfully looked over at the row of the other boring shoes.

"Can we go someplace else then?" I asked.

"No. Your mother can take you to someplace else. This is the best place for shoes."

"What about another Payless?"

"This is the only one."

That was a lie. I knew there were others. The ad listed four stores in the Greater Detroit Area, but this was probably the only one he knew how to get to without being shot and killed by black people.

"Put your shoes on, let's go."

"They fit. Grandpa! Look!"

"They don't. Let's go."

I took off the shoes and we left. On the way out Grandpa shot the saleswoman the same dirty look he brought into our house the day he yelled at my mother in our messy living room.

I tried not to pout. Pouting was practically pornographic to Grandpa and he would never take me anywhere lovely again if I got caught wearing a face full of feelings. I crossed and uncrossed my arms as Grandpa made his way quickly on, and quickly off, the expressway. He wanted to stop at the place he knew of where they sold the best, and cheapest, motor oil. It was a small gas station owned by a white guy, a friend of his back when my grandpa was a crane operator. He had taken me, Matt, and Hope there a year before. The owner had given us Twizzlers for Charlie, who had been home sick with the flu.

We pulled in to the same garage, but everything looked different. It seemed smaller and messier, and there were stray young black men hanging off the broken cars littering the lot. They weren't wearing uniforms, either.

Grandpa rolled down his window. "Is Jerry here?" he asked no one in particular.

Nobody answered.

My stomach cramped and twitched.

"Excuse me, I am looking for the owner, Jerry. Is he here?"

One of the black guys who was sitting on a stool jumped off and walked to the car, wiping his hands with a rag. Grandpa's own hands were still at ten and two o'clock, kneading away at the steering wheel.

"Who you looking for?" the black man asked, leaning his arm on the car and looking at my grandpa with amusement. He must have found it stupid that I was sitting in the back seat instead of up front, because he kept looking at me, then Grandpa, then me.

"Jerry, the owner," Grandpa said.

"He don't own this place no more. I do. You need somethin'?"

"Well, I used to buy Valvoline Gold here. You still sell it?"

"Yeah, hold on."

The man yelled toward a kid, about my age, who had been staring at me.

"Jace, go now, get this man the Valvoline."

The man turned to my grandpa and said, "It's hot for June."

"Yes, it is," Grandpa replied.

I had to pee really bad, but I was terrified of what the bathroom here would look like, or what the black men would do to me on the way to it.

"Hey, I got something for her," the man said to Grandpa, pointing right at me. He hurried back into the kiosk. I didn't know where to look or what to do with my hands, but my lock was pressed down, my window up, my grandpa's was only open a crack. We were doing everything right.

It was getting hotter. My thighs were stuck together damp.

The man and that boy Jace, the one about my age, both came out of the kiosk door. The man was holding the oil, Jace a melting Fudgsicle.

"This the oil?" the man asked, holding up the can to my grandpa's window.

"Yes, how much?" Grandpa replied.

"I'll give you a case for ten."

"I'll take it," Grandpa said. "Thanks."

"Go on, Jace," said the man to Jace. "Give it to her."

He was nudging Jace to give me the melting Fudgsicle while the man went to get more oil. Jace held the Fudgsicle up against my window. I could see the chocolate was already covering his own hand and I didn't want it on mine. When I caught my grandpa's eye in the rearview mirror he nodded to me, stiffly, to accept. I slowly rolled down my window and reached for the wet tips of the Fudgsicle stick.

"Well, that's nice of you. Isn't that nice of him?" my grandpa asked, in an totally unrecognizable voice. "What do you say, Faith?"

"Thank you," I said.

Jace nodded and ran away.

We were alone in the car with the Fudgsicle and my sick stomach.

"Grandpa, it's melting really fast," I said.

Grandpa shifted around in the front seat looking for his hankie, but he couldn't find it, probably having left it at Payless.

"Hold it forward, away from you," he ordered.

Too late. A big chunk slid down my finger and landed by my hip, lodging itself under my bum. I made it worse by shifting around to get at it, which sent another chunk flying down between my legs. I unbuckled and lifted myself up so I could grab the chunk before it melted underneath me. It had already made a large stain on the seat, and I noticed its matching stain on my crotch. How did it melt so fast, without my feeling it spreading coldly? The stain continued darkening warm between my legs. I realized a cruel God who couldn't wait until I got home to curse me had caused this stain. I didn't have to pee. My period had arrived. I had started my period all over Grandpa's tweed car seat.

Another chunk of the Fudgsicle shifted down on the stick and landed deep in the folds of my lap. I was left with little option but to eat what I could, and let the rest melt all over the back seat around me.

"Grandpa," I cried, "it's getting all over the car. Can I throw it out the window?"

I didn't want to tell him about my period. He'd make me go to the bathroom at the gas station. The men and Jace would see my bloody bum, and they'd laugh at me.

"No, don't throw it out the window, Faith. Don't do that!"

Jace was standing next to someone, still staring at me. I hated this Jace. Look at me, I wanted to yell. Look what you did! Look what you did to my grandpa's perfect car, asshole stupid idiot! Look what you made me do! You made me start my period out of stress and fear of you. I hated that black boy for his Fudgsicle, and I hated God for this mean timing.

The man with the case of oil was taking his time, so Grandpa got out of the car to find him.

"Wait here, honey, I'll get you some napkins."

Sanitary ones, please, I wanted to yell. I was practically choking on the Fudgsicle, which was becoming the worst thing I had ever put in my mouth.

"Okay. Hurry up, I want to go home," I sobbed, as the final chunks fell and dissolved on my crotch. The dark blood looked the same as the chocolate, which was all over my T-shirt, all over my cords, and in at least three spots on Grandpa's car seats. We were told in Health, your period will happen when you least expect it to, and the teacher was terribly, awfully right.

When Grandpa finally came out of the kiosk, the Fudgsicle was completely eaten or melted. Knowing we were only a few blocks from Auntie Linda's house, I decided to convince Grandpa to bring me there so I could clean myself up. I would take Auntie Linda aside and tell her about my period. She would definitely understand why I couldn't tell Grandpa.

Grandpa opened my side door and told me he couldn't find a napkin.

"Say thank you and get into the front seat," he whispered, before putting the oil into the trunk.

But if I moved to the front, I'd expose my fresh stain, a stain he'd know for sure hadn't come from any Fudgsicle.

I croaked, "I can't, Grandpa." Think. Think. "It's just my pants are full of chocolate and I'll make it worse up front."

"That's true, honey," he said, slamming my door and getting into the driver's side of the Comet. He looked over the front seat at the damage. Five big stains about the size of tea bags surrounded me. I knew I was sitting on top of the biggest one. I was officially a woman, but I felt and looked more like a greedy baby after a birthday party.

"I'm sorry," I said, clenching my thighs together to stop the flow.

"It's not your fault. You were being polite."

"Maybe I could clean myself up at Auntie Linda's? She lives just—" I offered, pointing.

"No. It's okay, dear. I'm taking you straight home."

When we passed under Auntie Linda's high-rise apartment

building, I looked up and wished she could pluck me from this rotten humiliation, using the tips of her manicured fingernails. I imagined us cuddled in a soft-focus Kotex commercial, side by side on a swing, me cupped with cotton, having just started my period in a blurry meadow full of swishing daisies. Instead I was bleeding freely in dingy Detroit, surrounded by bombed-out cars and sweaty black men.

Grandpa headed back to the blessed expressway, while I sat rigid. I didn't say a word to him the rest of the way home in case he turned around and saw my hand shoved down between my legs.

When we pulled up to our house I felt relieved. Yes, it was filthy and unpredictable, but now so was my body, and my body belonged here. Thanking Grandpa, I ran into the house, covering my bum with my purse. I went straight to my dresser, stuffing shorts and clean panties under my armpit. Matty was in the bathroom, so I slapped the door and screamed, "Get out. Now!"

Matty opened the door at the same time Hope came running down the hallway. My hands were shaking when I grabbed on to Hope's, pulling her into the bathroom with me.

"Calm, girls!" Matty yelled, as I shut the door on his stupid face. "Jeez, who's on the rag?" he said, through the door, not knowing I could have easily answered that question.

Hope gasped, "Faith! What happened! Are you all right? Did you get the shoes?"

"No," I whispered. "God gave me my damn period, instead of the damn shoes."

She covered her mouth with one hand, hiding a smile, digging under the vanity with the other, keeping her eyes on me.

"Oh, jeez, Faith. You just started?"

"Yeah. I didn't tell Grandpa or nothing, he'da killed me."

She pulled out one of my mom's super-absorbent pads, and handed it to me, a horrible-looking, tiny diaper with two long tails on either end. There was no "self-adhesive strip," like I had seen on TV, so I placed the pad into my panties and started tying down the long tails onto the crotch.

Hope smacked it out of my hands.

"You need a belt for these, retard. Don't you have a belt?"

"A belt? For what?"

"Oh, God, Faith," she said, looking at me with my mother's impatient expression stuck on top of her own features. "Hold on, I'll get mine."

I sank onto the floor and started pulling off my pants, thinking my twelve-year-old sister was ahead of me on this, would be ahead of me on everything, probably, for the rest of our lives.

THAT NIGHT, my mom called Auntie Linda and told her the story. I listened carefully how it became a funny, not terrible thing, and Oh, those black people, and Dad must've shit, and poor Faith gets her period. Poor Faith, Dad should've brought her to your place. My mom giggled and said she'd find out about the stains, right away, and she'd call Auntie Linda back. When she hung up, I told her it wasn't funny, but she said, You're wrong, Faith, it's funnier than you know.

When she phoned Grandpa, he told her, oddly, most of those stains seem to be coming out, except for one stubborn splotch right in the middle of the back seat.

"Well, Dad, keep at it. You just keep at it. They'll come out." She could barely breathe.

When she called my auntie Linda and told her what he had said, I could hear Auntie Linda's cackle from the dining room table.

My mother had tears in her eyes from laughing; the next day, more tears in her eyes from crying. The phone call was from my grandpa's friend, Mr. Marentette. He was calling to tell us that he found Grandpa dead, on the couch. For sixteen years, they played checkers at exactly noon every Sunday. Mr. Marentette told us that when Grandpa didn't answer the door, he knew right away something was wrong. He mentioned that Grandpa had been wearing flannel pajamas. They looked to have been ironed, a fresh crease down the leg. Also, the shirt was done up right to his neck. Mr. Marentette said he didn't know why that struck him so deeply, but wasn't it so like Grandpa not to take that top button for granted?

My mother agreed and blew her nose hard, nodding and sobbing.

GRANDPA WAS BURIED on the second last day of my first period. When I overheard my mother joke to my auntie Linda, after his funeral, that what happened to me in the back seat of my grandpa's car was probably what had killed him, I was furious. She was kidding; I knew it wasn't my fault Grandpa had had a heart attack. So I needed to blame God, and that black kid Jace.

"Oh, Lin, he couldn't get those goddamn stains out—" My mother laughed so hard she couldn't finish her sentence, Auntie Linda doubled over in pain. At the funeral, the neighbors told us when he got back from Detroit, Grandpa had mixed some potent, stain-removing paste in the garage and was scrubbing away at the seat until the wee, wee hours, his work bulb suspended over the windshield.

My mom said, "Poor Faith. Can you imagine? Two old men in three years," which made my aunt laugh even harder. Assholes, the both of them. I reminded myself to pray for their eternal souls. Somebody had to. And maybe now that I was a woman, God would finally, finally listen to me.

"Stop, Nan!" Auntie Linda begged, calming down, lighting a cigarette. "You know, none of this would've happened if the stubborn fool had just let Faith stop by that day."

It's not that my mother or Auntie Linda was happy about Grandpa dying. Just the opposite, you could tell. They only laughed because they were grieving drunk that hot afternoon, sitting on top of Grandpa's picnic table. They started with white wine out of a box, then beer out of the bottle when the wine ran out.

Auntie Linda had brought her new boyfriend to Grandpa's funeral, a Polish guy named Paul. He was uncomfortably chuckling along with them, and their inside jokes about their strict dad, now rigid in death, because he was rigid in life, Auntie Linda explained.

After the funeral, and my graduation the next day, she and Paul were driving to Niagara Falls to get married, then off to live in New York City, well, Greenpoint, nearby. Paul and his Polish family lived there, running a Polish restaurant, a real one, with tablecloths and candles. They were eloping, since, at her advanced age of thirty-three, Auntie Linda said she'd look ridiculous in a big white dress. A formal wedding didn't matter anyway, now that Grandpa was dead. But Auntie Linda was sad about the fact that her father died thinking she was a spinster slut.

"And here's a man gonna make an honest woman out of me and he never knew my soul was saved," she slurred, slapping Paul on the chest. Paul nodded and smiled.

When Auntie Linda got even drunker, she pulled me into the conversation, and raised a familiar finger in front of my face.

"You. This is not your fault, Faith, sweetie. Grandpa died because his heart was busted. Me and your mom broke it first, not you."

My mom said, gently, All right, Lin, that's enough of that, okay? Let's talk about something nice. So Auntie Linda described how when I'd visit her in New York, we'd see the Statue of Liberty and Radio City Music Hall and eat sandwiches at a real deli counter.

My dad couldn't make it back for the funeral. Too sudden. Too far. Too expensive. He had been laid off for the third time, and was waiting for news of a job on an oil rig. I had read one of his letters to my mother where he said, Hang on, Nancy. He described the great "munny" he'd definitely make drilling for precious oil in the middle of Alberta.

"You will see," he wrote, "we pay back your dad and buy a house, I promiss."

But since Grandpa was dead, we no longer owed him anything.

"That's one good thing to come out of this," Auntie Linda said. "You're off the hook, financially."

"Yes and here's to a similar fate for the rest of our creditors," my mother said, clinking Auntie Linda's beer, them laughing like hell, a place I would now surely end up, if I didn't get the chance to tell God my side of the story.

* * *

I WORE BUTTERFLY BARRETTES, my butterfly necklace, and my ugly striped Pepsi-Cola platforms to graduation the next day. As consolation, my mother let me wear the butterfly pin with the two authentic diamond chips. Auntie Linda came with me to church. Adam took Hope and the boys to the arena.

"We only have three periods in hockey," Matty teased, in front of Adam. "Not like yous girls who get them the rest of your life, ewww."

Adam grimaced and winked at me.

"Boys," he said. "What can you do?"

After the regular mass, the priest said a homily and a special prayer for Faith DiNapoli's Grandpa Franco, who sadly was buried the day before. Auntie Linda squeezed my wrist. Though I was grateful for the acknowledgment, I felt ill that we were standing out again. Or maybe it was the fact that I had found out that Hope had had four whole periods before me. But mentioning Grandpa made me sad, especially because anything like order and classiness disappeared along with him. He could be mean and I didn't know very much about him as a person, but I had looked up to him, and taped a picture of him on the wall next to my bed. In it, he is standing in his garden after I had helped him cover his rosebushes with upside-down giant glass jars. Even though they made the garden look like a science project, he said the jars protected the roses in winter. I made a note to talk to Adam about my grandpa in a way that would express my love for him, but with a level of mystery I sorely lacked.

The priest blessed the graduating class, then the fourteen kids making Confession were told to remain at the front after the host part.

"I'll meet you outside, kiddo," said Auntie Linda, making the motion of cigarette to mouth.

I recognized Serena Agora, who was in my grade, but in the remedial level. Matty said he once saw her coming out of the tavern with a guy who must have been at least twenty. She was for sure having sex, he said. But she was around my age, fourteen, I protested. That's not too early for out here, he said. County girls have sex all the time because there's nothing else to do, he said.

Serena didn't look like the other Michelles and Lauries who populated (or as my mother said, polluted) the town. She was dark, like me. Hair, skin, eyes, everything. She had wild, curly hair and she hardly looked around when she walked.

After the priest closed mass, and said go on to high school in peace, we were told by an altar boy to organize ourselves into alphabetical order. I sat two down from Serena in the first pew.

After a brief costume change, Father Joel returned for the Blessed Sacrament of Confession. He motioned to the first girl to follow him to the velvet booth at the back of the church.

For a few minutes, no one said a word to each other, then Serena whispered, "Hey, you really *can't* hear anything."

I had been thinking the exact same thing and wished that I could have been sitting next to her.

The first girl was in there for two minutes.

I had four things to confess, only three before yesterday, but the trip to Detroit caused me to question much about the way I thought of black people.

Father Joel was waiting for me behind the curtain.

"Are you Faith?"

"Yes."

"I'm Father Joel. I wish to congratulate you on this day—your graduation, and on this Blessed Sacrament. I would also like to offer condolences regarding your departed grandfather."

"Thank you."

"So, where shall we begin? Would you like me to start?" he asked. Confession at that age is mostly fill in the blanks. We could add sins if we wanted to but there was no pressure.

"Yes, please," taking the easy way out.

"Faith, when you're angry do you take the Lord God's name in vain?"

"I have, Father."

"Have you lustful thoughts?"

"I have, Father. Sometimes. I guess."

I couldn't tell him they were specific thoughts about a specific boy, Adam, and those thoughts had caused me to started touching myself down there with no specific skill or goal.

"Have you spoken back to your mother, thwarting her authority over you?" Father Joel asked. It was a small town. Everyone knew that my dad didn't live with us anymore.

"I have, Father," I said, and left it at that.

The other day, I had told my mother to get lost when she pinched my arm after I told Hope to screw off even though Hope had really only kicked me under the table. I was sent to my room until I could come out with an explanation for my actions. Later, I told my mother that it was because I had had my period, that I had been under a lot of stress with Grandpa dead, and that I needed to take the edge off. She shook her head and put the rest of the groceries away.

"Faith," Father Joel was reading aloud from a piece of paper, "the Lord forgives you and calls you to His bosom. Repeat after me. Forgive me, Father, for I have sinned, I have sinned in my heart and in my soul . . ."

I thought about Jace. He didn't do anything wrong by offering me a melting Fudgsicle that did permanent damage to Grandpa's Comet, but it was like he was daring me to say no. It wasn't a simple gift and I could tell he knew that. He wasn't trying to be nice, he was trying to tell whether or not we were. But I confessed none of this racism. I was an adult now, with a period and everything. Besides, I knew we were equal to the black people and they were equal to us whites. Period. I would just have to raise myself to be nonracist and try my best to stick up for all black people everywhere. After all, one day I wanted to live in America and there were a lot of black people living there. This could be another good topic of conversation with Adam. He was smart about things and treated me like I was at least sixteen sometimes.

We made the sign of the cross together and he recommended four Hail Marys and four Our Fathers and I would begin to see him one Wednesday a month, at the high school, which was down the street.

On the way out, I caught a glimpse of Serena in the parking lot. She was dark-skinned and that hair—it crossed my mind that she might be part black. I was going to make friends with Serena, even if she was part black—no—especially if she was part black, to prove to myself that I was not a racist person.

The next day we drove to Grandpa's lawyers in Windsor. He had left us a bit of money, which went straight to creditors. The Comet was intended for Matty, his oldest grandson, and the most responsible of us four. After Matty turned sixteen, it didn't take long for the Comet to take on the characteristics of an old La-Z-Boy: Sour man-smell in the back seat, duct tape holding up the rearview mirror, Led Zeppelin stickers on the bumper, work shirts and hockey equipment littering the trunk, and the ends of Matty's joints stuffing the ashtray.

Chapter Seven

I REMAINED MOSTLY barefoot during the summer months that passed after Grandpa died, and Dad couldn't afford to visit. Despite the heat, Hope joined the Sea Cadets, marching in a thick, dark uniform, covering her own feet with heavy, shiny boots. Matt began to drive, and roll exquisite joints, often at the very same time. Charlie disappeared into his room after school, the sound of deathly wails echoing out of his portable tape player. The music he chose to love had nothing to do with singing or dancing. It was music to writhe to, or murder by, but we ignored him.

During all these tiny changes, when little spaces formed between us four, my mother wrote letters to my dad. When she was done, she'd ask me to bike into town and mail them. On the way back I was to pick up a newspaper and a carton of cigarettes. She had no reason to believe that I opened these letters and read them, afterward copying out my dad's address on a new envelope, imitating her handwriting the best I could. I'd restamp, reseal, and mail it, promising myself that each was the last I'd ever open, like each of my mom's cigarettes I had begun to steal would be the last I'd ever smoke. But the information in those letters was as addictive and as vital to my bloodstream as nicotine was starting to become.

The first letter primarily concerned money, and this line, *Let's just be honest with each other, Joe, we both know our marriage was over long before you left.*

My heart busted for my dad. I knew he missed us, but he also wrote that coming home without money for a new house would be a bigger defeat than losing the old house had been. I had read that in one of his letters that my mom had thrown in the trash, the week it was my turn to take it to the road.

I cheered my mother in my head when I read, *And yes, I am grateful you're not being an ass about child support but what do you want, a prize? Back-to-school clothes are important here, shoes especially, so I need more money around this time. Period. I don't want to justify it, and no, just because they wear uniforms does not mean we're off the hook. Bad enough they struggle to fit in, I want them to have the things that other kids have. Let's not fight about this. I know how much shoes cost. I am not making up this number.*

Shortly after that letter, my mom took me to buy a pair of Nikes with the baby blue swoosh. Hope got a bomber jacket. The boys chose jerseys, their names ironed on the back with velvet letters.

The second letter was even more gratifying, though Hope was with me, so I had to calm her down before she let me pry it out of her hands.

"No, it's wrong," Hope whined, holding tight.

"Jesus Christ, Hope, give it to me now or I'll kill you!" I hissed. Maybe because I sounded like our mother, she let go. We crouched down on one of those cement parking lot dividers.

"This is a fucken sin," Hope warned, pulling her HMCS Hunter Sea Cadets baseball cap down over her darkening eyes.

"It's not. What's the sin is them lying all the time to us."

I read it out loud twice, while Hope kept a lookout for familiar cars or people.

Joe a formal separation is important for tax purposes, for me, yes, but who's got the kids? Me. Not you. So that's all I'm saying. As for seeing other people, ha don't worry, that's a luxury I don't have, though no doubt one you're enjoying. Fine as far as I'm concerned but I think we have to sit the kids down and tell them outright.

We cringed. Gross, our parents are dating, or talking about it.

As it stands, I think the kids figured it out, but next time you're in town, tell them you like it out there. Like your oil rig job. That you have friends and a life you enjoy. Be honest, they're not stupid. I know you say you feel like a failure, but you are doing more good out there, with that job, than you could do back here. We both know that. But if you decide to move back, it's not back with me. I won't live like that again. I don't hate you. But I don't feel married anymore. Nor am I anxious to ever marry again, but I want to be straight with the kids and I want you to back me up. I won't say bad things, I know you won't. Let's be good about this. We can do that much, can't we?

Hope was clutching her gut when I rewrote the address and stuck it in the mail slot.

"Fuck," she said, "don't you ever do that to me again, Faith. I feel totally sick."

She was nothing like me. I felt great.

The third letter I mailed was the last I read because my mother never wrote my dad again, as far as I knew. It was six pages. Her longest ever. In it she suggested that his next visit be extended. Our grandpa, the one who spent time with us, and did things with us, was dead now. She wrote that we now had no father figure whatsoever in our lives, *Unless you count the kid across the street who is a big help to us, especially to Matty.*

Eww, there she goes about Adam again, I thought.

So let me know the dates you're coming and I'll tell the kids. Do stuff with them. They love you, you know.

THREE WEEKS LATER, my dad came to town.

That first night, he stopped by for dinner, like my mom asked him to. She cooked a stew, bought dinner rolls and candles, and told him where stuff was. She left saying she was going to the movies. Have fun with your children, she said.

I set the table awkwardly and we five sat around it even more so. My dad was all, How's your marks, Fate? You, Matt-eew? Good. Charlie, you are seeming so tall. 'Ope, how come you cut-a your hair? No, eets very pretty, but I prefer hair long.

He didn't talk about not being married to Mom anymore. He didn't talk about his feelings of missing us, and failing us, because we didn't sit there itching with the need to know. Because of me, the dinner was awful. I had told my brothers and sister about the things I had read, so we had a hard time acting like ourselves or being curious about anything, for real.

After supper, Dad hinted for me and Hope to clean up, and we did. The boys snickered, since that was not the regular way we did things. Matt said, So, Dad, you're staying out there? You like digging for oil? My dad said, yes, very simply, and suggested that when we were a little older we could come out and stay with him for a whole summer if we wanted to.

"If your momma she say so," he added, clearing his throat. "You gonna hafta ask her."

She was in charge of us now. I had read that kids from broken homes are a sorry lot, damaged and angry, and generally up to no good whatsoever. Most criminals are raised alone by their mother, I had read. I also read girls like me screw up their own marriages, if they're lucky enough to get a proposal in the first place. I looked at Matt, Hope, and Charlie and I figured they were thinking the same thing. But I felt a kind of bottomless possibility take over me. It wasn't that I set out to be bad right then and there, but all incentive to be good completely disappeared.

MY DAD STAYED at the motel in town, but every day for that week, he picked us up in the morning and took us somewhere. Often the things he chose for us to do were for kids younger than we were, or way older. He took us to the tavern for dinner. The menu offered limited fare, but unlimited fascination. I recognized people from the pizza parlor and church and hoped for them to recognize me. I felt adult and sordid sitting in that dim, smoky room.

Another time he took us to the Farm, in Essex, which was a kind of miniature theme park based on all things farmy. The people who worked there dressed like farmers or milkmaids and you could touch all the animals. The only rides we weren't too big for were the tiny Ferris wheel, and the long hay ride, where we were all bitten by fleas. The Farm also had a miniature albino horse named Princess, who couldn't stand up anymore because her front legs were crippled, bent underneath her body. You had to pay a dollar extra to see her. The four of us leaned over the pen and stared down at Princess for a long time. Charlie put a piece of gum in front of her face, but she never lifted her giant head. She just looked at the gum and sneezed. It made me want to cry about my family for the first time, but I couldn't do that in front of the very people I was sad over.

My dad took us to see three movies that week, though he never stayed to watch them himself. The theater had a steakhouse right next door, so he'd instruct us to meet him there afterward. Dad would hand Matty money and leave. Matty would take a twenty off the top of the stack, give me the rest, and wander the mall. In the theater, Charlie, all in black, would fall asleep on my shoulder, drooling like a baby. I don't remember what movies we saw.

THE NIGHT HE was flying back to Calgary, my dad brought over a large pizza, which was a little cold. When he said he couldn't stay to eat it with us, I could tell he had been drinking. So could my mother, by the way she frowned hello. After we kissed and hugged him and thanked him for the week of trips and movies, he took my mother out on the porch to talk. We watched them from the big front window, behind the sheers, eating the slices, not bothering with plates or napkins. They looked like they had just met at a small party and were stuck chatting with each other. Finally, my dad reached out and kissed my mom hard on the side of her head. She kept her arms wrapped around herself. As he backed out of the driveway, she waved goodbye to him, gently, but he wasn't looking.

Matt threw his crust into the box and went downstairs to hit foam pucks into a net. Charlie got on the phone to find someone to go be with, and Hope searched for a show on the TV. I went to my room and lay on my bed next to sleeping Gigi. She had her feet tucked under her like that little horse from the Farm had. I stared at her for a long time before petting her wide awake, to get her to stop me from crying.

I HAD A FAVORITE OUTFIT that I wore every other Friday when we didn't have to wear our uniforms. I received many compliments on it. The blouse was pink, ruffles at the wrists, plaid vest, pink and blue highlights, baby blue corduroys, and white Nikes—baby blue swoosh.

Those year-old shoes were the only parts of the outfit that weren't stolen.

By the time I was in high school, I had become a talented and prolific shoplifter. I was daring about it, and fairly unrepentant. I never told anybody—except Hope, because it was hard to hide my new clothes from her, and easy to avoid my mother's notice if I spread the treasure between the two of us. We babysat and made a bit of money doing odd jobs for our landlord, Mr. Meloche, so it wasn't unusual for us to buy things without my mother knowing. Plus I needed these clothes. They provided insulation and comfort, not from the cold, but from being left out in the cold to begin with. We were poor, something my mom reminded us of almost daily. But I refused to believe we were poor—or worse, to dress as though it was a fact.

Stealing came naturally, I think, because I had coveted everything around me so badly and for so long that it had become a simple extension of that need. I was like that girl from *Carrie,* but instead of moving knives into my enemies' hearts with my eyes, I lifted outfits that mirrored them with my hands.

After a while, to not steal became harder than to take whatever it was that I wanted. Stealing made me feel better, like if I was falling down a hole, and needed to grab what was dangling in front of me, the things I lifted cushioned my fall. The bigger truth was that my parents couldn't afford to keep me dressed in a manner I was becoming more and more accustomed to. And recognized for.

"Faith, I love what you got on," people would say those Fridays.

"You look amazing today, Faith, I love those barrettes, where'd you get them?"

"Oh my God, I want that shirt it's so great."

I would not, could not, give that up.

Besides, my mother never went into our rooms, and even if she did, she wouldn't be able to make out the separate bits of clothing on our bedroom floor. It got so that you couldn't see our carpet anymore. It had been replaced by a solid, colorful mass of mating, writhing pant legs, shirt arms, leotards, and belts. She called it a "Junior Miss" snake pit. What she didn't know was that my slobbiness was strategic. How could she see exactly what I owned if she couldn't make out the individual stolen pieces? Plus we wore a uniform almost every day. For those Fridays, I put on my outfits in my room, then made a run for my coat. If my mom became overly curious, I'd just say I borrowed it from Nicole. Our friends never came over, so there'd be no cross-examination.

I thought I was developing a genius mind.

The first thing I ever stole was a pair of gloves, in church. I noticed them when we kneeled. They were in the little shelf where the hymnals went, so I thought that they must have been left behind by someone attending the earlier mass. They were gray and soft as flower petals. Hope saw me fingering them.

"Take them," she whispered.

So I did.

Hope was as astonished as I was when I put them into my coat pocket. And for the first time in my life I was glad Mom didn't go to church with us anymore. Not only would she have caught me, stealing would never have entered my mind in the first place. Who was watching me now? God? I began to find that more and more laughable. So far, in my life, God had ignored every single one of my pleas and prayers, so now I was looking out for myself. And besides, I didn't go to church to worship anything except for the back of James Newhouse's beautiful head, and the Gilroy boys, who generally sat next to him. Church was an opportunity to show off my excellent clothes, and that was all.

I knew for a fact that Hope only came with me to get out of the house, though I couldn't figure out what great powers she mustered up to prevent her from giggling when I first grabbed those gloves. But the high I felt was so new, it was holy even. Maybe because I did it in a church? I don't know, but I couldn't wait to take something else.

I started small, garage sales mostly, and I focused on things such as salt shakers or doorknobs. I stole odd household goods, things we either didn't have (a bent sieve, stained oven mitts, unicorn book ends) or didn't need (a garlic press, candles, dirty novels). Sometimes my mother would be right there, asking for a price on a set of vinyl chairs.

When I babysat, I began to look around the houses with a very different eye. I was less focused on good food, or how a family lived, and more focused on obscure drawers and shelves. I'd take an old tea towel, say, or a number-two pencil. Once I took this skinny suede tie I had seen a few times at the Mitchelssens'. The tie was hanging in the downstairs closet beside a couple of musty dress shirts, so I felt very strongly that it would never be missed.

But a week later, Sue Mitchelssen called my mother and asked her to ask me if I might have accidentally borrowed a suede tie, brown, with a black tip. She said she was pretty sure Faith might have it because the last time she had seen it was before Faith came over to babysit Toddy. My mother snorted, said this was impossible, what would Faith do with something like that? And how could you ever accuse Faith? She's been watching your kid for more than a year now, and if you think she's watching your snot-nosed brat ever again, forget it.

She hung up the phone and stomped toward me at the kitchen

table. I was fake-concentrating on a paint-by-number. Also stolen.

"Did you steal something from Sue's? You better tell me." She was holding one finger up to my face.

"Noooo. I didn't. I don't know what you're talking about," I said in the most casual way possible, not looking up from my artwork. I was on the heavenly sky part, but just dying inside.

"You know what I'm talking about. If I go in your room and find what she's looking for, I'll kill you."

"What's she looking for?"

My mom turned and hurried down the hallway. I ran after her declaring my innocence.

"You can't go in my room. It's private. Mom, I didn't do nothing wrong. Why are you going in there? Why won't you believe me?"

She shut my bedroom door on my face, so I went into the bathroom next door. I could hear her rifling through my dresser and closet. There was a long pause, then more frantic slamming. I was desperately trying to remember where I had put the tie.

After a while I didn't hear any more movement so I came outside. I tried to duck around into the living room where Matty was, but my mom yelled for me to come here. She was in the kitchen holding the tie and smoking a cigarette.

"I called Sue. I told her we were dropping by because it looks like you have something to give back to her."

I started to cry, "Don't kill me, Mom. It was by accident."

"Tell Sue that. Let's go."

"I can't."

"Let's go. *Now.*"

I felt like I had lost a small, private business. Like I had gone bankrupt. I had been stealing for a while, big things, too, like a winter vest from the Bay. Once even a bathing suit plus its matching wrap. My mother had dropped me off at the mall, since it was what the other girls did, and it seemed like a harmless place to spend a Saturday. Plus I told her I was meeting a bunch of friends that I did not have.

I didn't always take for myself. The potted spider plant was a gift for my mother on Mother's Day. It was just sitting there, in the garden center, outside of the grocery store. But I get caught for this? A dumb tie? I needed to feel like I should be doing a penance, but I was angry, filled with gaseous rage that hurt my middle.

When we got in the front seat of the Comet, my mother pivoted toward me and I instinctively covered my face with my hands. She smacked at us a lot now, not too hard, and not always landing her shots. Smacking wasn't as bad as grounding. That was worse; humiliating and dull.

"Oh stop that, I won't hit you," she said, "but you tell me where you got that stupid teddy bear."

She must have noticed him sitting on Hope's wicker chair. It would've cost thirty dollars, and I couldn't believe it when I saw it in the floral shop window. Thirty dollars for this?

My reply was, "What bear?"

"Jesus, Faith, you're a thief and a liar?" Her voice was cracking when she added, "Dammit, do you realize you have probably busted every single Commandment except maybe adultery."

She was appealing to an old sensibility, but she was right. And though she always insisted the deaths of the Old Man and Grandpa were not my fault, sometimes she'd joke that they were.

When we pulled up to the Mitchelssens', Sue was standing behind the screen door with her arms crossed. Todd Junior, now more than two, was next to her, holding on to her pant leg. I thought to myself, He will grow up to be a big, fat man someday.

My mom slapped the tie in my hand.

"Here, give it back," she said, looking over at the field next door, probably because she was unable to meet Sue Mitchelssen's eyes.

I got out and walked up to the door trying to be casual. I was the exact same size as Sue, which was why I tried on all her clothes, but this was the only thing I had ever stolen from her. Except for the hand cream samples. And those little things you stab on the ends of a corncob, but I only took one, so it was useless for eating corn. It was ornamental. But I'd also been watching Toddy much less lately, ever since Sue's husband, Todd Senior, acted all weird on me one drunken night. He had insisted on walking me home, after I babysat, despite me saying I'll be all right walking home by myself. On the way, he kept tickling the back of my neck, and when I'd slap at his hand to stop, he'd laugh and do it again. He thought it was some funny game.

"Stop it, Todd," I had yelled, hitting his hand in the dark.

"Oh, you ticklish, Faith, huh?" he teased.

"No, I'm not. But you're drunk enough."

"I am not," he said drunkenly. "I'm just doing my duty seeing you home safe. What's wrong with that? Why you gotta be all bitchy to me?"

"This is good enough, thanks," I said, trotting away, not realizing until I had arrived home that he hadn't paid me, that fucker.

Sue moved out onto the porch mouthing to Toddy to stay in the house.

"Hi, Sue," I said, almost whispering. "Sue. Jeez. It looks like this got in my bag by accident. So my mom says she thinks it might be yours."

"Yes, it is, Faith. It is mine," she whined. "And I would like you to go in my house and put it back on the hook, right exactly where you found it, please."

I looked at her and thought how impossible it felt for me to do that. The tie was difficult to find beside all those shirts and I could just picture her little face glowering at me while I dug into the back of the closet to return it. I couldn't allow her to watch me do that. I whipped the tie on the ground and walked back toward our car.

"Just take it, Sue, okay?" I stammered over my shoulder, nearly crying.

At this, my mom opened her door, while Sue stomped toward me. I was sandwiched between two women, who both felt wronged, who both were determined to make me feel like the giant sin that I was. I hadn't been trying to be mean. I just wanted that damn tie out of my damn hand. And I was scared because of shame.

"Faith . . ." my mom seethed through her teeth, "pick it up and *hand it to her in her hand! Now!*"

"Yes, Faith," said Sue, more calmly, "I want you to hand that tie to me right in my hand."

You bitch, Sue, I thought. You think you're so great. You are pregnant again, even though Todd Senior does not have that job at Ford's that you're always talking about.

My mother turned to Sue and said, "Sue dear, just shut the fuck up, okay?"

"Oh that's nice, Nancy," she huffed, "real nice. Now we know where your kids learned to talk like trash the way they do. You be careful, I'm telling everyone not to hire Faith as babysitter because she's a thief and I just got off the phone from the Scotts and Shirley said that Faith stole a beach towel, she's sure of it."

Mr. Scott was our dentist. I stole it because they were rich and had seven luxurious beach towels. I counted. In our entire house of five people there were four regular towels. Period.

I mouthed, "No, I didn't," to my mother, who had tears in her eyes, but to her miraculous credit, they were not falling out of her face.

"Get in the goddamn car, Faith," my mom ordered, in a weary voice. She sounded almost asleep when she turned to Sue and said, "Sue. Dear. There's your goddamn tie, okay? Please, I need you to just choke yourself with it."

As we pulled out of the driveway and with nothing to lose, I rolled down my window and yelled, "Yeah, Sue, and your husband is a pervert!"

My mother punched my arm hard.

"Ow. It's true!" I said, rubbing where she hit me.

"What'd he do to you?"

"Nothing. Yet. He was just drunk one time and teased me."

"Why didn't you say something to me?"

"I don't know."

"You better start telling me things, Faith, or I'll kill you, you hear? I'm your mother, whether you like it or not." She added, "Maybe I'm not doing a good job." She was saying this into the windshield, as though something or someone on the other side could answer her back. In a voice haunted by a TV mother, she added, "I think it would be important for you to bring me all the things you took."

"Forget it," I mumbled, calling her bluff.

Smack, hard on the face, for the second last time in my life.

"Don't you dare speak back to me. Don't. I am trying here. I'll sell you to gypsies or something," she threatened, half-laughing. Her own mother used to threaten to sell her and Auntie Linda to gypsies when they were little, and she was alive. I prayed for a band of them to pass through town.

"Go ahead," I said, crying, terrified of the things coming out of both our mouths. "You could probably get a decent price for me!"

"Probably," she said, choking up. "You're clearly good with your hands."

THE EXTENT OF MY thievery broke my mother's heart in a way that I had never intended. My mother had started reading psychological books and developed deep theories about my needs, needs I had no idea that I had until she told me. The day after the showdown at the Mitchelssens', my mom came into my room, holding one of those books. She sat down on Hope's chair, not bothering to remove the pile of dirty clothes.

"Faith, listen to me. I have this idea. Maybe it's that you got off on a wrong foot because of Dad being gone and everything. Plus with me working so much now, it says here . . ." She opened a paperback with a picture of a lightning bolt separating a mom and a girl and cleared her throat.

"'A father's absence in the family has separate ramifications. However, a mother's absence is often never discussed in an overt way, but it manifests itself in acts of unbridled aggression and anxiety in the offspring. In boys you can find an acting out, through violence. In girls, sometimes nail-biting, or often stealing, in order to garner attention.'"

She took a deep breath, like a kid wrapping up an oral exam. "And then with Grandpa dying, maybe you feel like you have, well, a need to stand out in the middle of everything. You're crying out. For stuff. Maybe? You think?"

I felt that her suggestion that I stole because I wanted to feel like the center of attention wasn't wrong, but I felt that I was the center of attention in a family that had no center, or ability to pay attention.

I said, "Maybe so, but still, it's important to have nice things, Mom. I hate how we're poor all the time."

She closed her eyes and said, "So do I, but stealing is wrong and bad and it's gotta stop, Faith, or else."

"I'm not going to steal anymore," I said, though really only intending on a leave of absence. I hadn't felt the least bit bad about the things I took while taking them, but felt horrible that my secret habit had been revealed. Mostly, I was embarrassed by my mother's attempt to be a mother. Part of me could tell she wanted to be anywhere else but here, in the claustrophobic chaos of this bedroom and our lives.

"Maybe we can get you a job," she said, finally. "You can buy nice things with money you earn, legally."

Though I deeply resented the solution, another part of me liked the way she was concerned. It was mostly my dad's idea. My parents had a long discussion on the phone that night. My dad talked to me, too. He offered to talk to the priest on my behalf. We couldn't have me stealing anymore, he said. He phoned Father Joel about my stealing and Father Joel told my dad that perhaps, since I didn't go to church all that regularly, I stole because "Jesus was no longer living in me." When my dad told my mother this, me listening in on the downstairs extension, she replied that my stealing was more likely because my dad was no longer living with us, not Jesus. Whose fault ees dat? my dad asked. Oh God, don't start, she replied. My dad said that Father Joel felt it might be time for me to make "a weekend" with the church.

The weekends were called Christ in Others retreats, or COR. Adam said he had gone on one, and that it was nothing but brainwashing for wayward Catholics as a way to keep us in line, like sheep. Ever since Adam started going to the university in the city, he had more sinister ideas about the Pope and the Church than I ever thought possible. He'd come over after school sometimes, and talk to my mother about the things he was learning. She'd smoke and nod and tell him to stay in school, because she never did, and look at her. They'd laugh and he'd say, it's always good talking to you, Mrs. DiNapoli. Then this one time, she said, Oh Christ, Adam, call me Nancy.

I almost vomited while she lit his cigarette.

We were sitting next to each other on the porch, both watching him walk away that night.

My mother looked at me looking at Adam, and said, "Jesus, close your mouth, Faith."

MY FRIEND NICOLE volunteered to go with me to COR. There was no such thing as too much religion in her family, she said.

"Promise you won't become a stupid gaylord on me," I said.

"Yeah, doy," she said.

My mother dropped us off and we smoked two cigarettes in a row before entering the rectory doors. I hadn't stolen them from my mother's purse but I had bought them with the change I found in it. I had chosen my own brand by then. Different than hers.

We were told to bring one nice outfit, the only bright side to my packing. I made sure that that outfit consisted entirely of stolen items. To hell with them and their brainwashing, I said to myself. These are nice leotards, and this is an amazing velvet T-shirt that I hadn't had the opportunity to wear yet.

Because enrollment in COR was a secret, we had no idea who would be there. I noticed James Newhouse, the guy from church with the perfect hair, Elizabeth St. James, the biggest loser in school, and two or three other people who had frightened me since we had moved to Belle River. I didn't want to talk to anybody about anything, let alone my little problem with stealing.

We were handed envelopes. Inside were the rules and regulations, songbooks, notepads, and a name tag that we were instructed to wear all the time. Also there was a fake letter from Jesus. "Dear Friend . . . I saw you yesterday as you were talking with your friends. I waited all day hoping you would want to talk with me also. . . . and I waited. You never came. Oh yes, it hurt me, but I still love you because I am your friend. Today you look so sad . . . so all alone. *I love you!* I want you to meet my father. He wants to help you too. My father is that way, you know! Signed, Jesus."

I remember thinking, Jesus had a father, a mother, and twelve friends who were always around. Maybe that's why He was so good.

There was another letter from "Everyteen" called "Please hear what I'm *not* saying." We had to each read a chunk out loud. "Honestly, I dislike the superficial game I'm playing, the superficial *phony* game. I'd like to be genuine and spontaneous and *me,* but you've got to help me. You've got to hold my hand, even when that's the last thing I seem to want and need."

At the end of this "letter" everyone clapped and three or four people broke down and cried. Hands over our hearts, we were sworn to secrecy. The COR weekend was never to be discussed. *Ever.* No problem. This being the stupidest thing I had ever been a part of, I wasn't anxious for it to get around.

Dinner was hot dogs, chips, and orange pop. Cult food. After supper a few of us sneaked into a bathroom to smoke and roll our eyes. I vowed no way was I going to open up to these people. Someone had the idea of entering the boys' dorm room, but it was locked from the inside.

Curled in my borrowed sleeping bag, I felt as though my religion was turning funny on me. What was once private and kind of holy now had the feel of a school play, with bad actors and worse food than a bake sale. Same with stealing. It was my thing, my way of soothing myself, and now I'd be left with nothing. Then it started. I began to try to remember things about the COR weekend that would make my mother laugh, as opposed to things that I could tell my dad to make him proud. By morning I realized I had completely adopted my mother's posture, arms crossed hard across my middle, kept there unless a hand was needed to move hair off my face, or to hold a cup of sugary pop.

Saturday, after breakfast, we divided into groups for the most awful aspect of COR, "Sharing in Jesus." I remembered my mother's advice when she dropped us off.

"Keep your trap shut, Faith. It's nobody's business what goes on in our house, hear me?" Besides, she said, we didn't have any problems that couldn't be solved by the lottery. "Pray for that, why don't you."

Our senior COR "brother" started off the group by talking about a drug, sex, or alcohol problem that was a result of a "separation from Jesus." Clockwise, we were asked to share a similar story where we "lost Him." We could pass at first, but eventually we had to face up to Christ.

When it came around to me, our senior guy paused and took a deep breath.

"Faith. You're not saying much. How do you feel?"

I told him I was very moved.

"What do you need from us, Faith?"

"I don't know," I said. I didn't.

"Well, how about telling us about a crisis, something that happened to you that made you feel alone and afraid. We all have those moments."

Everybody in the circle nodded and leaned in and I felt like I had taken something precious from them and left a lump of coal in its place.

"I steal things and get in trouble and then I feel bad," I said, really fast.

Silence.

"Faith, why is it that you are stealing?"

I said I don't know and started to cry. I hoped to God that Nicole couldn't hear me from her group. I felt like a faker since stealing was lovely, I was good at it, and I had collected a lot of nice things. But for some reason, with everybody riveted on me, I could not hold back my tears. People started to hug me. I must have been in a lot of pain, they reasoned, to cry out by stealing. I nodded and collapsed into a weeping pile of teenaged hypocrisy.

For six more hours, I heard about beatings, pot smoking, and diddler uncles and babysitters. By bedtime, fed only processed meat and orange pop, I was bleary-eyed and in a trance. People told each other things about themselves that only a priest should hear, and God should take good care of. And there I was taking it all in, trying to make it matter to me, and it didn't. We were supposed to be touched but I was shocked, at myself, and at them. I washed my bloated face and looked at myself in the mirror, under blue, heavy light. I was wearing pajamas stolen from the Bi-Way. They were two-piece flannels, no buttons, strawberry appliqués trimming the sleeve. I thought to myself, These are so, so pretty.

SUNDAY WAS A DAY of reflection. We put on our nice outfits for the bishop, who came and hugged all thirty-five of us. Our folks were meant to come pick us up at noon and hug us too. We sang a song about how losers like me, and popular kids, were all the same. "Take my hand and let us walk no more as strangers in this land . . ."

I looked sidelong at people, thinking, She knows, and he knows, that I am a thief. But her brother touches her. He thinks he's probably a gay. She played with herself in her sleeping bag, because I heard her wrestling around. That other guy smokes pot, and she lies. If we are all going to hell, what's the point of being here? Maybe just to introduce ourselves so we'd have someone to clink beers with when we all landed down there.

We were given another giant envelope, stuffed full of letters from people who had attended past COR weekends. They wrote that they were filled with love for us, because they were supposed to write that. I received at least ten letters from these liars, plus some from my family. My dad wrote that he missed me and hoped the weekend away helped me see how wrong stealing is, because Jesus never stole anything. There was one from Hope saying, "People told me I had to write you to tell you about Jesus and His love. Whatever that is. I love you even when you're not nice to me anymore." Adam wrote me that he hoped that if I ever needed to talk, I wouldn't hesitate to talk to him. "You're a very special girl and I hope the best for you and your family. I don't think you're going to find it here at COR, though. Come see me. I'm here for you."

It sounded vaguely like a love letter, because that was the way I needed to read it.

My mother wrote, "Your brother's coming to get you. Being in a room full of love and happiness makes me itch. Your mother, Mom."

When I got home, she was glad to see me and unfolded herself off the chair and took herself away from the crossword puzzle she hadn't really been working on. She hugged me loosely and reminded me that it was the longest I had ever been away from her, not counting the time she spent in the hospital, after my Communion. She poured herself a beer and settled down in front of me at the dining room table. She seemed tired, but interested.

"Well. So. Have you thought about the things you've done?" she asked in an overly practiced way.

"I did," I said, gently. "And it's not like I like to steal, Mom, but I do like to have nice things though."

"Like what?"

"Things that other kids have, like shoes and stuff."

"And you think that'll make things easier?"

"It does make things easier," I said, beginning to weep a bit for real. My mother put her hand on my forearm and squeezed while I let my stupid tears fall until I couldn't avoid wiping them away. To break the mood, I stole a sip from her beer. She slapped my hand away, not hard, then tugged at my hair, playfully.

"I missed you," she said. "Thought we'd lost you to God."

There was a roll of toilet paper on the table. I realized we had never bought a box of Kleenex in our lives. She unraveled a little pillow of it for me and while I blew my nose she asked me what was in the big yellow envelope. I showed her dad's letter and she rolled her eyes. She took particular interest in Adam's.

"Yeesh," she said, reading it. "Maybe that boy doesn't need to come around here so much anymore."

"Mom. He's only being nice," I said. But maybe, I thought, just maybe, she's jealous, something that made me feel kind of better, kind of sadder.

My mother looked at me like she was assessing facts. Brown hair, five feet four. A-cup boobs. Not too skinny but a little too sad, for being only almost fifteen.

"Still. He's got friends his own age," she said, folding the letter. "And so do you. Besides, you can come talk to me. Or priests, I guess, if you prefer."

I didn't prefer priests to anything anymore. The weekend was like being given a backstage pass to a show that was put on for the benefit of my doomed soul.

MONTHS LATER, we heard that a girl in a town just south of ours killed herself after a COR weekend. Rumor was she had admitted that her mother sexually abused her. Her mother? I remember thinking. How's that possible, her mother?

When I told my mom this, she lit up a cigarette. She was a little drunk when she said, "You know, Faith, I bet that everyone cried and hugged that poor girl that weekend and once that spark wore off, people just had to tell everyone down Main Street that poor girl's pathetic story. The whole town probably knew what happened to her and she probably just fell the fuck apart. Gossip is the worst kind of sin, Faith. Hope's not going to that damn COR, period. Hope's not going and neither is Matt and neither is Charlie and I'm sorry you ever did."

She asked me if I knew that girl and I said no. My mother shook her head, picked up her drink, and walked out onto the patio barefoot, even though it was October and cold out.

Shortly after that, I stopped stealing and going to church so much, two things I used to love doing more than anything else in the world.

Chapter Eight

Hope and I always joked that our entire sex education consisted of four sentences from my mother, repeated throughout our entire adolescence.

"Only sluts call boys. Wait until you're married to have sex. Don't do like your stupid mother. Period." We counted "Period" as a full sentence because anytime my mother used it, which was often, it substituted as a discussion about menstruation.

This was our joke:

Hope (after I'd have a big fight with Mom): How did your "talk" go?

Me: She said I'm not allowed to use the phone ever again, after ten o'clock. *Period!*

Hope: She said, "Period"?

Me: Yup, she said, "Period."

Hope: God. You guys are so close. She never talks to *me* about *my* period.

Every month my mom bought a super-size bag of sanitary napkins and wordlessly threw them under the vanity in the bathroom. What more is there to say? she'd ask Auntie Linda. They know what to do. It didn't occur to me that my own mother did not have a mother around to teach her these things. I just figured we didn't.

As for sex, she knew we were approaching an age where boys could call, come over, and eventually make us cry. But my mother was superstitious and probably felt the mere mention of sex might make sex erupt in our house. So she'd leave her self-help books around, opened to chapters that advised girls to "Save It for Marriage: True Love Waits!"; "Avoid Mr. Wrong: One Woman's Tragedy"; "Get a Man to Treat You Right"; or "Looks Aren't Everything. Honor Matters More!"

She'd say, "Girls, look at your mother. Number-one thing is to do the opposite of me." She'd be hosing off the oil stain on the driveway, or soaking Matt's hockey socks in the sink, or scooping out Gigi's litter box, or paying long-overdue bills, in the way that would make us laugh. "Ta-daa," she'd say, taking the bank statement and rubbing it against the phone bill, really, really hard. "There. Paid!"

But she never talked to us directly and delicately about all that stuff in the middle. Poverty and unpopularity. Cellulite and discharge. Heartbreak and fury.

And I couldn't talk to Hope about these things because she wasn't sensitive, like me. She was organized and distracted. She folded and marched and one time spent a rainy Saturday changing lightbulbs, polishing the brass doorknobs, and trying to train Gigi to answer when called.

My mother once wrote in her diary: *I never worry about Hope because she doesn't waste time worrying about anything. She's a doer. Faith, on the other hand, I worry about, because she's around all the time, worrying about everything.*

MY MOTHER DIDN'T wake up one morning to find herself unhappy; she expected to be unhappy. What do you want, she'd say to Auntie Linda, when you marry the first man who asked you? Well, you were pregnant, Auntie Linda reminded her, so Joe had little choice but to do the right thing by you. I'd be listening on the basement extension. Matty had rigged a room for himself down there, consisting of a bed, a dresser, and for privacy he stacked boxes on the cement floor around what he called, the "sleep area." He and his new girlfriend, Trelly, would spend time down there with the door locked. My mother would nervously tap on it when dinner was ready, then step away quickly, like whatever was going on behind it was catchy.

"Nancy, it's time for you to get out there," my auntie Linda said on the phone one day, the sound of her lighter flicking in the background.

"I know, but how and who? There's no one in this town I'm interested in. And I got these kids around all the time. It's not so easy."

"Shop around," Auntie Linda said. "Just keep your eyes open. You never know."

But my mother didn't shop around, and now that she was mostly single, she barely looked in the window. She told Auntie Linda that she didn't date because she didn't want her kids to think she was a "slut," didn't want to set a "bad example" for her girls. But especially the boys. "Can you imagine Matt's face? He hates me already, he'd hate the guy's guts more! Plus who would want a thirty-five-year-old with four teenagers? Especially these four, I barely have a handle on them. In fact, I bet I don't."

And she didn't. She had no idea we waited for her car to disappear down the driveway on a night shift before boldly whipping out our own cigarettes and prancing around the house. It was Matt mostly, smoking while talking on the phone, or lying on the couch. Dad called once and Matt cracked me and Hope up by blowing smoke rings between reciting his list of school marks, all notched up by ten percent. Fridays, one of Matt's friends or his girlfriend Trelly would produce a thermos of booze of some kind. Sometimes they'd let me join them. Those nights, I felt like a million dollars. I would get a little buzz on and Matt and his friends would take off in the Comet to a party. I would phone my friend Nicole and tell her that I was drunk. Charlie'd be in his room listening to weird music. Hope would fall asleep in front of the TV, after eating all the good food.

We never squealed on each other. What would we have said? Mom, don't go to work anymore so that we can stop having fun falling apart like this?

Those nights Adam would stop by and play Scrabble with me and Hope. He'd bring licorice and doughnuts and three or four beers dangling off a picked-over six-pack. Sometimes a movie, now that we owned our own VCR, secondhand. He once showed me his new tattoo of a skull with two crossed hockey sticks. It was low on his hipbone and you couldn't miss the brambles of hair that came out of the top of his pants, a trail of darkness that led "down there."

"Go ahead touch it, Faith, it won't hurt me," he teased, poking his hip toward me, almost spilling his beer. I moved my hand slowly toward the tattoo. When my hand brushed his skin he screamed, "Ow!" and I yelped, almost crashing backward through the patio screen door.

"Oh, Faith, I'm kidding," he said. "God, your mom's right, you're wound up so tight!"

I didn't get mad, but my heart took a long time to calm down and unbreak over the fact that they had had a private conversation about me. And maybe my mom's psychological books were right, that it was true that I craved boys more because we didn't have a dad around to make a man's presence seem anything but profound and exotic and fleeting. And I learned that men leave if it gets to be too much. So maybe that's why I started to make myself seem smaller, my voice weaker, my body much less mine than theirs, in case I could delay their departure a little while longer, with the ease of being with me. Faith doesn't want much. Just a call, a pat on the head. Stay. Faith won't bother you at all. She doesn't need anything.

"Faith, do you just see me as a father figure?" Adam had asked one night over a Scrabble game. He stopped in after dropping Charlie off. He had found him hitchhiking back from the old pinball place in Emeryville.

Charlie said, "I do, Adam. Thanks for the ride, *Dad.*"

I got embarrassed by his question because it coincided with me spelling the word "lust."

"No," I said. "You're being gross. Maybe it's you who sees me as a daughter figure, loser."

"I mostly definitely don't see that," Adam said. My face burned easily when the sun, or sex, was anywhere near it. I had just turned fifteen. Adam was a little over twenty, but it was way past ten, and we were drinking a bit too much in the dining room that night. My own beer was in a discreet coffee mug, since Charlie was playing with us.

Charlie teased, "Why don't you tell us what 'lust' means, Adam?"

Adam said, "Ask your sister. It's her word."

I kicked him under the table.

"Ask Denise, why don't you?" I replied, without looking up from my letters. Adam had dated Denise French, on and off, for years. He used to kid me that she was his temporary girlfriend, until I was old enough to marry him. That was before I started wearing a bra.

"Yous two suck," said Charlie, leaving us in disgust for his room.

We finished the game after I spelled the word "hare." Adam stuck an "m" on the end of the word, laughing when he explained what it meant. But it was too late. I had already won.

ONE THING ABOUT that summer was the animals. At home, even though my mother wasn't, and I couldn't conceive of it, Gigi was having sex all the time. She didn't even want to sleep in the house anymore, because there was always a new cat to smell and crouch under.

"What a slut," my mother once said, watching Gigi squirm and scream in the back yard. "Dammit. She's getting fixed, just like me."

My dad came in from Calgary for a month. The rigs were dormant, and so was a regular paycheck, so Dad arranged to work on one of his uncle's animal farms, out in Leamington. He was to bring us out there for a whole week, leaving my mother alone, with Auntie Linda. Days earlier she had shown up, minus Polish Paul, in a dangerous mood, carrying an entire box of wine, and a carload of shiny clothes for my mother to borrow or keep. Though time with Dad was fun and needed, and I always liked how he asked us easy questions and gave us plenty of spending money, I would've rather spent time with

Auntie Linda. It had been a while since I'd seen her, and she was the most fun of all. Plus I needed someone to talk to about sex. It was on my mind almost constantly, especially when Adam was around and my mother wasn't.

When I announced my decision to stay with "the girls," my mom looked at my aunt and said, "It's all yours, Lin."

Auntie Linda turned to me and said, "Faith, honey. Your dad's taking you to a real farm for a whole week. There'll be horses and cows and things to do. Your mom and me are going to have a little break from everything. It's not that we don't love you, it's just that we need to spend some time being girls."

"But I'm a girl too. Why can't I hang around yous guys?"

My mom leaned over the table.

"Faith, you should spend some time with your dad. It's important for daughters. We talked about this," she said, with a kindness dipped in impatience.

"I don't want to. I want to be with yous guys. Here."

"Well, we're not going to be here, dear. We're going to take a little trip," Auntie Linda said. "I'm taking your mother to Niagara Falls, and maybe Toronto for a couple of days."

The idea of them experiencing those exotic places without me made my brain's drawers spill out good reasons for me to accompany them. I ransacked my head for that last best sentence that would convince them I needed to stay. But when my mom said, You're going, don't break your dad's heart, Faith, he wants all four of yous to be with him, I knew she meant she didn't want any of us with her.

HOPE WAS THRILLED with the farm animal idea and packed accordingly.

"No skirts, no nylons, no bras, yippee, man!" she said, throwing flannel shirts and khaki shorts into a garbage bag we used for luggage.

Matty brought weed. Charlie brought his tapes and sunblock.

We did nothing special at the uncle's farm, bothered the wild barn kittens, threw ripe tomatoes at each other, and at the Portuguese neighbor's laundry. We helped our dad help his old uncle with all the heavy stuff, like stacking wood and repairing fences. Dad's old uncle was married to an old lady we called Nonna Tree, on account of their last name being Triasi. Nonna Tree taught me and Hope how to roll gnocchi and layer lasagna because she didn't need much English to show us how to do these things. But we were bored. Some afternoons we'd fall asleep, one of us curled up on each of the four couches lining the four walls of their hot, crowded living room.

My favorite place was the shed. I loved sneaking in there to steal Uncle Triasi's cigarettes, the unfiltered kind, which he had rolled himself and hidden away on the very top shelf. We'd crouch in the back room, under the swaying hocks of prosciutto and the giant purple wine jugs stacked side by side on the long, saggy shelves. We'd peek through the slats at the uncle doing nothing, maybe smoking, or flipping through his *Playboy*s from the 1950s.

Sometimes he'd catch us, and yell, "I'm-a tell you once-a more, getta da hell out. I'm-a no *like*-a dis!"

We'd run away laughing because we couldn't understand a word he yelled at us. I couldn't understand much about anything else he did, either. He had two kinds of personalities. For instance, he tenderly grew all his own vegetables and had successfully raised an exotic plum tree, imported all the way from Italy. These were the normal things about him. But other days, we'd watch him strangle his own chickens, slice open the bellies of his own pigs, using his own hands, which had generously fed the unsuspecting animals only hours earlier. The animals would have no idea.

My dad and the boys would help with all this murder, while I spent time wondering what my mother was doing. I pictured her and Auntie Linda in a fast-paced, restricted movie; them racing down a highway, whooping it up with truckers and hitchers, knocking back beers in taverns studding the side roads, on the way to the sexy Falls and seedier Toronto.

My mother slow dancing. Laughing.

My mother writing down her phone number and lying she was childless like Auntie Linda.

Imaging my mother happy without us made me sad. What if she fell in love and stayed forever in one of those cities, like Dad did? Would we be stuck on the farm with the plants and animals? Would Nonna Tree be my new mother? Would I learn Italian and wipe my hands on an apron, waiting out afternoons like Nonna Tree did in her faded sundresses, craning her neck at cars passing by the farm?

On the third last day, and counting, Matty took the uncle's truck into town for hay and I went with him. Hope and Charlie stayed behind to give the only horse, a shabby mare, its first brushing in probably a decade. Dad handed me a ten-dollar bill and told me to bring back ice cream for everybaddy.

Matty pulled over at the end of the gravel road and rolled a joint.

"Having fun?" he asked.

"No, are you?"

"Yeah, it's cool." He shrugged, lighting the end and sucking deeply. It took a few seconds for him to offer it to me. I took a long drag and was surprised at how little I choked and handed it back.

"Wonder what Mom's doing."

"Let's hope she's getting laid," he said.

"Matt! Asshole! Don't say that!"

"Why? It'd be good for all of us if the old lady got some."

"Fuck off, jerk," I said. "And since when did you call Mom 'old lady,' like you think it's so cool or something." I was sputtering slightly, but laughing a little at the idea of my mother being "our old lady."

"Relax, Faith. Look how beautiful it is," he said, opening his arm to the scenery around us. The trees lining the fields were spaced out, with long, frustrating breaks of land between them. They were low and brambly and seemed suddenly to be the most interesting things I had ever seen. The tops of the trees weren't popcorn-shaped, like in drawings, or in orchards. They were gnarled like old hands, and the leaves were a deep, chromy green.

Fuck, it is beautiful. And I am high, I thought.

When we got back, Dad did not ask for the change, and I ate the ice cream like it was the greatest thing for mouths, ever.

My dad didn't have a girlfriend. He said as much when he showed us pictures of his life on the oil rig. He lived on a bleak platform that jutted out of a northern lake like an otherworldly contraption from a *Star Wars* movie.

"I sleep-a under dis tower, me and alotta odder guys," he said.

He showed us where the chapel was. He told us they eat four times a day, because the work's so hard, they need the energy. Someone cleans their rooms for them, he said, and does all their laundry, folding it too, can you beeleeve dis? And every other weekend the company pays for them to go to Edmonton for steak and live music. I wondered about whores but didn't ask if he knew or had any. And when Matty asked him if he had himself another wife, he laughed and said, "As a Catholic, I'm-a only allowed one, and your momma, well, she was enough for me."

He seemed lost and found at the very same time, talking about his home more in-the-middle-of-nowhere than I ever thought possible. And I knew he loved living life far away from everything, and that he was never coming back to us.

THE WORST DAY at the farm was the last day. The uncle brought home a writhing, burlap bag. Little animals of some kind were bumping around inside. The bag was sewn shut and me and Hope asked if we could open it and let them out.

He took a hammer off the wall, and said, "Get adda here, Fate. 'Ope. Yous two no gonna like-a what I'm-a hafta do."

The boys stayed. We ran around the back of the shed to the meat and wine room, crouched down, and watched.

The uncle felt around the outside of the bag and carefully isolated each bobbing head. He located the perfect spot and knocked it, once, hard, with the hammer. He did this over and over again, until whatever was in the burlap bag had finally stopped moving. He must have hammered fifty times. When he cut open the bag and shook the limp bodies out onto the workbench, there was not a smidgen of blood on any of the pure-white, dead, bunny rabbits.

"Cool," Charlie muttered.

The uncle skinned the rabbits, pickled the meat, and gave each of us a foot as a gift. The boys threaded a string through their bloodied stumps and wore them on their belt loops. Me and Hope, holding the feet with the very tips of our fingers, just threw them onto the barn floor. We couldn't stick around to watch the cats fight over them, either.

That, I learned, was the difference between boys and girls. But I could eat Nonna Tree's cacciatore dishes, pork skewers, and pickled rabbit with a shameless appetite, because I had begun to force my mind to forget the connection between the meal on my plate and the necessary slaughter that men committed for it. Because sometimes murder is done in the name of love, and sometimes it's done in the name of regular old lunch, and there was me, a girl who always came back for seconds.

WHEN DAD DROPPED US OFF, he handed me a check, all the money he had earned at the farm that month, and said, Geeve to your momma, with my best. He pinched my nose, shook the boys' hands, and wrapped his arm around Hope, because she was sitting closest.

My mother came running out of the house, flapping her hands and jumping up and down. My dad waved to her. She waved at him, smiling. He didn't get out of the car because she didn't motion for him to do that. And the four of us tried our best not to mangle our mother with our happiness to see her fresh face and new haircut. She had lost a bit of weight and brought us silly gifts; super big pencils with erasers shaped like the CN tower; coffee mugs from Niagara Falls with our names on them. She asked very few questions, except, did we behave, and how was it being around all those animals?

A WEEK LATER we were officially from a broken home. My mom filed formal separation papers and went for a drink with Mr. Delgado, her lawyer in town. Matty teased her that she had a date, that maybe she was on a roll. She snapped her index finger in front of his face and told him to shut his trap. They were just friends. Mr. Delgado was a big help. He was working for cheap.

"I'll bet," Matt huffed.

Almost immediately after my mom slapped him hard across his newly seventeen-year-old face, she apologized and started to cry. Matty pretended not to feel anything and the rest of us backed up like we hadn't seen what happened.

Later, when she cleaned herself up and went back to the diner, I dug out her diary, hoping to catch up on our brief separation. I could tell she hadn't brought the diary on her trip with Auntie Linda, since the last entry read, *Lin and I had fun this past week, and I was good about not calling the kids. I know I needed a break, but damn if I wasn't up so early every day, waiting for her to wake up. I think I frustrated Lin. She was mad that I wanted to get back early. When she has kids, she'll know what it's like to miss them. I just told her my only advice is not to have four like me. Our consolation was Adam. We all got a bit too drunk that last night before the kids got back, and Adam taught us to play poker. I won forty dollars. I mean he's twenty-one or something, so it's not such a crime. And I'm only teasing, nothing would ever happen, but I can't tell you how flattering his attention is. But the little bugger just got a bunch of tattoos on his back which I warned him not to show Matt. First thing you know, he'll want them too. Let alone Hope or Charlie. Charlie's spooking me these days. He's very ghoulish in his clothes and thoughts . . .*

Nothing about me. Again. And her going on and on about Adam was sending me into a deep, internalized rage, which I reminded myself not to express, in case she figured me out by accident.

But she was right about her advice to Auntie Linda. Four kids is too many. Especially four like us, in a row like we were. And though we weren't bad, we began to avoid anything good. Not enough stimulation from things like varsity sports and good marks. Matt chased the feeling of oblivion. So did I, more and more, even going to church stoned once with Nicole, both of us vowing never again, because we couldn't handle the singing.

When Hope entered high school, she followed me around, and I let her, even though I was older and was meant to start acting cooler. Then she joined cadets, and disappeared into a blue van, which took her, and everything I knew about her life, to the HMCS *Hunter* building, in Windsor, two nights a week.

Charlie gravitated toward a group of freaks who grew their bangs long to one side, pierced their ears, and listened to music from England that sounded haunted. The only thing that saved him from being beaten to death in our town was that he told decent jokes and he was a good hockey player. Plus had found himself a girlfriend, as soon as he got to grade nine, a chubby, quiet girl named Cheryl Demaris. They were inseparable, though they barely held hands, or touched for that matter, so people still called him a faggot. Charlie and Cheryl talked about music constantly, looking at the rest of us with impatience and pity when we tried to join in on the discussion.

And Matty, now officially called Matt, had Trelly. At first, she scared me half to death with her revealing clothes and the way she chased Matt around the house. He'd be genuinely screaming. But my mother liked having Trelly around, if only because she helped her with the cooking and the dishes, rising out of her chair like a zombie housewife, well trained for this kind of work, right from birth.

If my brothers did well with the girls, me and Hope were the opposite with the boys. But at least I tried. Hope was a failure. She never wore makeup, never hiked her plaid skirt, and wore her uniform exactly as we were supposed to. Walking next to her sometimes made me feel like a Halloween version of a St. Francis schoolgirl, with my rubber necklaces, feather combs, and colored leotards. I'd see Hope at school, walking the crowded hallways as though she was completely alone, despite all those people hitting at her shoulders. She never took her eyes off the top inch of the folder she was carrying, as though it was the most fascinating thing in the world. I'd have to punch her in the arm twice to get her attention before she'd go, "Oh hey, Faith."

* * *

LIKE MY MOTHER, I met my first boyfriend in church. Nicole and I were sitting in front of James Newhouse, which made it difficult to stare at his perfect hair, but easier for him to slip me a note that read, "My friend likes you."

I turned around to a giggling James pointing at a pitch-red Chuckie Pound next to him. The Pounds had moved here from England. Chuckie wasn't so much cute as he was nicely put together. I was flattered, but hid this fact, faced front again, and thanked the Lord for the attention from a boy. Finally, someone for me. It didn't matter that he was short and pink and had a stupidly thick English accent. What mattered was that he liked me, nobody Faith DiNapoli.

Our three-day relationship consisted of Chuckie and me meeting rather purposelessly in the hallways. After a soccer game, in which our side won, I let him walk me up to the school buses along the fence where no one would see us.

"I want to kiss you real bad, Faith," he said.

"So what," was my reply. I wanted him to kiss me too, though I was unsure how to involve myself. He shoved me up against the fence, hard. He was pushing my hand, by the wrist, down the front of his shorts. I was fighting it, but terribly curious. His other hand held on to the fence, and the rest of him was pressing up against my entire body. He was saying my name over and over again in an English accent ("Fyth") and rubbing himself, furiously, for about thirty seconds.

I wondered if I was getting raped. Is it rape if you giggle? They never taught us this ordeal in health class, and all the pictures of the penis faced down like a shy disappointment. This penis was definitely different. First of all it was bald and smooth and it had a hard weight to it, like a water balloon. Chuckie was my first European boyfriend. I figured that this was what they all did in Europe. So I let him spoosh wet all over the back of my hand, and take off.

"Call ye later," he yelled, zipping his pants and running toward his bus.

"'Kay."

I wiped my hand off on the grass, careful not to get any of his stuff on my uniform, or near my privates. I walked home, slowly, smelling my fingers every few minutes. I was confused about this sex we had just had, which left me damp between my legs. I was more confused when Chuckie began to completely ignore me in the hallways. It was just before break, the best time to have a boyfriend of any kind. Even this strange English boy would've done the job for a while.

"Is this Chuckie boy ever going to call you again, Faith?" my mother asked while cleaning the stove. I had told her about Chuckie, mentioned his interesting English accent and his cool way of acting like I wasn't really there, even though I was his special girlfriend.

"Yeah. He will."

"Sounds like an asshole, Faith."

Call me, call me, call me, I prayed into the phone, the phone that was studded with filthy handprints, the phone with a sticky seven and a faded eight. I memorized everything about the phone that kept on not ringing for me. It wasn't that I was in love with Chuckie; he treated me like I was just a stupid girl with a silly hand he needed wrapped around his ridiculous penis. Sure, he pressed me against the fence against my will, a little, but it seemed like he was the one who had been overcome, not me. He was weakened, by me, grunting and running away like he did. I felt great about it, filled with a new kind of power from doing nothing but being in possession of something boys wanted so badly, they risked feeling weak and destroyed to get at it. I wanted to feel that again.

My mother hated seeing me wait by that phone, which I was trying hard not to do. She also thought that my need to pine after uninterested men suggested that I had "father figure" issues, and I wondered if she had been talking to Adam again privately about me.

"Well, they say here that all your life you're going to be looking for a father figure. Looking for some guy to raise you," she said, looking up from one of those psychological books.

"Raise me? That's stupid. I'm already being raised by you."

"Still, you should call your dad, you know. Just because he hates my guts doesn't mean he doesn't love his children. After all, most of you are his, you know," she said, smirking back down into her book.

* * *

CHUCKIE POUND never called me again. His dad got a job in another city and they moved. But I told everyone that he had called me the night before they left, his mom pulling the receiver out of his hand, him calling me just to say how much he really, really loved me and that the reason he had to break up with me was that he knew in his heart that it was the right thing to do, the easier thing to do, the smarter thing to do, because of the amount of the way he loved me, until he died. The alternative was "futile at best" and "against the animal want of his basest nature's soul, which resided in a place he dared not venture." I nicked that theme from *The Thorn Birds,* which I loved, knowing not one of my friends would have watched it for the entire week. Least of all Matt's girlfriend, Trelly.

"Me and Chuckie are going to try and keep in touch, but it's going to be very, very hard, you know?" I explained to Trelly, while she was painting my fingernails with Sally Hansen Hard as Nails, Candy Apple Red. She got free samples at the salon where she worked.

Trelly replied, through watery eyes, "It's going to be real fucken hard, Faith. But if it's really, really meant to be, it'll be," she said, placing her hand on my hand, careful not to touch the drying nails. "Like with me and Matt, hon, it'll just be, right? Like it is with us two, right?"

TRELLY AND MATT met at the salon when he started getting his hair cut and feathered professionally. She was nineteen, two years older than Matt, and she had a MasterCard, which Matt bragged about. And although she was sort of terrifying, Hope and I actually liked Trelly because she provided comic relief, and someone to talk to about sex. And the fact was, Matt really didn't treat her all that well. Mom once suggested that Matt might have "anger issues" with women. Her self-help books had turned her into an amateur psychologist, scrutinizing our lives like some Freudian detective. She told Matt it was common for boys to act aggressive with their girlfriends when they were really super-angry at their own mothers. Matty would just shrug at her and disappear into the basement to smoke another joint.

Trelly was also known as the kind of drunk people resisted driving home in case she puked. Also, she came from a set of folks who were so stupid they let her quit school when she was in grade ten, simply because she said she was bored and didn't like the math teacher. But Trelly was very pretty, though weirdly muscular, doing the Jane Fonda workout tape every morning, a Christmas present from Matt.

Hope once described Trelly like this: "Take the head of a Barbie and put it on the body of a GI Joe. Give her beer."

One night at a giant bush party, Trelly had had many, many beers, and came stumbling up to me and Hope. She was wearing a Pittsburgh Steelers jersey, Terry Bradshaw's usual number crudely written over by black Magic Marker into a "69." Her lipstick was smeared badly, her hair pushed flat to one side, her shirt bunched up and untucked.

"Faith, Hopey, you guys walk me home, 'kay? Your brother's being a total fucking a-hole. I'm through with him."

Hope rolled her eyes at me and we each took a side of tippy Trelly. She and Matt broke up all the time like this, every other month.

"I didn't do nothing," she wailed, half holding on to me, half falling off me, clutching her roadie, a warm sloshing Old Vienna. "Like, not to be offended or nothing, but your brother never says nothing good about me. All my friends say I gotta be more defensive on my needs about him and stuff."

She talked so badly I sometimes doubted my own halfway decent grammar.

After we watched Trelly stumble up to her parents' farmhouse, we turned back toward the party we weren't supposed to be at. Serena Agora was there, sitting on the hood of the truck owned by the guy she seemed to be going out with. He was leaning on the front bumper, between her legs, facing away from her, and talking to his friends. Serena was resting back on her hands, her spread legs kicking out every once in a while on either side of his waist. She looked so relaxed having a guy between her legs, his butt so close to her own privates. She was almost sixteen and now I knew, for sure, she was having sex of some kind, just by her cool way of being around boys.

I learned to tell when a girl was having sex. Boys were always around them. For instance, Lauren Verdun, a total slut in town, was always surrounded by boys. She hung out in front of the pizza parlor that had two kinds of pinball machines. When we'd pull in to pick up our order, my mom would tsk-tsk Lauren Verdun.

"See that girl, Faith? Her parents don't love her enough to let her be out here acting like that. If she was my kid I'd smack the shit out of her."

Somebody'd be tickling Lauren Verdun down to the ground; she'd be laughing so hard she'd drop her cigarette. My mom would carefully walk around the pile of rustling teenagers, not looking at them. I once overheard a guy say they should make up T-shirts that said, "I've Done Verdun."

Out in the county, you were either nice or you were a whore. Unlike in the city, here there were few places to disappear into. How you behaved between fourteen and eighteen determined the rest of your life, especially if you stayed in town. Lauren, Serena, and Trelly seemed to be heading one way. I had been trained by Jesus and my mother to head the other. But staring down that bleak and dull road made me yawn. I saw a life of baggy clothes, boring friends, Sunday church, and getting off the phone at ten o'clock sharp. I saw me helping with yearbook, volunteering at old people's homes, being teacher's pet, and having piano lessons. I saw corsages being pinned so carefully that the guy didn't brush my breasts. I saw me dating a guy who didn't even want to brush my breasts to begin with.

Worse, I saw myself being good at it.

I looked over at Hope, who was digging two beers out of Matt's cooler. When we had pulled up to the bonfire, Matt had said, "Don't hang around with me and don't tell Mom and don't puke or I'll kill you."

"Shut up, I had rum, you know," Hope said. It was true. The night of her fourteenth birthday, me and Matt fed her some we stole.

We laughed at her as she laughed at us for laughing at her, keeping the noise down, though my mom had long ago fallen asleep after a few drinks of her own.

I had started to love drinking and was good at it. Worse, I had started to understand why my mother drank, too, and stopped thinking she was a bad parent while I was suffering slowly in the role of being a good daughter.

When the sun dropped, Adam Lauzon pulled into the bush party with Denise French sitting in the front seat of his Gremlin. I hadn't seen him since he had moved into Windsor after his first year of university, only coming home weekends and summer vacations. My mother said that he had had a big fight with his parents because of his new tattoos. She said they were religious-themed, including a snake, plus Eve on his arm, and a Jesus face on his chest. I asked her how did she know, and she said, Mrs. Lauzon told her. Liar. Adam must have shown her that night he played poker and she won money. God, maybe they played strip poker.

"There's Adam," Hope teased, "and his wife-to-be, Den-eeeee-eese."

"He's not marrying her. He's just using her for sex because she's a slut is all," I replied, pretending not to care, looking around for a place to sit and hide and watch them. I hadn't thought much about him, because of Chuckie Pound, until just then, when his showing up had charged the atoms in the dark around me. And just seeing the car seat that I had sat in so many times, now occupied by Denise's thighs, bum, waist, shoulders, head, and hair made my face screw into a knot of jealous tension. I once saw Denise at the arena, when Adam was away at school, and she was wearing his Red Wings bomber jacket. He had thrown that very jacket around me a few times in the dark of his car, when he'd drive me here or there, as a favor to my mother. I had imagined my skin cells, still stuck on the insides of the coat, breaking out, multiplying, and attacking Denise with wicked purple hives. And now I was projecting fresh hatred toward her, through the night air, thinking as though the embers from the bonfire were my feelings perfectly, floating red-hot, and spazzing out in all directions.

When I grabbed another beer, Matt eyed me.

"Don't go getting wasted, Faith, I'm not carrying you home, too."

"What do you mean, we practically carried Trelly home, asshole."

"Well, hello there, Faith DiNapoli."

I turned around. It was Adam.

"Hi, Adam. When'd you get back?" I was blushing, and blessing the night for being here so he couldn't see his effect on my face.

"Just the other day. You look taller. So does Hope. Hey, Matty, look at you, little man!" They punched arms and clinked beers. "Your little sisters are your dates? Lucky guy, Matty."

"Get off my back," Matt grumbled. "I got no choice. I can't go nowheres without them."

Matt walked away from us toward a few of his other friends. He was going through this stage where he felt the world was on his back. Every day, for no reason, he'd say, "Get off my back! Would you just get off my back? Stay off my back." Poor Trelly, she'd say one stupid thing like, "Can you drop me off at the salon first?" and Matt would go, "Yeah! Jeez, would you just get off my back?" Maybe because Dad was gone, Matt felt he had to be the man of the house, but you'd never know it, since Matt was never in the house. He disappeared for entire weekends, phoning from Trelly's to say he was staying at a friend's house. My mom figured the fewer kids around, the better, so she didn't object. Plus he was a boy, my mom said. Boys had the special ability to have sex without getting pregnant, unlike us girls who she had to keep a stricter eye on. That was stupid reasoning, I told her. Matt could get someone else pregnant. She said, Yeah, well, there are options, options I don't want you and Hope to ever have to contemplate.

Maybe me and Hope were too young for this party, but Adam at twenty-one was definitely too old for this high-schoolish drinking and smoking and necking. There was something pathetic about him being there, but his presence did lift the party a cool notch toward mature, and I was a little proud how he hovered nearby, all congenial and adult.

Adam introduced us to Denise as his "little sister-neighbors."

"I've known them since they were this big, before they started wearing bras and drinking beer."

Denise recognized someone behind us and left, but not before kissing the side of Adam's head, which forced me to step out of her scummy way. She was older than me by a lot, and probably felt a stupid fifteen-year-old was no threat to her. I thought to myself, She probably shouldn't think that too, too much.

"Well, I gotta go," I said, following Hope, who had wandered away from the conversation.

"Where you going? Will you be around later?"

"I don't know."

"I'll come find you," he said, smiling. "You look great tonight, Faith. Really great."

True, I had on my Jordache jeans, which made my bum look high and round, and I was the first in my group with all-white, leather Reeboks, a birthday present I paid half for. True, my hair was feathering perfect these days, people said so at school. But all I offered Adam was a quick "Whatever," tossed over my shoulder as I walked away. My mother might think it's all right to flirt with another woman's man, but that was almost adultery to me, and the only Commandment I hadn't yet broken.

BY NINE-THIRTY, the small party had bloated into a giant crowd. There must have been a hundred people clustered in fours and sixes and eights around the growing fires. The beer and coolers I had drunk made it hard for me to concentrate on anybody's face in particular. I had been standing around in a group Nicole knew, from the French high school. From there I could easily watch how Adam acted with Denise. I noticed his body curved away from hers, and she kissed him a lot more than he kissed her.

Things darkened, and the fires got skinnier. I looked around at the teetering pack of us there that night and knew in the base of my stomach there could be no saving anybody in this kind of crowd. I didn't even know where my own baby sister was. Matt was gone too, though the Comet was parked, stereo blasting something by Def Leppard, so he couldn't be far away. I was so drunk that everything seemed like a movie underwater and I wanted to go home before I drowned in it, for good.

Then I saw an outline of Adam walking some girl around in a little circle, until she struggled awake and puked. At first, I thought it was stupid Denise, but it was actually Hope. Adam was gently singing to her, "Just put one foot in front of the other . . ." which got people around them laughing at poor drunken Hope. She smiled a little, shoving her hair off her face and begging Adam to take her home now, please, because she was done.

"Where'd you find her? Jeez, Hope!" I said, stumbling up to them, not knowing she was lost.

"In a car, over there," Adam said. "Let's get her over to yours."

I took Hope's other arm and she said, "Hi, Faith, Hiiiii. Hi. Hi."

We found Matt, and I said, Look at her, let's go, now, dammit. But he said we couldn't leave, reminding me that we had told Mom we were going to the drive-in, and were meant to all arrive home together, after midnight, stuffed full of popcorn and stories of how good the new *Star Wars* movie was. So we folded sleepy Hope into the Comet. Adam and I finished our drinks, watching her pass out again in the familiar comfort of the wrecked back seat of Grandpa's once- perfect car. I was studying her cuteness. Hope hadn't looked like that since I could remember. We were all so close in age we didn't have enough space between us to take in each other's babyness. Hope looked just like a baby there, and I suddenly felt like a shabby guardian angel who should be fired from the job.

"I should've kept a better eye on her. She's only fourteen," I said.

"She puked. She'll be all right," Adam soothed. He protects us, I thought. He's a bigger help to my mother, and to us, than we really are to each other.

"Well then, I would like another beer," I said.

Matt shrugged that he was all out.

"I got something in my car," Adam said. "Come with me."

Matt gave me the eye that said Matt was there instead of Mom.

"What?" I huffed at him, sticking my tongue out, skipping on after Adam.

"Don't be long, we're leaving soon, Faith, I mean it," Matt yelled after me.

TOO MANY PEOPLE saw me leave with Adam that night. There were a couple of long, slow whistles following me out of the crowd, coming from people I didn't know. I owed nothing to Denise, and besides, this is Adam Lauzon, the neighbor's boy. He wouldn't do anything to me that I didn't want done.

When we reached the paved part of the road, I steadied myself on the black, flattened surface. We climbed into the Gremlin, and Adam popped in his *Eagles Greatest Hits* and started to roll a joint underneath the overhead light.

"Faith DiNapoli," he said, sprinkling pot into the "V" of the rolling paper.

"Yeah, that's me."

"Little Faith DiNapoli, the girl across the street."

"Yup," I said, nervously.

"You still going to church?" he asked.

"No, not so much."

In truth, not since there were no more boys to look at. It used to be Jesus was enough of a man to draw me in. Now they needed to be earthbound, with nice hair, or I slept in like the rest of my family.

"Too bad. I used to like watching you leave on Sundays. It was very sweet to see that."

I wanted to scream, delighted, You watched me? You noticed me?

Instead I asked, "What about you? Still hating the Pope?"

"Yup. I made my own religion, all over my body," he said, licking the joint closed. "I'll show you my tattoos, if you want."

"That's okay," I said. I couldn't ask him to take his shirt off because where would that leave me and my shirt?

Adam lit the joint and leaned against his window looking at me in a way that made the cells in my body burn and divide. The shadows from the overhead light made him look mean. I wondered how the light made me look. Mean too? Older? Pretty? Afraid? He took a long drag and offered me the joint. I pulled on it with a little too much strength, hoping the joint would give me some.

"Denise'll be mad at you, eh?" I said, hopeful.

"I don't care," he said, shutting off the overhead light.

"That's not a way to talk about your girlfriend," I said, turning the light back on.

"Yeah, well, I'm not sure how much longer she's gonna be my girlfriend, Faith," Adam said. "I like being with you, a lot, you know."

"Yeah, and I hear you like being with my mother a lot, too."

I slapped my hand over my mouth to prevent the air coming out of my mouth from sounding too much like a gasp.

Adam thought for a few seconds.

"I do. Your mom's really cool. One day you'll agree with me."

"But you like being with me better, right?" I was stoned and drunk and pushing this somewhere treacherous.

"Hmm, that's an interesting question, Faith, one I'll try and answer," he said, almost laughing, me leaning in anxiously.

"Well, thing is, I love the way you are so young and everything. I feel great being around you because you're not mean to me. You don't get sarcastic. You're not all bitchy and needy, like Denise and her fucking friends."

"I would never be a bitch like Denise," I said. Immediately feeling that I sounded too eager, I added, proudly, "Besides, I don't have any needs!"

Adam laughed right into my face, trying to see my eyes in the dim light of the car. I was shrinking away from him, making myself a part of the door. He jammed the rest of the joint into the ashtray, put his hand on the side of my head, and started to gather a fistful of my hair.

"You're hurting my hair," I said, not really meaning it.

"Sorry," he said, letting go. Both his hands were kneading one of my thighs. He was saying my name, first and last. Over and over. Faith DiNapoli. Faith DiNapoli.

"Adam, don't," I said, feeling small.

"How about us doing this? How about just one little kiss?" he asked gently. "One? It'll be fun. Funny."

"Okay, one."

What's the harm in one kiss? I thought, until he gave me a dirty kind. His tongue went straight for the back of my throat, his moaning covering mine up completely. He flung my arm around his neck and grabbed my other wrist with his hand, since I myself was doing nothing with them, not knowing what you do with hands. He pried open my fist and placed it on his penis, through his jeans, and made a sandwich out of my hand, with his body and with mine. His other hand was touching my ears and shoulders, ribs and thighs, lighting little pilot lights underneath my clothes—doing all the doing. He was expert, and I was his Faith-sized doll.

Finally, the attention on areas that were not on my face and neck, but on my hyper breasts and searing middle, became too much to handle, manage, and stop.

"Adam!" I growled, low in my throat, like I was falling under water. I mashed my forehead against his chest away from me, removing the hand he had on one of my breasts.

"Fuck! Sorrysorrysorry!" he whispered into the top of my head. He lurched back, the hand that was on my breast now covering his mouth.

I was shaking but recognized him, again, at that better distance.

"Fuck!" he said, holding on to my shuddering forearm. "Don't be scared of me, Faith. Okay? I'm the last person in the world you gotta be scared of. It was just a stupid kiss."

What he didn't know was that it was my first real kiss. And while Chuckie's had left me stained and bothered, Adam's made me feel like I could've done this better if I had had time to catch up. I was starting to get the point, that we were supposed to be trying to make each other feel the same way.

"It's okay. I'm not scared," I said, with a voice stuck high in my throat, where all the air had stayed.

Then he leaned into me again, asking, almost kidding, almost scolding, "How about one more then, hey?" he urged, like he was a swimming instructor coaxing a kid into a very warm but very deep pool. I pictured myself shivering at the edges, arms wrapped around me like my mother wrapped hers around herself. My mother. God. She would die at knowing this, which thrilled me more.

I said, "I gotta get back, Adam. Matt'll kill me. Hopey's got sick. We have to go home."

"All right, I can take you home," he said, snapping himself out of this thick moment.

"No, we gotta go home together, or else. We're supposed to be at the movies. We were supposed to see the new *Star Wars* movie."

And maybe the mention of that movie, meant for kids like me, caused him to open his arms in defeat.

He exhaled loudly.

"Listen, Faith, don't say anything about this, okay? I acted badly. I'm sorry. It won't happen again. I swear. It's just my life's been crazy for me lately. I'm not acting like myself. I don't know what's wrong with me."

He told me he had quit school, moved home, and didn't know what he was going to do with the rest of his life. All I was concentrating on was the top of his pants. They were open, and his penis was peeking over his underwear like a soldier's head over a trench. He didn't cover himself. He just lay there splayed and tense and talking at me. Then he hummed a sound like he realized who he was confessing to, and was about to cry because it was me, the little neighbor-girl.

"It's okay," I said, "nothing happened, Adam."

I felt protective of him, despite the fact that both my body and soul had been in jeopardy, moments earlier. I got out of the Gremlin and ran down the road toward the bonfire, using legs that no longer seemed like mine. Behind me, I heard Adam start his engine and squeal away. I felt that feeling rush through me, again. It started at my feet and came out the top of my head, so by the time I found Matt, it seemed like all the molecules in my body had been replaced by older, though maybe not wiser, ones.

* * *

IT WAS ALMOST MIDNIGHT when we bumped up the driveway.

"We're home," Matt said to Hope. "Act okay."

"I'm okay," she said. "I'm fine."

There was no light on in our house. Charlie had probably gone to bed long ago, followed by my mom, thinking her kids would be filled with stories of space battles and evil villains and real comets, not the earthly kind we were driving. And if Adam was supposed to be the bad guy in the movie playing out in my mind, what did that make me, a girl who was now feeling all lit up with a different kind of light? A light that did not come from outer space at all.

Chapter Nine

Serena Agora was at my house, in my bedroom and putting on my makeup in my mirror. I could hardly believe my luck. I was sitting on the stool staring at her like a lover.

I snapped out of this lucky trance when my mother knocked on my bedroom door. She was leaving for work, she said, looking at Serena. I introduced my mother to my new friend and was impressed how Serena shook her hand. My mother took in Serena's green eyeliner, her gum-chewing, lip-glossed mouth, and the long skinny braid, which hung six inches lower than the rest of her fuzzy hair.

"Well, nice to meet you," she said to Serena. She turned to me and said, "Don't get into too much trouble, Faith."

And she meant it, because she called half an hour later, because it was slow at the diner, because she was bored, because she was just wondering what we were up to, because Saturday afternoons were long in summer, because we should stop by for lunch, why don't we?

"Tell Serena it'll be on me," she said.

"That's okay, Mom, we can make a sandwich here," I said, sensing her insecurity, sensing my own lack of it.

"Well, all right then, but I'm just thinking I haven't spent much time with you lately, eh?"

"I guess not," I said, impatient, wanting to get back to Serena. "But you gotta work, I know."

"Yeah, well, maybe I can get off earlier today and we can rent a movie or something. Is Hopey around?"

"She's got cadets."

"Well, how about Matt?"

"He's at Trel's."

"Charlie home?"

"Him neither."

"All right. Well, anyways, remember, Faith, I don't think Adam should come around, if I'm not home, okay?"

She was referring to a little talk we had had a few weeks after the night of the bush party. I breathed a different kind of air the first time Adam had come around; the first time since he had burned that permanent kiss onto my mouth. She had noticed me slowly rocking on one hip, mesmerized by the chat that Adam was having with her about the riding lawn mower. I was willing his eyes to meet mine. I wanted to prove the kiss happened and to suss out whether I'd be getting another one, but his eyes wouldn't meet mine for more than one empty second. After my mom thanked Adam for doing the whole lawn that day, she yanked the chunk of hair I had been chewing out of my mouth. She wrecked my daydream. I had imaged Adam had offered to mow the whole lawn that day because he loved me. He wanted to be around me as much as possible, not because Mr. Meloche was paying him to mow all the rental lawns, and trim all the rental trees, as a summer job. He did it because I wasn't a bitch, and I didn't need anything. And he loved me for that, he said as much. I also felt that he had said, "Bye, dear," to me, with secret specialness, and, "Bye, Nancy," to her, with absolutely none.

When Adam got to the end of the driveway, my mother had looked at me and said, "Faith, forget it, he's too old for you."

"Mom, that's stupid, I know that. I don't even like him."

"No, it's not stupid. I'm telling you he's too old for you, and I'm thinking I don't want him around here when I'm not there."

"Why?"

"Because."

"Because why?"

"Faith."

"Mom," I teased.

"Faith, Jesus *Christ.* I mean it, period. Or else, I'm going to tell him myself."

I shrugged so what.

SCHOOL HAD LET OUT the week before. Serena and I had only met a week before that, in detention. We both were in grade eleven, but I was in advanced classes and she was "with the retards," as she put it. It had been my first detention ever. Her third that year. I had sassed Mr. Payne-Johnson for no other reason except that I was from a broken home, my new excuse for everything. Serena had detention because she had let off a firecracker in the baseball dugout. Detention for us consisted of cutting out giant doves and crosses from colored felt for the church banners. When the supervising nun wasn't looking, Serena cut out extra letters so her banner read "Hosebag" instead of "Hosanna in the Highest." She made the doves look like they were humping each other.

I fell in love with her for that, but not like a lesbian or anything.

Serena's parents were veterinarians who drove matching Thunderbirds. They were the most interesting people in town, because of their education and their beepers. She had also been to New York City, visiting cousins who lived on Manhattan Island. I had only ever been as far as Manitoulin Island, on our one and only vacation.

That Saturday was the first time Serena had ever been over. We had gotten high a half hour before, so I was still buzzing all wonderful, when she was at that stage in her makeup ritual where she would carefully separate the thick stubs of mascara with the end of a filthy safety pin. Serena explained that mascara goes on the last because it takes the longest. The catch is that if you fuck it up, sometimes you have to start all over again—eye shadow, liner, everything, right from scratch.

Serena's chin was one inch from the mirror. She was pulling out the hairs between her eyebrows, thick, she explained, because she was Greek. I asked her if that meant she was part black and she said probably.

"We're all from around the Egypt area anyway, as people. Greece is pretty close. Italy is not too far either, really. I bet you we both have black in us, we get so tanned easily." Still stoned, I giggled at the idea of telling my mother that we could be part black.

Serena leaned back from the mirror regarding herself with a deep sigh. She stretched her neck and looked out the window at the Lauzons' cornfield next door. Corn detassling didn't start for another month. It was a horrible job, but the only one available to teens without driver's licenses, out in the county. Mostly girls detassled corn because at fourteen or fifteen, we were taller than the boys our age. You had to be at least five-two to reach the top of the stalk to properly yank the tassel straight up, neutering the corn. That's how regular corn became feed corn, though I only found that out later. My focus was on the $3.40/hour part, and how much yanking I had to do in order to shop at Fairweather's and not stupid Kmart, for back-to-school outfits.

This year, Serena and I were going to get on the same detassling crew. Looking out the window, I could tell she was thinking the same thing I was: When the corn reached the chin, summer was coming to an end.

"The corn is getting high," she whispered. I looked at the corn, then our eyes met for two hot seconds in the mirror.

"So are wee—" I started but couldn't even finish. This was my first great pot joke, and it made her laugh so hard she had to run to the bathroom. I crossed my legs giggling at myself in the mirror, teetering on the stool. Serena came back holding toilet paper to the corner of her eye to stop her teary mascara.

"Faith, you are a fucken riot. A fucken riot. Holy shit that was funny!" Deep breath. "OhmyGod."

And for the first time, in a long, long time, I felt proud of myself.

We had half a bag of weed left and nothing else to do.

Adam had moved home, but his mom still hadn't left the house. From my brothers' bedroom window I could see his driveway and his mom's dark blue K-car next to his Gremlin.

While Serena plucked her eyebrows I went back and forth between bedrooms, checking the driveway every two minutes. I had told her about our kiss, and lied and said that Adam loved me more than life itself, but was trying to figure out a way to break off with Denise without killing her too badly. Also, I told Serena that I had decided to lose my virginity with Adam that summer. I didn't mean it for sure. I only said it for something to say, in order for Serena to like me more, because she had admitted that she was no longer a virgin. But that day, that morning, I wasn't thinking about sex, only love, for my new friend and our long summer. I saw beautiful calendar photographs of June, July, and August, each as big as my back yard, stretching flat, all the way out to the sunset.

Serena was eight months older than me and told me she had recently passed her driving test, though her parents wouldn't let her touch their matching cars. I only had my beginner's, so it meant that I could drive a car if I was accompanied by a licensed driver.

That's how we came to be on Ouellette Avenue, in downtown Windsor, later that evening. The effect of our afternoon pot session had worn off, so Matt said I could take the Comet into the city as long as I was home before eight. My mom wouldn't have liked it if she had known I was driving into the city with Serena, but she called to say forget the movie, she was working until midnight.

"I don't want my first time with sex to be with some stupid jerk, that's why I choose Adam to have my virginity," I said to Serena, on the way into the city. "He knows all about it and everything and he can't wait."

"What's cool," Serena added, "is that you can't get a reputation if he doesn't even go to our school, anyways."

"That's true."

My hand was fluttering out the window, stopping wind. This was the kind of grown-up conversation that I'd seen other people have with their friends on after-school specials. The kind of conversation I had never had with Nicole, the kind I could never have with my mom, or Auntie Linda, or Hope, for that matter.

We threw our spent cigarettes out the window because the ashtray of the Comet was overflowing with the roach ends of Matt's joints. He saved them, sometimes rerolling them into fresh joints if he was at the bottom of his weed bag.

OUELLETTE AVENUE, in Windsor, was where young people in cars, not their own, cruised alongside other young people in cars, not their own. Being a new driver was dangerous because it was hard not to be distracted by all those clean cars and all those strange people so freshly out of showers that the backs of their necks were still shiny.

Serena and I had no intention that night except to say, Look at us in this car. We are moving. We are heading somewhere.

It was exciting to be driving alone with my new friend, but Ouellette Avenue didn't get exciting until well after nine. This was past my car curfew. It seemed that we were really just cruising in downtown commuter traffic, going in the opposite direction.

That afternoon, there were no boys, Camaros, Americans, or booming stereos, for us. But we drove the loop twice.

"This sucks," Serena said.

"Well, we have to get the car back by eight. But things'll pick up in an hour," I said, full of hope and fake knowledge.

"But then we have to turn around and go back to Belle River. This sucks."

I almost blurted out, "Well, at least I got us a car," but we weren't that close of friends yet. I was still in that worship stage where I would've done anything Serena Agora wanted in order to keep Serena Agora interested.

It was a shame there were no boys to see us, because we really did look great that night. We had finished getting ready at Serena's place, her parents having been called away by a farmer whose cow and horse were both giving birth. We put on our super-short miniskirts, rolling the waistband up an extra inch. We plastered on a heavy layer of makeup.

My mother wasn't stupid. She knew I owned this miniskirt, she knew I had bought the hot-pink spaghetti-strap tank top, she had seen my high-heeled, cloth wedges, which tied around the ankle. She bought them with me, scowling slightly, but still, she let me pay for them with babysitting money, proud I didn't steal them, and telling me that. She also saw me spritz my hair with Auntie Linda's Sun-In, once, to lighten it, though she said the color it turned my hair was closer to Kraft Dinner orange than "California Blond."

I had introduced these items little by little, strategically pairing them off with boring stuff. For instance, I would wear that miniskirt with dark leotards, and my flat Mary Janes, and a thick turtleneck. I would wear the tank top, braless, but under a sweater with my baggy painter pants. The lip gloss? Maybe to church. And every time I got away with wearing something slutty, it felt like a little victory.

That night, heading down to Ouellette Avenue the first time, alone with my new best friend, in my grandpa's old car, I had on every single sexy thing I owned, and some of Serena's things, too. The centerpiece of my outfit was my three-inch feather earrings I had bought at a carnival stand, with my mother right there, stiffly nodding like Grandpa used to.

"Fuck, I love this song," said Serena, cranking up the volume on a Foreigner slow song. We sang out loud, "I've Been Waiting for a Girl Like You," as though it was meant for us to sing to each other. Not like lesbians though. The radio announcer said Foreigner was playing at Cobo Hall across the river in Detroit that night.

"Don't you wish we were going?"

"Yeah," I said.

The announcer described the madness in downtown Detroit, something to do with the Freedom Festival, and people were everywhere, unlike Windsor, where they were deserting the streets.

So when Serena said, "Let's go, Faith. Let's go to Detroit. This sucks," all I had to do was turn the wheel toward the Canada/U.S. tunnel and fish out my birth certificate.

"Yeah?"

"Yeah, plus I know my way around Detroit like it's the back of my hand. We'll drive up and down, and if it gets to be too scary, we'll leave. Simple. It's better than this," said Serena, dramatically sweeping her arm out toward the empty sidewalks. "This sucks."

I hadn't been to Detroit since Grandpa died and Auntie Linda moved to New York. But if we stayed on one street, Jefferson Avenue, Detroit's equivalent to Ouellette, and if we kept the Windsor skyline in sight, we couldn't get lost.

"Oh my God, what a good idea," and I thought it was. I really thought it was a good idea. I thought that Serena Agora was brilliant. I thought my life was already becoming more interesting.

I was only right about that last part.

"Oh my God, maybe we'll see Foreigner walking around," she said, squealing. "Let's go, let's go, let's go."

Another Foreigner song came on the radio and Serena turned up the volume even more.

"As if they'd just be walking around downtown Detroit," I said.

"You never know, Faith."

Serena was playing the air drums to "Cold as Ice," on the dashboard, when we pulled up to the black woman at the booth.

Without even looking at us, she asked, "Citizenship?"

We yelled, "Canadian!"

"Turn down the music, ladies."

We both scrambled for the volume dial at the same time.

"Sorry. We're both Canadian."

"Going to the concert?" She leaned out of the kiosk, looking down into the car and, deeply, at us, at our outfits.

"No. We wish."

"Then what exactly is your destination, ladies?"

We started to answer at the same time, Serena with, "Nowhere really, we're—" and me finishing with, "Just driving around. You know, nothing really—"

"One at a time," she yelled, as impatient as a babysitter. "You two just gonna drive around Detroit? Got nowhere to go?"

"Uh-huh."

"Right. And do what?" By now she was dialing up someone on what looked like a walkie-talkie or a large phone.

"Nothing, we just wanted to take a drive. We were driving on Ouellette and thought—"

"You thought wrong."

She was asking someone on the walkie-talkie if there was a parking space available at Inspections because she was sending a rust-colored, '72 Ford Comet . . .

I began to shake.

"You know, ma'am, we'll just turn around if it's not all right for us to—" I started to plead, Serena crossing her arms hard across her chest.

"No you won't. You will take this car and park it up there by that bench, get out, hand your keys to that porter, and go into that building. Give me your birth certificates."

She was acting very mean.

Two men and a woman came out of the building and guided the Comet into the empty parking spot.

Another black woman, dressed in uniform, came around to the driver's side.

"Please get out of the car," she said, "and hand the keys to that gentleman."

My knees were knocking so hard, I almost toppled off my wedges. Our outfits, such assets in Canada, were now our greatest liabilities in America. We looked like hookers and the innocence of our destination, "Nowhere, just driving around," rang in my ears until it sounded pornographic. My mother will kill me, I thought. My mother will, literally, kill me using her two hands.

"Follow me," the woman said, motioning to Serena. I started after them. "No, wait here, another woman's coming for you."

When I finally spoke up I sounded hoarse. "Why can't we go together? I would like to call my mother."

I had the urge to yell for my mother into the American air, which was now smothering me.

"Be my guest," the woman snorted, and off she went with Serena.

Another woman, this time white, came out and guided me by my upper arm into the building.

"This is all a mistake," I said to her.

When the porter started up the Comet and drove away with it, I peed my underwear a little.

"You should have thought of that before," she said. Suddenly, her being white was no longer a comfort to me.

She led me into a small office where there was a desk, two chairs, a high window, a big bulletin board with almost nothing tacked onto it, and a small changing room with a shower curtain suspended around it. It looked like a Confession booth, minus the velvet and privacy part. Totally minus Jesus.

"Can I call my mother?"

"In a minute. Sit here."

She asked for my name, address, birth date, birthplace, mother's and father's name, friend's name.

"Place of employment?"

"What?"

This was like a movie and Serena and I were all wrong for these parts. I had heard stories like this. This happened all the time, but usually to Canadian shoppers heading back home, caught and stopped on the Canadian side, after a long day of shopping and smuggling.

"Where do you work?" she asked again.

"Nowhere. I'm sixteen. But I'm gonna be doing corn detassling soon. I do some babysitting, still."

"And you're the driver of the vehicle? Who owns it?"

"I do. Me and my brother do. I have my beginner's license. My friend has her license. I can drive so long as she's in the car with me. Why am I in here? Can I call my mom?"

"In a minute. I'll be right back."

And I sat there in that cell, that brick room, feeling far away from my mother. Phoning home would be my first long-distance call. And though I knew the diner's number by heart, I wasn't sure how to dial it from Detroit. I was thinking, How could I have never made a long-distance call in my life? Because, Faith, idiot, you have never been anywhere, and now you will never go anywhere again. Least of all to hateful America, responsible for murdering Grandpa, using your own cursed blood. And no doubt more will spill, later.

I began scanning the room, desperately and instinctively looking for a cross to pray to, or for some Jesus face to comfort me. When's the last time I'd been to church? Two, three months? God, I am sorry, I thought. I am so so sorry. Is my absence why this is happening to me? Is it because I let Adam, a neighbor-boy, and a big help to my mother, kiss me on the mouth, leaving a taste for more on my lips? Jesus forgive me. I will go to church, I prayed. I will not kiss anyone again. I will carry my virginity to my grave, if necessary. At the very least, I will not allow Adam to come over if my mother's at work. I will listen to my mother. I will love her and never leave her again. And if You promise me these people won't touch my body, I won't let Adam touch it either, ever again.

There was a calendar, but no crucifix, so I had to make do with murmuring these prayers into the arms of the giant wall clock, now screaming seven fucking thirty.

Ten minutes later a different black woman came into the room. She said words to me that arrived long seconds after leaving her mouth.

She instructed, "Faith DiNapoli, step behind the curtain and remove all your clothes including your underthings and hand them over to me please. We need to search your body for drugs."

At first, I pretended that I could not understand her language. When she repeated herself, like I asked her to, I pretended that I really would not understand her language.

I made a sound; not quite a laugh, not quite a cry.

"Nha. Heh . . . nha," I moaned, rocking, grabbing onto the bottom of the chair, looking down and shaking my head slowly, no, not possible. My skirt was so short I had to press my legs together to hide the white crescent of my underpants. I tried crossing them but the posture made me look too adult and wary, like the hooker-druggie they thought I was. The feather lengths of my earrings rested spent on my collarbone, their weight pulling my head down. I was wilting under all this cruel attention.

I started to cry.

The woman knelt down beside the chair and in a steady voice that, despite her uniform, was kind of loving, said, "I am going to give you a Kleenex and I am going to tell you something, Faith DiNapoli. You two girls are very stupid. You do not dress like this, or drive a car without ownership papers. Honey, the ashtray is full of marijuana, or at least evidence that marijuana is in use while operating the vehicle. You proceed to pull up and tell us that you two, neither licensed drivers, are going to just drive around downtown Detroit City. You understand that we are going to be suspicious."

"I told you Serena has—"

"No, honey, Serena does not have a license to drive."

"But she said—"

"Well, whatever she said she lied. You two look and smell and sound like a couple of drug smugglers. Or prostitutes. That's how it looks to us. And you're probably not, but do you understand why we think so?"

"No. I swear. We're not—"

"We don't know that. We don't know that and, frankly, neither do you two. Drugs get into this city in ways that would shock you. You two may not even know that you are carrying drugs. Understand? We need to look at your clothes and we need to ensure, on your bodies, that you are not carrying drugs into this city. This city does not need any more drugs. You understand me, dear?"

"Please can I call my mother?"

"We've already called her, she'll be here shortly. With her lawyer."

"How'd you know how to find her?"

"Your friend told us where she worked. Your friend can't seem to remember her own parents' number."

Serena Agora's smart and I'm a stupid ass, I thought. Serena Agora's also a fucking liar. I hated Serena Agora's guts.

God, my mom was bringing Mr. Delgado? Her divorce lawyer? That's funny, I thought, what's he going to do, divorce me from America? Probably when I tell my mother that this wasn't my idea, she will divorce me from Serena. Then she will divorce me from our family and send me to live with the gypsies, or worse, with Dad on the oil rig. The lonely, stranded oilmen would tie my dad up and throw him over the platform. Then they'll take turns at me, ripping my miniskirt to shreds. My lipstick would be permanently smeared, just like a whore's. There was Auntie Linda, but she lived here in horrible America. Maybe Nonna Tree would take me in and teach me how to be calm, how to make bread, how to wait. I could sit on her porch, in one of her roomy sundresses, watching for visitors, since I'd never wander any farther than the mailbox at the end of that long, dusty driveway.

"Fuck, shit," I whined out loud, lost in the certainty of my banishment.

"Hey now," both women said to me. One of them even put her finger in front of my face the way my mother always did, when words weren't enough.

"Watch that mouth, you're too young to be talking just like an old bitch."

They both cracked up over this warning.

I thought about yelling out my denunciation of future dreams in their mean land, but the only thing I could say to them with any conviction was, "I hope you know that yous two will both go straight to hell for doing this."

I pictured their naked souls lifting out of their uniforms and sinking down in front of me like two pieces of bread in an eternal toaster.

"Well, if stupidity is a sin, girl," one said, pulling the rubber gloves high up over her wrists, "then you and your dumbass friend is gonna be joining us for dinner with the devil."

She held open the vinyl curtain like I had won something excellent behind it. But there was only a small bench, a plastic hook for clothes, and two disturbing yellow handprints painted on the wall, shoulder height. Facing that wall, two yellow feet were imprinted on the linoleum floor.

"After you have disrobed, place your hands on the hands on the wall. Place your feet on the feet on the floor."

It took fifteen minutes to remove my skirt. Another fifteen minutes to take off my shirt. But they were patient. They said they had all night. This gave Mr. Delgado enough time to drive four blocks to the diner, pick up my mother, and make it to the border in a record twenty-eight minutes. The hot air from my mother probably screaming, "For fuck sakes, hurry the fuck up," directly into the dashboard, would've helped to physically propel the car faster toward America.

I got to know that wall, and all its flaws. I stared hard into that wall, even while I heard my mother ripping loud and hard into the desk clerk down the hall.

"Where's my goddamn daughter, for chrissakes? You better fucking tell me where the hell she is, for godsakes!"

She couldn't have been more than a few feet from the door behind which I stood, arms straight ahead, legs spread-eagled three feet apart, naked, losing my virginity to a black woman whose name I would never know.

MY MOTHER DROVE the shattered Comet home. Serena and I bundled up into Mr. Delgado's LeBaron, because my mother said for me to go with Mr. Delgado, I can't look at you right now, because I don't know what I will do to you, she said.

Mr. Delgado's initial legal assessment of the case of *Faith and Serena vs. The United States of America* was that there was no case. Border laws are strict and unassailable, he explained, especially in President Reagan's "War on Drugs" era, a policy that affected us Canadians because of our proximity.

The ride home was very quiet, our mascara, beyond smeared, just completely gone, which was a miracle of physics considering how many coats we had applied. Serena stretched out in the back seat, limp and distracted. I sat in the front, Mr. Delgado's cologne-soaked blazer wrapped tightly around me. I had taken off my feather earrings and folded them into one of his pockets. I never saw them again.

We dropped Serena off and she kind of poured out of the car into her darkened house, not even saying goodbye or good night to either one of us.

There was the part about the fine. Serena did not, indeed, have a driver's license, which cost me a $150 penalty for driving without one.

Grandpa's Comet would fare worse. My mother had stuffed what was left of the back seat into the back seat area. The border guards had removed all of the bottom cushions in their search for drugs, slashed them apart, and left the seat strewn about the customs lot like *Sanford and Son.* That was how my mother described the scene to my auntie Linda on the phone that night, in a story that took a long time to sound funny to anyone, especially me.

My mother drove back to Canada in a speeding hot rage, hurling expletives, both religious and racist, and big tufts of cotton, out the window at the black Americans. Later, I overheard her tell Auntie Linda that she was relieved she had been pulled over by a county cop, an attractive man by the name of Dennis. She was grateful that he had given her a speeding ticket, and a quiet pep talk, because she was able to calm down enough before arriving home, fifteen minutes after us.

I watched our wounded Comet bump up our dim driveway. I had put my pajamas on, and my face was scrubbed and murder-ready, though when I saw the headlights shut off, I ran to my room like a scared dog.

My mother padded down the hallway and stopped in front of my bedroom door. Seconds passed before she knocked, not hard, not soft.

"Come in," I said, in a voice soaked in resignation. Come in, Mom, and hit me, hard, please, I thought. Mom, please hit me hard, because I can't feel anything. I was more afraid of this numbness, than of all the blood I ever spilled in America. The red spot, the size of a thumbprint, in the panties that I had I thrown out, would be the last drop I would ever spill in that country, I vowed. From now on, I would do all my dying at home, or within walking distance of it.

My mom opened the door and stood there. Her face was beautiful, maybe from the crying, which caused her eyes to puff out, making her look almost my age.

"At least they got the stains out," she said finally, crossing her arms hard and leaning on the doorjamb.

"What?"

"The stains in Grandpa's Comet. They used a carpenter's knife, I guess, to cut open the upholstery, so you can't see the stains anymore. Come see."

There was no friendliness in her voice. No meanness. Just information.

I got up and walked behind her, passing Mr. Delgado, passing Hope, who was still sitting in front of a big bowl of something she was no longer eating. They watched me walk behind my mother, and follow her out the door. I was thinking that maybe, once she got me in the garage, it would be all over; a hail of smacks and screams or some such punishment would rain down on me, but I wanted it. I needed it. I didn't care one bit if she actually killed me with her hands because a big, fat black woman had put her finger up my vagina looking for drugs in another country. I couldn't imagine anything worse coming from a woman who loved me so much that crying over something terrible that happened to me actually made her beautiful.

I peered into the back seat, now an unrecognizable mess of cuts and stuffing, like a bunch of starving, bladed roosters had been let loose inside for days with all the windows rolled up. This couldn't be the same back seat that only a few years earlier I had sat on, bleeding, holding a melting Fudgsicle, feeling as helpless as I ever had in my entire life. Until today.

"It looks awful, Mom. I'm so sorry." I meant it.

She was gone for a long time and when she returned, struggling with the sewing kit, and two lit cigarettes dangling from her mouth, I wasn't sure what to grab first.

"Here."

She handed me one of the cigarettes. For a second I pretended like it was the first time I had ever seen one.

"Quit being a phony, I know you smoke. Now . . . let me see . . ." she said, fishing around in the wicker basket, her cigarette hanging from her lips. She pulled out a curved upholstery needle and dug back inside for the extra-strength thread she used to repair Matt's hockey equipment.

Tears hung off her eyelids while she knotted the thread, and stabbed the upholstery. She pulled the two sides of the gashed-open tweed together, yanking and stitching and stuffing in the cotton as she went.

"You're going to need more thread than this. I'll get some tomorrow. But I think it can be fixed. I'll show you a basic blanket stitch which I think is the only thing that'll pull and hold that tweed together. There's also that cotton stuffing in the basement, remember, from when you made that Valentine heart pillow for me, in Home Ec?"

I watched silently. There were at least a dozen open wounds in the back cushion, and a few longer ones in the two front bucket seats.

"Faith, you can start tonight. Dad left that lightbulb thing. You can hook it up over the garage handle. Leave the door open because it's hot, right? Now I'm going to go back in and talk to Mr. Delgado about all this. Start on the front so it's at least drivable for us. Okay?"

She walked toward the garage door. I noticed she was still wearing her black waitressing pouch. On the top step, she smoothed down her hair and T-shirt, then turned around to face me.

"Faith," she said, holding up that finger, pronouncing every single syllable carefully, "promise me this one thing. Promise me that you'll make what happened today the worst thing that ever happens to you in your life, because I just don't think that any of us could truly survive anything bigger. Least of all me. Okay? Promise me that."

I nodded, clenching my teeth to stop from bawling, grateful that she had spared my life.

I waited for her to shut the door before taking a deep, long drag off the blessed cigarette. I'll never be sure whether it was relief that my mother did not murder me with her hands, or the rush of nicotine sailing into my bloodstream, or that Adam Lauzon drove slowly by our house, honking and waving, which caused me to faint down hard onto the cool garage floor.

As I WAS COMING TO, I saw the face of Our Lord Jesus Christ. At first I thought He needed a shave, but Adam had removed his shirt and balled it up under my head, so for the first time, his tattoos were visible to me. The hair on his chest was minimal, but provided his Jesus tattoo with a kind of beard, so an added realism. Then I saw Adam's concerned face. Then I saw Eve, also tattooed on the outer part of his upper right arm, the serpent covering her boobs and privates, winding around his elbow, finishing up at his right wrist.

He was slapping my cheeks, saying, Faith, Faith.

Adam had left his Gremlin running in front of our garage door, so for a second I thought a vengeful Comet had run me over and killed me.

I heard my mother's voice before I saw her face.

"Jesus Christ, Faith, what happened? What the hell's happening? Jesus, Adam, what did you do to her? Go home. Please."

"I was just—she fell. I saw her go down!"

"Just go home."

"All right, I was just trying to help her."

"I know, but we need more help than anyone could give us, right now," she said, impatiently tugging me up onto my feet, pulling my pajama top down over my belly, brushing the dirt off my bum. I felt starving. I hadn't had a thing all day except for pot and cigarettes.

Adam scooped his T-shirt off the garage floor, and shoved it into his back pocket.

"Whatever you say, Nancy. See you, Faith," he mumbled.

I waved, and let my mother lead me into the house, dumbly looking over my shoulder at Adam's spattered back. The cross tattoo started at the base of his neck, extended to his waistband, and spanned both shoulder blades. A garland of flowers wound around the bottom. I must have only been out cold for a few seconds, but it seemed like hours, because the sun had sunk, making everything around me seem much, much darker.

Chapter Ten

My mother lifted my grounding early, when corn detassling started. She always reached a point when punishing her kids at home would eventually backfire against her.

"I'm not sure if groundings hurt anyone but me," she said, coming home to my angry, buckled face, night after night. "Don't you have a book you can read in your room, so I can make a phone call, or watch what I want on my TV?"

In total, I only suffered two weeks of moping around the house, treating every chair I sat in like it was a permanent wheelchair. I exaggerated my imprisonment by pretending I couldn't feel my legs, couldn't walk, so wasn't able to fetch a beer or answer the phone. In truth, I cherished being stuck home. Sewing up the car cushions passed the hours quite decently, and provided front-row seats in the comings and goings of Adam Lauzon's Gremlin.

Hope signed on for detassling with me, eager to develop her arm muscles, to better execute color guard duties at cadets.

"God, Faith, those flags are heavier than you'd think looking at them."

"Yeah, I was up all night thinking that same thing, Hope."

Matt lied about his age, and got a job at the Ford's plant, summer help. He was hoping to stay on permanently. Charlie was still too short to detassle, and now that he wore black almost entirely, my mom joked that the sun beating down on his Sex Pistols T-shirt would likely cause a heatstroke.

SERENA HAD BEEN GROUNDED, too, after my poor mother told her rich, animal-doctor parents how their precious handful had brutally corrupted me that night. I overheard her tell Mrs. Agora that it was my "passive personality" that got me into trouble.

I cringed, later, when she described me in her diary. *Faith's a bit of a follower and stupidly impressionable, way too willing to please, and I gotta figure a way to hammer that out of her.*

To my face, she suggested that Serena might not be a good match, that Nicole was a better friend, since there had been no imbalance of power between us. I told her that Nicole was a bit of a geek, and that hanging around Serena should be better for me, if I needed to gather more gumption. How could I learn that from Nicole, when she didn't have much herself?

"Faith, I'm just saying that you should pick your friends more carefully."

"I would," I said, "if I had a selection of friends to choose from."

My mother looked at me and frowned, pity peeking out from the corners of her mouth. Neither one of us had much talent in making friends, less so in keeping them. As it was, Serena was my only friend and my mother couldn't take her away from me. She had already banished Adam from the house, with no explanation, and only a light suspicion that it was the right thing to do. She once wrote in her diary that she still couldn't believe that she had two daughters, *A fifteen- and a sixteen-year-old, filling out their bras, and probably doing even worse things behind my back. I just wish the two of them would talk to me more. I see other mothers and daughters looking like they're friends with each other. We're all more like roommates. Is this my fault? It's probably my fault. But what to do about it I don't know.*

My mother was convinced that the boys we detassled corn with were retarded, due to their big ears, and extra-long farmer arms.

"Would you look at that one!" she'd say, dropping us off in the morning, her pink rollers sticking out of her kerchief, her red eyes peering over her giant sunglasses. "He'd be quite a catch, Faith, if you could train him to stop scratching his privates in public."

At six-thirty, a yellow school bus picked up me, Hope, and Serena from the church steps, and transported us detasslers deep into the middle of nowhere. Every evening at the same time, it dropped us off, filthy and exhausted. That drive, from the endless cornfields, to the town center, began to make Belle River seem like a busy metropolis.

Corn detassling was the worst kind of work if you hoped to stay pretty all day long. That didn't stop me and Serena from decking ourselves out in bright tube tops, to avoid tan lines, and waterproof mascara, in order to stay fresh during afternoon thunderstorms. I'd put makeup on while waiting for the bus, Hope next to me, rolling her eyes. But there were no cute guys on our first cycle of fields, so I'm not sure why we bothered.

The stiff corn leaves cut shallow lines across our cheeks. Bug bites sometimes popped up in weird patterns on our arms and shoulders. When I got home, my mother would joke that I had an almost-Orion, or a near–Big Dipper, spelled out in black-fly welts in the middle of my back. My fingers were impacted so deep with dirt, I'd have to scrub them outside using the hose and an old hairbrush.

My clothes smelled always of corn.

But I loved the work because it evened everyone out. We were all equal in the eyes of the corn. Even the rich kids, whose parents owned the farms, worked beside us in the sticky heat. The only thing I hated about the job was Marie, our crew boss. She was my mother's age, and acted like she was ours. She never failed to butt her smushed-up French-Canadian nose into our whispered conversations.

"Oh, and wit har yous two talkin' ha-bout?" she'd say, turning around, eagerly facing me and Serena. Hope sat far away from me on the bus, reading, pretending she didn't know me.

"We're not talkin' HA-bout naw-ting, Marie," Serena mocked.

"You girls har trouble. I watch hout for you two!"

I'd crack my mother up imitating Marie's accent, both of us giggling, surrounded by French-Canadians. She'd snap a wet rag at me, sitting on the diner stool.

"Don't fuck this job up, Faith," she'd say. "You need to work off that fine, and you need to buy clothes, not steal them. The only other option is that I get you a job here. With me."

So I tried to get along. But Marie did keep extra eyes on me and Serena. Serena thought maybe she was a lez, the way she'd hover back if one of us had to pee.

People rarely lasted for the entire four-week cycle. Even Hope quit after the Wednesday we worked overtime, because she missed cadets. That bus ride home was the first time I ever saw Hope bite her nails until they bled. I had the fine to pay off before I saw a penny for school clothes, so I vowed to last. Serena promised she'd last too, but after the second week, she started skipping days, or she'd show up after lunch, one of her parents driving around the county roads, spotting our parked yellow bus, dropping her off, pouting, in full makeup.

One rainy morning, we snapped, somewhere out in Comber, after waiting out a wicked lightning storm inside the all-metal bus.

Serena said, "Faith, I can't do this no more, I feel like a Negro or something."

The rich girls, who didn't have to work, spent their days at Sandpoint Beach in Tecumseh. And look at us, she'd say, slaving away for nothing.

But Marie wouldn't take us home. She promised the storm would pass soon enough for us to finish the field we had started. She had a quota, and dammit if she wasn't going to fill it.

"This is my last day," said Serena, looking angrily out the window at the mucky field. "I am not getting out of the bus."

"Fuck it, then. I'm quitting, too," I said. Visions of the diner danced in my head; my mother bossing me around; me cringing while my mother flirted with businessmen, introducing me as her oldest daughter, and her little helper, in that fake perfect-family way she acted when we'd visit her at work. Also, from reading her diary, I knew how hard waitressing was. Probably harder then detassling. Mostly I wondered how would I have time to read her diaries if we were always working together?

Still, she would understand that being struck by lightning for $3.40 an hour was not a great first job, and a decent enough reason to quit. So without leaving our seats, both of us shivering in our rain-drenched green garbage bags, Serena yelled, with a mouth full of cheese sandwich, "Hey, Marie! Guess what? Me and Faith, we *quit!*"

The bus exploded.

Four other people yelled they were going to quit, too, and Marie had a full-scale mutiny brewing.

She looked panicked.

"Shut hup heveryone!"

She paused, covered her little face with her little hands, taking a few shallow breaths.

"Hokay," she reasoned, "HIF yous get hout and finish dis field, I pay yous time and a half. But HIF yous don't want to do dis, den get HOUT of dis bus NOW, and get home on your hone. Ryde *now!*"

She was looking directly at me and Serena.

We were in Comber, a twenty-minute drive to our pickup spot, and at least a half-hour walk to the nearest highway. The rain had subsided, but the lightning hadn't quite let up enough to make it safe for walking. It thundered like crazy, too. These conditions must have been exactly right for two girls who had spent the early parts of their summer getting fingered by lady border guards, then grounded because of it. I promised my mother nothing bad would happen to me, but what could be worse than this?

I rose and stretched easily. I wished that my mother could've seen me acting so not passive. See, I'm not impressionable, Mom! Maybe just a little bit unemployable is all. And I'm only following behind Serena because she was sitting on the aisle.

"Bye, losers," sang Serena, climbing down off the bus and right into a whack of thunder. We screamed and pulled the garbage bags over our heads, leaving little holes for our faces. There was no climbing back into the bus just like babies. I would rather die, get hit by lightning, or drown in a flash flood.

If anything bad had happened to us we couldn't have sued the company. We had signed a waiver that said, more or less, that even if we fainted on a dried-up cornstalk stump, and split open our skulls, we should simply pray that the six-inch gash doesn't scar. That's what happened to Sarah Narmont. She stayed on for the rest of the day with a wad of bloodied toilet paper stuck to the side of her head, detassling like a zombie.

"She must come from much poorer folk than us," my mom had said, when she picked us up at the church that day.

Serena and I had accidentally left our water jugs and lunch bags on the bus, but I had four cigarettes sealed in a Baggie in my back pocket, and Serena had the Van Halen Zippo we shared.

The rain was gentle but cold.

"We are fucked!" Serena laughed, wearing only a tube top under her garbage bag, shuddering with a chill.

The fact that we had on very short shorts under those bags, made us look like shriveled, life-size pickles, jogging arm-in-arm down a dirt road.

"This is hilarious," I said. And it was, until a semi truck passed us, honking madly, nearly running us off the road. It became less funny when another one did the identical thing one second later.

The storm still threatened in flashes of spooky light. The tall corn looked bluish and the sound of stalks rustling had a rhythm to it that was almost sleepy. We passed a line of sunflowers swaying like skinny, damp blondes.

Then Serena had a delicious idea, one I could taste on my mouth like another kiss.

"Faith, let's call Adam Lauzon. He'll come get us. You always say he'll do anything for you. We could walk up to a farmhouse and borrow a phone."

"I guess, if you want."

At the crossroads we passed a well-cared-for scarecrow, freshly stuffed and crucified, wearing a newish-looking plaid work shirt.

"Ooo. Look! I'm taking that shirt, dammit," said Serena, as she threw off her garbage bag and ran up to it like it was a mannequin at the mall. She began stripping the scarecrow down like a lover would, bumping and grinding it, and cracking me up hard.

"Thanks, Mr. Scarecrow!" she yelled over her shoulder as she buttoned the straw-spattered shirt around her tube top. "Eww, it stinks, Faith, and it's got bird shit on it."

Lightning struck too close by us, with a crack.

"Fuck," we screamed, making a run for the nearest farmhouse, as though lightning wouldn't strike us if we were running away from the last place it hit, as though I had any way of knowing where lightning would strike next.

OUT HERE, it wasn't much of a coincidence that the farmer we met at the first house we stopped at tilled the cornfield we bailed out on, and owned the one next to it. The one with a now-topless scarecrow standing guard. But the farmer didn't mind at all and told Serena she could keep the shirt. It didn't fit him no mores, and if I was cold I could have one too. Go right in my room and pick one out, he said. His wife had died, breast cancer, rest her soul, not so very long ago, so it was just him out here, alone, now that the kids were grown and gone to university, learning how to do anything else but grow corn. But I told him I was fine and that our ride would be here in fifteen minutes tops. I said thanks for giving my older brother, Adam, directions, as I hadn't a clue where the hell in the county we were. And we'll just wait outside on the porch, hope you don't mind if we smoke. No, no, he said, maybe I'll join yous, don't get many visitors, especially young and pretty ones, ha ha ha. Quite a storm. Yes, quite a storm.

But the farmer was nice, despite his belly poking out from underneath his shirt. He even offered us a lunch of yellow pea soup, which was thawing in Tupperware under the running tap in the kitchen. His sister made it, divided it into meal-sized portions, and drove it out here, once a week, imagine that. People helped him out, so it's not too bad, he said.

I thought of my own dad, living alone, like this farmer. But unlike my dad, this man didn't choose to be alone. People died or left him, with fields and fields of corn to grow. He probably wondered, How could people leave a place as beautiful as this, for school, or heaven, or Calgary, even? So there's me thinking the farmer's thinking, "Who's going to take care of the corn when I'm dead and gone?"

But we were just here by accident, and now, we were just waiting to leave him, too.

When Adam finally pulled up and honked, we thanked the farmer for the scarecrow's shirt, for the offer of yellow pea soup for lunch, and we left him alone, with a million stalks of swaying corn and the hundreds of storms that would hit them.

The sun burst out hot. It wasn't even noon yet.

On the way back, before we reached Belle River, Adam said we were going to stop at a friend's for a quick visit.

"You'll like him," he said. "He has an in-ground pool, and his folks are at the cottage."

I could smell beer on his breath. My mother told me he was spending his summer break drinking beer, reading magazines, and dangling his feet off the rotting dock of his dad's homemade pond. She had heard that he was falling apart over his breakup with Denise, and was kicked out of the university for drug use and spending tuition money on tattoos instead of textbooks. People were talking about him at the diner, and she reminded me he was no longer welcome at the house. I reminded her gossip was a sin, and she said, Not if it's true gossip, and unless there's a damn good reason, he was not to come over. Being stranded in the middle of a Comber storm seemed as good a reason as any. But she'd say, You could have called me, I'm your mother, she'd say, while nailing my bare feet to my bedroom floor, grounding me, literally, for eternity.

"Faith, I'm glad you called me. This'll be fun," Adam said, rolling into the beer store. With the Gremlin idling, he hoisted some empties out of the hatchback and carried them in, a cigarette bobbing between his lips.

Serena shoved her face between the bucket seats and whispered, "Now's your chance, Faith. Today could be the day."

"I know," I said, sinking deep into the seat.

I watched Adam pay for the beer. He wasn't wearing any shoes.

Turned out Serena knew Scott Demeter, Adam's friend. He and Serena's older brother both sold pot, but Scott decorated his plastic bags with band logos and sayings such as "Die young, leave a beautiful corpse" and "Here's to the road less traveled," all carefully spelled with Wite-Out.

I didn't like Scott because right away he asked Adam just how the fuck old are these two. Adam said, Older than you think, guy. Scott had the spoiled mouth of rich kids, which pointed down and mostly away from me and Serena. His T-shirt was too tight, making him seem far too large to be living with other people, especially his own folks. He was talking about how at the university, where he was studying philosophy, in order not to be a farmer like his dad, he just couldn't get his head around the damn morning schedule.

"They had me in *early* classes and I had to get to Windsor from all the way out *here,* if you can believe it, Adam. My only option is residence for third year. But fuck that. You did it, and you hated it, right?"

Adam nodded while rolling a "fattie," as Scott called it. Scott warned me and Serena not to "nigger-lip" it because it made him want to vomit, sucking back on a wet "hoolie."

I looked around, wondering why Scott would ever want to leave this house. It was a terribly perfect, utterly clean, entirely new mansion farmhouse. His mother had a duck theme running throughout the kitchen. Ducks on tea towels, ducks on napkins, ducks on trays, oven mitts, and kettle. There was a white ceramic crucifix hanging above the sink, that Scott said his parents bought in Portugal. And frankly, I had never seen a bigger TV in my life than the one in the "formal living room," staring at us glossy black and dead-eyed. You could also see the in-ground swimming pool from the "breakfast nook," something I had never heard of.

Adam had the idea of taking the party "poolside."

"Let us repair to the deck, shall we?" he asked, in a fake British accent, giving me his arm. "Faith DiNapoli? Would you do me the honor of accompanying me out to the deck where I am going to hurl you into the deep end and hold your head underwater."

Serena squealed and ran out the door. Scott chased after her. I allowed myself the stoned fantasy that this mansion was all mine and Adam's, and Serena and Scott were visiting friends.

I pictured Serena saying, "Hi, what you all up to this beautiful day?"

"Why nothing but reading this science fiction novel which Adam just wrote," I'd say. "Join us for a cold beer, why don't you?"

Adam would be flipping steaks on our gas barbecue. He'd shake Scott's hand firmly and disappear with him into the shed, which substituted as his office where he wrote all day, as I cooked and cleaned in our mansion. Look at me, Mom, I'd scream. I'm in a fucking mansion, with a goddamn in-ground swimming pool, dammit! And look here, I have all the beach towels I'll ever need. Not stolen.

Adam grabbed my free hand and forced his thick fingers between mine. He held our mutual fist under his chin, punching himself gently in the face with it.

"Faith DiNapoli," he said, "I'm glad you called. Nobody else is these days."

"I know. I'm not ever supposed to neither."

"Yeah, what else aren't you supposed to do with me?" he asked, grabbing my other hand.

"Well, everything. People say you've gone all crazy, with quitting school, and losing Denise and everything."

"Fuck them, fuck Denise," he said. His mouth found my thumb, he sucked it for a second, then he pulled me closer. "I don't give a shit what people say. Gimme a hug, Faith. You'll always be my friend, right? Tell me you're gonna always be my little friend."

"I will. I promise," I said, me feeling scared saying it.

Adam's skinny torso folded over one of my shoulders, his nails gently scratched down my back. I poked my head out from under his armpit and my eyes found the ceramic crucifix again. I closed them, praying, Please, God, forgive me for being here. But we had a deal and You didn't hold up your end. Somebody else got to my virginity first, in the most unkind way. I will remove that shitty memory with this better one and I am going to love this man because nobody else does. I am going to kiss this man, so please make me kiss him good. I will use my arms and my legs. I am going to have sex with Adam, and if it can't be lovely, make it feel at least a little like love.

I hiccuped and opened my eyes and watched Serena through the kitchen window. She took off her tube top and shorts, flinging them onto the deck with a harsh slap. Scott jumped into the pool, shoving armfuls of water at her. Both of them were laughing and naked.

"Okay. Let's go," Adam said, smacking my back, unfolding himself from me. He didn't grab my hand as I followed behind him out to the deck. Serena didn't seem to mind that we could see her breasts flashing above the surface, the dark "V" of her privates shimmering below the waterline.

Adam put his arm around my back and started to tug me gently toward the pool.

"Let's go, baby girl," he coaxed.

"NOooooo," I whined, as he pulled me by my tube top. "Adam Adam Adam, I can't go naked. I can't go in."

I'm not like Serena, I wanted to yell. I want to be alone with you, I thought.

"Then don't go naked, Faith," he said, shoving me hard into the shallow end of the cold pool. I hit the bottom with my knees. I surfaced with my thumb over my beer and held it up. Everyone cheered my accidental feat, though I was pissed at the tumbling mess Adam had made of me. He walked over to the deep end, whipped off his T-shirt, pulled off his shorts, and dove in. I caught a glimpse of his penis and his tattoos, which for an instant made it seem like he had been wearing still another shirt.

He started gunning like a missile underwater, toward me, his frozen target.

"Faith, he's coming for you," screamed Serena. She was holding on to the side of the pool, taking a sip from the fresh beer Scott had handed to her. Scott was being nice to us now that one of us got naked, I bet, and the other was half-stoned out of her mind.

When Adam broke through the water in front me, I panicked, and at the moment of his first inhale, I threw my shaken beer directly into his face.

"Ow! Fuck!" he gasped. He threw his head back underwater, shaking it fast back and forth. Still underwater, Adam stroked to the side of the pool. He came up, his back to me, his cross tattoo dripping shiny. He rested his face down on the deck, breathing fast and deep.

"Oh, jeez," said Scott, tsk-tsking me. Serena had a hand over her mouth, stifling a giggle.

"Adam!" I yelled, "I'm sorry, I didn't mean—"

"Leave me alone!" he yelled, wiping his face with his hands.

"Want a towel, buddy?" asked Scott.

Adam didn't reply. I swam hard through the water to him, holding up my soggy tube top with one hand, the rescued beer with the other. My blood was racing into my heart. I had never been violent with anyone before. Didn't Adam come get us in the middle of the day, in the middle of nowhere? Didn't he make a party out of nothing but a case of beer and one new friend? Didn't he love being with me because I wasn't a needy bitch like Denise?

"Oh my God, Adam, I am so sorry." I placed a hand on his back. He was heaving. Crying, maybe?

"I said, leave me alone."

I backed away. And before I could turn and get out of the pool, Adam pounced on my back and shoved me down underwater. In my struggle, I could hear muffled laughter coming from Serena and Scott's direction, but I was busy fighting for the surface. Adam batted my head down under every time I'd almost make it up. I got the feeling he was trying to murder me a little.

"Stop," I sputtered, finally forcing my head up between his legs. "Stop it! I mean it, Adam!" I pushed him hard away from me, and caught a handful of his stiff penis, only by accident.

He was laughing, swimming backward away from me.

"You could've killed me, asshole!" I screamed, while fishing for the bobbing beer bottle.

"Yeah," said Serena, "you don't have to fucken kill her."

Adam was calming down. I was calming down, too, from the other side of the shallow end, where I balanced the bottle on the deck, unsure of how to escape the pool with my tube top intact.

Scott said to Serena, "Let's leave these two lovebirds alone."

"We are not lovebirds," I said, never taking my eyes off Adam, who was still smiling over at me. "We are hate birds."

Adam started chirping angrily at me, crazed. He is insane, I thought. Adam's not well in the head. Or maybe it's me who's nuts to be out here with him.

Scott pulled Serena out of the pool. I saw how Adam looked at Serena's naked body before Scott swallowed it inside a giant beach towel, and steered her toward the air-conditioned mansion.

"We'll be upstairs if yous two need anything," Scott yelled, while Serena wordlessly ducked under his arm, into the open patio door. She would have sex with him, for no good reason except that we were there. What to do with Adam? I could call my mother. She'd still be at home. But how to explain this? Besides now that we were alone, there was part of me itching to adjust to this scene, to see how it all played out.

For a minute or so, we remained on opposite sides of the shallow end, both of us bobbing our eyes above the waterline, spitting mouthfuls of the pool at each other. I was counting the years I had known him and thinking about his grown-up naked body and mine. I felt the water was dangerous, and if I fully dunked my head underneath, I'd never resurface again.

After a few seconds, Adam crooked his finger for me to "come here." I shook my head back and forth, saying "no." Boldly, I crooked my finger for him to "come here." I would follow his lead, I thought, because he knows better about what to do.

"Let's meet in the middle," he suggested.

My heart was pounding, my tube top stretched out and falling down around my waist, and my terry-cloth shorts felt like a loose diaper, barely draping my bum. My tiny breasts were floating.

I glided slowly toward Adam, who was already in the middle of the pool. When I reached him, he dove his hands under the water, separated my legs, and threw them around his waist. His arms around my back, he held me up, but mostly I was supported by his hard penis prodding the cheeks of my bum and the underneath part of my thigh. It only very innocently poked the area around where I knew it really wanted to end up.

"Adam, I don't know about this," I whispered.

"Shhh, shhhh. I'll show you. It's cool. Everything's cool, Faith."

Then he kissed me softly like I always wanted to be kissed, minus the smoke and beer on his mouth and breath. He kissed my cheeks and my neck and my shoulder. He bit down on my ear, slightly, which made me clutch him harder. I shut my eyes from the heavy sun, and a God who had never been very watchful.

I weighed nothing in this water.

He looked at me with mild shock, which made his face melt into someone younger and finally recognizable to me. I felt what had shocked him, the very second after it happened. His penis was inside of me, using the pressure you'd use with your thumbs to separate an unripe peach away from the center of its own self. He started pushing me down hard on to it, his forearms on the tops of my hipbones, my body floating against my will, up away from his hard, hard penis. I didn't know what my body needed me to do more, fight the force of the water holding me up, or the force of a man who wanted to bring me down to his level. Adam looked at my face for orders he had no intention of obeying, since I'm sure my eyes were screaming, "You can't do this!"

He moved me up and down slowly, holding my waist tighter to fight the water's natural urge to float me. Our bodies were making the sound of a human-size plunger that was pulling out something stuck deep inside me.

But it hurt. The water wasn't as helpful as water looks like it should be. I thought about the time in science class when I tried to force rubber gloves over my sweaty hands. The ladies at the border had used a fast, medical finger. But this sex was all squeaky friction, like my insides were lined with a skinny, dry balloon and I was giving reverse birth to a rubber baby doll's arm. We were having nothing like the sex I'd seen on soap operas, where the lovers slide into bed, then fold around each other with such ease and joy, making a happy tent out of their white satin sheets.

"Stop, okay? Adam?" I whispered, but he couldn't hear me. His chin was jammed into my collarbone, his ear pressed up against mine, his penis stuck directly up the center of me, so far up, I could feel it behind my belly button, probably picking a fight with one of my lesser organs and winning.

He moved us over to the side of the pool, so my back was smacking rhythmically up against the baby-blue cement wall. Water splashed up between the vacuum of our chests. Then he stopped, though the sore feeling between my legs hadn't, so I couldn't tell if he had pulled himself out of me. He stepped back and looked down. I looked down, too, and watched his hand jerk his penis quickly and skillfully. A tiny, milky jellyfish escaped out of the opening and floated away.

Adam threw his head back, squeezed his eyes shut, and patted at the surface of the water lightly with his free hand.

"Jesus . . . fucking . . . Christ . . . Faith," he said, collapsing toward me, leaning very gently up against my little body.

I didn't know what else to do but wrap my weak arms around his wet neck and stay like that, for as long as it was that he wanted to stay like that with me. Even if it was forever. And even though I hated him a little, I held on to him a lot harder than he held on to me.

"Don't tell anyone," I whispered.

"Amen to that, Faith," he said, without lifting his head from the crook of my neck.

EVERYTHING AFTER THAT, I did like a robot. I crouched behind the barbecue, wrung out my wet clothes, and slapped them back on. I found my garbage bag and threw it over me to hide the way my wet shorts clung to my bum. Adam got himself dressed without drying himself off. It was almost five o'clock. My mother would be at work.

I yelled upstairs for Serena but there was no answer, so Adam drove me home in silence, both of us smoking one cigarette after another.

When he pulled the Gremlin into my driveway, I felt stuck to the seat for a second.

"I'll call you," he said, leaning over and opening my door for me.

"Okay," I murmured, thinking, Is that it? He will call me? And then what?

It hurt to walk. Later, it hurt to eat, to think, then to sleep.

ADAM WAITED A WEEK and a day before he called, and I just waited, remembering that only sluts ever call boys. But during that week, I pined sick for some kind of explanation about what I was supposed to do next. Shouldn't Adam love me more? Shouldn't I love him a lot better too? Why didn't I? If sex was so sacred, why did my body feel like a junkyard?

During those days, the phone rang only once for me. It was Serena, calling to say she had had sex with Scott and passed out, then he took her home after supper. She lied about overtime in the fields that day, which forced her to finally quit. I had told my mother something similar, that I quit detassling because it was too hard, and she said, Well, I can't really argue about that, the first time out's always hard, but good try, Faith, next time maybe you'll find it easier.

That same week, the phone rang three times for my mother. It was Dennis the cop, who had pulled her over the night she drove the battered Comet back from Detroit. Once, when he called, she was home, once she wasn't, and once she only pretended not to be there.

"Why don't you want to talk to him?" I asked, after enviously taking a message.

"Because I don't want to seem too eager. You should never seem too eager, Faith, guys don't like that."

"What else don't guys like?" I asked, casually, hoping to dissect this silence coming from Adam, a man who had taken my virginity but didn't seem to want anything else to do with it.

My mother looked at me, thinking for a second. We were sitting at the dining room table, my face covered in her cold cream to help with the breakouts I was experiencing right after my period started. I didn't mind the cramps or zits that month. Though Adam was careful with his sperm, all the pregnant girls at our school always said that they had been careful too.

"Well, number one, guys don't like it if you're too easy. Or if you smoke," she said, blowing rings. "Umm, they don't like it if you drink," taking a sip, "or if you're loud. Let me see . . . they don't like it if you swear, goddammit," she said, stubbing out her cigarette, giggling.

"Yeah, so, except for being easy, Mom, you do all those things."

"Hey now," she scolded. "Well, anyways, that's why I have to not be easy, with Dennis, because it's my only card."

I did all those things too, but unlike my mother, I had played my last card. Though nothing felt easy about what we did in that pool.

HOPE AND I were the only ones home to meet Dennis the cop. Matt and Charlie had gone to the mall, anywhere, so as not to be around when her date arrived.

"That's normal. Boys get like that when their moms start dating," my mother said. "They'll get over it."

I sat in a daze, on the bathroom vanity, as I watched her apply layers of Arrid Extra Dry and mascara. She even borrowed my Daniel Hechter button-down shirt, and matching belt. But why did I feel jealous? Of course the shirt would stretch perfectly across her much fuller breasts. I knew that would happen when I offered her the shirt, didn't I?

She kept saying into the mirror, "Oh, Faith, are you sure? This looks okay? I don't look like an idiot? You promise? You swear? It's not too small?"

"No, it's fine, you're fine, Mom. You look real great," I said. She did.

My mother asked me to open the door when Dennis arrived. She introduced me as the girl she had told him about, who had had that trouble at the border.

"Yes, heard about that awful business," Dennis said, his big head glancing around our clean living room, using a cop's eye for details. My mother had spent the whole day scrubbing and shining, probably knowing this fact about him.

"Yeah, but I'm all right."

"Good to hear, it's good to hear, yes." He nodded. He seemed nice, but he was using a fake voice, probably reserved for stupid kids getting themselves into stupid trouble, like I had.

My mother said, Bye, I won't be late, don't you stay up too late either, there's fish sticks in the freezer, let Gigi in tonight, I love you, she said, to us, in front of Dennis the cop.

"Us too," we mumbled.

Before Dennis's car could reach the road, before Hope and I could spew icky opinions over him, the phone rang and Hope grabbed it first.

"Hey, Adam, stranger . . ." she said, eyeing me. They chatted for a bit before she handed me the phone, making a face.

"He's not allowed over," she whispered.

"I know that," I hissed, covering the receiver. "Why don't you go polish your boots, loser."

"Hi, Faith, it's Adam."

"Hi," I said, terribly low.

"Listen, um, I saw your mom leave, and I'm heading off for a bit, going to some auctions with my dad. I'm, ahh, leaving tomorrow and I just wanted to say that, uhh, sorry I can't spend more time with you, but I just wanted to say I'm good at keeping secrets and I sure know you are, too."

I paused, then said, "Maybe."

Gigi came by to rub herself against my legs. I grabbed onto her tail, hard, until she fought to break free.

"Listen, you know, it's important. No fooling around when I say it's between you and me, what happened. You know, Faith, it was great, and everything, but in a way, it shouldn't've really happened. We could get in a lot of trouble. Fuck, I could get in a lot of trouble. So I'm just hoping we're friends for life."

"Yup. Friends for life," I mimicked.

Hope was looking at me, rolling her eyes.

"So, bye, Faith. We'll see each other around."

"Bye."

I waited for him to hang up first.

I replaced the receiver on the holder mounted to the small wall that divided these four clean rooms; the living room, dining room, kitchen, and bathroom. Hope walked by me and disappeared down the hall that led to the two messy bedrooms. There was no place for me to go, so I slid down the little wall with my bare knees up and thought about the summer before, when my dad had taken us to the animal farm, where I had learned this sudden cruelty, this swift-hammer-to-the-head feeling, was something only visited upon those that didn't see it coming.

LATER THAT NIGHT, I heard Dennis's car pull up. I listened as he shut the engine off. Though I tried my best, the hardest ever, to stay awake, I ended up falling back to sleep before I ever heard the car door open, or the front door slam shut.

I found my mother in the morning, raking the garden, talking to Trelly. Trelly had probably slept over. Since Matt had begun to make more money at Ford's than my mother did at the diner, he was allowed to act much older than seventeen.

Trelly was wearing one of Matt's baseball hats, and smoking.

"Hey. How was your date?" I yelled from the patio.

My mother turned around and made a visor with her hand. I felt my heart crack at the remembrance of Dad doing that.

"It was nice," she said. Trelly punched her in the arm, teasingly. My mother slapped at her hand for real, which made Trelly tiptoe a few feet away.

Matt came around the side of the house with a bushel basket of dirt. Without looking at my mother, he dumped the dirt where her hand was pointing, turned, and went back for more. That was all I wanted to know about the date in front of Matt.

Chapter Eleven

For the next few weeks, then months, after what had happened in the pool, I began to feel like one of those limp bunnies that Uncle Triasi shook out of the burlap bag. I became soft and flexible in the arms of the boys I'd meet at the parties I'd drink at. I had no visible signs of abuse on the outside, but inside I was a mash of barely functioning bones and organs. I didn't blame Adam, my mother, or anyone. I climbed inside that dark sack willingly, my beating heart an easy target for boys to find, hammer, and stop. And each time, I never really saw it coming.

So it was kind of appropriate that my plaid skirt was bunched up around my waist, and my underwear was down around my ankles, when I first read the words "Faith DiNapoli is a slut" on the wall of the stall I was peeing in. I was in the girl's bathroom, the smaller one, by the cafeteria. I hadn't noticed the graffiti right away, because I wasn't in there looking for information about myself. I was just looking for toilet paper. The words weren't large, thankfully, and the person had used light blue eyeliner, so I was able to easily spit-wash it off with a wet wad of grainy paper towels. But I wasn't sure how long it had been up there. Wasn't sure who would write something like that. Wasn't sure whether it was true or not.

I left the stall and found Serena, sitting alone, eating her sandwich, and looking into a book that she probably wasn't reading.

"You took long enough," she said.

"I found something," I whispered, not looking around, in case whoever wrote it was watching me in the lunch crowd.

"What did you find?"

I told her. I choked on the "slut" part but kept my steady eyes on Serena. In the bathroom, I had unrolled my skirt at the waist, bringing it back down to knee-length. I had removed my hoop earrings, too. The less attention on myself, right now, the better, I thought.

"Oh, jeez, Faith," she said, biting down on her sandwich and chewing slowly.

I felt how vulnerable I was to an abandonment. Serena had become my only friend, happily, but unintentionally so. If she walked away from me because I was a slut, I'd have no friends, and a harder time making any new ones. There was Nicole, but she had transferred to the French high school. Hope—she didn't like me all that much anymore.

I thought, for one unholy second, that maybe Serena had written it. Maybe Serena had put that up there to force me into her kind of club, a club I didn't fully belong in, as I hadn't had sex in the real way, since that day with Adam, in the pool. I had done a number of other things, with several boys, who had probably counted what we did as a kind of sex. But still, I felt undeserving of this baby-blue title.

"Who would write this?" I asked, my voice quavering.

"I honestly, honestly don't know. I really don't," she said.

Her hand was on mine, and by the way she kept chewing, and not taking her eyes off me, I could tell it was not Serena who had written it. She wasn't mean enough for this. I could also tell she didn't think being called a slut was all that big a deal.

I wiped my mouth with the back of my hand. I wasn't wearing lipstick, but it felt like there was something on them, like spit, or bile, or the remnants of a rough, scummy kiss.

"I feel sick," I said, grabbing my books and standing up. "I'm going outside. I don't want to sit in here. Come with me."

Serena followed. We went over by a tree near the smoking area and lit two cigarettes.

"Oh, Faith. Don't feel bad," Serena soothed. "It's not true. You know it and I know it. So fuck them."

She motioned over to the crowd by the dugout, the crowd of people whose hair shone whiter in the sun, who all suddenly seemed to be talking only about Faith DiNapoli and what a slut she was.

I noticed Joey St. Pierre smoking and motioning wildly about something, to his girlfriend, Lea Marks. Maybe she wrote it because maybe he was talking about me, and what a giant slut I had been over Christmas break. Maybe Joey was telling her our one kiss was my fault, not his. Joey was in grade twelve and not particularly cute, but he was the best lunch DJ, and I liked his hair. A few months earlier, I had been coming out of a party, weaving drunk, but not wasted or anything. Joey was on his way in. He grabbed my coat arm and said, Hey, Faith, where are you going? I said, Leaving. Too bad, he said, I was hoping to talk to you. Serena said go ahead, talk to Faith, as she made her way toward Joey's friend Tony Levesque, who was coming out of the dark behind us. I saw Serena stop Tony and kiss him. Joey looked at them, then at me. I shrugged and laughed. He put his arm around my neck and dipped me. I said, Go ahead, if you want, copying Serena. He kissed my mouth. Then I jerked away from Joey and walked toward Tony Levesque, who Serena had abandoned. Tony said, Hey, where you going so fast, Faith? Nowhere, kiss me, I said. So he kissed me, too. Serena was honking in the Comet because we had another party to go to.

As we drove away, they both screamed, Where are yous two going? Nowhere! we screamed back.

Okay, then, March break, I slept out at the bush with Serena and Nicole, and her friend Elly, from the French high school. We were inspired after reading *Roughing It in the Bush* in English class. It was boring, but the things the characters did were cool, so we thought, Let's try it since we can't afford to go to Florida like the rich girls.

We were supposed to camp for three days, but we barely lasted one night, even with the Coleman heaters and piles of wood. We told a few guys where we'd be, guys each of us liked. I chose to tell Andrew Fortin, who I'd had a crush on since the day he had worn red-and-white-striped socks to school, as a joke, for the whole day. He tucked his uniform pants into them pretending he didn't know what you were talking about when you'd pointed them out. It was funny. When I told Andrew about our experiment in the bush, he said, Sounds fun, I'll try to make it. But he didn't.

Serena's guy, who lived in Ridgetown, brought his friend Davey Laurier, a popular forward on their Junior "C" hockey team. At first Davey didn't pay any attention to me, until people paired off, so we went walking down the path that led to the river. He grabbed me from behind and I put my feet on top of his shoes and he walked me like a doll for many steps. We were laughing drunk, so I didn't mind his hand on my breast or the other one cupping me hard underneath. He started shoving his face into the back of my head, leaning me forward. When I tried to turn my body around to let him kiss me, he wouldn't let me do that. No, he said, like this, he said, and he knocked my knees in with his, bringing me down onto mine. His body covered my back, but my back was arching him off me. I was struggling to face his face. He just kept saying, No, let's do it like this. But I didn't know what it was that he wanted me to do, not facing him, or kissing him, like that. So I opened his arms from around my waist and said, I don't know what it is you want me to do, not facing you like this. So he said, Forget it, Fran. I said, My name's Faith, *Danny.* And he said, Right, *Faith.* My name's *Davey,* he said. I know, I said. Then he said, Forget it, let's go back. I said, Okay, fine by me.

We ended up back in the tent, lying on either side of Serena and her guy, trying hard not to listen to the sounds they were trying hard not to make.

Then there was Thom Faubert, at the hockey dance. We kissed behind the Zamboni. And Lenny Pellisier, who worked at the store, but I only ever showed him my boobs for cigarettes. And I wasn't the only girl who did that. I was just the last to find out it was an option for payment. It only happened once, since Lenny said they weren't worth more than licorice, or a bag of Fritos.

And then, Luke Trottier. A friend of Matt's from Ford's. I had seen him every once in a while, pulling up our driveway. I hadn't noticed him especially, until this one night I saw his horrible, horrible scar. It started at the outside of his right eye and went up, like a thick "C," to the middle of his forehead. Someone had hit him over the head with a beer bottle, at the horse track. It was an accident. This guy was mad about losing a bet, so Luke didn't sue him or anything. He had also lost a tooth, and had a fake one that he moved in and out of its slot, absently, while concentrating on his cards. We were playing Hearts at the dining room table. It was me, Luke, and Charlie. Hope was at cadets. Mom was at work. Matt and Trelly were in the basement with the music loud. They had yelled, Luke, you're early, we'll be up in a while, relax, have a beer.

Charlie left to go uptown to do his laundry. I made him take two of my white uniform shirts and two of my black jerseys, which I said he could wear as a trade-off for washing them.

Luke rolled a joint and asked me about school. Siphoning off some of my mom's vodka, and using flat ginger ale as a mix, I told him I was doing okay, hated gym and my trig teacher, but what are you going to do? He drank his vodka straight. I asked, How are you doing, Luke, as I inhaled, swallowed, and leaned back with my arms crossed, feeling grown up from the cocktail and alive from the pot.

He said, I'm doing really bad.

His brother had leukemia, and Luke had to work overtime in order to pay for the hospital bed that they had just set up in the living room. They wanted him to die at home. He said it was awful. I didn't know any of this. Matt never told me any of this.

Luke asked me if I could imagine ever wiping Matt or Charlie's ass, as that is what he did some nights when he stopped by to do what he could to help. I said, No way could I imagine that, and he said, You'd be surprised at yourself, the things you can do when you love someone. He said the saddest part was his brother was only thirteen, had never even had sex yet, and was going to die without having it, and because of that, Luke was going to have all the sex he could get his hands on. He said he felt like he was having sex for his brother.

I got high listening to the story, so my eyes started to water for Luke and his brother. I placed my arm on Luke's forearm and let one of my fingers caress it, back and forth like a grown-up would. Luke placed his hand over my hand and tugged slightly at my sleeve, laughing a little.

Five minutes, we stayed like that.

He said, Thank you, thank you, for being so sweet, so special. Wow, Faith, is it ever good to confess how I've been feeling to someone like you, thank you.

For some reason I was grateful for his gratefulness. So it's no surprise that I was the one that got out of my chair, and I was the one that went up to him and put my thigh over his and straddled his lap, facing him. I was the one who took off his baseball cap and placed it behind me on the table.

He whispered with a laugh, What are you doing to me, little girl? And I shrugged because I didn't know. I was happily giving him comfort, and it didn't feel totally sexual, what I was doing, until he started kneading my bum softly, his head resting back on the chair. He was looking down his nose at me, glassy-eyed and calm. He began grinding me on top of him saying, Jesus, this is so sweet, Faith. Can we go somewhere? he asked. Faith, take me to your room. Come on. We tiptoed down the hall. I shoved the clothes off the bottom bunk, placed my drink of vodka and flat ginger ale down on the floor, turned, and sat on my bed. He stood in front of me and took off his pants, and asked me to take off his underwear for him, and I did. His penis flung out and dropped into my hand, which was cold from the drink I carried in with me.

His hands began helping my hands help him. Maybe he wanted me, but I felt more so that he needed me, which was a better way for a boy to get into my pants, back then.

When I got my hand down to a perfect rhythm, he told me to put my mouth on it, which I did. I had to make myself resist the urge to bite it, not because I was mad or scared, but because it was the first thing I had ever put inside my mouth that wasn't food.

At first he moved my head with his hands. Then he stopped, and left his fingers trailing through my hair, and under my chin, until he was done, and came into my mouth, deep into the back of my throat, before I even saw it coming.

I fished around for my drink, to wash it permanently down, and he fell on his knees before me. He prayed into them, saying fuck, that was fucken great.

Now take off your pants, Faith, now, he said. I took off my pants and stood in front of him while he slid off my underwear. I fell back down on the bunk and he kissed my knees and my thighs, and he said, Anyone ever done this to you, Faith? I said, No. You want me to do this to you, Faith? I nodded, Yes. I do. And he found me with his mouth and it took all of ten seconds for his tongue to bring me somewhere I had never been before, and I screamed by accident, because I was terrified, and glorified, at the same time.

"Wow, that was fast," he laughed, wiping the wet of me off his mouth.

"Jeez, sorry," I whispered, trembling. What was fast? I wasn't sure I was done, or knew how to finish what he had started. What we did to each other felt worshipful, both taking turns on our knees. I felt I had healed him, simply by giving over bits of my body. It was Communion again, only earthbound and far more fun.

The music shut off downstairs. We jumped off the bunk, threw our clothes on, and ran out to the dining room, flopping into the chairs, each of us smelling an awful lot like the other one. My sticky fingers gathered up the cards and I dealt us both a sloppy hand.

Trelly came upstairs first.

"Well, we're ready to go, Luke," she announced, picking at her sweater.

"I bet you are," said Luke, winking at me. I think I started to feel as though it might be possible to love this Luke, despite his tooth and scar and dying brother, or maybe because of them.

"Luke, let's go, man," said Matt, coming out from behind Trelly. "Sorry for the wait, but it takes Trel so looooong to look this ugly."

Trelly smacked him hard on the arm.

I wanted to go with them, and was kind of hoping Luke would ask me.

"Where are yous going tonight?" I asked Matt, pretending I didn't care.

"Well, it depends." Matt was addressing Luke. "Luke, do we have to pick up Stacey at work, or is she just meeting us at the Keg."

"I'll call her and see when she's off shift. Excuse me, Faith," mumbled Luke, dropping his cards without looking at me. He got up from the chair, walked over to the kitchen, picked up the phone, and dialed a number by heart.

I mouthed to Trelly, "Who's Stacey?"

"Luke's wife," she whispered. "It's their one-year anniversary tonight, so we're gonna go all *out.* Steak and lobster at the Keg. Whoo-hooo!"

I was in the bathroom when they left, sitting on the vanity, watching myself smoke the rest of the joint. This is what a bad girl looks like, I thought. You have to have broken every single Commandment to get this smeared, wary expression. And now that I had busted those tablets, I wasn't sure what there was left to do with my life, let alone with the rest of my summer.

Luke yelled, "Bye, Faith, thanks for the game!"

I said nothing back. I was afraid blood would bubble out of my mouth after I felt the whack of that familiar hammer to the head. My sadness fought for the surface, but I shoved it down by cleaning. I hid our empty beer bottles out back, near the brush. I washed out our cups, after pouring the remainder into one plastic glass, with ice. I emptied the ashtrays, even Matt's and Trelly's from downstairs. I put the cards away, wiped the table, and refolded the clothes I had thrown off my bed. I scrubbed my face and put on my pajamas.

I sat at the dining room table, teasing Gigi with a line of dental floss. If someone had been looking at me through the patio window right then, they might have said, "Now, here's a nice, clean, young woman playing with her kitty cat, waiting for her mom to come home from work."

But if that same person had seen me an hour earlier, straddling married Luke, kissing his married scar, and grinding away on his married lap, they would've said, "On the other hand, what you're looking at here, ladies and gentlemen, is nothing but a filthy little slut, who has broken every single Commandment."

I SAT NEXT TO CHARLIE on the bus ride home from my first day of being labeled a slut. I didn't want to settle into an empty seat first. I didn't want to give anyone the opportunity to avoid sitting next to me, the slut. Although there were countless times I'd watch my little brother Charlie sit alone, today I was happy to be associated with his spiked hair and six earrings, hoping they'd obscure the blue neon "slut" sign that seemed to be flashing over my head.

"Hey, Charl."

"Hey."

"How was your day?"

"Total crap. Yours?"

"Same."

Hope wasn't on the bus. She had gone to a friend's house after school, and she told me to tell Mom she was going straight to cadets from there. Matt had quit, three weeks into grade twelve.

"Charlie, can I ask you something?" I whispered.

"Yeah."

"Do you ever hear anything about me?"

"Like what?"

"I don't know, opinions, or rumors, or anything?"

"No, why?"

"Nothing."

"Faith, don't worry about stuff like that. You can't worry what other people think of you."

He was almost fifteen and wiser than I was.

"Do you hear anything about me?" he asked.

I had. I heard people call him a "faggot" and a "freak" behind his back.

"Nope."

"See? Who cares. Everyone's an asshole at that school anyways. Me and Cheryl can't wait to get the fuck out."

"Hey, Charlie, are you and Cheryl boyfriend and girlfriend?"

"Yeah, doy, what do you think?"

"Nothing, I was just asking."

I guess it was just us two now, me, the slut, and my fag brother. We never really asked Charlie outright if he was gay, because it didn't really seem to matter to my mom. So why would it wouldn't matter to us? But I just couldn't picture my mom beaming down at me with anything resembling pride if she saw what had been written about her oldest beloved daughter on the bathroom wall.

When we got home, my mom was finishing spicing a big pot of something on the stove. My mother sometimes worried we weren't getting enough nourishment, but she long ago gave up the idea of working nine to five. Money was better at night, she liked having days to herself, and we were old enough to be left alone. Besides, Dad had cut back on the child support when Matt started at Ford's full-time. It made sense to my mother, but she was trying to save up money for a house.

She wasn't counting on Dennis to help. After a few dates, he called once more when she was home, but I was told to take a message. In her diary she described him as *nice, but a little dull, and I'm sure he hates that I work at the diner, among other things about me. He asked me why do you have to be so friendly to guys there? Like I was some kind of slut for working as a waitress. I told him that's how I make my tips for crying out loud. Three dates and he thinks he owns me. Lin says that's typical man behavior that I should just ignore. Easy for her to say, her husband owns the restaurant she works in.*

One time, my mom told me she waited on Bob Seger, and some of the Silver Bullet Band. She said he owned a cottage in Stoney Point, just west of Belle River, and they gave her a fifty-dollar tip. American. I was in awe and wondered what she had done to earn it. I told both Serena and Nicole on the phone that night. My mother picked up the extension by accident and must have heard me vow to find his place that summer, to try to party with Bob Seger and his band, in order to get famous. Later, when I casually entered the living room, day-dreaming of a life on the road as Bob Seger's special girlfriend, my mother put her finger up in front of my face. She told me she had heard us, and she'd kick my ass but good if I so much as hummed one of their "goddamn tunes" around the house.

"You hear?"

"We're just kidding, Mom, jeez!"

"I mean it, Faith, no kidding. If I ever catch you catting around, I'll ground your ass until we arrange a goddamn marriage for you! I don't want any trouble from either one of yous girls."

Hope sometimes got sucked into the vortex of her threats against me, just for sitting there.

"What are you looking at me for, Mom?" Hope whined. "I don't even like Bob Seger!"

"Why do you have to be so goddamn nosy?" I yelled.

Smack on the arm, not too hard.

"Watch your mouth. You four are all lucky I'm nosy. I'm probably not nosy enough."

It's true. She knew nothing important about us. We were spreading out into secret lives. There were times I would stumble on my brothers or my sister doing something particular to their own life, Hope shining her boots, Charlie tracing out the cover from a Depeche Mode record, Matt sweeping cigarette butts off his bedroom floor, and think, Who are you? Where did you grow up? How come you enjoy this music or that TV show, and I don't, and we are from the same folks? What are you doing to your hair? Didn't we have the same past? Then how come you are so different?

Hope, especially. She had grown more serious and somber as I became more scattered and stressed. She didn't waste her time worrying about the things that concerned me, like boys and outfits, parties and money. She was cool, but not in a popular way. She was cool in temperament. She had cultivated a kind of delayed reaction to life, that, if you didn't know her, would make you think she was slow. At school, she had fewer friends than even I did. And more often than not, I'd find her in the smoking area, talking to one or two people that no one else seemed to much bother with. The friends she had, the ones she'd speak to on the phone, were people I had never met. They were fellow cadets who lived in Windsor, and they hardly ever came out to these parts of the county, unless Hope desperately needed a ride into the city and had convinced someone kind enough to oblige her. Sometimes, when I'd offer to drop her off at the HMCS *Hunter* building, on Ouellette, I'd only catch a quick glimpse of her cadet friends before they'd stub out their cigarettes and fall in behind Hope, for head counts.

I asked her once why she never bothered introducing me, and she said, "Why would I? You just laugh at us anyways."

I did, that's for sure. But how could I help it? Look at you in your little outfit, I'd say, on the way into Windsor. Boots shiny enough? Ooop, you got something on your shirt. Made you look!

But the only reason I teased her was that I knew for a fact she didn't really care what I thought, and she knew I was being more funny than cruel. None of us had the ability to be deliberately mean. We'd wail and lash out at each other, but we'd pull back our insults long before they'd ever stick for life. We were all a little different than the people around us, in more ways, and for more reasons, than even we were aware of back then. That knowledge didn't ensure closeness, but it was great insurance against us ever being too far away from each other.

"Raising teenagers is like trying to train house cats," my mother once told Auntie Linda, to cheer her up for not getting pregnant easily. "I tell them what to do, they listen, then they wander off and do what the hell they want anyways. The cat listens to me more than these four. They're my kids and sometimes I don't like them at all. You're lucky."

There were times my mother had an idea, something she thought she'd like us to do all together, but it became harder and harder for her to just ask outright. Especially as each of us developed a special type of personality, which demanded she ask four different ways for the exact same thing.

The time she wanted us to go to Sears Portrait Studio for a photo, me, she asked outright. I said yes, easily, to many things and people. Hope she begged, Charlie she bribed, and Matty she ordered, switching from simple chauffeur to frantic shepherd, herding sleepy teenagers, with her words and hands, into the idling Comet. Come on, come on, let's go!

I still have a copy of that picture. In it, my left hand is on Charlie's shoulder, he's sitting in the middle, at fifteen. Matt's eighteen, standing next to me. I'm almost seventeen. Matt's hand is on my shoulder. Hope's slightly in front of Matt. Her hand is on Charlie's other shoulder. She'd just turned sixteen.

She yelled, "Kids! Like this, be happy. Show your teeth. Charlie, smile, dammit. *Charlie!* Smile or I'll kill you!"

My mom framed a giant copy and hung it on the living room wall, next to Matt's hockey pictures, Charlie's soccer pictures, and me and Hope's curtsy shots from long-ago dance recitals. She sent a smaller framed copy to my dad, with a note that read, "Here are your four children, Joe, all grown. In case you have forgotten, that is Faith, Matt, and Hope. Charlie in the middle. Display prominently."

Chapter Twelve

Our landlord, Mr. Meloche, was talking fancy about Adam to my mother. When he talked fancy, it made my mother talk fancy, too.

Mr. Meloche said, "Well, it seems Adam's mother erupted when she saw his tattoos! They pollute his entire body! And he never attended one class the last semester, either. He frittered away his tuition on those blasphemous tattoos! Religious ones! Imagine that."

"No, my Lord, I just cannot," my mom replied, hand over her heart, glancing over at me.

"No, I cannot, either," I said, robotically.

Mr. Meloche said that Adam's parents had no choice but to take him in, because his dad needed help with the fields. But Adam's mom had just called Mr. Meloche to see if he had any other rental property, in case Adam wanted to move out on his own. He told Mrs. Lauzon nothing was available right now, though he'd certainly let her know if anything came open. Mr. Meloche told my mother that even if he had anything available, he'd not rent to "the likes of Adam."

"He's a bad element, I believe," said Mr. Meloche, somberly. "Perhaps he fell in with a bad lot at the university and they spoiled his character."

"Perhaps. Well, alls I know is I don't want his element around our place, neither," said my mom.

I almost laughed out loud.

She added, "I don't want him around here displaying his religious tattoos, because I would fear, the next thing you know, Matt's gonna want one. I just don't trust him anymore, as I once did."

"I don't blame you, Nancy," said Mr. Meloche, "not one bit. When he's not with his father, I see him drinking heavily at the tavern. He is no longer in my employment. Gosh, I see him parked at the tavern, some days, for all the livelong day."

My mom shook her head. Imagine drinking all the livelong day away. I pictured her and Auntie Linda pouring out big glasses of wine from the box in the fridge and shaking their heads at Adam. Tsk-tsk.

Mr. Meloche's funeral home was right across the street from the tavern. He had stopped in at the diner to inform my mother that he was entering our house, his property. My mother let him store his special blend of embalming fluid in our basement cellar in exchange for a cut in the rent.

"And by the way, the lawn looks stupendous. Truly. You have a bunch of really wonderful children! They do a far superior job than even Adam did."

I expected her to spit her coffee at him. True that Sunday I had helped with the trim, and Hope drove uptown for more gasoline. But Matt slept in and Charlie went out, saying goodbye to Cheryl, in town, who was spending the summer in the Soo, with relatives.

My mother had mowed most of it, pushing with the strength of ten martyrs.

"Yup," she nodded, "they're not such bad kids." She made a face at me, while I was stuffing mine with mashed potatoes and gravy.

That day, I went to the diner to talk to my mother's boss, Angie. They were looking for part-time help. And though I cringed at the idea of working with my mother, I cringed harder at the idea of detassling corn the next summer, especially without Serena there to make it fun. Her folks kept her closer to home and put her to work at the clinic bathing dogs and changing cat litter.

* * *

WAITRESSING WAS HARD FOR ME, because I was missing the thing that makes people want do things for others without expecting anything back. I hated that part of the Bible. Always did. And I couldn't fathom why a customer would ask me to hand them an ashtray when there was a clean stack *right there!* Two feet away. Not that I was mean or lazy, I always obliged, kindly and quickly, then later, in the bathroom, I made faces to myself about them.

Me, scrunching my nose, imitating Mrs. Lebeouf: "Oooh, take dis hegg salad sandwich back, Fate, it's got too much salt in it."

Me, answering back, in my dreams: "Why don't you just take that sandwich and shove it right up your ass, ma'am!"

Me, for real: "Gee, sorry, Mrs. Lebeouf. I'll tell Angie. Want me to get you something else?"

My mother trained me for two weeks, using a kind of pride that made me queasy.

"Faith, I always get to the table within the first two minutes."

"Faith, don't forget to wash down the menus with vinegar and water, every night, after every shift."

"Wash your hands after you pee."

"Anticipate their needs. Like if they order French fries, put ketchup on the table, right away. Before the fries are ready."

It was as though she was using the training session as a substitute parenting seminar. She found it easier to tell me what to do if someone else was paying me to listen. I could have been a better waitress, but when she was around, I acted slightly retarded, just to make her anxious.

I'd drop a glass and my mother would wince, look at Angie, and say, "She's learning."

I found I stalled with the ketchup, and "totally forgot" that they had asked for separate checks. All for no real reason except I had started to feel comfortable about being a disappointment to my mother, so it mattered less and less that I might be disappointing others.

There was nothing wrong with people paying me to bring them a meal that they didn't feel like cooking themselves. It was the other stuff that bugged me. Hanging their coats for them. Cleaning up vomit in the bathroom. Splitting a meal into two plates for the kids, because they're small and can't eat the whole thing, but most likely it's because the parents couldn't afford two burgers, as their welfare check hadn't arrived. That's the kind of information my mother gathered for me and sometimes shared with the cooks back in the kitchen.

"Table ten," she said one day, inhaling on a cigarette.

I leaned out of the kitchen doorway into the dining area.

"No, *don't* look! Jesus, Faith! Anyway. Table ten. Her name's Terese Trembley. Bonnie Trembley's niece, in from Quebec for the summer."

Apparently she had been convicted of credit card fraud. She was too young to go to jail, so she was put under some kind of house arrest. Her dad beat the shit out of her. The whole town knew about her crime, so they thought she deserved it. I couldn't imagine my dad hitting anything. Sure my mother slapped me. Not so much anymore. And I had had my share of being chased around the house with an orange Hot Wheel track. But a downright, slow-motion beating? Couldn't imagine it. Terese became "Number One Fascinating Person to Try Not to Stare At."

"Mom, that's gossip," I said, lording her own words over her head.

"It's not. It's information. That's different."

My mom got the best information, because she was on the night shift, so people drank and talked a lot more. I worked weekend days. It was slower and easier for a beginner. Also we served less alcohol, and since I wasn't eighteen, I wasn't really allowed to serve any at all, really. But Angie barely abided by that rule.

"Too many people drink 'ere during the day, and besides when da guys got hoff shift, and stop in for beer, 'oo are we to say no?" she reasoned.

I loved serving beer, loved mixing drinks more. I always dropped that little bit of extra booze into them. I was known for making them strong. I was also known to hardly ever ask for ID, and developed a bit of a powerful position in town. I didn't serve little, little kids. But eighteen-year-olds were as good as nineteen in my book.

I actually started to look forward to the hour or so that my shift would overlap with my mom's. She'd arrive and start taking new tables as my late lunch crowd stumbled out, slightly drunk, shielding their eyes from the late-afternoon sun.

She'd ask me, How was lunch? Busy? Make good tips? If I made bad ones, she'd consider it an omen for her evening.

"Damn, means my tips'll probably suck, too."

"Maybe not. I think it just means I'm bad at my job."

"No, you're not. You're getting better every day. Angie says so."

I wasn't really. Because I wasn't trying all that hard. I think I was afraid of being good at something I hated doing, because it might mean I'd be doing it for the rest of my life. Just like my mother. She hated her job so much she wore herself out from hating it, to the point where she no longer hated it anymore, she just did it.

"This is what I do," she'd say. "It's just a fact and, oh well, I try to make the best of it."

My mother once told me that people who do the same stupid things over and over again do it because they simply know how to. They get good at it. It's not that these people want to screw up, it's just that screwing things up gets to feel familiar to them. And if people get good at even bad things, they'll repeat themselves, because it's something they do really well.

"Is that why there's sluts and murderers and thieves and drunks?" I had asked, before I was a slut of any kind, and before my mother's drinking turned daily.

"Well, remember drunks are alcoholics and alcoholism is a disease," she said, pouring her beer into a coffee mug. "But pretty much 'yes' to the rest."

That wasn't going to be me.

Some nights, after I'd get off my shift, I'd stick around and eat something for free and watch my mother. I remember thinking, It's weird when you know someone who's out in the public eye. Actresses and politicians probably have family members who stand on the sidelines thinking to themselves, "What a faker Dad's being!" "Look how Mom's pretending to be happy when she's not." That's what I felt watching my mom skip around the dining hall, topping off coffees and messing little kids' hair. She flirted too, not in an overtly slutty way, but she was nicer to men than women, so it was no wonder she didn't have all that many female friends in town.

But she looked like a different person to me, a person not fully mine, but not fully her own person either.

I wondered how I must look to her, her daughter, having regular customers, who weren't too perverted. Her daughter having duties and conversations and exchanging numbers with people. Her daughter also flirting with men and boys. She only mentioned me once in her diary, saying, *"Faith's working with me now. I like the company, and frankly it's good for her to know how hard I work."*

I used to play this game with myself. I used to pretend I wasn't my mother's daughter, and I'd ask myself what I really thought of her, from an outside point of view. Reading her diary was an unfair advantage in knowing about this "waitress called Nancy."

My mother had talents, like making people laugh easily. But sometimes her jokes were at the expense of others. I think she was attractive, for thirty-seven, but not in an overly feminine way. She wore pants and T-shirts, but a cloud of Moonwind perfume hovered around her. She touched up her lipstick four or five times a night. She was friendly, especially if she sensed a big tip lodged in a customer's pocket. When it got really busy, she sometimes looked like she could fly off the handle at any moment, from the way she had of never sitting still, always seeming ready to pounce. This quality was formidable when she was holding hot coffee. She loved when Matt, Hope, and Charlie stopped in. She'd run in the back like celebrities had arrived, saying, "Oh, Faith, Hope's in, how about you go get her order," as though I'd be as thrilled as she was to feed her kids. She'd sometimes look over their shoulder at their homework, though rarely offering suggestions on this or that problem, especially if it was math.

Would I be friends with her? Probably. Maybe not best friends but I would hang around my mother, see a movie with her, go for a coffee, confide some lesser secrets, if I wasn't her daughter.

Waitressing was far better than detassling, even though it was more difficult to daydream. You need your brain for storing orders on how a person wants his goddamn eggs.

Then there was a lovely lull between three and five o'clock, when the sun sank lower and shone bright right through the big front windows facing west. It was the time when the lunch drinkers either paid up and left, or had "one more." For the "one mores," I'd keep their tab open and pass it on to my mother. They were not going home anytime soon.

It was during those hours that I'd get the restaurant ready for the supper crowd, get it ready for my mother, and do all my thinking. I'd refill the ketchup and think about being an actress.

I'd give the bathroom a quick wipe down, and think about Adam falling apart. I used to want to be his wife, now I didn't even like being his neighbor. I was positive I was called a slut because of Adam. He started me down that littered road, and I vowed to turn back and find that fork again. It was not too late to choose the other path.

I'd wash glasses by hand and think about my mother's unhappiness.

I'd bleach the countertop and wonder what was to become of us out here.

If I was bored I'd smoke out the window, the one over the kitchen sink. It offered a great view of the other half of town. I could see the funeral home, but not the tavern, as it was on the same side of the street as the 2–4. But I could see the corner store. I could watch half the town's comings and goings without having to stare out the front window the way my mother did, craning and peering, absently wiping a table, giving herself away as wanting or waiting for something or someone.

Once, I watched Adam run across the street, from the tavern, into the store, probably to buy cigarettes. He had a plaid jacket tied around his waist. He was wearing a white undershirt. He looked skinnier. His hair was longer. He had sunglasses on. When he exited the store, he removed the plastic wrapping from the cigarette pack and released it like so much onion skin, into the wind. He stood in the middle of the road while trying to light one. Flick, flick, flick. His whole body was saying, "Dammit, light!" He gave up, turned and ran back to the store, probably to grab matches. He reached the middle of the street, where he, again, stopped and lit a cigarette.

The soy had been planted, so all that was left for him to do was weed and wait. And drink. And so that's what he did.

It was July, noon.

He was barefoot.

While I sulked and served, my mother had a date with a sports fisherman, a guy from Michigan, who used to stop in at the diner on his way back from Lake Erie. She switched shifts with me on that slow Saturday. I came in at five and found her applying makeup in the bathroom, completely ignoring her customers.

"Mom, people are asking for you."

"Oh. Faith. Do me a favor. Top off the Derosiers' coffee and give them their bill? They're my last customers and I want to get off now and have a drink to calm down my nerves."

I obliged, with a huff.

My mother sat down at the counter I was now bleaching. She had poured herself a beer.

I lifted up her glass, wiped, and plopped it down.

"I noticed you didn't restock condiments," I said.

My mother paused from lighting her cigarette. "Oh gee. That's right. I'm sorry. I'm not used to the day shift."

She lit her cigarette and made a "sorry" face, she shrugged a "sorry" shrug. She looked nice. I didn't tell her.

"No, I guess you're not used to days," I scolded. "I guess you're used to me doing it all day. Also, I saw the bathroom's a mess."

"Oh, yeah. Sorry, Faith. I forgot."

"Also you didn't take out the lunch garbage," I said.

"Oh, is it today they pick up?"

"Yeah! And you didn't make up the coleslaw."

"Faith!"

"Mom!" I hissed.

"Faith! Sorry! Give me a break," she hissed back.

"I'm just saying. Now I gotta do all that, and waitress. You know, it's a lot, Mom."

"I'm sure you'll live," she said, almost talking to me like we were home. But she caught something in her voice and sent it back down, with a gulp of beer. "Faith, I'm sorry, truly, I am. I got away from myself today. But I'm all dressed now and he's going to be here any minute, otherwise I would go and take out the garbage."

"I'll do it. But why's he have to pick you up here?" I asked.

"Because I don't want him knowing where I live when I don't know much about him. He's an American. At least with Dennis, he was a cop from around here."

"Doesn't this guy have to drop you off?"

"No. I'm going to get him to drop me off here, and I'll go home with you."

This situation felt so weird, my waitressing shift bracketing the parameters of her date with a guy. My mom felt a little embarrassed about it too, I could tell. Though she seemed more excited to be going out with the sports fisherman than she did with Dennis the cop.

Things should have been the other way around. I should be the one going out on a date. Not my old mother. I should be the one carefully reapplying lipstick in the rusty washroom mirror. I should be anxiously adjusting my blouse, and twisting my rings around on my fingers, now tapping the bleached countertop. I should be enjoying a nerve-calming beer, this dusky Saturday afternoon. I should be on the other side of the counter waiting for a guy, who my mother would kindly greet, size up, and bless.

Matt pulled up to the diner in his new Mustang. He enjoyed a discount, working at Ford's, so he got himself a blue one with all the trimmings—a two-door coupe, with sunroof and air-conditioning. Trelly got out and leaned her seat forward, letting Charlie and Hope out of the back.

"Oh, jeez," whistled my mom, "I guess he's going to meet the whole family."

"I guess."

Charlie and Hope came for dinner. I already started to write up their orders. Charlie, shepherd's pie, with fries on the side. Hope, macaroni and cheese, tomato slices instead of coleslaw, but only if the tomatoes were ripe.

Trelly said she and Matt were only staying for a beer, as they had plans in Windsor.

"You look just great, Nancy," said Trelly, my mother making a face saying "as if."

"You do, Mom," Matt muttered, after Trelly hit him in the arm.

"Well thanks, kids."

The sports fisherman's name was Martin. His sunburned face was hidden under a low-riding baseball hat. He looked to be in his forties, far too old for my mother, but she was probably not so picky anymore. When she introduced each of her kids, Martin touched the rim of his hat and nodded stiffly, four times. Matt stuck out his hand. Martin looked at it for a second like it was the first time he had ever seen one. But he shook it anyway.

"Well, this is quite a brood here, Nancy."

"Yup, quite, and this is Trelly, who's probably gonna be my daughter-in-law, someday."

Trelly squealed and showed him the "friendship ring" Matt had bought for her at Zeller's department store for her twentieth birthday. Matt reminded Trelly it was not an engagement ring and we all groaned, showing him we were on Trelly's side.

"Well, looky that," Martin said, not really looking at it.

My mom left with him, without kissing us, without paying for her beer. When I handed Matt and Trelly each a roadie to drink on their way into the city, Matt tipped me five dollars.

"Here, for Mom's drink," he said.

I felt bad for Matt. He had a harder time seeing Mom out the door with strange men than any of the rest of us did.

"That guy's gross," said Hope later, biting down on a tomato.

"Very gross," said Charlie.

"He might end up being our new daddy," I said, batting my eyelashes.

"Ewws" to that notion, all around.

THAT SATURDAY NIGHT was busy on account of the weather being so hot, and few people in town having air-conditioning. It was so busy, in fact, Angie asked Hope to stick around and help bus some tables. I said I'd pay her twenty dollars, or half the tips I would make that night. Charlie decided to walk home by himself. Cheryl had been gone two weeks now, and he still hadn't escaped the sad funk of her absence.

"Poor little guy," said Hope, as we watched him trudge off.

We had fun, though, me and Hope, for the first time in ages. Angie even let us put the music up a little bit and a table of cute street-hockey players came in, and they were nice to us. They left us a great ten-dollar bill as a tip, folding it like a paper airplane, leaving it balanced on an empty coffee mug. Hope sailed it at me, standing behind the counter. It landed on the blender and we laughed.

When Angie wasn't looking, I poured the rest of their leftover beers into two coffee cups and we toasted each other on the great job we did handling the dinner crowd. Only one screwup with Old Man Artie's soup. He hadn't ordered the soup, wanted the salad, and I let him have both. No charge.

At nine o'clock, it died down some, but it still wasn't fully dark, so I easily made out Adam's Gremlin pulling in to the empty parking lot. Terese, the beat-up French-Canadian girl, was with him. They staggered out of the car, both drunk and laughing.

Adam walked in and waved at me like he had never seen me naked. He just grabbed two menus from the stand and pointed to a table by the window, indicating where I could find them. I nodded back, pretending he was any old asshole customer with the balls to come in so late for dinner, with a criminal bitch like Terese as a date.

Angie was scraping the grill clean, but when she saw we had two more, she rolled her eyes and fired it up again.

Adam seemed to be fully in Terese's company by the way he held out a chair for her and handed her a menu, not once looking over at me for a reaction.

Hope was sitting at the counter, pouring more beer into her mug. Her work was done. That left just me to wait on them and it was the last thing in the world I cared to do. My knees were not happy about it either, and they felt so wrong they could've almost bent backward, like a cat's.

"God," Hope whispered. "I haven't seen *him* in a *long* time."

I wasn't jealous, so much as furious, because I was captive to his sordid presence, which was the crappiest part of being a waitress. Sometimes the dining room would be filled with people I wouldn't have in my own house, and though I wanted to, I hadn't the right to ask any of them to leave. Worse, I had to be nice to them, and bring them the things they ordered me to bring them.

I carried over two glasses of ice water, as steady as possible and placed them on the table with as much gentleness as I could muster.

"Hi there, folks, what can I get you?" I said, overfriendly, looking down into my pad.

"Why if it isn't Faith DiNapoli!" Adam exclaimed. "I do believe it is!"

"Hi there. What can I get you?" I repeated.

"To start, bring us two OVs, please," instructed Adam. "And know what? I'll have a shot of rye on the side."

"Me too," said Terese to Adam. *"Moi aussi,"* she said to me.

"Oh, don't bother with French, Faith's not French. Faith's eye-talian. Aren't you?" he said, not looking up from the menu.

"I'll be right back with your drinks."

Terese looked at Adam funny, then she looked at me. She had wide blue eyes that made her look stupid, but in a pretty way. Her bruises were gone, but her fingernails were bitten bloody and stained yellow from chain-smoking. I wanted to warn Terese about Adam, but she seemed to be the type that could handle herself in ways I hoped never to get accustomed to.

Adam ordered for the both of them, pretending to be fascinated by every tick and shudder coming from the freak across from him. I stalled in the kitchen waiting for their meals. When Adam came out of the bathroom, he made his way over to the counter where Hope was sitting doing a crossword puzzle. He poked her sides and Hope jumped, smiled, and hugged him loosely.

I waited a beat before I sprung out of the kitchen, pretending I really needed to find the ice cream scoop stowed in the drawer across from them.

"Oh, here it is," I said, one hand resting on my hip, the other on the scoop. "You want that ice cream now, Hope?"

"Uh, no thanks. Hey, Adam told me he saw Mom at the tavern with that Martin guy."

"Yeah," said Adam. "Your mom and her date are over at the tavern," he said, smiling and swaying.

"It's not her date, it's a friend," I said, too defensively.

"Well, I just saw them there, as friends, looking pretty cozy."

"Why don't you just shut up and go sit with your date?" I said, slapping a hand on the counter, a little too loudly. "I am closing up soon," I lied.

"Faith, you've been closing up ever since I met you."

Adam made me sick now, with his stringy hair and scrappy ways. He was falling apart at the exact moment I was trying terribly to hold my life together.

"What's that supposed to mean? You're the one—" I stopped.

Hope looked at Adam, then at me, then at the scoop, then at the newspaper, as though she was trying not to overhear the rest of what wasn't being said between us.

When Angie dinged the meals, I headed to the kitchen.

"Wad is going on out dare, Fate?" she asked, as I grabbed the burgers and garnished them as sloppily as possible.

"Nothing. That guy's just been drinking too much."

I dropped a side of coleslaw on the floor, kicked it out of the way, then grabbed another one.

"Is he boddering yous two? Want me cut 'im off?" she asked. She liked doing that to people, it made her feel bossy and probably taller, as she only came up to my shoulders, even in a set of heels.

"Maybe. We'll see after they eat, okay?" I said, popping a pickle into my mouth.

Angie snapped a dish towel at my thigh.

"You're just like your mudder," she said, shaking her head and smiling. She meant it as a compliment, but I didn't take it as one. I thought, Maybe I am like my mother, in some ways, but the difference is, I'm not slutting out at the tavern, am I? I forced out the image of my mother giggling at something Martin said, picking the lint off Martin's corduroy jacket. God, why couldn't he have taken her into Windsor? We know people at the tavern, starting with Adam. And those are the kind of people who go there. Adam-type people, local drunks and budding whores.

When I came out of the kitchen, Adam was sitting at the table but Terese was gone. Adam's shirt was hanging off the back of her chair, and the chair was now occupied by Hope.

"Where's your date?" I asked, keeping my eyes on Hope. Hope was covering her mouth with her hand stopping a laugh.

"I think she's left. I think she's gone home," said Adam, with a shrug. "Oh and, Faith, watch your step." He pointed to a spot by the door. It was vomit.

"Fu-uck!" I said, dropping the burgers on the table. "How fucking perfect that your date would puke and that I would have to clean it up. Fuck, Adam!"

Hope burst out laughing. "Oh my God, Faith, she is just so wasted. You should have seen her."

Blessed Angie came out of the kitchen with a mop and pail and told me she'd clean it up, it's been that kind of night. I said, Thank you, thank you.

"You go home, Fate," said Angie. "Marian is coming on at heleven and I can 'andle it from 'ere.

But I couldn't go home. My mom was meeting me here after her date. I had to drive her home in the Comet. Sure Angie could tell her I had gone home early, leaving her stupid American date to take her home, but God knows how much longer she'd be out with him, having no deadline or daughter looming. Plus my mom said she didn't want this Martin to know where we lived, in case he turned out to be an American pervert. Bad enough he knew where she worked. Plus there was a lot to be done. I was opening up the restaurant the next morning, too, and I wanted to stock it well, to give myself a head start. And I assumed Hope would stay and help, waiting for Mom with me.

But when Adam asked Hope to drive his car home, I nearly threw up myself.

"Perfect. I wanna go home anyways," Hope replied.

I said, "No way. I need you to stay with me."

They both looked at my face.

"Faith, really," Hope said. "I'm tired. I wasn't going to stay this long."

Hope took a fry from Terese's plate and trailed it in the ketchup. She swigged off Terese's half-full beer. Everything she did with Terese's abandoned meal was so ominous and awful, it felt like there was a full set of teeth clamping down on my heart.

"Hope, can I talk to you in the kitchen?" I was seething.

Adam leaned away from the table and tucked a napkin in under his chin, grinning at his sloppy burger. Hope seemed confused but shrugged and followed me.

When we got to the kitchen I was shaking.

"What the hell is wrong with you?" Hope asked, still holding a handful of fries that she was shoving, one by one, into her mouth. She stared at me like there was a movie playing across my face.

"There is nothing wrong with me. But there is definitely something wrong with you going home with Adam."

"Why? He's drunk! I'm driving. You are not the boss of me."

"I'm telling Mom."

"So what! I don't get this!"

"Listen to me. Very carefully. He's dangerous. Adam is dangerous."

Hope looked at me, still chewing. "What'd he do to you?"

"Nothing," I said. "It's not that. But . . . he sure tried enough."

"Tried what?"

"Oh you know, this and that. It's just . . . don't go. Stay with me. Please? I'd love the company!"

"Oh Christ, Faith, Angie's here and I am awful tired. It's no big deal. I'll call as soon as he drops me off. Okay? Calm down already. Besides, nothing can happen with us, because I'm not like you."

"What's that supposed to mean?"

She popped the last fry into her mouth, turned, and walked slowly back to where Adam was waiting by the cash register.

I followed, stomping.

"Here," said Adam, handing me two twenties. "Keep the change."

It was a twelve-dollar tip. My biggest ever.

"Thanks a whole bunch for your patronage," I said. "Hope, call me as soon as you get home!"

"Jesus! You drive me nuts, Faith," she said, punching open the door.

It took her four attempts to start the Gremlin, but I made myself turn away as they pulled out.

Ten minutes later the phone rang. Angie reached it first and handed it to me. It was my mother calling to say she'd be late.

"That's okay, I'll wait," I said.

I wanted her here. Now. Lord only knows what Adam's doing to Hope, let alone what Martin's going to do to my precious mother. If he doesn't molest her against her will, he will make her fall in love with him against her will. Then he'll want to move her to America. We will not want to follow her. That would leave me here to finish raising Hope and Charlie, which didn't feel like such a horrible idea, because maybe I'd do a better job.

"No, don't, Faith. You gotta open up early tomorrow. So go home and get some rest. I'll call you at the restaurant tomorrow morning if we miss each other tonight."

"Well then, I'll wait up for you at home, okay?"

My mother paused.

"Faith, you don't need to do that for me. But thanks, honey, I'll be home later."

She hung up without saying goodbye.

My eyes stung as I scrubbed the bathroom floor, and splashed bleach across the counter. I threw the garbage bags into the bin, landing them hard, on the first toss. I killed a half hour in a steady-moving trance, and Hope still hadn't called. And she kept on not calling, on purpose, I bet. I waited five more minutes, cashing out slowly. Still no call. Hope should've been home, would've been home by now, but if I called her I'd seem even more paranoid and unhinged. I didn't want to go home either. I was afraid to find Charlie playing solitaire on the floor in front of the TV, Gigi perched on his thigh, Hope's top bunk and Adam's driveway empty.

I said good night to Angie and braced myself for whatever I'd find at the end of our long driveway.

The house was dark when I pulled up. I found Charlie asleep on the couch, Hope asleep in her bed, Gigi asleep on Hope, and I fell asleep before Mom came home from her date. Again.

Chapter Thirteen

I wasn't the only person in our family to notice that Trelly was pregnant a few weeks before she and Matt made a formal announcement.

"She's fat, Faith. Our Trelly's getting a little belly," my mom whispered, throwing a pan into the soapy sink with a bang. She put her hand on her waist, hard, and looked out the window at the overgrown garden. Every year she had big plans for it, and every year it ended up looking like a bad home perm.

That night was a special occasion. Charlie's girlfriend Cheryl was back from her aunt's place up north, and Hope was made corporal second class at cadets. So my mom cooked a ham with scalloped potatoes, and we all got to drink a little wine.

Trelly was wearing one of Matt's normally roomy concert jerseys, but it seemed to fit her a little too well. What was also different about Trelly was that she said almost nothing the whole night. Trelly was the kind of person who'd tell long rambling stories about her sister's ex-boyfriends, and how this one had smacked Rose, that one had come on to Trel, or about her second cousin's new house payments, and how they couldn't afford to make them on account of the hot tub they installed. Once she spoke for hours, and in great detail, about Madonna's plans to marry Sean Penn, and why it was such a bad, bad idea. She thought her ability to pass time by talking was what made her a great hairdresser.

But that night she just sat there, damp-faced and teetery, nodding at Cheryl's dull description of her dull vacation, keeping one hand draped over her middle.

"I noticed it too, Mom," I said, easing a spatula under the suds.

"Fuck. I knew it. She's pregnant," she said, lighting a cigarette. She looked down at her stained pink slippers. "What else do you know? Tell me what you know."

"Nothing. I'm just guessing too, is all."

I felt conspiratorial but a bit insulted. Yes, I was the nosiest of us all, but it didn't mean I knew every single little secret. I did know that my mother wasn't in the best of moods that night. She had invited the sports fisherman to dinner but he had politely declined. The night before, I read, *It took everything out of me to call that guy. I was not raised to do that. But I figured what do I have to lose? Lin says this is the eighties, after all. So he picked up after seven rings and I asked him would you like to come to dinner and he goes "Oh well, you know, I'll take a pass, thanks anyways. I'll give you a call later." Doubt I'll ever hear from him again.*

But even before she confronted me in the kitchen about Trelly, I knew from her diary that she had her own suspicions. She had closed that entry with, *I am probably stupidly hoping this will all go away. I am kind of hoping that Trel's tummy will just shrink, that I will have been wrong, or they will have done something about it. I'm going to hell. I don't want to say anything to them probably because I don't really want to know. Plus I am a coward! I pray I am wrong, but I know about these things. God, they are both too young and too ignorant to be parents of anything. Matt can't even keep his damn car clean!*

Three days later, me and my mom were in the back yard. She was hosing down the back patio. I was taking the laundry off the line. I remember because my seventeenth birthday was coming, and I was kind of proud about the fact that we weren't going to make a big deal about it. There was to be a small cake and one present of a rabbit's fur bomber jacket that everyone chipped in for, followed by a beer each, and TV. Also there was no wind that day so my dark green sheets hung straight down like empty chalkboards. I was playing teacher in front of them and making my mother laugh.

"Now tell me, Nancy DiNapoli, what is the square root of nine?" I mimicked.

"Ummm, Bucharest!" my mother yelled from the patio.

I would not say we were friends or anything, but I really didn't have any other one besides her those days. I worked Sunday days, and two nights at the diner, leaving me little time to go to church with Nicole, or to be a slut with Serena.

Matt and Trelly pulled up in his Mustang. We hadn't seen either one of them since that dinner. Matt disappeared every morning, early, for work, coming home even later.

They sat in the car for a few minutes until my mom waved them over.

"Here we go," she said, rolling her eyes.

Matt stepped out of the car first. Trelly trailed behind him smoking a cigarette, the evidence of their news barely hidden underneath her shirt.

"Hey, Mom. Faith. Hope and Charlie home?" Matt asked.

My mom shut off the hose and said they were both out. I stayed over by the clothesline.

"Well, we got something to tell yous two," Matt said, looking over at Trelly. "Thing is, it looks like Trelly and me are going to have a baby."

"You're right, Matt, it looks exactly like that," said my mother, making reference to Trelly's billowy "Rush" T-shirt.

"Also," said Trelly, coming around from behind Matt, "we're going to get married as well."

She was the only one smiling.

My mother began rubbing her face hard and pulling her cheeks down in an exaggerated way. I was waiting for her to say something before I said something.

"For chrissakes, Matt, you went and knocked up Trel, you stupid ass!" she said,

Trelly stomped. "Mrs. DiNapoli! Jeez! You don't gotta put it that way."

I stifled a giggle, and my mother laughed the laugh of a person who didn't get her own joke.

"How the hell do yous two think you're going to do this?" she asked.

Matt motioned to Trelly like she was the main act, and he was just the warm-up band.

"Well, we pretty much got it figured out," said Trelly, waving her hands in the air.

"This'll be good," said my mother.

While Trelly spilled out their plans in great detail, my mother kept a hand over her mouth, nodding and grunting.

". . . and so, we're getting married. But after the baby's born. 'Cause I wanna wear a nice dress. Not a maternity dress! That would look terrible."

"Uh-huh," said my mom. "Terrible."

"And then we'll probably get our own place in town. Eventually. After a little while. It's just we gotta save some money first."

"Uh-huh."

"And we'll make enough money with Matt just working, for, like, a little while. Until we can put the baby in day care. Unless my folks wanna take care of it during days, or something. Hey! Unless you do? I don't know, just thinking, 'cause it's your grandchild too, and everything. But we'll see, it's a long way off and stuff, and alls I care about is that I sure hope it's a girl, don't you?"

"Uh-huh."

"Okay, so, I hope it's all right if I move, like, a few things into the basement but only for a little while. Oh. Heeee-eeey. Maybe should I call you 'Mom' now, d'ya think?"

Imagining Trelly as another daughter broke my mother's spell.

"No. Nancy. Trel, you just call me Nancy. Plain old Nancy."

"Nancy."

"Just Nancy," my mom said, through her fingers, which were still over her mouth.

"All right, Nancy, then. Well, hi, Nancy!" she yelped.

After a moment, my mom looked down at Trelly's belly. Trelly put her cigarette between her lips and lifted up her shirt.

"Ta-daa," she said, her stomach sticking out like a small, sideways soup bowl.

My mother put her hand on Trelly's little belly, and with sympathy she said, "Yous two have no idea."

Matt put a solemn arm around his wife-to-be and said, "Probably not."

Trelly shrugged and threw her cigarette into the damp grass. It was so quiet outside we could hear it "tshhhh," and expire.

TRELLY WAS INCREDIBLY HAPPY about the baby, but she smoked more than ever, saying that some pregnant women crave pickles and ice cream, but all she wanted, around the clock, were "smokes, smokes, and more smokes!" Besides, the only side effect she had heard of was low birth weight, which she said was an excellent one, since the smaller the baby the easier the labor, right?

My mother tried to be a good sport about her oldest son having an illegitimate child, under her very own roof, but the reality of Trelly's living belly was hard for her to face on a daily basis. I overheard her talking to Angie at the diner, crying about the fact that she was too young for all this, let alone Matt.

"Goddamn it. I'm going to be a grandma before I'm even forty, for chrissakes. Angie, I could kill them both and that damn baby, too. And if they think they're living with me, with *me* doing all the work, they are terribly, terribly mistaken. Poor Matt, he has no fucking idea what he's got himself into. No idea. Charlie's on my side. He said something about not needing another mouth to feed on this overcrowded planet. Jesus, I agree. I really wish the baby was getting born on another planet, not mine!"

* * *

I DIDN'T CARE one bit about the baby, but I was excited as hell about the wedding because Trelly asked me to be the maid of honor. She said her own sister was a "two-faced, stupid bitch." Hope would be a bridesmaid, along with Trelly's girlfriend Marie-Claire, who didn't speak very good English. Trelly told me that part of the challenge of being a maid of honor was helping the bride with anything she needs, from the time she is asked, to the time of the wedding, which was to take place after the baby was born, roughly six months away. My duties included running uptown to buy Trelly cigarettes, and rubbing her swollen feet during *The Price Is Right.*

In our town, unwed motherhood was as common as tonsillitis. But the stigma of being pregnant lessened considerably when you were no longer an official teen. At twenty, Trelly wasn't thought of as a slut for getting pregnant, then getting married because of it. She was really only considered a young mom, maybe a young bride. Not to her own parents, though. Once they were informed of her pregnancy, they all but kicked her out. So she stayed at our house every night after the announcement, and showed no signs of leaving. My mother hinted that since they were going to get married anyway, maybe she and Matt ought to finally find their own little honeymoon place, in town. Sooner. Like now. She even asked our landlord, Mr. Meloche, whether he had any other apartments coming available. He didn't, but he asked her why on earth was she wondering this? Is everything okay with our house? She told him she was just wondering for Matt, as he wants to move out, now that he was working full-time at Ford's, and things with Trelly were serious. She couldn't bring herself to tell him about Trelly having a baby. Planning a wedding, yes, having a baby, no. Not yet.

TWO DAYS BEFORE CHRISTMAS, Trelly came home with an ultrasound photo. Matt and Charlie looked at it like it was a snapshot of a car accident scene. We all agreed the fetus looked like a cracked peanut shell, with bits of limbs sticking out of it. And though the doctor couldn't tell its sex yet, he did say it was perfectly healthy.

To celebrate, Trelly opened a beer and my mother said if she kept that up she would be giving birth to an actual peanut, or to something equally intelligent. Trelly shushed her and said it's just the one, the baby wouldn't know, wouldn't be able to hear anything going on outside for a few more weeks. She did promise to quit smoking as soon as the fetus developed its sense of smell. I had to sometimes remind myself that Trelly hadn't finished high school, so she was never privy to the health class warnings about prenatal care, or the dangerous effects drugs and alcohol have on a growing fetus.

"Besides," Trelly said to my mother, inhaling on a cigarette, "you smoked and drank when you were pregnant with your kids, didn't you say so?"

"Certainly enough to know that these four should be a warning to you."

BEFORE WE CHOSE FABRIC for the bridesmaids' dresses, before we booked the hall for the wedding, or picked out a menu for the reception, there was the matter of making the unfinished basement more livable for a newborn. When my mother could no longer avoid telling Mr. Meloche about the baby, he said, Well, isn't this nice news, and offered to spring for carpeting and wall covering if we provided the labor. He also sent over a wreath of flowers on a three-foot tripod, the word "Mother" strapped across it, the words "To Be" written underneath with black marker. My mom said it was probably left over from one of his recent funeral services and that it was very fitting, as our lives would be officially over once the baby was born. She placed the wreath in the basement next to the chipped white crib that Trelly had picked up at a garage sale.

"There," she said, "rest in peace."

Matt worked nights and weekends on the basement, as soon as his shift at Ford's ended. Hope and I helped with anything involving cutting and measuring. Trelly did a lot of resting in front of the TV, eating Ritz crackers with cream cheese and sardines, drinking dozens of cans of Vernor's ginger ale, and smoking.

Charlie, however, boycotted the existence of anything as chaotic and inevitable as birth. At school, they had screened a documentary about a nuclear holocaust that was soon to be visited upon our heads. Charlie felt that this was a bigger thing to worry about than the arrival of a stupid baby, and the subsequent marriage of its ignorant parents. He often ended his sentences with, "It doesn't matter because we're all going to die, anyways," even if we were just asking him what ingredients he would prefer on his side of the pizza.

I concerned myself with sketching our bridesmaid dresses. I felt Hope and I would both look good in pale green satin, on account of our dark hair and skin. Hope felt navy blue polyester was better since it photographed well, kept its shape, and resisted all manner of stains. Her wardrobe strength revolved around ironing a military uniform and polishing big stupid boots, so she might as well have suggested camouflage.

Marie-Claire's parents forced her to drop out as the second bridesmaid after they found out that Trelly was pregnant. They claimed that because the child would be born after the wedding, it would officially be a bastard, according to the Church. Some French-Canadians took Catholicism to the kind of heights and depths I had never imagined God really meant for us to go with our religion. But when I asked Matt why they didn't prevent the baby's illegitimacy by marrying sooner and having the reception, with the dresses, later, he shrugged and tamped the carpeting down harder.

"I think we want to wait a bit and see," he said.

The carpeting Mr. Meloche provided was actually three huge swaths of leftover shag remnants. Matt had laid a base over the cement floor, and trimmed it with one-by-ones. He was wearing my dad's kneepads, which were too big for him. Dad sent them, then called with instructions on how to do this by phone. Sometimes they stayed talking for a few minutes. I don't know if they got all "father and son" because Matt would take the call on the extension downstairs, always catching me if I accidentally picked up the kitchen receiver.

"Wait for what?" I asked, cutting out a corner with Dad's work knife.

"I don't know. Wait and see if everything's okay, I guess."

"Okay with what?"

"Wait and see if things are okay between us," he said, "after the baby comes." He stopped stapling and looked right at me. "Can you believe this is all happening?"

Matt looked thinner than normal, and his chest caved in a bit, probably from the weight of his knobby shoulders, or the burden he looked to be carrying on top of them. We were almost finished. The only thing left to do was hang the paneling and throw up some curtains.

"Matt, are you sure that you're okay with everything?" I asked.

He put down his staple gun, took off his baseball hat, and ran his fingers through his sweaty hair. He reminded me of Dad for the first time ever. And when he said, "No. I'm not, Faith. I wish I was, really wish I was, but I'm not," he reminded me of Dad even more.

"Jeez. Matt. Don't you want this baby and to get married?"

"Yes. And no. But I don't see a choice, really. What else is there to do now that she's something like seven months along? I just gotta do the right thing by Trel, and hope for the best, is all, I guess." He whispered, "You know, Faith, we thought about having an abortion, but Trelly just couldn't go through with it. She backed out at the last minute. Don't tell Mom or anything. If I was her, I couldn't do it either," he said. "But I tell you, Faith, I wanted her to. I betcha anything Mom wanted her to have one, too."

"What a thing to say! Why would you say that?"

"She hinted."

"How?"

"Oh, like, this one time she goes," he was imitating her with his finger in my face, "'Matt, I hope yous two are using something, and I hope if you ever do something stupid with Trelly you know there are ways out of it, you know.' Something like that."

"She didn't mean abortion," I said, defending her.

"Trust me, she wasn't talking about adoption."

I wondered how bad a sin my mother committed in counseling her son toward abortion, if indeed that was what she had meant. Not only is abortion a sin against the Ten Commandments, it's one of the

Sins That Cry Out to Heaven for Revenge, a special category we memorized in grade school. "Sodomy" and "oppressing the poor" were also included on that list. Those two were the same thing, my mother once joked.

Girls who had abortions mostly went to the public high school. Girls who kept their babies always went to mine. I knew so many girls who had babies, my mother nicknamed my high school "The Slut Day Care Center." The public school girls did seem a bit godless and doomed, but some were so well put-together, I figured they, at least, had a fighting chance at heaven. They looked incapable of doing anything worse than not hand-washing their woolens.

Thinking about whether I would've had an abortion, if Adam had got me pregnant that day in the pool, made the hairs on my forearms stand up, and my nipples hurt. A baby wasn't in my plans. Not until I became a famous actress, or a fashion designer, at least.

But Matt wasn't stupid either. So I figured Trelly was responsible for getting herself into this kind of trouble. That's because once she entered her twenties, Trelly wanted to be done worrying about what the rest of her life would turn out like. According to her, she was "getting up there in years." Motherhood and marriage were the last two items on her "things to do with my life" list. In her case, these things would probably happen a little bit out of order.

"Well . . . Matt, just to tell you," I said, stroking a piece of carpet resting across my knees, "I think you are doing the right thing by Trel and I think everything is going to be okay. Because what else is there to do now but get married? Right? And I'm going to help with everything. All the wedding plans. Everything. It's going to be okay. Even with the baby."

Matt wasn't crying, he was sniffling, probably in order not to let himself cry.

"Don't tell Trelly about us talking, okay?" he said, looking up at me with blurry eyes. "I don't want her to think I don't love her, because it'll freak her right out."

"What are you saying, Matt? That you don't love Trel?" I asked, scared for the answer.

"Sure. Yeah. I do. She's great and everything. She wants all this, you know? But I am still pretty young for what's happening. I don't know, I always wanted to do stuff."

"Like what?"

"I don't know, like travel. I always wanted to go to Florida. The guys from work are going next week, and there's no way in hell I can go now. Trel would freak and plus I can't spend the money."

"You'll still be able to do stuff. You just bring the baby. Or leave it here! With us!"

I thought he was about to crack up laughing, but he just sat there, slumped in his kneepads.

Maybe the answer was simple. Maybe, I thought, they should just marry sooner, to secure the eternal fate of the baby, and worry about themselves later. Plus I had been making drawings of this pale green maid-of-honor dress I was hoping to wear. They were simple spaghetti-strap designs that would be both figure-flattering and reusable, if we took them up at the knee. I felt genius about them. So all this talk of fear and doubt and abortion sent me into a panic about whether their wedding would ever really happen at all.

"Matt, like I was saying. Why don't you guys just go ahead and get married in the Church, right now, before the baby's born? I can help a lot. And that way, once the baby's born, then things could be more right with you, with Trelly, and with the Church. Everybody would feel a whole lot less guilty about it. Have you thought of that?"

Matt picked up his staple gun.

"More right? What do you mean by 'more right'? I'm more worried about making things just a little bit less wrong! Jeez, Faith, I don't give a fuck about a church wedding. God, Mom is right. Alls you care about is wearing a goddamn bridesmaid dress! But I'm telling you, the Church has done our family no favors. I've had enough of this 'guilt' crap to last me a lifetime. Haven't you?"

I whimpered, "I guess. I was just thinking of a way to make things better is all," and I went back to cutting the carpet. But Matt, and things my mother had said to him, made me feel worse than the Church ever did.

* * *

LATER THAT NIGHT I overheard Trelly arguing with Matt in the basement. At one point, her voice made the floorboards by the fridge tremble slightly. They were still at it when my mom came home from work. I said "Hi," quietly, from the darkened kitchen, pointing down toward the muffled noise. She tiptoed over to me, took a sip from my water, handed it back, and tilted her head like a smart dog. We heard the words "wedding" and "bastard" float up from below, and stayed close like that, for a few more interesting minutes.

When it got quiet, I muttered a good night, and for the first time in a year, kissed my mother on the cheek.

She stopped me by the elbow.

"Faith," she whispered. "Know what downstairs sounds like to me? Sounds like we should probably get started on those bridesmaid dresses."

"You think?" I said.

"Yup. *I do,*" my mother joked, in a deep, churchy vow.

THE DATE WAS SET for late April, timed roughly six weeks before the birth of the baby. The doctor told Trelly there was a chance it would arrive early, completely wrecking all my careful wedding plans, so I prayed it would want to fully develop itself, a wedding being no place for a baby. Especially this baby.

"You stay in there!" I kidded to Trelly's belly. "You're not invited!"

Despite the fact that it was to be rescued from Catholic bastardom, I believed, by the last-minute intervention from its soon-to-be favorite auntie, Trelly left Marie-Claire off the invitation list. She said she was also a two-faced bitch, like her sister. So it remained me and Hope, and a half a dozen yards of light green satin we found on sale in Windsor.

"They can fuck right off!" Trelly said, standing on top of the dining room table. "We are going to look so fucken beautiful, they're all going to die from jealousy because of us!"

My mother was pinning up the bottom of her old wedding dress, which she had sliced down the middle with an X-Acto knife to accommodate Trelly's belly. Trelly was kind of wearing it like a cape, except for the intact bodice. Her now-huge breasts spilled over the top and she couldn't seem to keep her hands off them. She reminded me of the Statue of Liberty, but trashy. And stacked.

I witnessed the idea for this bridal concoction ripple across my mother's face one morning. First thing she had said to me was, "Faith, tell the truth. Have you ever thought you'd want to wear my wedding dress when you get married?"

"I never thought about it," I said, and I hadn't. Besides, I always assumed I wouldn't be three months pregnant, like she was, when I got married.

"Good. Then let's dig it out. I think I can make something out of it for Trel."

She never bothered asking Hope if she had plans for the dress. Between cutting her hair really short, and borrowing more of Matt's clothes than mine, we figured the bridesmaid dress would be the last girly thing we'd probably ever see on Hope. Her "military career" was slowly swallowing up everything recognizable about her, and it was replacing her with someone more particular than Grandpa Franco used to be.

My mom bunched yards of sheer material under the slit she made in the front of the dress, arranging it carefully, like drapes, over the belly part. She was trying to avoid the look of a back yard puppet show. But whenever the baby kicked, my mother would laugh and say, "Look, Trel, Punch and Judy are rehearsing!"

Trelly would groan, "Don't let me look stupid, Nancy, I'm a fucken bride for godsakes!"

I was getting nervous. Our bridesmaid dresses were next in line at the mad scientist's sewing table. The wrinkles of our carefully folded satin suddenly made the material look worried about itself. But my mother was captivated by what she was doing, like she'd been possessed by a second-class fairy godmother sent here to try to do the very, very best she could under the circumstances. And her trance was contagious. I cut out what she told me to, measured like she said I should, and handed her hundreds of pins and sequins.

Hope happily ironed.

Finally, with a gauzy panel successfully covering up Trelly's eight-month-old "bastard bulge," as my mom called it, the dress was declared finished. We made Trelly stand on the table for pictures. My mother stood next to her with arm around the back of her knees. She kept a bunch of seamstress pins in her mouth for effect. Trelly looked like she felt beautiful in it, until Charlie, who took the shot, said, "Trel, it's like some short kid with a giant head was hired to stand really, really still underneath the front of the dress."

My mom kicked him in the butt and sent him away. Trelly shot him the finger.

Charlie was Matt's best man, and since he owned no less than three black velvet tuxedo jackets, Matt and my dad were the only ones who had to rent their outfits. My dad gave my mom his measurements over the phone. He was flying in the day of the wedding, but out the very next, because of work.

My mother felt that it was important for her to have a date, and since the sports fisherman no longer called, she got up the nerve to ask Dennis the cop, and he said yes. The only glitch was he'd be on duty, so in uniform. Fine, said my mom. Hope's date, from cadets, would also be in a uniform, so maybe they could sit next to each other.

I wasn't bringing a date. I had a job to do, which I did not want to be distracted from.

Hope and I fared better under my mother's nimble, callused fingers. Our dresses were near approximations of the many drawings I had been making of the floor-length A-lines. Bows tied gloriously behind. Except she wasn't very good with zippers, so we had to slip them over our heads, and cinch the waists with a sash. Also, Hope wanted thicker straps, and because of her bigger boobs, she got them. My only disappointment was that we didn't have enough material left for the ten-foot train I had planned for. But my mother reminded me that even though I was the maid of honor, my dress should not take attention away from the bride. Then she laughed and said, "God, the only thing that could possibly compete with Trelly's dress would be something like a big, pornographic Rose Bowl float."

I couldn't say a bad word about the dress, except that it was "original," which I meant as a compliment. I was very proud of my mother, and what she had generously created for Trelly, and I told her so. She thanked me, bashfully, while plucking up loose threads from the carpet.

I felt like I was on a roll, making her feel good like this.

"I totally love our bridesmaid dresses too, Mom."

"Yeah?"

"Yeah. Just imagine how you're going to feel when you see us walk down the aisle."

It never occurred to me that my mother wouldn't be at the church ceremony, so when she said, "Oh, I'll probably skip that part, Faith," I smashed the iron down hard on the board.

"Mom! You can't be serious!"

"Faith, don't start with me. I have done my duty, and I will meet everyone at the reception."

"You're gonna break Matt's heart when he finds out," I said, not caring about my scolding voice.

She stopped picking up the scraps and looked up at me with slitty eyes.

"Like I said, Faith, I've done my duty and I've already had a long talk with Matty. Trust me. He understands."

I grabbed my dress off the ironing board and clutched it to my heart. Without saying anything more, I stomped into my bedroom and slammed the door.

Matty. She called him by his baby name, which felt like both an intimate and a sad thing to hear. What did he know? When did they talk? How had I missed that, too?

I hung up my dress on the back of my door thinking of all the times I tried to save my mother from hell, when I should have been worrying about my own soul. Ten Commandments, all busted in my wake, and this dress would be my salvation. Maybe my mother had made them with her own hands, but I had willed the wedding to begin with. I saved this baby from hell, and that would just have to be good enough for God.

I've done my duty, too.

Chapter Fourteen

On the day of the wedding, Hope ended up being the one to pick Dad up from the Windsor Airport. I remember my mother wouldn't, and I couldn't, due to the many important things I was in charge of. Charlie didn't have his license, and wasn't planning on getting one. He felt there were already enough cars on the planet, and hitchhiking made him feel sort of noble. Auntie Linda's Polish husband drank too much to be counted on to drive.

"Besides," Paul said, cracking himself up, "I don't know my way around Canada too good."

Matt was trying hard to be a decent groom, but he held his stag at a friend's house the night before the wedding, and just like an idiot, stumbled home as the sun was breaking over the freshly plowed field across the street.

"Faith, how the hell are you?" he said, saluting me with a weak smile. He slunk down into the basement after making me promise to wake him up one hour before the time he was due at the church. No sooner.

Trelly had been sleeping at her two-faced sister's house for the week leading up to the wedding. I suggested a brief absence would make her feel a little new to Matt on their honeymoon, something else I had totally arranged for them. After the reception they were to spend the night at Leamington Motor Inn, the one with the big indoor pool. Then Pelee Island for two nights. Matt couldn't afford more time away, plus the baby was due in a few weeks and they didn't want to travel too far from Trelly's doctor or any hospital.

I finished my hair and makeup early so that I could supervise Trelly's, but when her friends from the salon arrived at our house balancing the kinds of hairdos that my auntie Linda said needed scaffolding, I became worried. Not just because you wouldn't have wanted to light a match anywhere near them, but because I thought they'd do up Trelly like a whore. I urged them both to take it easy with the lipstick, hairspray, and blush, as the bride was now a very gaudy eight months along.

"Don't forget," I said, "Trel's going to be someone's mother soon."

"Jeez, Faith, fucken relax," said Trelly, barely visible under her coworkers' arms, which surrounded her head like thick, pink vines.

I had promised myself during the planning that I wasn't going to get mad at anyone, wasn't going to yell, wasn't going to turn myself directly inside-out over my family's laziness when it came to anything holy. But nobody seemed to grasp the importance of this day, the day the baby was rescued from hell, from being picked on as a bastard kid, which was the same thing in my book. After today, the baby would be a legal citizen in the eyes of the Church, and the parents would seem a lot less seedy too. I was responsible for that. I was also responsible for successfully shooing Matt down the church aisle and for having Hope done up in a way that made her closely resemble a girl. I also booked my dad's flight, leaving him enough time to change into his tuxedo in the back seat of the Comet on the way to the church. But because we were so late in firming up our plans, the only time St. Francis's was available was at four sharp. And we had to be out by five, sharp, as the church was to be decorated for the next couple, who no doubt were doing everything exactly the right way. The day's schedule was a fragile thing, with no room for error.

So when Trelly and her friends poked their heads out of the

church doors to say "Let's get going already!" I lost my last pinch of composure.

The ceremony was held up because of waiting for Dad and Hope.

"Hope had just the one goddamn job to do this whole day!" I screamed at my mother, who was checking her pale pink lipstick in the rearview mirror of Auntie Linda's rental. I was leaning on the door, chain-smoking, knowing full well it took away from the elegance of my pale green dress, French braids, and baby's breath crown.

"Jeeee-zuzz Keee—ryst, Faith," my mom hissed, "they are ten minutes late is all. You need to relax yourself." She smacked her compact shut and plucked the cigarette out of my hand. "I'll see you at the diner. This is where I get off."

Nothing I could say could convince her to attend the ceremony. As a Catholic, she joked, she was so lapsed, the rafters would come crashing down upon her head if she so much as entered the sacred ground of St. Francis's. I told her that was an arrogant thought; as if Jesus would remember her anyways.

"Oh, He would," she said.

"You wish," I said, before she pinched me hard on the arm.

I watched her drive away. She had on a baby pink suit she had borrowed from Auntie Linda. (Later, she would tell the cops the wrong color of her suit, saying light green, which was the color of what I was wearing. Not that it mattered. It never mattered.)

She seemed as relaxed as four Bloody Marys generally make a person who hadn't eaten a recognizable meal, unless you count the celery Auntie Linda was famous for garnishing them with. I also knew my mom wasn't particularly nervous about seeing Dad, before she had even said anything to Auntie Linda. By now, I could pick up my mom's internal thoughts effortlessly. I knew her so well from working with her, and poking through her diaries, I was bored by the things that used to slay me. So what if she forgot to ring in a second coffee and pocketed the sixty-five cents. Big deal that she became all different around men with a little money. Okay, I was kind of shocked when she bought a joint from Trev Monroe. In her diary, I read that she toked off it, once, just to see what her kids were all about on it, but she ended up nearly puking and left Angie to finish the rest.

I hadn't been reading her diaries much. In the weeks leading up to that day, I had other things to worry about. After the wedding, then the baby's birth, my own soul was next on the list of things left for me to fix. My mother and her soul were entirely on their own.

WHEN HOPE AND DAD pulled up in the Comet, I didn't notice the back left bumper right away. It was smashed in, the rear window also completely out, making the Comet into a near convertible.

Hope clambered out of the car saying, "I'll tell you later, Faith, okay? It's no big deal, no one's hurt, no worries, let's go."

"Jesus Christ," I said, ignoring my dad, who was waving at me and running toward the rectory. I took the front steps in twos, extending my hand out to Hope, like I was next in the relay, the baton was her forearm, and I wasn't letting go.

We had practiced a slow march down the aisle, but the late start meant that we had to keep everything moving at a faster pace. The best part of the wedding march was watching everyone's reaction to Trelly's dress. My auntie Linda kept her hand over her mouth, but you could see deep admiration in her eyes. Polish Paul wore bifocals so he had to tilt his head forward to peer over the top of his glasses, which added to his overall expression of disbelief. And you could have cooked an egg on Trelly's mother's flushed, hypocritical face. I wished my mother could've seen her turn deep, deep red. She'd be no doubt thinking, "It was worth slicing my own wedding dress in half just to see this stupid cow burn up like this."

Trelly floated strangely by and above us all, the way that truly happy people do sometimes.

Father Joel looked at his watch and read the service like a 33 record running at 45 speed.

"RepeataftermeIMatthewMarioDiNapolidotakeTrellisAnneMarietobe . . ."

Yup.Yup. Matt said. Same with Trelly. She did, too.

"OkayInowpronounceyouhusbandandwifeyoumaykissthebride."

They necked using tongues, like at a drive-in, which was slightly embarrassing, so I looked at the colorful banners and the fourteen beautiful windows.

The second best part about the ceremony was being Catholic again. Not once did I hesitate during the recitations of creeds or prayers. Also I knew precisely when to stand, sit, and kneel. I hadn't forgotten the words to the psalms or songs and the host stuck to the top of my mouth in that gummy, familiar way.

Hope came up behind me wrestling the host down with her tongue and continued to whisper the story of the Comet.

"*So.* I *got* Dad at the airport. Gave him his tux. He changed in back, like you *said.* I put the rearview mirror *up* for *privacy.* We were on the way *hee*-re, *bu*-ut, we forgot the *dress* shirt. Stopped home. *Ran* in. *Got* it. Backed *out* of the driveway. Left the mirror *up.* Didn't see *pickup truck.* Sma—*ash.* Fuck."

"Christ, Hope! You don't have to swear!" I whispered.

"I'm just *say*ing. Anyways, I think I broke a *rib.* But the window came off in two big chunks, so we left it in the ditch and swept out the back seat best we could."

My dad was returning from receiving the host, rubbing the side of his head.

"I think Dad broke his head," whispered Hope.

"Nowgoinpeace," said Father Joel.

The ceremony was over so fast that I didn't get a chance to cry the way I was hoping and practicing to. And maybe because Matt was still a little drunk, he bent down and placed a big kiss in the middle of Trelly's belly. Everyone clapped. Trelly, in her excitement, yelled, "Wooo-hooo, I'm so happy! Let's party!" launching her bouquet into the pews, me scrambling to retrieve it, so she could retoss it, the right way, later.

THERE ARE BETTER PLACES for a wedding reception than a damp, twenty-four-hour diner with broken air-conditioning. And if we had been rich enough to have saved some money, and smart enough to have booked ahead, we might have held it at the Stoney Inn by the lake, or even at the church hall, with its stackable chairs and paper tablecloths. But that was not how we did things in our family. We were last-minute, barely-avoid-disaster kind of people. So we were the recipients of Angie's generosity of spirit, and of salt, especially in the egg salad sandwiches, crusts taken off. Also, she made chili and potato salad, hot dogs and orange pop for the kids. Beer bobbed in the melted ice in the buckets along the counter. It was hot for late April, so Angie removed the big front window, leaving the restaurant open to the street. This made the diner look like it came from Europe, like it was a café in one of the framed and mounted "Paris Streets" puzzles lining the hallway to the bathrooms.

It got hotter as the day got older, so by the time the last of the stragglers from the church walked over to the diner, it was eighty-five degrees. Heat and the crowd in the tiny diner caused the people and the decorations to wilt. One corner of my hand-painted banner loosened and sank, its new message reading, "Congrat— Matt and Tre— Way to . . ."

My own hairdo disappeared without a fight.

Poor Trelly. She had horrible sweat rings under her breasts and every once in a while she'd lift one of them up and fan the air underneath. Because of the heat, I missed Adam's entrance. I was standing very still in the walk-in cooler. Eyes closed. My mother didn't object to Matt inviting Adam to an event that she would be able to maintain a watchful eye over. Adam brought Terese, the beat-up French-Canadian girl, as a date. (Hope told the police later that Adam was already drunk by the time he arrived at the reception. Maybe high too, she said, but it was hard to tell.)

I was surprised that I was more jealous of Hope having a date than Adam bringing one. The most attractive person at the reception had to be Chief Petty Officer Sam Lougheed. Hope introduced me to the officer. I shook the officer's hand firmly. I noticed the officer's beautiful blue eyes, long, dark eyelashes, and short, glossy crew cut. The officer had large smooth hands. The officer's uniform was pressed and impressive. The officer was pleased to meet me, and for a second I imagined myself shining boots, my own and his, and being good at it, starting as soon as the next week.

But then the officer leaned into my ear and asked, politely, did I have a tampon, or a pad, as the officer had just started her period, and can you believe it, Hope didn't bring anything either? The officer's full name was Samantha, though people just called her "Sam," a name she preferred.

I pointed Angie out to Sam and said she'd be happy to fix you up. I turned and grabbed Hope's arm.

"Hope! Jesus Christ! Mom is going to kill you if you're being a lez with Sam!"

"Faith, we're just friends," she said, her eyes following Sam, Sam following a slightly stunned Angie into the kitchen.

Adam came by and said, "I can't wait to meet your date, Faith. The DiNapoli girls never fail to amaze me."

We exchanged a longer than normal look, me and Adam. His drinking seemed to make the skin around his eyes look papery, and the rest of him dusty, like he had been dipped in a vat of gray sadness, then left to dry under cold, pale sun.

Hope kicked him in the shins, playfully, as he handed her a fresh beer.

"You two look really, really pretty, Faith," Adam said.

I said thanks, and I meant it. He walked away from us, backwards, dipping in a low bow, and spilling some of his drink down the front of his dress shirt.

"Well, that's nice of him," said Hope, "and that's all that matters to you anyways." She was straightening out the folds of her satin skirt, arranging them just so. "You gotta learn to lighten up, Faith."

"Yeah, you gotta learn to like boys."

"So do you," she replied.

"You."

"You."

* * *

THE BEER DIVIDED MY ATTENTION into little pie-shaped slivers. A big part of it was devoted to watching the spectacle of Adam and Terese, who took turns holding each other up, dancing and drinking at the same time. I also found myself trying not to stare at Sam in full military regalia, and Hope in her long green dress. They seemed to be chatting happily about things I knew nothing about—the sea, sails, boats, war, being lez. And it's not like they slow-danced or anything, but you could tell they were a couple, the same way you could tell my parents weren't. My mom and dad mostly kept to different sides of the room, Dad catching up with relatives he hadn't seen in a while, Mom trying to ignore them. At one point my dad seemed to be enjoying a conversation with Dennis the cop, who was hovering and smoking by the door. But when my mother tugged Dennis onto the dance floor for a Johnny Mathis number, my dad's face fell a little and scanned the room to find someone to lift it up again. His face found Hope's and they met in the middle to dance. At first this seemed lovely to me, standing there, tipsy and sensitive. Then I noticed Hope was nearly as tall as my dad, and it made me sad because of all the years that seemed to flood the tiny space between them.

The only person who wasn't pretending to be happy was Trelly. She was as graceless and tippy as an amateur clown, and danced like her big belly was a figment of our imaginations.

When the sun mercifully dropped, and took some of the temperature with it, my mom and I went into the kitchen to start dessert.

"Everything went really nice, Faith. You did a good job," she said, shoving her hair off her sweaty forehead with the back of her hand. "But too bad you didn't bring a date like Hope. Hey, what do you think of Sam? He seems nice. Young, but nice. Maybe a little girly-looking."

"Girly-looking? Mom, doy! Sam *is* a girl!"

I regretted my tattletale almost immediately. We had been hoisting a cardboard cylinder of chocolate ice cream onto Angie's chopping block, but my mother stopped lifting midway, forcing me to drop my end.

"Hey! You all right?" I asked.

Her face was slightly flushed. We were all drinking way too much that night.

"Jeez," my mom said. "All this time and we were worried about Charlie."

"Well, I'm sure they are just friends," I added, echoing Hope's words.

My mother looked around, focusing her gaze about six inches in front of her face. Then she said, "Oh hell, what can you do, right? What can you do but just go ahead and serve dessert anyway, right?"

"Right," I said, handing her the scoop.

The screeching whine of microphone feedback caused us both to cover our ears.

"Excuse me, excuse me. I have a few words I wanna say," Trelly yelled, squinting into the back of the room.

My mother moved me over to the kitchen door and nudged me in front of her.

"Here's your chance to take a bow, Faith," she whispered.

Trelly unfolded a tiny piece of paper.

"First off, I want to thank Angie for doing all this, and to my dad, thanks for paying for it, like you're supposed to anyways. But I really want to thank the person who made this day really special for me and Matt . . . Mrs. DiNapoli . . . Nancy to me!"

Everyone clapped. I saw my dad clap toward my mother, while my mother kept her eyes on Trelly, shyly shaking her head. Trelly carefully read out the rest of her prepared speech.

"I am wanting to thank you, Nancy, for giving me this beautiful dress as a gift that you made from your own hands and for making me feel like I am a special person in the eyes of your family and especially in the eyes of you. Thank you so much for everything that you did for me to make my wedding day the most beautiful day of my life, until I have this little baby. And I would also—" But she choked up, put her hand on her belly, and said, "Oh my God, the baby just fucken kicked just now!"

The whole room exploded, laughing and yelping, at the same

time. The DJ spun a stripper song, and Trelly hammed it up on the stage, modeling the silly dress with her giant belly, my mother getting caught up in the excitement, joining her on stage, before anyone had a chance to realize they had totally forgot to thank me.

Adam must have read my face, because he kindly mimicked it back to me. He pushed the corners of his mouth up, suggesting that mine do the same. Before I could smack Adam's foolish face, or thank him for noticing my sad one, Charlie grabbed my hand and pulled me out back with him, the sexy stripper song funneling smaller behind us.

My younger, kinder brother took me by the shoulders and looked up into my eyes, hidden under a wilted hairdo. Only my mouth, a tight line welded shut with anger, remained visible.

"Faith, don't get upset they didn't thank you," Charlie said. "They forgot in the excitement is all. Let me go in when the song's done and tell Mom. You know and they know that you did a great job in all this."

"No—do not—" I said, my eyes following his arms, now motioning through the window at the ungrateful bunch beyond. I would've finished my sentence, saying I do not want a thank-you if I have to ask for it, but we were both frozen by the spectacle of Trelly throwing the bouquet. Without me. I watched the bouquet that I had made sail over Trelly's shoulder. All two dozen pink carnations (including stems, carefully covered in a wet Baggie, neatly rolled with florist tape, like the bridal magazine said you should, "to maintain a certain puffy buoyancy") were launched into the undeserving crowd. The bouquet smacked the side of Terese's head, bounced off, and hit the ground. Hope's date bent to scoop it up. Chief Petty Officer Sam Lougheed held the flowers aloft, like a beauty pageant queen, celebrating her victory wearing a war hero's outfit.

I was just set to all-out bawl, to bring the diner down around everyone's ears, brick by rude brick, when Adam's date Terese came stumbling out of the back door.

"Good par-dee," she said, feeling her way down the brick wall of the diner, making her painful way home. Adam followed seconds later holding two plastic glasses, brimming over with pink Spumanti.

"Just in time for a toast," Charlie said, grabbing the drinks out of Adam's hand.

Before Adam could say, "Whoa, no they're for me and Terese," Charlie clinked my cup and we downed the drinks, Charlie saying, Here's to you, dear Faith, I love you like a sister.

Adam scratched his head while me and Charlie squeezed the now-empty plastic glasses. For effect, we whipped them over our shoulders, me feeling a lot better right away.

Adam said, "Oh, Jeez. My God. Um . . . Terese left?"

I nodded, wiping my mouth, thinking, yup, first Denise broke up with you, then my mom stopped liking you, then I stopped loving you, and now Terese is sick of you, too. Women will leave you, Adam, because you're too much to bear.

Instead I said, "She wasn't feeling very well."

When Charlie said, "Maybe it's Angie's egg salad," I laughed hard and long, not because I was drunk, but because it was the damn funniest thing I have ever heard. Or maybe I was just going to let Charlie make me laugh on a night where I was too sad to make my myself cry.

Adam looked at my shoes, at Charlie's shoes, at his own shoes, and then, grinning, he turned and marched inside. We heard him break out laughing in the kitchen. And he laughed and he laughed and he laughed, all the way back into the dark reception.

"It wasn't that funny a joke," said Charlie, with a hiccup.

"Yeah it was. It was perfect."

If it wasn't a mortal sin, plus a bad notion all around, I would've kissed my baby brother on his mouth.

After our toast of Spumanti and the wonderful joke, the evening started moving like a euphoric play, staged by the happiest of actors, in slow-motion detail with everyone standing at weird angles, wearing all-wrong colors.

WITH MY EYES CLOSED (one blackened shut that way), I told the police the things I knew to be true, and some things I wish were not. I remember someone had been holding me. I was turning.

Matt was drunk, Trelly was across his lap talking to Matt's friend Luke and Luke's wife. Her name is Stacey, I was thinking. I walked up to her and said, I know you, but Luke said to Stacey, I don't think you've ever met Faith, Matt's sister. Trelly kissed Matt a bunch of times on his neck, which cracked me up, so I turned to Luke and said we did that, didn't we do that too? Someone grabbed my arm ("That's enough of that"), which made my dad's face smear. He had been sitting next to Angie, waving her smoke from his face, but he was listening. Trying to. A kid (I don't know who he was) climbed into Dad's lap. Dad smiled at him and tickled him and wiped his face. I recognized Dad in his own face again. Then Mom and Dennis the cop, they were in charge of coffees; Mom first pouring it out of the machine, Dennis—he handed the cup over the counter to takers. Dennis said, Sugar's here, but only Coffeemate, no milk, all out. Mom said, Yup, all out, unless you wanna go to the store and get some milk for us. Takers? Any takers? They laughed. My mother wasn't being so mean to Dennis the cop. ("Do you know him?" I asked the cops. "No, he's OPP, we're RCMP," they said. "Oh," I said. "I didn't know there were different types of police.")

Right. Then Hope and Sam. They were picking up the empties off the tables. They dropped some. They were moving slow. Hope looked at Sam, every once in a while, through her bangs, or maybe she didn't look at her like that. I don't know. What if she did? Does it matter? I'm not sure. Then Charlie and Cheryl were arguing with the DJ over the next song to play and dance to. The DJ looked like a judge in a booth. He'd never heard of Charlie's request. Charlie knew this before he even asked, so why did he do that? Why did he bother? Auntie Linda and Paul, her Polish husband, they were dancing next to me, but my face just missed Auntie Linda's face at every turn, which made me laugh. Auntie Linda wasn't drinking, because when I handed her a beer, she said, No thanks, taking it easy, Faith, because guess what I'm having a baby! But don't say anything yet, because it's not even three months along. I was happy because they've been trying for a baby for years. And I hugged her hard and she asked me if I was all right. I said, Yes, more than all right. I was the happiest I had ever been, I think.

She said, Maybe you should ease up on the beer, dear, and I laughed because it rhymed. I kept saying beer dear. Then I remember her dancing with Paul again, and he squeezed the back of Auntie Linda's dress and put his face in her neck while they were swaying. Auntie Linda kicked her leg up, laughing. I was thinking to myself, I like the way they love each other because it looks like the way people should. (The cop listened, but he didn't write that down.) Then Hope handed me the bouquet and said, Here you take it you deserve this most of anyone. I said I love you, and Hope, she went, Whatever, I love you too you're a mess and go home. Oh yeah, there was also Trelly's mom adjusting her nylons, right in the dining room, in front of everybody. I could see her crotch panel when she pulled them up her thighs. I remember pointing at her and someone hit my hand. (I know the cop didn't write this down.) I could feel myself being held. Practically being held up. Then I was watching Charlie falling asleep, then his head bobbed awake. Then asleep. I turned on the dance floor. Who was holding me? I didn't know at first. Nope, then Charlie was awake. I turned again. Oops, now Charlie's asleep. My dad went to him. Then I remember Adam Lauzon. He had been far away from me, at one point, five feet away from me, then four, three, two, one. Then there he was. He was the one who was holding me. Right? Adam was the one who said, Who's dancing with Faith? I said, I don't know. I told him, My God, I am very drunk. He said, Yes you are. I asked him, Why am I like this? This is not what I meant to be like, I said. He told me that he gave me something special to drink by accident. It was supposed to be for him and Terese. He said, Let's get you some air. He said I felt clammy, which I laughed at. Clammy. We passed Charlie in the chair, he looked up at me, and he seemed like he would cry if I said anything to him. Dad had his hand on Charlie's back and said to me, Wait, Fate. I laughed at them and then I snapped like I'm a clam, like Adam said. Adam told my dad, She's okay, she's fine, Joe, she just needs some air. Adam hid me away me from my mother. Then I was outside, and it was all dark. And that's what I remember.

"Thank you, Faith, get some rest."

The cops left the hospital room. I cried, then slept.

* * *

ALL THIS, all these people doing all these things, I saw them while I was dancing with Adam, his weak shoulders and the one side of his sweaty head were such an unsteady frame, I couldn't be exact. I don't really know how long we had been on the dance floor. Could've been for one song, like Hope thought, could've been ten, according to my mother. I couldn't answer that question. Also according to my mother, Uncle Paul came upon me sitting on the hood of the Comet, kissing that neighbor-boy, Adam.

I wish I could remember that kiss more than anything else in the world.

Uncle Paul told my mother that he was startled to see that the Comet was running and he casually reached into the vehicle to shut it off, taking the keys with him. No, he told my mother, who had been still serving coffee, Faith did not appear to be putting up that much of a struggle. Yes, he said, it looked like it was her intention to drive with him somewhere. No, he said, she is in no condition to do anything of the sort. Neither is that neighbor-boy. Uncle Paul playfully dangled the Comet's keys in front of my mother's face before shoving them back into his suit pocket. My mother came running out to the car, probably to beat me, but instead she found me in the back seat, sleeping against Adam's chest, mouth open, Adam's arm lazily draped down my back.

We were both out cold. I was holding the bouquet so tight, she said she couldn't pull it out of my hands.

Uncle Paul offered to drive the Comet home, as Adam would be in need of some manly dragging; my mother offered to follow behind in Paul's rental car, as I was in need of some motherly slapping, hard, she said, across my drunken face.

My mother also told me at one point, Auntie Linda had climbed into the back seat of the Comet with us, but when she came across a healthy shard of glass left behind from the earlier bang-up, she thought better, and rode back to our place with my mother. My mother told me Auntie Linda dozed off slightly, while talking about how beautiful the wedding was, how much Paul had drunk, how terrible Grandpa's Comet looked, how tired her pregnancy was making her.

Auntie Linda's eyes were blessedly shut when the Comet smashed into the tree after Uncle Paul swerved to miss the rabbit that my mother hit and killed. But my mother's eyes were open, so she was the only person who saw me fly out of the Comet, in my pale green dress, clutching that bouquet, one second later.

Chapter Fifteen

Because of those sad weeks following Matt and Trelly's happy wedding, I came to believe that how a person handles tragedy is really the most important thing about them. I had always been taught that's how saints are chosen, that's why martyrs don't mind dying, and why Jesus Christ was picked to be the Son of God to begin with.

Now I was getting the practice. But it was nothing compared to my mother's ability to negotiate every level of hell imaginable. I think the worst was seeing her oldest daughter soar out of the spinning Comet. Second would be seeing Auntie Linda watch her young husband die stuck inside.

Adam was thrown too, and landed alive, but badly broken when the ambulance arrived. All in all, I am glad I hit the road, far away from the crash, because it would have been such a rotten thing to see. Trelly's bouquet cushioned my head, they said, and I was grateful that I had made it huge. I was more grateful that the tulips Trelly wanted were too expensive, as carnations made for a kinder type of landing pad.

During those days, when Paul died, and Adam fought for his life, my coma broke twice while I was alone.

The first time my eyes opened, it was dark in the room, but light came from the area of the door, which I knew by the sound of nurses was located on my left. My body felt like it was encased in warm cement, almost fully set. My arms felt like they had been tied down by someone weak and lazy. I couldn't move my head. I hadn't been told about Paul or Adam, but I felt tears for them falling out of the wrong corners of my eyes, the outside ones, and I was helpless to prevent them from flooding my ears.

The second time I awoke, daylight blinded me. I could hear Auntie Linda crying in the little bathroom. She was saying, Oh Paul, oh Jesus, and throwing up. Out of fear of her sadness, I willed my brain to shut itself off as I didn't want to know why she was crying; didn't know what to say to make her feel better. Before I blacked out, more tears came to my eyes. And even though I could have moved my arms to wipe them off my face, I left them there for Auntie Linda to see, and fell asleep again.

I fully came to consciousness at Hotel Dieu Hospital, fourth floor, a week later while Charlie was holding my hand.

He said, "Faith . . . Faith . . . you're gonna do fine, they say. But Uncle Paul, he died. And Adam's not doing so good."

My reply was, "Uncle who?"

Afterward, they said, I fell asleep for many days, during which time it rained and rained and Adam died from the injuries he sustained in the crash. He was buried on the Tuesday that Trelly gave birth to a boy, a little early, two floors down from me. They named him Marc Jean-Luc, a French-Canadian homage to my mother's attempt to name her brood after the New Testament.

I missed all that.

Later I learned that Charlie and I drank from drinks that Adam had spiked with an unkind drug. Luckily, the acid had relaxed my body, making it possible for me to fly, then land with a kind of elasticity.

Terese told my mother "dey didn't mean any 'arm, dey were just 'aving fun, and it was a haccident, what 'appened." She told my mother that she had bought the acid off a guy in Detroit. If my mother had owned a nuclear warhead, or knew how to build one, she would've taken aim at that entire city and the country surrounding it. She would have killed Adam too, if he hadn't done the job himself. Her only vengeful option was to slap Terese's face and body a whole bunch of times in the emergency room. She was given some Valiums and a stern warning from the police officer not to make things worse. She handed Auntie Linda only one of those damn pills, because she was going to have a baby, after all.

Poor Charlie. He was fined for walking into the variety store naked and gathering up an armful of potato chip bags. Afterward he plucked four pink flamingos off someone's lawn and carried them to the park. He said he saw them walking on their own, just before he passed out laughing at a Canadian flag. At one point, Charlie was positive, absolutely positive, that he saw God. He said God didn't say anything to him, really. God was just standing there being calm.

"What did He look like, Charlie?" I asked from my hospital bed, curious, though cracking up slightly.

Charlie thought about my question for a second, and said, with deep seriousness, "God . . . well . . . He looks exactly like Jesus, only older."

Two minutes later, my mother found us there, me sitting up in bed, trying to turn down the volume on the suspended TV, Charlie drinking all my juice. She put her hand over her mouth, yelped, and left the room. She returned a second later tugging Hope. Hope smiled and said "Hi, there" and asked me if I felt like having a sip of her coffee, if I felt like having anything at all. Anything, my mother repeated, sitting on the edge of the bed, inching herself nearer to me to rhythmically move my too-short bangs over behind my right ear. Then again behind my right ear. Then again. Behind. There. Stay. She did this for five whole minutes and I let her.

My dad poked his head around the door and said the longest "hi" I ever heard. "Hiiiiiiiiiiiiiiiiiiiiii," he said. "Where you have been?" He was joking to hide his fear.

"Heeeeeeeere. Where have yoooooou been?" I said, following his joke.

He looked startled for a second, glanced at my mother with concern, then gently grabbed my hand and said, like I was retarded, "Sweet-art, Fate. Maybe you doan 'nember, but I leeve out west. But I tell you dis. I stay here as long as you need me."

My mother turned to Hope and said, "Jesus Christ. I'm going to talk to the doctor. You let me know how this ends."

My short, necessary coma, was brought on by a large concussion, which left me with a three-week headache in a very specific location behind my left ear. There was no permanent damage to my neck, sprained was all. One broken rib. Twelve stitches on my upper lip. Black eye. My right wrist hurt, but the X rays revealed nothing but a deep, sorrowful bone bruise.

Other damage was that the Comet was a write-off, I would never be able to wear my bridesmaid dress again, Auntie Linda's baby would be born fatherless, and the Lauzons were left childless.

People called. I ran the inventory six or seven times a day, listing one broken rib, sprained this, banged that, nothing else, I'm fine, thanks for calling, thanks for the flowers, for your concern, your visit. Yes, it's a miracle. Lucky the back window broke earlier that day, I know. Could have been worse. Much worse. I'm lucky I'm alive. My own mother could've run me over. Mostly, I'm lucky I can fly. I wish it were so for the others.

The Comet's crash became my least favorite story about me. And there were parts I overheard my mother tell people on the phone, and parts she had written in her diary, that were so awful, I understood why she would never say these stories to my face, and why they would never become funny, even in my own faraway future.

She looked like she was flying . . . almost . . . soaring in the air . . . like an angel . . . I was praying . . . right over the car . . . beautiful . . . sleeping on the road with flowers . . . I prayed, Dear God . . . I almost ran her over . . . killed my own daughter . . . Poor Paul . . . instantly . . . Poor Adam . . . God bless the many drinks they drank . . . out cold before he landed . . . God I prayed . . . Faith and Luck and God and Luck and Jesus and Luck and Faith and Luck and God and Luck and Jesus . . .

* * *

THREE DAYS LATER, after unnecessarily carrying me up the stairs of our home, my dad flew back to Calgary for his job. Before he left for the airport, he brought me the nicest carnations I ever saw (my lucky flower, he wrote) and handed me a personal check for $150. He promised to call every day, and he did, for a week. Also, he promised to take us all on a good vacation the following Christmas. Florida, maybe.

"I'll believe it when I see you all in mouse ears," my mother said.

I was stretched out on the couch next to her, watching TV. Gigi was sitting vigilantly on my chest, sniffing the stitches on my lip.

"Maybe Gigi thinks you're growing whiskers, too," she said, which made me laugh so hard I split one of them open.

"Ow! Ma! Look what you made me do!" I yelled, laughing. Happy. Sad.

That missing stitch made it difficult to form a proper seal around a cigarette, so I ended up quitting smoking, by accident, for the three weeks it took my face to heal.

Serena called a lot at first, then she called sometimes, then rarely, then not at all. Nicole, just the opposite. At first she called a little, then weekly, then twice daily.

My teachers talked to my mother and figured they could give me the year as a gift for living. Summer was coming in two months, so they prepared home exercises and Hope and Charlie delivered them. I finished each assignment, but the pressure to excel was so light it was almost ticklish. The biggest side effect was that I refused to drive a car. Even the new Escort my mother bought with the money she was saving for a house could not tempt me.

At first my resistance brought me attention. People looked at me like I was interesting when I whispered, not too dramatically, that I just didn't want to. Simply couldn't. But the power of my fake inertia turned itself into a full-blown phobia. I wasn't concerned at first, because I couldn't think of any place I wanted to go, so I began thinking I could do like Trelly and learn to cut people's hair and stand around in the same place, in the same town, all my life. I wasn't thinking much about my future because the thing is, I almost didn't have one, and it was difficult enough to avoid contemplating that.

WHEN I BEGAN to unstiffen and crave the sun, Hope took me into town to visit my mother at the diner. When we pulled up, Angie was waiting for us, the front door held halfway open by one curtainy arm, the other one waving and flapping at us while we parked.

She placed her hand on my cheek and said, "Oh, Fate. We pray so 'ard."

At first I thought she meant let us pray, now, and I almost dropped to my knees on her command.

"Oh, Faith," my mother said. "This is good. It's good you're getting out. It'll make you feel better."

She winked at Hope. Hope rolled her eyes, but kept them on my profile, still bruised slightly. Though the stitches on my lip were long removed, a lobe of skin dipped over my teeth, and the split had been badly matched, leaving a pink zigzag scar running to my nose. But I liked my scar. It was better than the one Hope was left with on her thigh, way back, the day Old Man Chaumier had chased us to his own death.

Later, at the counter, Angie and my mother orbited me like two moons, fetching grilled cheese and ketchup and water, and placing them all within my reach. My mother touched my hair or arm or shoulder every time she left the counter to bring me something else to eat. And I believe she would've kept on doing that as long as I had hunger, even if it was bottomless and it meant my mother would never sit down again.

AFTER BURYING HER HUSBAND in Brooklyn, Auntie Linda came back to stay with us for a while. She needed to figure out what to do with the rest of her and the baby's life now that Uncle

Paul was dead, and I was spared whatever was left of mine. Auntie Linda talked about Detroit a lot while she rubbed her stomach with cream to help with the stretch marks. She said, Remember that bank I used to work in? Way back? The one your mother used to work at too? She said that job was like heaven, being around all those tall buildings and all that money. She and my mom would go to lunch counters and gossip about cute managers and racial tension between the black and white tellers. Auntie Linda took the bold step of securing an apartment downtown and urged my mother to join her, to escape Canada and become a free American. But my mother didn't want to leave Grandpa. So living in Canada, and afraid of America, she one day met my dad, and the rest of her life all kind of happened to her.

Auntie Linda, however, had concentrated on her career. She had made good money at the bank and bought armfuls of beautiful sweater sets and her first piece of good jewelry. It was a butterfly brooch pin, studded with two authentic diamond chips, surrounded by several other pretty good gems. Auntie Linda gave it to my mother on her wedding day, the day my mother went one way and Auntie Linda went another. I told her I remembered the brooch, which I used to carry to a window so the diamonds would glitter better in the light.

"I wonder if she still has it," Auntie Linda said.

I didn't tell her that the brooch was once the most important thing in the house to me, until the silverware box that it was housed in began to share space with my mother's diary.

"I don't know," I lied, not wanting to give the diary's hiding place, and myself, away.

"I sometimes thought about that brooch, and knowing your mother, I thought, Oh, she probably never even wears the damn thing. And I almost asked for it back, but Paul bought me this big diamond, Faith. I can't wear it now that my fingers are all swollen. So one day, I just forgot about the brooch I bought with my own money and started to love my husband."

She laughed. It wasn't because he bought her nice things, she said. It was just the idea that he tried to make her happy. She told me she had met Paul at a salsa club in Detroit. She was there with girlfriends from work. Paul was in town for a class reunion. Auntie Linda had long given up on the idea of marrying, as she was in her thirties, and was contemplating buying cats.

"A lot of them," she said. "Maybe a tiger even."

They didn't date for too long before they decided on getting married. She explained that Uncle Paul was rational. He didn't want to waste time and money living apart from her, so he asked his brother to run his restaurant in Greenpoint for a month so he could remain in Detroit for a few weeks to see about this Linda woman. Paul stayed in hotels and with friends, decided he was right about this Linda woman, and asked her to come back to Greenpoint to be his wife. She quit her job at the bank and stuffed her things into the back seat of his Ventura. It was around the time Grandpa died. I remembered the postcard they had sent us, having stopped in Niagara Falls for as long as it takes a couple to find a chapel and some witnesses. Then they drove straight to New York City.

She really loved working at Paul's restaurant, doing the books, wiping the menus, and seating the guests. She loved it more after he renamed it Paul and Linda's as a wedding present, and a nod toward his favorite Beatle and his own beloved wife.

"I wish Grandpa could've met him. He would've loved Paul. He should have seen Paul's kitchen. So clean and shiny and organized. I even did his spice racks like Grandpa did, with all those nails in those jars. Remember, Faith? How Grandpa kept that damn garage? Paul's kitchen is something like that. It's really something."

I told her their lives sounded very romantic and she said, Nah, marrying Paul was the least romantic thing she had ever done, but burying him was probably the most. Then she bent to cry into a pillow that she kept on her lap all day. I circled Auntie Linda's back with my hand, unsure of how much pressure to apply when comforting someone who is almost entirely uncomfortable.

* * *

SOME PEOPLE IN TOWN thought it was creepy that the brother and sister-in-law of the "Tossed Girl," as I had become known, would want to live in a dead guy's place. Others understood the practicality of Matt and Trelly and the baby moving into Adam's now-vacant apartment on the lake. Besides, it was Mrs. Lauzon's idea, and a good one, as his landlord returned Adam's deposit, and the newlyweds bought most of Adam's furniture. Trelly promised once they painted inside and planted new flowers outside, no one would remember what happened to the guy who lived there before. Except for me.

For the days and weeks I stayed close to home, the Lauzons' empty driveway fascinated me three, maybe four times a day. Adam's parents sold the Gremlin to Scott Demeter, and I thought I could hear it drive by because I knew the sound of the engine by heart, but I never, ever looked to see if I was right.

One time my mother caught me looking over at the Lauzons' while I was holding baby Marc. She took him from my arms, placed her lips on his fleshy belly, and blew hard until his skin farted. The noise made Auntie Linda stir. She often stayed sleeping on the foldout until well toward the noon hour.

"Well, hi, little baby," Auntie Linda said, half-awake and stretching. "How's my cutie?" She stuck her arms out and my mother poured the baby into my aunt's now-chubby belly.

"Why don't yous two do something today?" my mother said. "Get out of the house a bit. Something. I have to work but you can drop me off, Faith, and you and Lin can take the new car into Windsor. See a movie or go shopping or something."

Neither one of us said anything.

"Maybe tomorrow, Nan," said my aunt. She knew about my vow. I told her late one night when I couldn't fall asleep and I knew she'd be up. She said she understood but refusing to drive would severely limit my life's experiences. She said for a person to be happy living in the middle of nowhere, they had to know that they could leave it whenever they wanted to. I told her no problem. I never wanted to leave.

The baby started to rub his eyes. Auntie Linda pulled the blanket over his head and made a little tent around him.

"There . . . isn't that better? Is the sun too, too bright today, baby?"

THE DAY AFTER the Lauzons had cleaned out Adam's belongings from the apartment, I drove. Trelly made me, saying, unless I want to breastfeed the baby myself, there was no way I could go with her to see about Adam's place, something I had wanted to do, badly.

The Escort carried us to the apartment on a kind of rail, that's how safe and smooth the drive felt. My organs had grown used to jiggling around on the Comet's crappy suspension, or vibrating in the bucket seats atop the Gremlin's poor exhaust.

Trelly folded the baby over her shoulder and we took the tender, rotting steps slowly, me keeping my hand on Trelly's back. The apartment was above a large garage that used to be a tackle shop. Inside, Trelly poked at the cigarette burns on the rug between the couch and coffee table. I noticed only one of the two tiny bedrooms had a decent-size closet, but there was a long skinny one in the hallway, the handle almost completely camouflaged by paneling. That was probably why the Lauzons missed the contents. When I opened it, the smell of Adam, his cigarettes and Polo cologne, came wafting out. His leather Red Wings jacket hung alone above two or three pairs of old black shoes. They were piled next to a box of dusty magazines, mostly *Playboy*s and *Penthouse*s.

I put my face into the jacket and smelled him. I held the jacket in front of Trelly's face and she smelled it too.

"What?" she asked.

"Can you smell him?"

"No, I smell stinky ."

"I'm keeping this," I said, pulling the jacket off the hanger. "This I want. We can throw the rest out."

"Yeah," she said, tenderly kicking at the old shoes by the box, "doubt his parents need porn magazines to remember him by."

I dropped the jacket on the ground, placed Marc into the middle, gathered him back up into my arms, and kissed the baby on the mouth.

THE FACT THAT people became more interesting when they were dead than when they were alive made me understand Jesus Christ a lot more, and my alive self a little less.

In church, sitting beside Auntie Linda, on the Sunday she flew back to New York, the priest said a memorial prayer, in the name of a good American killed on a bad Canadian road. The priest blessed the baby, yet unborn. We made the sign of the cross, and I kept my eyes on the crucifix. I thought about the sick luck of Jesus' sorry execution. Before He was hung like that, He was on His way to becoming nothing but a really eccentric preacher man. But He suffered, and because of that we wore crosses and prayed to crosses, Jesus sadly staring down at me from the walls of the many Catholic kitchens I had been in. Imaging Jesus as aging and rusty, dying of natural causes, is to imagine an unremarkable life at the head of a pretty boring religion. And the symbol for Christianity could have easily been an old man slumped in a rocking chair, clutching at his sacred, stopping heart.

Like with Adam. Before his death he was becoming a cartoon nightmare of this small town. A local drunk, selfish and sad, cursed to be pitied and ridiculed as he got older and more pathetic. And for months after he died, I thought about him often and wondered where he was. Wondered if he could see me. If he hated me. If I'd see him again. If I wanted to see him again. He almost killed me, after all.

But I didn't die, and that's why people were losing interest in me. While I allowed my floaty sadness to linger longer than I felt it, my family had begun to drift back into their lives, doing the things they had done before I became the center of attention. Just as I was getting used to the feeling of being a miracle.

Hope had been the first to treat me normally. Two weeks before Auntie Linda left, Hope had refused to go uptown to buy me some cigarettes. I started bawling helplessly, but, still, with real conviction.

"I'm sick of her," I could hear Hope scream in the dining room to my mother. "Faith's gotta snap out of this, Mom, or we're all gonna go fucken nuts!"

I slapped the door and yelled, "Lez!"

My mother knocked and opened it without waiting.

"Faith, listen, enough! Everyone's finished with this business," she said, holding a finger up. "I know you're still sad, and that's okay, but stop bringing everyone down with you. And stop calling your sister a lesbian, for chrissakes!"

"I'm still sometimes afraid to drive uptown!" I whined.

But my mother knew I wasn't afraid of the lovely Escort and its dreamy ride. It was just that I wanted a few more moments under their attentive glare. I was loving their need to know how Faith was feeling. Maybe it was making up for all the years I felt ignored in my mother's diary, snubbed on the bus by Hope, left to stand alone at a party by Matt. My dad began calling only as often as he ever did, two Saturdays a month, when he and the guys landed in Edmonton, for drinking, and possibly, for whoring.

Charlie had always been kind to me, but even he had begun to take guitar lessons with Cheryl, spending less time searching my face for a mood to talk about. My mother, once soft with my emotions, and so generous with the Tab and the phone privileges, began to work Sunday mornings, early, leaving me to organize the mowing of the lawn, despite my still slightly sore wrist.

That's why I didn't want Auntie Linda to leave, taking her kind eyes with her. But she said she had to, that she was contributing too much depression to our already tender home.

"I want you to think about something," Auntie Linda said, loading her bags into the back of the Escort. "I want you to think about coming to stay with me for a while."

We both looked at the back of my mother's head as she sat on the driver's side. I could tell she had heard Auntie Linda, but she didn't add or subtract anything from the statement.

"I don't think my mother would let me do that," I said into my mother's head. "I probably have to stay here."

My mother was distracting herself, looking for cigarettes in her purse.

Auntie Linda kissed my forehead and whispered, "If you want to. If you ask. I think she would."

"Let's go," my mother said. "We're running late."

"If you want to," Auntie Linda repeated, rubbing her belly. She was wearing one of Trelly's maternity sweatshirts, decorated with teddy bears and hearts, the opposite of Auntie Linda's style, but nothing fit her anymore.

"I'll think about it."

My aunt blew me a kiss and climbed into the car.

My mother turned to me and said, "Faith, I want to talk to you about something, so be home when I get back, okay?"

I nodded, waved until the Escort disappeared, and went into the house to dig out her diary. I hated surprises.

I read her last entry once. Then I put her diary away, smoked five cigarettes, cried, then grabbed the diary and read it over again just to make sure I had been reading a diary and not a novel.

Faith has to leave, my mother wrote. *She can't stay here. If she stays here, she'll end up like me. The accident's shocked the life out of her. It's made her scared of everything. But I am thanking God every day. And I'm sticking to my bargain. I said to God if Faith died I was dead too, and that He would certainly be forever dead to me. But if she lives, I will make a deal to ask for forgiveness for all the bad things I have done. I will go to church again. I will ask for forgiveness for the sin of not having that baby way back, when Faith made her Communion, and Joe made himself scarcer, and when I knew a fifth kid would finish me off for good.*

My mother wrote that she had started to go to nine o'clock mass, even though she told us she was working the early shift at the diner. My mother wrote that she did not find religion, or become reborn under the watchful eyes of Jesus. Her new weekly attendance at church, her earnest attempt to quit smoking, plus her successful denunciation of drinking, during the day, was brought on by a bargain made the moment she watched me sail out of the window of the

Comet. She wrote that in exchange for all the things she'd need to do in order to clean up the mess she felt she'd made of her soul and her kids, in exchange for all that, she had asked God to please save Faith.

And in the matter of my future, she wrote: *Lin wants Faith to come live with her. Maybe I owe Lin that. Owe her my Faith. It's my fault, the accident, because I did not have a good enough handle on my kids. But, my God, I don't know. I don't want to let Faith go but—*

Smack.

That was the last entry I read, and the last time my mother ever slapped me hard across my face. And the tears running down my cheeks made the slap hurt more than my mother probably meant it to. I was so absorbed by my mother's pact with God, and the sacrifice she'd made of me, I didn't hear the Escort pull up.

I looked up at my mother's face, but I couldn't tell what level of anger she had reached because her hands were covering it. I looked down at her diary in my hands. She always bought the same padded red notebook and she never kept them once they were filled. She'd just throw them away and buy another one. We had no place in our house to hide an inventory and knowing this, at times I'd copy passages on little pieces of paper, like the one that read: *Today Charlie gave me a bunch of dandelions with a note that said, "You are pretty to me" and it melted my heart, he does that to me sometimes.*

I remembered doing that exact same thing a year ago on Mother's Day, tying a similar message to a bunch of daisies. For weeks I checked her diary, but she never, ever mentioned it. I was thinking, I have always looked for me in her diary, and now I was afraid because after today, where would I go to look for myself?

I couldn't move. My mother fell to her knees. She was crying and pulling the diary out of my fingers. I wasn't resisting her tug, it's just that I felt for a fearful second that she'd hit me harder, in the head, if she got it free.

"Jesus Christ, Faith, this is mine!" she screamed, like we were in a schoolyard, fighting over a skipping rope. "How long have you been doing this? Eh? Reading my personal things? These are my things. These are personal for me, for chrissakes! God, Faith, I could kill you!"

She said this with a weird warning in her voice that scared even her. She yanked it from me, and closed her diary gently around her finger, which she kept in the place where I had been reading.

"How long. Tell me! Oh, I can't believe you!"

"I haven't been doing it for long, Mom, I'm sorry," I lied, sputtering, spraying spit and tears all over her. "I feel bad, but you didn't have to hit me. I'm almost eighteen!"

"I know how old you are. God almighty, I know," she said, standing up, using the wall to support her back. "This is my life, Faith. Right here. Mine." She was shaking the diary in the air. "You need to get your own damn life, or you are just going to die, if I don't kill you first. Now, get lost. I don't want to see you for a while."

She said this walking away, keeping her hand on her face in the place where she had smacked mine hard.

After she opened the patio door and safely disappeared into the garden, I yelled after her, "Fine, I don't care where I go as long as it's far away from here! I will get out of your sight, I swear it, and you'll never see me again!"

Through the window, I saw her open her diary to the spot I had been reading, then she walked down to the river. I don't know if she threw the diary in, but it was the last time I ever saw it.

THAT NIGHT, she called Auntie Linda. She wanted my damp, white face to be sitting next to her at the dining room table. Lin, she said, Faith wants to come and live with you, after all, like we talked about. Then she handed the phone to me and walked away. Before I could protest, Auntie Linda said, Oh Faith, thank you so much. I need you here so bad. This is good. This is the right thing for you to do. She described my new room, which would be my own room, occupying the entire third floor of their brownstone. And the school, though not Catholic, was a decent one, and walking distance from the restaurant. Plus her baby would be coming in a few months and she wondered if I'd like to be the godmother, a very important job, which I would be needing a lot of practice for. Auntie Linda also whispered to me on the phone that my mother wasn't so much mad at me as she was sad to see me go. But give her time, she said, because time is really the best thing of all.

"I think this'll work out for the both of us."

"Yeah, I think it will too," I said, my voice cracking with doubt.

I hung up, went into the bathroom, and leaned over the vanity. I thought I was just going to burp, but instead I threw up in the sink, by accident.

THESE ARE THE THINGS I overheard my mother telling people, and my dad. Fact is, her sister, Lin, needed me in Greenpoint. I needed a change of scenery. It would be good for me to work at the restaurant and help with the baby and finish high school in a place where no one knew about the fact that I had once almost died in a crash that killed two others. I heard her tell my dad, "Faith wants to be an actress and that's the place to do those sorts of things and I could use the space plus she's old enough."

These are the things she told me, when I went to the diner, to look around one more time and say goodbye to Angie.

"Faith, do us a favor and take out the garbage. Marian's late. Then could you run to the store for us? We ran out of lightbulbs. Get the forty-watt kind so the light's not so harsh in the bathrooms."

Angie made a sympathetic face and handed me a crumpled-up $100 bill.

"'Ere, you go buy the lights wid dis, and you keep da change, Fate."

That whole week, my mother talked to me about everything except why she felt I had to leave Belle River, the overcrowded house we rented, and the sagging couch I had been lying on for four months, balled-up tissue surrounding my feet like dead flowers. She told people that I wanted to go, but I knew I had to go, because my mother had lost a bet with God. Or won. It was hard to know. She was sending me off on a wave of her leftover hate. And maybe, though I really didn't think this at the time, maybe hating me was the only way she could have ever put me on that plane.

* * *

FOR THE ENTIRE WEEK before I left, it rained the hardest it had ever rained in the history of Essex County. The downpour was thrilling. The river was upon our back yard within days. Between packing my own bags, and saying goodbye to Nicole, I was filling the sandbags, right along with the Lauzons, who came over to help stop the water from swallowing up our little house.

The morning of my flight, my mother poked her head into my room. Hope and I were bargaining over the good feather pillow that we took turns enjoying every other month. I told Hope, You keep it, Auntie Linda has millions like it.

"Cool," Hope said, before she left to join the rest of the people stopping the water out back.

"You have everything?" my mother asked.

"Yeah, I think so."

She turned to leave, then stopped. "No second thoughts?"

"Nope," I said, folding a sweater. "You?"

"Faith, the trouble is I have second thoughts about my whole life. I don't want you to have the same ones. You understand?"

"I guess," I said, refolding the sweater.

My mother looked at her watch and clapped. "Okay, let's get going. We're gonna have to leave everyone here to finish bailing us out."

Charlie, bare-chested and full of mud, kissed and hugged me hard and said he would be next to New York and I made him promise me that. Hope stuck her wet hand out for me to shake and pulled it away at the last minute and said, "Psyche." Then she said, Just kidding, come here, Faith, and we held each other for a long time. I whispered "lez" in her ear and she put her hand on my bum, and we laughed.

Dad called and said, Are you sure, sweetheart? And I said, Yes, Dad, leaving will be very good for me too. I did not say it in a mean way, though he took it as such, for a second, then said good luck, you'll do great.

I gave him my new number, which I already knew by heart.

We only had time for my mother to idle the car in front of Matt and Trelly's apartment. I ran through puddles as high as the drowning flowers and was glad that their home was above the flood. I kissed the both of them, the young sleepless parents, and then I hugged the baby until he cried.

My mother and I silently passed the gray buildings and the broken highways surrounding soggy Detroit. We parked the car far away and took our time walking to the departure lounge, our umbrellas keeping our cigarettes dry. Inside we checked my luggage, found the smoking area, bought coffees and muffins, and sat and stared, neither of us having ever been inside an airport before.

"Scared?" she asked.

"A little," I said.

"Me too."

Then she handed me an unwrapped gift of my own diary. It was different than the ones she always used. It was smaller and blue, with a little lock and key and the word "Diary" written on the cover.

"Here," she said. "Use it if you want. I don't know. I find it helpful to put my thoughts on paper, because sometimes it was hard all those years not having someone my own age to talk to."

She shoved the book into the side of my carry-on bag, which did not match my makeup case, since we had bought them at two different garage sales.

"Thanks," I said, fingering the spine, a little afraid of it. What would go in here now, I thought, me no longer in my mother's life? What could I possibly have to write about without Matt, Hope, and Charlie around?

"Thanks," I said again. "I mean it. And, Mom, I'm sorry."

"Just hide it better than me, okay? Auntie Linda can be nosy, too. In fact, that's probably where you get it from," she said, staring down at the diary.

Then she stood up with her arms wrapped tightly around herself, looking at the people boarding my plane. She was squinting at them, probably trying to spot perverts in order to warn me about them. For a second, I thought she might just walk away without saying goodbye, because it suddenly seemed to me like she was here to do anything but say goodbye. She opened up her arms to me and made a noise in her throat that sounded like my name. When they called out my flight for the last time, my mother was not the first to let go. I was.

I always knew my mother still liked me, maybe loved me even, but it wasn't until I read the inscription in my new diary, flying thousands of miles above her, that I felt she had finally, fully, forgiven me.

"To my little Faith, who gave me back some of my own."

SO THE FLOOD WON, my mother wrote, in her familiar curly handwriting. The letter was waiting for me on the stoop, a week after I arrived safely, and called my mother, long-distance, twice, to say that I had.

I read the letter out loud to Auntie Linda, who was gigantic pregnant. (When I met her Polish husband's relatives, tall pink people, with large soft hands and pale hair and eyes, I figured that's what was growing inside of her belly.)

According to the letter, my mother got home from the airport, and the foundation looked to be neatly protected by the sand and the sweat of her leftover kids, and all the people who helped. The rain subsided enough that my mother went on a date with Dennis the cop, who's not so bad, and Hope stayed in Windsor after cadets. Charlie went to a party until late.

Before midnight, she wrote, another storm hit, and that sneaky river reached the windows of our empty house and broke in. We laughed at my mother's description of me trying to save my Communion dress and Trelly's wedding dress from floating away with all the other things we still kept for nothing.

There's you, Faith, who would have probably been the only one home, frantically shoving back that river with your two little hands (something I think you've been doing your whole damn life).

Those words came out sounding thicker than the others. My aunt put her hand on my back, and I continued.

Next day, our back yard looked like someone had tipped over the house and shook out the insides. We managed to save some of the toys and that one bike, and, Gigi, though slightly traumatized, sort of likes to sleep on top of the fridge now. But the books, some pictures, and the old hockey equipment are gone. Faith, so were those dresses.

But Monday, I convinced Hope to take a drive with me. Most of the roads were reopened and I wanted to go get mail, and groceries. Plus I needed to talk to Mr. Meloche about fixing the basement before it got even colder out.

So there we were on County Road 42. Now when have you ever known me to pass a garage sale? Hope said, I'll wait here. And too bad Hope stayed in the car because I would've paid money to have seen her face when I saw those two dresses hanging off a damn tree, for sale, as is, looking just like something old ghosts would wear. Your little Communion dress, Faith, was a baby version of Trel's big wedding dress.

My mother didn't have the heart to tell the lady selling them that they were ours to begin with. Besides she was asking only five dollars for both, so my mother paid, laughing, and dragged the smelly things back to the car.

Hope did not believe they were our dresses until my mother washed them in the sink, changing the brown water twice.

And she got them clean enough to use the material again.

So the next thing to expect in the mail, she wrote, *is a little christening gown for the baby, which I am hard at work on. Nothing fancy, something that you could pull over its head, appropriate for a boy or a girl, doesn't matter, so long as it's healthy and happy, and yous two do your goddamn best to not screw that kid up too, too badly. Just kidding* (underlined three times). *Love, your mother, Mom.*

ACKNOWLEDGMENTS

LOVE AND THANKS TO MY FAMILY: Susan, Dave, Sean, and my dad, John Gabriele. And to my mom, Joanne Elizabeth Gabriele—we miss you so. Also thanks to Melissa and Karen, Elizabeth and Jamie, Michael, Selina and Ryan, Megan and Marissa, Kathy and Aldo Maniacco, Maria Gabriele, and Rita Paliani. In memory of Guido Gabriele, and George and Marie Erdelyan.

Thanks to Deborah Bach, Gillian Dobias, Steve Erwin, Jenn Goodwin, Cori Howard, Greg Kelly, Lisa Laborde, Gary Lang, Julietta McGovern, Gavin McInnis, Lynne McIntyre, Shannon McKinnon, Joanne McPherson, Madonna, Ola Pelka, Becki Rose, Natasha Stoynoff, and Michael Wilcox.

In memory of Tim Renaud.

Special thanks to Cathie James for the early advice, Jameel Bharmal for the constant patience, Tracey and Leslie Paul for the fun, Lydia Ghanam Morrow for the memories, the Ontario Arts Council for the timely money, Lianne Conner for the wisdom, Cindy Witten, Mike Goldbach and Becke Gainforth for taking care of Chicky, and Christopher George List for being at the finish line.

Thanks also to Dave Terry for the original guidance, Peter Mansbridge, who said, "Get an agent," Jae Gold for providing a number, and Helen Heller for taking that call and for everything after. Eternal thanks to Maya Mavjee, Martha Kanya-Forstner, Lennie Goodings, and Antonia Hodgson for keeping the faith.

Undying gratitude to Marysue Rucci.

About the Author

Lisa Gabriele is a television producer, cinematographer, and writer. Her work has appeared on the CBC, The History Channel and The Life Network. Her writing has appeared in *Vice Magazine* and the *Washington Post*, among other publications, and she is a frequent contributor to *Nerve* magazine. Gabriele lives in Toronto.